Adam Matlow

Dark Sentinel

Acknowledgements

To my wonderful wife and two children, for putting up with all the late nights, and rushed mornings.

And to my friends and beta readers, for their help and encouragement, without whom this book might never have been finished.

Chapter One

A meteor streaked through the early morning air. *Marcus* shielded his eyes against a bright flash as the rock burned across the sky. A sonic boom scattered birds from the dead branches of nearby trees, shattering the morning peace. Large chunks of the meteor split from the main body and exploded into smaller fragments raining burning debris over the land below.

He cursed himself. He'd been outside the settlement for far too long. He should have been back hours ago, while it was dark. Now, in the light of the new day, he would be much easier to spot.

Marcus slowed as he made his way along the chain link fence that marked the outer boundaries of the settlement. Fifteen feet high and bristling with razor wire, climbing it was not an option. The gap he used to get outside was nearby, he must be close. Thankful for the event happening above him Marcus pushed on. He glanced at the guard post protecting the main entrance. The guards stood motionless, their heads tipped back as they followed the course of the meteor through the sky, oblivious to the lone figure skulking along the fence.

Clambering along the rusted fence he spotted the damaged section which had been his exit point. Disguised by a few dust-covered bushes it was barely a tear, but it was enough for him to get through. Footprints in the dust on the far side of the fence were evidence someone, probably a guard, had been past here recently.

He stopped, held his breath and listened. The fence clinked and groaned as it swayed gently in the wind and the meteor roared in the distance as it passed over the horizon. With no sign that whoever had made the footprints were still around he quickly pulled back the damaged section and shoved his way through.

When on the other side he quickly concealed the damaged section with whatever was at hand and dashed for the safety of the nearest building, concealing himself behind it, out of sight of the sentries. His pulse raced as he rubbed his sweaty palms on his jacket. He needed to put some distance between himself and the outer fence. He wasn't in the mood for a visit from the Legion.

The meteor vanished, leaving only a thick trail of smoke in the orange sky above the ruins of the cities below. There was a bright flash, followed some seconds later by a deep rumbling boom which shook the dust from the tin roofs of the settlement.

New Hope. He hated the name. It had been chosen by the first people to settle this area after stumbling out from the bunkers they had lived in for the better part of a century. The asteroid that caused the devastation a century ago sent people scurrying into underground bunkers. The lucky ones at least. Everyone left on the surface died, along with almost everything else. When dwindling supplies forced people above ground they found a world almost incapable of supporting life. Yet they had little choice and so here they were. Fifty years later and life was still a daily struggle for survival. New Hope indeed.

More like No Hope. Most of the other settlements formed at that time were graveyards now. They all had equally optimistic names. Not that it did them much good.

Marcus relaxed as he entered the main square. The Legion hadn't detected his little excursion. The fact he wasn't currently surrounded by guards was proof enough. They didn't take kindly to people outside the city without permission and liked to make examples of those who defied them. Control by fear and violence.

He missed the good old days when he could come and go as he pleased. The rise of the Legion had taken everyone by surprise. They appeared from nowhere and almost overnight their soldiers were in every major settlement for two hundred miles. Wherever all these well-armed, well-trained soldiers had come from nobody knew. Their leader, a man who called himself *Davon,* was a virtual recluse and was hardly ever spotted leaving his well-fortified bunker in *The Forge.*

Marcus stretched his aching legs. A night of scouring the Badlands, areas bathed in swathes of radioactive dust and preyed upon by bandits had turned up nothing for the third night in a row.

He longed for his bed, but first, he needed to check in with Doc. He headed towards the centre of town, to the workshop where Doc was usually found, tinkering with his gadgets.

As he dragged himself through town the thick smell of charcoal pits and cooking meats drifted through the air, which served to remind him how hungry he was. The shouts of the townsfolk peddling their wares echoed off the corrugated metal sheets which made up many of the structures here. He located a stall selling food and selected a skewered piece of meat, suspiciously rodent shaped. His stomach turned. His eyes scanned the other stalls, but his options were limited. Relenting he bought two pieces, wrapped one of them up and put it in his pocket. He took the other one and gave it a cautionary sniff. It smelt like dirt. He took a bite. Somehow it tasted worse than he'd imagined, full of gristle and burnt almost beyond recognition.

He tossed a few coins in the direction of the owner, who gave him a toothless grin and muttered something about being woken up by 'some bloody great noise' which could only have been the meteor. People here were used to such events.

Marcus gazed into the early morning sky. The rings that encircled the Earth glinted with deep hues of brown and gold. They stretched halfway to the moon and rivalled those of even the outer planets and were a remnant of the asteroid collision all those years ago. Light scattered through their various layers and cast intricate shadows on the Earth below. Though beautiful, the debris ring was also deadly, raining down radioactive fragments of the asteroid daily. Luckily most were small, and almost never made it to the ground. Today's looked a little bigger than most.

Marcus finished his rodent kebab by the time he reached the warehouse and tossed the wooden skewer into the street. Piles of partially disassembled machinery, spare parts and half-finished inventions were scattered haphazardly around. Metal shelves were choked full of spare parts and lined with bottles of various chemicals, which gave off a pungent smell that made Marcus's eyes water if he lingered too long.

He slid open the large double doors and walked into the gloom. Despite the fact it was bright daylight outside, inside it was dim. There were few windows, and most were either covered up or encrusted with so much grime and dust no light penetrated them. It took a few moments for Marcus's eyes to adjust and he walked into a table. Something metallic clattered to the floor. He cursed under his breath, as he reached to tidy the mess.

"Don't worry about that," came the deep voice of Doc somewhere in the gloom ahead, "I've been meaning to move all this junk out of here for days now." His voice carried the faintest twinge of an accent, revealing his African Heritage. Doc wasn't his real name, but the nickname he'd acquired. He was regarded as eccentric by most people, yet his skills as a mechanic and inventor

4

were always in demand. Even if he was responsible for the odd explosion now and again.

There was a click, and a light hanging from the ceiling came on. Doc was standing a few feet away from Marcus, fiddling with a small silver object about the size of a coin. No doubt part of some invention or experiment. Despite being in his sixties, he was surprisingly light on his feet, and Marcus flinched at his sudden appearance.

After a few seconds Doc lost interest in whatever he was holding and put it into one of his pockets on his well-worn lab coat. He pushed his glasses onto his bald head and rubbed his eyes. One of his eyebrows was missing and there was a faint odour` of burnt hair, but he didn't seem to care. Marcus wondered if he even realised.

"You know, you should probably think about cleaning those windows some time," said Marcus. "Let some real light in here"

Doc grinned - it was not the first time Marcus had berated him over the condition of the warehouse.

"When was the last time you went outside?" asked Marcus.

"I'm far, far too busy for that my boy," he beamed. "Besides, why do I need to go out when I have you to bring me everything I need? Speaking of which, I don't suppose you managed to…"

Marcus reached into his pocket and took out the food he'd picked up earlier and tossed it to Doc, who caught it and carefully unwrapped it.

"Is this the best you could do?" said Doc. A frown crossed his face as he picked through the offering. "And I was in such a good mood as well."

"Slim pickings out there I'm afraid, and it's only going to get worse come winter."

Doc sighed and shook his head. "Any luck last night?" he said, as seated himself at a nearby desk.

"No, nothing. No trace, just like the others."

"Must be the third one this week now?"

"Fourth, counting last nights. As usual, nobody saw or heard anything, and I still can't find any pattern to these disappearances. It's just… random. I mean, I know we live in the middle of a radioactive wasteland, but still? Four in one week?"

"Whoever is behind these disappearances is certainly becoming more brazen. They don't seem to care how obvious they have become," said Doc. "Thanks for continuing to look into this for me. I know people around town appreciate someone doing something. People are too afraid of the Legion to pursue it themselves."

"Well someone's got to do something," huffed Marcus. "I don't fancy being the next one to vanish." He had made it known about town if anyone was to go missing they should tell him at once. The sooner he was notified the greater the chances of him finding something that may help explain all this.

"I thought I might find something this time," said Marcus. "I the guy had only been missing a few hours, but still, nothing. He was last seen near the city limits, so I thought maybe some of the drifters that live out in the Badlands might have something to do with it, or at least know something, but..."

Doc nodded along with Marcus. "I heard some people approached the Legion and asked them to do something about it. They made plenty of promises but I doubt anything will come of it."

"Hah," Marcus grunted. The Legion's only purpose seemed to be to enforce the rules and showed little interest in solving crimes, or investigating missing person cases. For all he knew *they* were behind the disappearances themselves.

Marcus walked over to the desk Doc was sitting at, pulled up a chair and sat down. He swung his boots onto the table and dried mud from his boots scattered across the table. Doc tutted and brushed the mud away and continued to eat.

"Everything that happens, happens for a reason," said Doc. "There will be a connection, a pattern you just have to keep at it. If anyone can get to the bottom of this mystery it's you."

"I appreciate the confidence Doc, but I'm striking out here," said Marcus. He leant back in his chair and closed his eyes.

"Don't give up," replied Doc. "You'll get to the bottom of all this, that's why I asked you to look into it in the first place."

Doc finished his food, screwed up the greasy paper and threw it over his shoulder. It hit an empty wastebasket behind him and bounced off. Several other balled up pieces of paper lay on the floor around it.

"I think you're getting closer," said Marcus.

"Bah!" exclaimed Doc with a wave of his hand. His eyes lit up and a grin crept across his face. "Anyway, how would you like to do me a little favour?"

These little favours tended to be nothing of the sort, but they usually paid well. A quick job done for Doc would be enough to feed him for a week.

"What do you need Doc?" He tried to sound upbeat, but all he wanted was a good meal and twelve hours solid sleep.

"I'm sure you're aware of the atmospheric disturbance this morning?"

"It was a meteor Doc. You don't always have to use big words you know. Especially around me. You know I don't understand most of them anyway."

"I'd like some samples to analyse. The magnetometric data I acquired as it passed overhead clearly indicated there was something quite different about this specimen."

"Big words again Doc, big words."

Doc sighed. "Believe me young man, when I start using 'big' words you'll know about it. Look, all I need is some samples. I want you to drive out there and bring me back some rocks. I assume I can count on you?"

Marcus was hoping to get a few days rest before going out again, but Doc was clearly excited by this latest event and he didn't want to let his old friend down.

"Right now? I really need some sleep Doc," said Marcus through a yawn.

Doc ignored Marcus and reached into his lab coat, pulling out a stained map. He pushed Marcus's feet off the table and laid the map out flat.

"It came down in this area," said Doc. He drew a circle with his finger on the map and jabbed at it with a stained finger.

With great effort, Marcus leant forward to examine the map more closely. The area Doc had indicated was quite remote and prone to bandit raids. He avoided it whenever possible.

"I wouldn't ask if it wasn't important," said Doc, sensing Marcus's hesitation.

"Fine." Marcus let out a deep breath. "I'm going to need a travel permit. There's no way I can sneak the truck out past the guards. It will have to be under the guise of a delivery or something."

"You leave that to me," said Doc confidently, "I can get you the paperwork. You just get yourself ready."

"The only place I'm going is bed. I'll be back after I've got a little shut-eye," said Marcus, and with that, he marched out of the warehouse, across a dusty roadway and into the rundown campervan he called home. Lap of luxury it wasn't but he didn't care. He flopped onto a stained mattress and was asleep within moments.

****

After a restless few hours' sleep, Marcus picked his truck up from Doc's warehouse. It was a safe place to leave it as Doc would always keep it in good condition. He was a tinkerer and loved to fix things. All Marcus needed to do was drop a few subtle hints about some strange sound he heard from the engine and he knew Doc would dismantle, clean and reassemble almost the entire thing.

The truck started life as a normal flatbed pickup but had been extensively modified over the years. Doc managed to install an electric motor, as well as an array of batteries, which could supplement the engine. Fuel here was hard to come by and expensive, so solar power was the preferred way to power vehicles. Doc built up quite a lucrative business converting old cars and trucks to use the power of the sun and his services were always in demand. Despite the reliance on solar power, the truck could still use its original engine in case of emergency. Marcus always kept a can of fuel on board, just in case.

The sun had sunk into the horizon before Doc called him back to the warehouse to give him his pass, which allowed him to get past the Legion's guards at the city limits.

"I've managed to get you a travel permit to Jericho," said Doc as he waved a sheet of paper at him. "You'll be delivering some equipment there, but you will *accidentally* get lost and end up at the impact site. Well, that's your cover if you get stopped anyway."

"Jericho is not exactly in the same direction as the impact zone," said Marcus, "in fact, it's fifty miles in the opposite direction."

"Have you ever been to Jericho?" asked Doc.

"No," replied Marcus as he rubbed the side of his head. It throbbed from straining his eyes in the dim light.

"Uh huh," mumbled Doc, "Well, that's the closest major settlement. Anywhere else would look suspicious, and I don't relish being under the scrutiny of the Legion."

"Fair point. Anything else I should know before I get going?"

"I've fixed the high gain antenna on the truck, so you should be able to keep in contact with me for at least part of the way. Try not to break it this time, will you? There are a couple of radiation zones you should probably try to avoid as well. I've marked them on the map for you. Oh, and take this," said Doc as he handed Marcus a Geiger counter, for measuring radiation. "Try not to lose this one. There's no way of knowing how irradiated the samples may be, so it's best to be on the safe side. Just remember, if the needle goes into the red, that's bad."

"I know how to work these things you know."

People didn't survive long in this world if they didn't know how to stay away from the irradiated zones. Nobody went outside without taking a Geiger counter with them.

"Be safe out there," said Doc as he helped Marcus load the last of his supplies into the truck. "And bring her back in one piece. I've spent all week getting her running again."

The last time Marcus had taken the truck out she'd sustained some significant damage whilst avoiding the Legion, which Doc spent considerable time fixing. Smuggling contraband to some of the outlying settlements was profitable but risky. Doc rubbed his hands over the bonnet of the truck, proud of his handiwork.

Marcus climbed aboard the truck and after a few last-minute checks drove out of the warehouse and into the dusty streets. The curfew would come into effect soon, and the Legion took a dim view of anyone out after hours. It only took him a few minutes to pick his way through to the city limits where he was stopped by the guards operating the checkpoint. The truck was searched and his papers scrutinised before the barriers were lifted and he was allowed on his way. Marcus suspected the papers Doc had given to him were forged, though he had no idea how he was getting his hands on them. He wasn't sure he even wanted to know.

He proceeded out onto the uneven roads and into the somewhat unpredictable areas between towns. Not everyone lived in the settlements - many people had been forced out of them either banished for a crime, or in hiding. Out here there was a lot more exposure to radiation, and it was not uncommon for those who were born in these zones to have physical deformities, and of course they could expect to live shorter lives. This made them more dangerous, more unpredictable. He would no doubt bump into someone on this journey. He instinctively reached for his pistol, tucked into a hidden compartment beneath the steering wheel. It was illegal for anyone but members of the Legion to carry firearms, but he wasn't about to get caught in the wilds with nothing to defend himself with.

****

He made good progress, only stopping when he needed to take a break or to shift some debris from the track he was using. He stuck to the route he was supposed to be taking for a long as possible before he deviated and headed towards the impact site. Legion patrols in this area were uncommon, but not unheard of. If they caught him out here with no good reason it might be the last thing he ever did. They were notorious for their brutality, carrying out their orders with no hesitation or sign of remorse. When one of the nearby settlements had refused to capitulate to him Davon sent in the Legion to make an example out of them. They massacred everyone, women and children included. None were left alive, and when they were finished the settlement was burned to the ground. Any resistance there might have been towards him from other settlements soon vanished after that.

But after driving late into the night Marcus was exhausted. His eyes weighed heavily and on more than one occasion he was jolted awake as he drifted off the track and drifted off to sleep. So, when the ruins of an old factory came into view he drove the truck inside its crumbling remains and parked up. It would be hard to spot him from the roadside and in the dark, someone could walk right past where he was parked and wouldn't see him.

He got out of the truck and stretched his legs. In the distance, a faint orange glow and small pillars of smoke rose into the night sky. He checked his map with a small pocket flashlight and worked out his current position. He'd almost reached the impact site. The buildings ahead of him were cast in silhouette, lit by small fires probably started by the burning hot fragments of meteorite hitting the ground. It would be foolish to head down there in the dark, it'd be much safer in daylight. Besides, it wasn't like the rocks were going anywhere and he needed rest.

He climbed back into the truck, took the pistol from the hidden compartment and tucked it into his waistband, before trying to get comfortable for the night. He fell asleep almost immediately.

****

Marcus was startled awake by a sharp cracking noise. He jumped in his seat and looked around, rubbing his eyes, his mind dulled from sleep. Had he imagined it? It was still dark outside, but the first rays of sunlight were starting to poke their way above the horizon, warming his skin as they refracted through the windscreen.

Another loud crack pierced the morning air and this time he recognised it at once as a gunshot. He pulled the pistol from his waistband, pushed the cylinder out to check it was fully loaded and snapped it back into place.

Gingerly he climbed from the truck, taking care not to make any noise which might give away his position. He hugged the side of the vehicle and kept as low as possible while trying to get a better view of what was happening outside. He poked his head out of the door of the warehouse where he'd spent the night and strained his eyes against the darkness. Two figures in the distance were making their way through the ruins of the small town below him. The first and taller of the two, stalked their way across the foundations of a collapsed building, armed with a rifle. The second clumsily picked his way across a patch of open ground, while trying somewhat unsuccessfully to remain concealed. More gunshots followed, which caused Marcus to duck for cover, but he soon realised the shots were not aimed at him.

The pair worked together to flush someone out. The figure shooting the rifle had somebody pinned down inside the empty shell of an old building. The clumsy one moved to try and flank whoever it was in there and squeezed his way through a gap in the structure. A few seconds later he reappeared, dragging someone behind him by the legs back towards his partner. The figure thrashed and screamed, trying to break free, but she was bound and gagged. Every so often the man would lose his grip on her, and she would try to squirm away, only to receive a boot to the torso for her trouble.

The sun poked up above the horizon, light spilling over the ruined town casting elongated shadows. In the light of the new day, Marcus saw the taller figure was a woman, who as well as being armed with a rifle, also carried a large, curved sword, sheathed on her back. Her dark skin shone in the morning light, her cropped black hair held in place with a white bandanna, stained with grime and dust.

Judging by the way the woman carried herself, she was an Elite the most loyal of Davon's soldiers, ready to die for him without hesitation. They almost never spoke and were rumoured to feel no pain or harbour no remorse. The man she was with was a regular. They were mainly used for less important duties, manning checkpoints and the day to day enforcement of the laws set down by Davon. Despite this, they were still not to be trifled with. Regulars were found in almost every major settlement and always seemed to have something to prove.

The man walked back up a steep incline dragging his struggling prisoner along behind. At the top, the outline of an old military vehicle, a Humvee, stood in dark contrast against the morning sky. The prisoner, stumbled as they reached the top and fell to the ground. The Elite dragged the scrawny girl from the floor, pulled back her hood and peered in, before quickly covering her up. Apparently satisfied they had the right person.

The prisoner was marched to the Humvee and bundled into the back of it. The two Legion soldiers climbed in the front of the vehicle and set off in a cloud of dust. Wherever they were going they were in a hurry.

What the hell was the Legion doing this deep into the Badlands? And not just the Legion, but an Elite. They were a rare enough sight in normal circumstances, to find one out here was almost unheard of. Nothing about this situation screamed *normal* to Marcus.

Should he have done something to help? He pushed the thought aside, there was no context for what he saw, for all he knew she was an escaped criminal and they were bringing her to justice. Still, something didn't sit right with him about the whole scene. His mind wandered back to the people who'd been going missing. He'd suspected the Legion might have something to do with it, but there was no proof, nor any explanation as to why they would even want to kidnap civilians.

Marcus tried to shake the thoughts and concentrated on the job at hand. In the now rapidly brightening morning the outline of a tall building became visible. Despite being half collapsed on one side and being held up by its neighbour, it appeared sturdy enough to climb. It would give him a good vantage point of the surrounding area. There was no way he was going down there until he was sure he wouldn't be disturbed.

****

At the top of the building, Marcus was rewarded with a view which encompassed the entire area. A long, deep trench gouged out by the impact signposted the way to his target. He scanned the area below him, checking for any hint of movement. When he was satisfied there wasn't going to be any surprises he climbed down and followed the trench. As he grew closer his Geiger counter sprung to life and hovered close to the danger zone. He wouldn't be able to stay here long.

He continued along the trench until he reached the object that had carved it. Piles of rock and twisted metal, still hot to the touch lay scattered around. The Geiger counter spiked, adding fresh impetus to his task. Almost at once it became obvious someone had been here before him. Recent footprints belonging to several different people were scattered around the site. Tire tracks crisscrossed the area and a large gouge in the dirt signified where a larger object had been dragged out and loaded onto a vehicle. With the earlier encounter still fresh in his mind it was a safe assumption who had been here first.

Not wanting to spend any more time here than necessary Marcus collected the blackened meteorite fragments which easily stood apart from terrestrial rocks. He took care to leave any that were showing high levels of radiation, scanning each one with his Geiger counter. With the samples secured in his backpack, Marcus headed back to his truck and set off back to New Hope. Doc would be pleased with the haul.

****

Less than an hour passed before Marcus spotted the Humvee from earlier parked in the distance. They must have been going in the same direction as him but had stopped for some reason. He slowed, hoping to avoid being spotted. The battery-powered truck was quiet, despite its size, giving him an advantage.

He pulled over a few hundred meters away, tucking the truck out of the line of sight behind an outcropping of rock. He made his way closer on foot and soon discovered the reason the Humvee had stopped. It lay beached on a large rock, fragments of glass and metal scattered nearby. The crash had immobilized it, and the vehicles back wheels span ineffectually in the air. The shorter man who was in the driver's seat, lay unmoving, crumpled over the steering wheel, blood dripping from a gash on his forehead. The Elite and the prisoner were nowhere to be seen.

Marcus cautiously made his way over to the crashed vehicle, keeping an eye out for the missing occupants. Upon reaching the Humvee he climbed into the passenger side and put his fingers to the drivers' neck. He felt the faint rhythm of a pulse under his fingers. The blood from his head wound trickled down the steering column and congealed on the instrument panel below.

Marcus searched the door panels and consoles inside the vehicle for any indication to what they were doing in the area. He

16

opened the glove box and a well-worn map dropped into the footwell. He unfolded it. A thick red circle had been drawn around the meteorite impact site. At least that explained one thing, but it didn't explain the prisoner.

He spread the map on the bonnet of the Humvee and backtracked the route they had taken, indicated by a series of checkpoints. Probably a patrol route of some kind. It took him a moment to discover they were from the Forge. Great, thought Marcus, he didn't want to get mixed up in this, it would only lead to trouble. He folded the map back up and replaced it where he found it and contemplated what to do about the driver. Without medical attention, he would be dead within a few hours. On the other hand, nobody knew Marcus was here. If he left now there would be no repercussions. He wasn't supposed to be here anyway so perhaps it was best if he snuck away.

He weighed his options. The safest thing would be to leave. There was nothing to be gained here. He felt a pang of guilt as he walked away, but he only managed to get a few steps away before a low moan from the injured man made him stop. He didn't have to do much, did he? Just enough to keep him alive until the other one returned. It was likely she would return because there were no other settlements for miles around. The vehicle, even badly damaged, would be the only way out of here. Against his better judgement, Marcus returned to the Humvee and searched for a first aid kit or anything he could use to help the driver.

It was then Marcus noticed the large object in the back. It was covered in a sheet and held in place by ropes. Curiosity got the better of him and he reached his hand through one corner of the sheet. He fumbled around, trying to get a feel of whatever it was hiding. He felt a cold smooth metallic surface and he pulled the sheet in an attempt to get a look at whatever was underneath.

There was a scream in the distance. Marcus span his head in the direction of the cry. The blade-wielding Elite dragged her prisoner by the hair over the rough ground and was heading back towards the truck. Perhaps she managed to escape in the crash, though evidently, she hadn't got very far.

The girl struggled, desperate to break free but to no avail. The Elite woman was so busy trying to keep control of her prisoner she hadn't spotted Marcus yet. Not wanting to be around when she returned, he ducked down the opposite side of the Humvee before sprinting several meters and diving into a small ditch along one side of the road. He pulled clumps of brown grass and branches over himself. It wasn't much of a disguise, but hopefully, with her hands full, the Elite wouldn't notice.

The woman reached the Humvee and after kicking the unfortunate prisoner in the ribs, hoisted her and tossed her, with apparently no effort, onto the back. With a length of rope, she bound her hands tying one end off on vehicle's chassis. The Elite checked the driver and when she discovered he was still unconscious pulled him out of the seat and sent him crashing to the ground with a sickening thud. He groaned and blood oozed from a fresh cut to his face, mixing with the thick dust.

Out here, leaving him would be a death sentence. Either from exposure to the elements or when someone stumbled across him. The Legion had no friends out here and there were plenty of people who would love to extract revenge on anyone who associated themselves with Davon.

The girl cowered in the back of the Humvee, her hood pulled back slightly, which gave him his first look at her face. She was young, perhaps in her early twenties, with long black hair matted with dust and patches of dried blood. Her face was thin, but not gaunt; skin smooth and unblemished, unlike many of the poor wretches which were forced to live out here. Her most striking feature however, was her eyes. A deep shade of purple, which glinted in the morning sun. Marcus had seen many deformities caused by the radiation in his life, but they usually resulted in hideous mutations. If this was a mutation she seemed to have fared much better than most.

Marcus froze. She was staring right back at him, her eyes fixed on his. His mind raced. Would she give him away? Cry for help? He felt for the gun in his waistband, running his fingers over the grip. If the Elite came at him he needed to be prepared to use it. He swallowed hard. His aim wasn't great, could he take her down before she made mincemeat out of him with that sword? He forced himself to look away, breaking the girls gaze. Don't be stupid, he thought, whatever the Legion want her for it's none of your business. Just stay out of it.

The Elite was distracted. The bonnet of the vehicle was up as she tried to get the engine started. Something must have been damaged in the crash and she wasn't going anywhere until it was fixed. The prisoner hadn't taken her eyes off him. People had been going missing and here he lay witnessing a possible kidnapping. He had to do something, perhaps the girl knew what was going on. He swallowed hard and glanced around. They were alone. If he was going to do something, it was now or never.

"Shit," he exclaimed under his breath and edged towards the prisoner. Staying low, and using the vehicle as cover, he slid along the side until he was parallel with her. He raised his head slightly and checked he'd remained concealed. The Elite grunted as she yanked something from the engine and tossed it aside with a clatter. She hadn't seen him yet.

Marcus pulled a small knife from a sheath on his belt. The girl flinched, her eyes wide with fear at the glint of the blade. He put his fingers to his lips and waved his hand to show he meant her no harm. She nodded and flashed her rope-bound wrists. The knife made short work of her bonds, and Marcus tossed them to one side. Quietly he helped her climb down from the back and took her hand to lead her back the way he'd come. She moved with surprising speed and grace, her feet leaving only the lightest of traces in the thick dust. It wasn't long before they reached his truck.

Marcus jumped into the driver's side and started it up. The girl stood by the passenger side door, glancing around as if she was trying to decide what to do.

"Get in," he whispered. He waited a few seconds before repeating himself. "Come on, get in. Unless you want to be left out here, cause' I'm sure as hell not sticking around."

She studied Marcus. She probably didn't trust him. He'd assumed freeing her would have answered that question for her, but he knew trust was a commodity in short supply. Even though he understood her hesitation, he wasn't willing to be caught by the Legion helping someone they wanted, to escape. He'd already stuck his neck out further than he should or normally would have. There was something about her that bothered him. Like an itch in the back of his mind he couldn't quite scratch. Something was going on here, and for some reason, he felt compelled to help her, but not at the cost of his own life.

"Fine, have it your way," grunted Marcus. "Head south," he gestured in the approximate direction as he spoke, "There are a few small towns down there that you should be able to hide out in. At least for now." He reached over to pull the door shut, but as he did she grabbed the frame, and swung herself inside, closing the door behind her.

"Well alright then," said Marcus, slamming the Truck into reverse.

"I'm Marcus," he said. "Time for pleasantries later, right now we need to put as much distance between us and your *friend* out there as possible."

The screech of metal being dragged across stone broke the morning silence. In the distance, the Humvee heaved itself from the rock it had beached itself on and crashed to the ground. Its suspension creaked as it struggled to cope with the manoeuvre. The driver gunned the engine as shards of rock spewed from underneath the spinning wheels. The downed guard - still unconscious, was unable to shield himself from the onslaught. If he wasn't dead already, he would be now.

"Ah crap," said Marcus, "What the hell have I gotten myself into. Hold on."

He spun the truck around and took off at full speed back the way he had come. The Humvee closed rapidly, it was much faster than his truck, which was built more for endurance than speed. Smoke billowed from the bonnet of the Humvee as it grew closer. The driver willing to destroy the engine in an attempt to catch up to them. Marcus knew his only chance was if her engine gave out before she reached them.

Sparks flew off the bodywork of the truck as bullets ricocheted off the chassis and Marcus made a mental note to thank Doc for adding the extra layer of armour. Behind them, their pursuer had her arm through the driver's side window and shot at them with a semi-automatic handgun. It was probably all she could manage to do whilst driving.

The girl was on her knees in the seat, looking back at the chase going on behind them.

"Keep your head down," yelled Marcus. "And for god's sake belt up."

She stared at him, apparently unsure of what he meant.

"Here," he said, tugging at his own belt, "put yours on, or the first bump we hit you'll be going through the windscreen."

A flicker of understanding flashed across her face. She sat back in her seat and fumbled for a few seconds with the belt. There was a click as the buckle fastened. He glanced across at her, she grinned back at him.

"I'm glad you're enjoying yourself," he said, as he threw the truck around a corner. He felt a jolt as at least one of the wheels left the ground before coming down with a thud.

Ahead the remnants of an old town came into view. Collapsed buildings and rusted abandoned cars littered the roadway. Marcus swerved around them, to put as many obstacles between themselves and his pursuer as possible. The Humvee took no evasive action and instead piled straight through them, scattering the wrecks like a bowling ball knocking pins around.

Marcus spotted a large stone building that was still mostly standing to his left and threw the truck behind it, granting temporary cover from the hail of bullets. They found themselves climbing a steep hillside.

The distance between the two vehicles closed fast. Marcus reached for his pistol. He'd rather not have to use it. It's not like there was much opportunity for him to practice since it was illegal for him to even own it. Never mind how expensive the bullets were. In truth, he only kept it around for emergencies and had never needed to use it before. He was pretty sure now classed as an emergency though.

There was a large bang behind them from the Humvee. Its engine, overtaxed from the chase, billowed smoke from under the bonnet. His pursuer dropped back into the distance. Conscious of the condition of his own engine, Marcus slowed down.

There was a loud crack. A bullet hole appeared in the windscreen directly in front of him. Spinning his head around he saw a similar hole in the window behind him. A bullet had missed him by inches. The shot had come from the Elite, who'd climbed out of the Humvee and had steadied her aim on the door of her vehicle. It was an impressive shot from that distance and Marcus sure wasn't sticking around give her another chance. They reached the crest of the hill and dived down the other side, taking them out of the line of fire. He drove on for several more minutes before skidding to a stop.

He let out a huge sigh of relief and checked himself and the girl for any sign of injury miraculously finding none. Someone must have been watching out for them today, he thought. The truck itself fared okay. It was still working, and the bullets appeared not to have hit anything vital.

An alarm grabbed his attention. It was coming from the dashboard and monitored the battery life of the Truck. It flashed urgently, warning him there was less than ten percent battery life remaining.

Marcus tapped the display as if somehow it would help and sighed. The chase had all but depleted the batteries. It wouldn't be too much of a problem though, he still had the fuel he brought with him. He reached into the back of the truck and pulled out the fuel can. His nose caught the pungent and unmistakable scent of fuel. He turned the can over in his hands to reveal a large bullet hole. Most of the fuel had leaked away.

"Great," he said throwing the can into the back. He kicked the side of the truck, which he instantly regretted. He hobbled back to the cab, the girl peered out of the window at him.

"There's no way we have enough charge to make it back tonight," he said. "We're going to have to find somewhere to hide while the batteries charge."

It would take several hours for the truck to charge enough to get them back to New Hope, but Marcus wasn't going to stop

23

now, not with their pursuer so close behind. He climbed back in and pushed on until the blaring alarms and warnings forced him to find shelter under a stone bridge beside a dried-up river bed. Thankfully it had started to rain. The water had already begun to erase the tracks of the truck in the soft dirt. It would make tracking him much more difficult.

He pulled alongside several wrecked cars and switched off the engine. It would be hard to spot them in the dark, and gave them some measure of protection. He was glad he had the forethought to bring some extra rations, it looked like they were going to need them.

The radio in the truck crackled to life. Through the static, there was the faint trace of a voice.

"I don't receive you, please say again, over," Marcus said into the radio. More static. "Doc, hey Doc is that you?"

A voice came over the radio, more clearly this time. A voice he recognised, but it wasn't that of his friend.

"You have something I want," said the man's voice calmly, "I'm giving you one chance, and one chance only. Hand her over or suffer the consequences."

Marcus did not reply, instead, he reached out a trembling hand and switched off the radio, leaned back in his seat with his eyes closed and sucked in a deep breath.

His stomach knotted up. Things had just gone from bad, to worse.

Chapter two

Marcus wished for the ground to open and swallow him whole. It had been six hours since the radio contact with the last voice he ever wanted to hear. Davon's. His chest tightened at the mere thought of his name. Whoever this girl was, Davon wanted her personally. Daylight streamed through the gaps in the bridge above them, hitting the solar panels on the truck and providing much-needed power to the batteries.

His instincts told him to run. To take the truck and drive as far away from this place as possible. Even if he complied with his demands to hand over the girl, Davon would probably kill him anyway, he wasn't known for his generous nature. Could there be any chance he didn't know who he was? Marcus let the thought roll around in his mind for a few moments. Could he take the risk?

The girl was asleep, tucked against the passenger side door, her hood pulled over her face. The gentle rhythm of her breathing the only sound in the cab. She still hadn't said a word to him, despite his efforts to coax something from her. Marcus drummed his fingers on the dashboard, his mind racing. Enough was enough. He'd risked his life for this girl, and in the process managed to get himself on the hit list of the most dangerous man in a thousand miles. It was time for some answers.

"Hey, wake up!" He shook her by the shoulder.

She woke with a jump and pressed herself against the door, eyes wide, like a frightened animal backed into a corner. Marcus held up a hand. "Whoa, it's okay. I'm not going to hurt you."

Her breath quickened, she pulled her knees to her chest and wrapped her hands around them defensively.

Marcus reached for a bottle of water and flicked the cap open. He took a sip and offered it to her. She reached out gingerly and took the bottle. She turned it over in her hands and sniffed at its contents, before taking several large gulps.

"Hey, steady, that's got to last us until we can find more," said Marcus softly. She stopped, wiped a dribble of water from her chin and handed the bottle back to Marcus.

At least she understands. That's something.

She slumped back and loosened her grip on the armrest which still bore marks where her fingers had dug into the fabric. He took out the food he'd packed back in New Hope and shared it with her. As they sat in silence eating, Marcus tried talking to her again.

"My name is Marcus," he said. "And you are?"

She studied him as if she was trying to decide whether or not to answer. She took a piece of bread from the container and nibbled on it. Her unblinking eyes locked on his.

"Do you understand me?" he asked

She gave a quick nod and shoved the bread into her mouth hungrily.

"Why were the Legion after you?"

"Vana," she said quietly.

"What does that mean?" asked Marcus.

"My name. My name is Vana."

Her voice was lighter and softer than he imagined it would be, and she spoke with a strange accent he couldn't quite place.

"Good to meet you Vana,"

He held his hand out in greeting. She simply looked at it. "We've got a major problem here, and unless I know exactly what is going on things are going to get worse. Now I need to know why the Legion were after you."

"I don't know," she mumbled. "They came after me for no reason."

Marcus wasn't convinced. There was nothing but radioactive wasteland this far out. If the Legion were here, they were here for a reason. It couldn't' just be a coincidence that they happened to stumble across her. They knew she was out there. He wouldn't press her on that though. He'd only just gotten her talking and he didn't want her to clam up again.

"What are you doing all the way out here in the middle of nowhere?"

"I got lost," Vana said, as she brushed crumbs from her clothes.

"Are you with anyone else?"

She shook her head.

Marcus slunk back in his seat, put his head back and closed his eyes. He knew a few places in the Badlands he could vanish into for a while - but he needed to offload this girl somewhere safe and pick up more supplies.

"I'm heading back to New Hope," he said after a few minutes of silence. "It's the closest settlement around here. You can tag along with me until then if you like, or we can go our separate ways now. It's up to you. If Davon is after you though I would suggest finding a rock to hide underneath for a few months and wait for all this to blow over. I for one intend to do the same."

She looked at her hands as she rubbed them absentmindedly.

"Well?" asked Marcus. He regretted his harsh tone, but this was no time for dawdling.

Vana reached out and opened the truck door, she half climbed out and stopped. A few seconds later the door closed and she was sat in her seat - belted up.

"Okay," said Marcus as he started the engine, it hummed quietly - the faint vibration of the motors rippled through the seats. He checked the battery levels: thirty-eight percent. If he was lucky it would be enough to get him back home. He wasn't prepared to risk taking the more travelled routes, choosing instead to take a long way around. It would be dark before they reached New Hope, but at least that should make sneaking past the guards slightly easier.

He wasn't looking forward to explaining any of this to Doc.

****

The truck moved silently through the night, only the crunch of loose rock underneath the tires betrayed its presence. Vana hung her head from the window and gazed at the stars.

Maybe it's the first time she's seen them.

Marcus recalled something he had been told years ago - about a group which had remained locked away in their bunker, not realising that people had once again taken to the surface. A group of scavengers happened upon them and murdered half the group for their meagre possessions. Whether the story was true he never found out, but it got him thinking.

How many others were out there, across the world? Buried away unwilling or too afraid to come to the surface.

Marcus dismissed the thought. It didn't matter in the end. He was only concerned with getting back to New Hope. He'd grab some supplies and vanish into the Badlands for a few weeks until the Legion got bored and moved onto something else.

They drove on through the night. Marcus kept a watchful eye on his surroundings and fully expected to be attacked at any moment. No attack came, and Marcus allowed himself a moment of relaxation. Hours of being on edge had taken its toll, his nerves were shot and his eyelids felt like lead weights.

A dim orange glow on the horizon caught Marcus's attention and snapped him out of his daze. It was far too early for the sun to be rising. Thick black smudges were mixed in with the glow, but from here he couldn't make out what they were. As they drew closer Marcus's heart dropped. It was smoke. Thick black smoke. New Hope was burning.

"Shit!" cried Marcus, "He wouldn't have?"

He pulled up and jumped out of the truck. One half the settlement was in flames. The inferno roared as it tore into buildings, and people scattered. Some fighting the fires, some trying to escape them.

Vana appeared beside him, rubbing her eyes. She surveyed the chaos below. What's happeni--?" she began.

"Your friend Davon is what's going on," snapped Marcus. "It's no coincidence that I stumble upon you and now this happens." He kicked a nearby rock, sending it crashing into the side of the truck, denting the panel slightly.

"What are you going to do?" she asked. Her posture stiffened and she took a few steps back from Marcus.

He unclenched his fists and softened his tone. His anger towards her was misplaced. Certainly, she hadn't asked for any of this. He took a deep breath and collected his thoughts.

"Doc's down there somewhere. I need to get him out. If they're looking for me they'll start at his place."

Vana stepped forward and reached out a hand towards his shoulder, but hesitated. She walked back over to the truck.

"I'm sorry if I caused this Marcus," she said softly.

29

"We can worry about all that later. Right now, I need to find my friends."

They climbed back into the truck and drove as close to the fences as he dared. The pandemonium going on in New Hope masked their approach, but they couldn't get any closer in the truck without the risk of being seen. The main routes into the settlement were heavily guarded. The Legion it seemed were not interested in helping people escape the inferno but instead were searching and detaining people trying to flee. He needed another way inside. It wasn't going to be a problem; this wasn't the first time he'd sneaked into town.

He hid the truck in the collapsed remains of an old church, a few hundred meters from the outer perimeter. It was nothing more than a pile of rubble at this point, but it was enough.

"I'm going to get my friend, and then we're getting the hell out of here," said Marcus as he jumped from the cab. "You should get out of here too. I hear there are a few settlements out in the East that are too small for the Legion to be bothered with. You might find someone willing to take you in. If you're lucky."

Vana didn't move, her face fell flat.

"I'll never make it on my own," she said. "And anyway, I'm heading north. There's something I need to do."

Marcus put his head in his hands and rubbed his face. She was right. On her own, with no supplies, she wouldn't stand a chance. She'd already been kidnapped, beaten, shot at and god knows what else.

"Fine," conceded Marcus. "Stay here, I'll be back in an hour, two tops. When I get back we can discuss where to go, but I can tell you now, it won't be north. Cause' that's where Davon is."

Vana smiled, and unclenched her fists, the colour in her palms returned and a flicker of a smile flashed across her face. She climbed back into the truck without saying a word and sat motionlessly. He would help her, just this once. After all, she was a long way from home. For some reason it didn't strike him as odd he should know that.

****

Guards lined the settlements checkpoints. People fleeing the flames were stopped and searched and those who tried to run past were knocked to the floor and restrained. A patrol loomed in the distance. Marcus flattened himself against the fence and edged along it carefully. He located his usual entrance and pushed his way through, this time he didn't bother to conceal it behind him. It wouldn't make any difference now.

Thick smoke burned his lungs as he ran towards the centre of town. The fire hadn't reached here yet. People weighed down by whatever possessions they could carry ran from the flames, funnelled towards the checkpoints and into the waiting arms of the Legion.

Marcus grabbed a piece of material as it blew by in the wind, and wrapped it around his face. In part to help filter out some of the smoke, but mainly as a disguise. This was all because of him - because he felt sorry for someone. Now look at what it had cost. He passed dozens of people as he ran. Some tried to put out the fires with buckets of water, some cradled loved ones and wept over soot covered bodies. Others were in shock and wandered around with no idea what to do. He pulled the disguise over his face as he passed them, kept his head down and ran.

All this devastation because he chose to help Vana. Was the suffering these people, and probably people in other settlements, were going through worth it? Something bigger was going on here, and he'd fallen square in the middle of it.

31

"Hey, you!"

The voice came from behind him. Marcus didn't turn but instead quickened his pace.

"Hey, stop!" called the voice again. Marcus spun his head around but kept moving. There were two men behind him, one was carrying a length of metal pipe. He doubted that they simply wanted a friendly chat.

"That's him, that's the guy," one said, as he pointed the pipe at Marcus.

Marcus wasn't waiting around to find out what they wanted, instead, he broke into a full sprint and ducked into the first alleyway he saw. He barrelled along several more side-streets overshooting one of them and careering into the wall. His shoulder bore the brunt of the impact and sent a wave of pain through his upper body. Winded, he scrambled to his feet and darted into the smoke-filled alleyway.

The shouts for him to stop intensified, the two men close behind. Marcus vaulted over a low wall at the end of the alley and landed on a pile of garbage. He lost his footing and fell to the ground. He cursed himself and got back up. He'd given them chance to catch up. He clawed his way out of the mess and got to his feet, only to be met by a dead end. Behind him, his pursuers flung themselves over the wall skidding to a halt a few paces away from him.

Marcus stepped back defensively and looked around for anything he could use as a weapon, but saw nothing that could help him.

"You," the big guy grunted, as he struggled to catch his breath, "Where's the girl?" He wrapped the pipe in his hands.

"How did you manage to keep up with me?" he said to the larger man. "I mean, carrying all that extra weight around?"

Antagonising a large man wielding a pipe was not the smartest thing he could have done, but he was angry. Angry for getting himself into this situation, and angry at being so careless as to be cornered.

"You're gonna regret that," he said, "We know who you are, and we know you were with her. Davon wants the girl and he's happy to kill all of us to get her. He's already burned down half the town. So, I'll make it real easy for you. Tell us where she is, and nobody else needs to get hurt."

"Look, I don't want any trouble. You've obviously mixed me up with someone else. So, I'll be on my way now."

"Oh, there's no mix-up."

The pipe wielder pulled a crumpled photograph of Marcus and Vana from his back pocket, apparently taken during the escape from the Elite soldier.

How had they gotten a picture of him? Was there someone else there, watching them the whole time? These were questions for another time, as Marcus's attention snapped back to the larger man. He was advancing upon him the pipe scraping on the ground as he dragged it behind him.

The smaller man, wearing a soot-covered shirt pocked with burn marks spoke in a thick broad accent. "The Legion was 'anding those pictures out, right before they set fire to everything. Now we don't 'specially like them much around 'ere, but we ain't gonna sit around doing nothin' while our homes burn."

Marcus's back hit the wall behind him with a jolt. There was nowhere left to go. The big guy swung the pipe between his hands, a menacing glint in his eye and the faint curl of a smile on his lips.

Even if Marcus told him what he wanted to know, he'd probably still get a crack around the head from that pipe. The guy was angry, his home was under siege and he wanted to take it out on someone. Marcus could understand that much at least. Still, he didn't fancy being on the receiving end of it.

"Last chance. Where's the girl?"

"Guys, guys! Can't we just—" The pipe struck Marcus and he was hit by an explosion of pain. His vision blurred and he fell backwards into the wall, crumpling to his knees. The pipe was hoisted into the air again before a hand came out to stop it.

"That's enough, he won't be any good to us if you splatter his brains all up this wall now will he?" The pipe rattled to the floor and Marcus felt himself being dragged into a standing position and pulled face to face with his assailant.

"He'll be fine, just givin' him something to think about," grinned the big guy.

"Bring him," said the small one.

Marcus tried to resist, but the blow to the head left him woozy. The world span and the voices of his attackers became distant and unimportant. His gaze drifted up - the smaller man's face filled his vision.

"Sorry about this."

The last thing Marcus saw was a fist heading towards him.

****

Marcus looks around. His arms and legs are in chains, he's in a dark room, but he's not alone. He can hear soft sobbing noises in the darkness. Suddenly, light bursts into the room. The silhouette of a figure stands in the doorway, before yanking Marcus to his feet, dragging him outside.

He is not in Jericho anymore, he's in the Forge. People scurry around and bump into him as they pass. He can smell burning, but there's no fire.

The man who he is walking with is ahead of him now, he's leading him to a building. His body won't listen to his cries to run, he continues to walk until he reaches the door. The room inside is dark, save for a surgical bed in the middle of the room, lit from above with a spotlight. A woman stands next to the bed, dressed all in white, wearing rubber gloves. She is carrying a tray with needles and scalpels, some covered in dried blood. Marcus suddenly finds himself on the table, he's terrified but he can't move or call out. The woman places a mask over his face, blurring out her features. There is a noise of escaping gas.

As suddenly as it began it is over. He is stood in the operating room, all his doubts and fears gone. Replaced by certainty, confidence of purpose. The door opened again, someone else is brought into the room. Marcus looks down, and now he has a surgical tray in his hands. A woman is brought over and placed on the table, Marcus knows her from somewhere, but doesn't dwell on it. Soon she will come to understand. She struggles as he places the mask over her face and switches on the gas. She tries to cry out, but the anaesthetic takes hold. Marcus reaches for one of the scalpels on the tray, selects the biggest one and raises it to her face.

A sudden feeling of cold comes across him, he feels wet. There are voices coming from somewhere. From the darkness.

****

"Wakey, wakey."

Marcus's vision started to clear. He rolled his tongue around the inside of his mouth and spat out a mouthful of blood. The side of this head pounded from where he had been struck. Another bucket of icy water hit him in the face, getting in his eyes and nose. He spluttered as he strained for breath. He tried to move but found himself immobilized, his arms and legs bound by a thick rope cutting deeply into his exposed skin.

"That's enough," came a voice.

Someone grabbed Marcus by the hair and yanked him up.

"I hope Clifton here didn't hit you too hard because we have a few questions we'd like you to answer."

The voice came from an older man, perhaps around sixty, he had a short scruffy grey beard and a fat face which gave him a 'Jolly old man' look, although there was nothing jolly about him now. The hand released him and his head flopped down.

"Clean him up, and bring him to my office," the man said as he headed for the doorway. "And make it quick. I want to get this dealt with before word gets out."

Clifton grabbed a machete from a nearby table and turned it over in his hands. He shot Marcus a sinister grin and swung the blade through the air. Marcus flinched as the edge streaked past his face and sliced clean through one of the ropes binding him.

Clifton laughed. "Now you didn't think I was gonna hurt you did ya?"

He cut the second rope and Marcus crashed to the floor. Clifton grabbed his arm and pulled him up.

"Walk," he grunted, "If I have to drag your sorry ass through here you'll come to regret it."

Marcus tried to summon the strength to break free of Clifton, but he was in no condition to put up a fight.

"You're lucky," said Clifton as they walked through a damp smelling corridor. "If it were up to me you'd already be on your way to Davon."

At the end of the corridor was another room, more brightly lit with the door half ajar. A heated argument was taking place inside. Clifton shoved Marcus through the doorway and into a chair. In front of him was a desk cluttered with paperwork and ashtrays full of cigar stubs.

The pressure on Marcus's arm slackened, and Clifton took a few steps back.

The bearded man sat on the other side of the desk, a cigar wedged between his fingers. A woman, hands splayed on the desk stood nose to nose with him. Her face was flushed and her clothes and hair stained with ash and soot. She pushed a fleck of blonde hair from in front of her eyes and tucked it behind her ear.

"Ah, speak of the devil," the man said. "I don't think we have been properly introduced, my name is Hudson and of course we already know who you are. Clifton would you mind waiting outside for me whilst we have a discussion with Marcus?"

Clifton opened his mouth to argue but appeared to change his mind, and simply turned and left. The door slammed behind him.

"Now, perhaps we can conduct a more civilised conversation. I'm sorry for how you were treated earlier, Clifton can be a bit…

overzealous. He has his uses but lacks subtlety," he pointed his cigar at the bump on Marcus's head. "If you get my meaning."

"May I introduce you to Kali? We were discussing our current situation."

"Discussing my arse," snorted Kali. "You're only interested in turning a profit."

She pushed some papers from Hudson's desk onto the floor and looked at him in disgust. "I saw those two clowns drag you down here," she said to Marcus. "I know Hudson. He intends to turn you over to the Legion, for a price."

"Everything… everyone has a price my dear. Even you," said Hudson calmly.

"Pfft, you can't afford me." Kali stood back from the table and leaned against the back wall with one foot.

Had he met her before? She looked familiar. His head throbbed from the earlier beating, he had trouble keeping his thoughts straight.

Hudson laughed. Cigar smoke billowed from his mouth and hung in the air above him.

Marcus wafted the smoke from his face and coughed theatrically.

"So, what is it you do around here *Mister* Hudson?"

Hudson grinned, took a long drag on his cigar and exhaled, before stubbing it out.

"You really can't beat a good cigar you know," he said. "Very hard to come by these days as well. Proper ones anyway, not the rubbish they peddle around here. Can I offer you one?"

He took a cigar from its container and wafted it under Marcus's nose.

"No thanks," said Marcus. "I'm not planning on staying long."

"Hah!" Hudson clapped his hands together in amusement. "I think I'm going to like you." Well in answer to your previous question, I *acquire* things. Things that are hard to get. Then I deliver them. For a reasonable price of course."

"You're a glorified thug Hudson," interjected Kali. "You act like you're some big mob boss or something, but you're just a two-bit player. You've proven yourself useful in the past, but remember, should things ever change you will find the nature of our *relationship* changes, quickly."

Hudson didn't rise to Kali's comments and instead waved his hand at her. He pushed his chair back and put his feet on the desk in front of him.

"Well, to business," he said. "Let me tell you about the situation you have found yourself in. Last night we had a visit from the Legion. They were looking for you and a girl who was travelling with you. They said you interfered with an operation - killed one of their men and kidnapped the girl."

Marcus slammed his hands on the desk, his face flushed red.

"First of all, I didn't kill anyone," he yelled. "And secondly, I didn't kidnap her, it was a rescue." Kali's eyes were burning into him. "You've heard about the disappearances? People vanishing never to be seen again?" A flicker of recognition flashed across Kali's face. *She knows.* "Vana, the girl," he clarified, "When I saw her tied up, thrown in the back of the Humvee I had to do something, I couldn't leave her like that."

"I understand," said Hudson, "I really do. You saw someone in trouble and you helped them out. You have a conscience, I can understand that."

Kali scoffed, "Yeah right. Like you were ever burdened with one."

"You wound me," said Hudson, placing his hand over his heart, "You really do, but this isn't about me now is it. It's about you, and how you can get yourself out of this situation."

"How was I supposed to know they knew where to find me?" Marcus protested. "I was out in the middle of nowhere. I could have been anybody."

Hudson leaned forward, jabbing the cigar at Marcus as he spoke. "Well, they did know who you were and where you were from. They came here and when they couldn't find you they started rounding people up for questioning. When they didn't get the answers they were looking for… well, you've seen their handiwork for yourself. The fires were brought under control last night, but they were only a warning."

"Stop pretending like you care," said Kali. "You see this as a business opportunity and nothing more."

"You're wrong Kali. I'm doing this to protect the town and my family. What Davon and the Legion are doing here is nothing compared to what they'll do if they don't get what they want. And we can make it all go away. My conscience is clear."

Hudson picked up a framed photograph from his desk and showed it to Marcus. It was old and yellowing at the edges.

"My wife, and daughter," he said, pointing to the picture. "This was taken a few years ago now."

In the centre of the image was a young woman, with dark hair and wearing a long flowing dress. In the background, a small girl played with wooden toys, a look of glee on her face.

Marcus let out a sigh and stared at the ceiling. He wasn't sure he wanted to know the answer to his next question, but he asked it anyway.

"So why exactly am I still here, and not being turned over to Davon?"

"He seems to want you pretty bad," said Hudson. "But he wants the girl more. Kali has persuaded me to let you go. All you need to do in return is to tell me where she is."

40

Kali walked over and placed a hand on Marcus's shoulder. Her grip was firm and she stared into his eyes.

"I suggest you cooperate with us, things will go a lot more smoothly if you do," she said as she released her grip and returned to the other side of the room.

"Wise words. I think we can all agree the first thing we need to do is to find this girl," said Hudson. "Once we have her, we will be in a much better position to negotiate with Davon for the safety of the town." He looked over at Marcus, "So, are you going to tell us where she is or not?"

Marcus weighed his options. They weren't numerous. If he refused to talk he was sure Hudson would have someone beat it out of him, and he was unsure if Kali would intervene to stop it. At some point she would have to make a choice, him and Vana over the rest of the town. He knew which he would choose if the roles were reversed. He knew, in the end, they would get him to talk.

But there was also something else. A deep-seated fear of Davon on an almost instinctive level. He wasn't willing to turn her over though, not to him. He needed to buy himself some time; string them along until he could figure out a way out of this.

"Okay, okay," he said, "I can see you mean business, so I'll tell you, on one condition."

"And that is?" Hudson asked as he leaned forward in his chair.

"You can have the girl, but not me. It's her he wants anyway, and I really don't enjoy the thought of what he may have in store for me. You can tell them I died in the fire or something, then I'll leave town and you will never hear from me again."

If Vana had any sense, she'd be miles away from here by now anyway.

Before anyone could answer, the door to the office burst open and Clifton barged into the cramped space, he was red-faced and short of breath.

"He's here," he gasped.

Hudson sighed. "Looks like we're out of time Marcus."

Chapter Three

A muffled conversation leaked through the office door. Marcus strained, but the voices were too distant for him to tell what was being said. One of the voices was clearly Hudson's; the other belonged to Davon.

Kali left as soon as she heard Davon had arrived, and with her went the only person he thought may be on his side. Marcus guessed she didn't want to be anywhere near him, a feeling he understood completely.

When the door finally opened he found himself face to face with Davon. He stood at least six feet tall. His thin face and sharp eyes gave him the look of a predator. He strode across the room, flanked by two big, tough-looking men. Behind him came the sword woman, stoic and silent as ever.

Marcus squirmed in his seat. The ropes used to bind him to the chair itched his skin.

"Mr Davon," clamoured Hudson, "It's a pleasure to meet you. I understand that you don't usually make personal visits, it's an honour to finally make your acquaintance. I have a business proposition if you're interes-"

Davon waved his hand at Hudson without ever taking his eyes off Marcus. Hudson backed away and remained silent. The bodyguards took positions near the door, while the sword woman stayed behind Davon at all times, her eyes darting across everyone in the room. Davon stared Marcus in the eye.

"Where's the girl?" he asked in a blunt tone of voice.

He was not in the mood to be messed around. Marcus wracked his brains for any way he could get himself out of this situation but his options were limited.

Yep, you're screwed.

Marcus dug his nails into the armrests of the chair he was tied to. The odds of him getting out of this alive were slim, and if he was going down, he wasn't going to lead them to Vana.

"Your Amazon warrior queen over there had her chance," spat Marcus, indicating the sword-wielding woman. "And I managed to outrun her in a glorified milk float," Marcus smirked.

He was going to die, but he didn't care anymore. Perhaps if he made them mad it would be over quickly.

Davon beckoned with two fingers to the sword-wielding woman, who grabbed Marcus's right hand, pinning it to the arm of the wooden chair he was tied to.

"Hey, come on!" yelled Marcus. He struggled to get free, but it was futile; the ropes gave no leeway. He felt a sharp pain in his jaw as an elbow smashed into him. He tasted blood and spat it out onto the floor.

"You haven't been properly introduced to Amara have you?" said Davon indicating the sword woman. "She's here to - *encourage* you to be honest with me." At this, Amara unsheathed her sword, brought it down, and pressed it against Marcus's wrist. He winced as a thin line of blood appeared where the blade contacted his skin.

"Do you like the sword?" Davon asked. "Guns are clumsy weapons. Efficient in some ways, but they lack a certain something don't you think? Too easy to use. A blade on the other hand, takes skill, and I find that people are a lot more cooperative when faced with one. After all, you can't see the bullet that will kill you. A blade on the other hand…"

Amara pressed down harder, and Marcus couldn't help but let out a cry of pain. A wide grin crossed Davon's face. "I recommend you be honest with me, or else Amara here will start removing bits of you. Now, where's the girl?"

Marcus spat out another mouthful of blood. "What's she to you?" he asked.

"I ask the questions," snapped Davon. He flashed a glance to Amara, who dug the blade deeper into his arm. The pain made him light-headed, he was on the verge of passing out.

"Last chance. Where is she?"

How long since he left Vana at the truck? It was daytime now, so it must have been a few hours at least. If she had any sense she would be long gone by now. He wouldn't wish Davon on his worst enemy, he'd just have to hope she'd left while she could. He was quite attached to his arm, and he'd like to keep it that way.

"She's hiding on the outskirts of town, I was coming to get supplies when Hudson's collection of inbred monkeys jumped me."

Hudson rifled through some papers on his desk and produced a map of the area. He brought it over to where Marcus was sitting. With his finger, he pointed to a spot nowhere near where he left Vana.

"There," he said. "I left her there."

Davon didn't look at the map, instead, he pushed it to one side. Hudson backed away silently.

"We already found your vehicle," said Davon, "She was nowhere to be found."

Marcus saw an opportunity.

I'll make myself useful to you.

"I don't know where she's gone," blurted Marcus. "I told her to stay put and wait with the truck until I got back."

"And what exactly were your plans for when you returned?"

We were going to hide out in the Badlands, find an abandoned building and hole up in there until this all blew over." he lied.

"What did she tell you about herself?" Davon asked. He brought his face down close and flashed his teeth. Marcus reeled back as Davon's hot breath hit his face.

"Nothing, she barely spoke, it's almost as if she'd never spoken to anyone before."

At least that much was true.

Davon considered what had been said for a few seconds before he spoke, "I have heard enough." He glanced at Amara and nodded. She released his wrist, which was now covered in blood from where the blade had cut into his skin. His relief was short lived when he saw Amara raise her blade, ready to land a killing blow.

He jolted back in the chair and strained against the ropes binding him. He turned his head and winced. "Good luck finding her without me," he spurted out desperately. "I know the Badlands, I know all the places she could hide. Let me live and I'll help you find her."

The first chance I get, I'm gone.

Amara grabbed Marcus by the hair and pulled his head up. He hoped he'd done enough to convince Davon. If not, at least it would be over quickly.

Davon stared at him, a strange grin on his face. He grabbed Marcus's head and tilted it to one side as if he was examining him. After what felt like an eternity, he released him and put his hand on Amara's shoulder. She lowered the sword and sheathed it.

"Perhaps you are right, you could be of some further use to me," said Davon as he turned to leave the room. "Amara, I'll leave this in your hands. Do not fail me again." Amara showed no outward sign of concern from his barely veiled threat.

"Davon," called Hudson, "I hope I have proven to be of some use in this situation," he said, the confidence in his voice betrayed by his body language. "I already have men out looking for the girl."

Davon stopped in his tracks, and promptly turned and strode back over to Hudson. He grabbed his shirt with both hands lifting him so he was at Davon's eye level, who was quite a bit taller. Hudson was not a small man by any means but the apparent ease at which he was lifted surprised everyone in the room. Clifton, who normally would have rushed to his boss's aid, stood rooted to the spot, his eyes darting between Davon and Hudson and the two men by the doorway. He shifted his feet back and forth but made no attempt to intervene.

"Listen to me very carefully, I want the girl *alive*," growled Davon.

"Should one of your half-witted men hurt her I will have Amara remove your head and have it displayed on a spike at the main gates. You, as well as anyone you may care for." Davon glanced at the photograph on the desk. Hudson swallowed hard and remained silent. Davon released his grip and he crumpled to the floor. He didn't try to get up but instead backed into the corner.

Amara swung the sword towards Marcus, who flinched, before realising the target was the ropes binding him to the chair. He really wished people would stop doing that to him. The remains of the rope fell away and Amara yanked Marcus out of the chair, jammed the cold, hard barrel of her gun into his back and pushed him through the doorway towards the exit. She wasn't taking any chances this time.

She marched him outside and the Humvee, now repaired, sat waiting for them. The dents from his previous run-in with it were clearly visible. Clifton was muttering to himself, kicking up dirt as he walked along behind him. He was red-faced, perhaps because he hadn't been allowed to rough Marcus up. They marched out into the morning glare, broken glass cracked under his feet. He stopped, and turned to Clifton, shooting him a look which said, *better luck next time.*

Marcus braced himself for the inevitable, taking all his remaining willpower not to duck out of the way as Clifton's fist hit him in the gut. He went down. He laughed through the pain, tears blurring his vision.

Totally worth it.

Amara came to his aid and dragged him up by his shirt. She gave Clifton a look which conveyed it would be a bad idea to try that again. Clifton, on the other hand, seemed to have gotten it out of his system and was grinning at Marcus.

"You're a dead man anyway," he snorted. "Enjoy what's left of your miserable life."

"Why Clifton, I didn't know you cared," Marcus retorted, blowing him a kiss.

Clifton raised his fist but was stopped by the point of Amara's sword at his neck. He lifted his hands in surrender and backed away, grinning at Marcus as he drew a line across his neck with his finger.

Marcus was loaded into the back of the Humvee and his hands were once again tied together with a thick rope. The two heavies that escorted Davon were also in the Humvee and they looked much more able and well trained than her previous companion. It would be harder to slip away from these guys. But still, every second he was alive was one more than he would have had. He needed to use his time wisely.

Marcus intended to wait until night time before he made his move. It was still early in the morning, so he would have to string them along for a few hours until dusk. Amara finally spoke to ask Marcus where they should start looking. By now, Vana would have a full day's head start on them. He asked to see a map and found an area he knew to be a day's walk away, in the opposite direction to anywhere anyone sane would want to go. It was an area he knew well, and one where he felt he would have the best chance of escape. It was also several hours drive, which was a welcome way of using up some of the daylight hours.

****

Marcus made sure to make them stop every few miles to check an area where he said Vana might be hiding. It was wasting their time, and more importantly making the heavies riding along with them restless and impatient. Even the unflappable Amara started to show some irritation. This served his purpose well; they would be more prone to make mistakes which gave him more of a chance. He wouldn't be able to keep this up for much longer, there was bound to be a limit to her patience and he didn't want to be around her when it ran out.

Finally, they reached the area where Marcus wanted to make his move. Dusk painted the sky a deep shade of purple. Out here with no artificial lights, it would be pitch black, even the light from the moon would be dim; scattered by the dust in the air.

The path was too difficult to navigate at night, and Marcus argued Vana would spot the headlights from the Humvee from miles away and would easily be able to avoid them. He convinced them it would be best to stop here for the night, as Vana surely would not travel in the dark.

Amara turned in her seat and unholstered her gun. She leaned into the back where Marcus was sitting and pushed the gun into his kneecap.

"If this is a trick, you'll be sorry," she said, digging the gun into him. "I won't kill you, but you'll wish I had when I deliver you to Davon. That is unless the girl takes your place."

They parked the vehicle beside a crumbling building. The two guards got out and secured the perimeter whilst Amara built a small fire. Marcus was kept locked in the back of the Humvee, his hands tied at the wrists. He tried to pull the knots apart with his teeth when the guards were not looking, but they were too tight.

Amara kept her distance from the fire and her eyes on the horizon, ever alert. Occasionally one of the guards checked on Marcus. He pretended to be asleep, hoping they'd eventually tire and become careless.

The doors to the Humvee were locked, but he had an idea on how he might deal with that. He coughed and heaved to attract the attention of one of the guards. After a while of listening to him retching in the back, one of them came over to find out what all the commotion was about.

"What's up with you?" the guard asked,

"I need water," spluttered Marcus through fake coughs.

The guard took a water bottle from his belt and held it to Marcus's lips, before squirting it onto his face.

"That's all you're getting, make the most of it," said the guard with an irritation in his voice. Marcus took his opportunity. Before the guard could slam the door shut, he wedged his boot into the frame of the door to prevent it from closing. The guard, who had already started to walk away, turned around a puzzled look on his face. He returned to the Humvee and reached out to slam the door shut again. With all his strength Marcus kicked the door, which swung out and caught the guard on the head. He staggered around for a few seconds, dazed, before Marcus dove out of the seat, knocking him over. The guard hit the ground with a thud, moaned and rolled over. He nursed his head as he tried to regain his footing. Marcus kicked out, catching the downed guard in the chest, knocking the wind from him, turned and ran into the darkness.

His escape attempt lasted precisely fifteen seconds before he was brought to the ground tackled by the second guard. Moments later he was looking up the length of Amara's sword, its point dug sharply into his chest.

"Pathetic," she spat. "I expected as much." She pulled her sword away and pointed it at the guard, still catching his breath.

"You. Tie him up, and make sure you do it properly this time or you'll have me to answer to."

His legs were tied, the rope cut deep into his skin. He considered protesting, but he knew they'd only tighten them out of spite. He winced as his hands were tied behind his back. The guards took a hold of him, each grabbing an arm and led him back to the Humvee.

"We're heading back to the Forge," Amara stated as Marcus was dragged across the dusty ground.

"It's obvious you were never going to lead us to the girl. She's nowhere near here is she?" Amara glared at Marcus and continued, "Davon will not be pleased you have deceived him. You can forget any hope you may have had for a quick death. He likes to make an example out of people like you. Failures."

There was nothing much Marcus could say in response, he would be watched like a hawk from now on. He would be thrown in front of Davon and god knows what he would do to him. He tried not to think about all the terrible things in store for him, but his mind tormented him with all the possibilities.

Marcus hit the ground in front of the Humvee, whilst one of the guards went to open the door to get him in. The other guard maintained a tight grip on his shoulder.

"Sorry about the head," said Marcus, gesturing towards the bandage wrapped around the guard's head. "No hard feelings eh?"

His head hit the metal framework of the Humvee, and a wave of dizziness came over him.

The faintest hint of a smile crossed the guard's face.

A loud bang and the crack of breaking glass broke the silence. The grip on his shoulder was released and he fell to the ground, cracking his knees in the process.

The body of the guard hit the floor next to him, a bullet hole in his temple. Marcus gagged, and dove for cover. Shots rang out as the remaining guard fired blindly into the night. The attackers returned the favour and a bullet ricocheted off the ground a few feet from Marcus. He felt a sharp burning pain in his left shoulder. He'd been hit. Instincts wanted him to put pressure on the wound, but with his hands still tied behind his back, it was impossible.

He wormed his way across the ground towards a large boulder and curled up behind it, pulling himself against it to get out of the line of fire.

The commotion in the distance drew closer.

Bandits. It must be, nobody else would be crazy enough to attack the Legion. Whoever it was, they'd caused enough of a distraction that he might be able to escape. He started to crawl away from the battle, inching through the dust on his hands and knees. A hand appeared from out of the darkness and grabbed his legs.

"Not so fast," huffed Amara, as she dragged him away from the firefight. "You're not getting off that easily."

"In case you haven't noticed we're being shot at. Untie me, give me a gun, it's our only chance to get out of this in one piece."

"You must think me a fool." She cocked her gun and pressed it against Marcus's head. The muzzle was still hot and it burned as it pressed into his skin.

"No comment," he said flatly.

She pulled the pistol from his head and shot several times into the night. There was a yelp as someone went down in pain. More shots rained on their position.

"Good shot! Can I have a go now?"

Amara reeled around. "I have two bullets left," she said. "Should they overrun us, one is for you the other is for me."

"You know, I'm starting to think you don't like me."

She ignored him and called to the second guard. "Cover me."

The man acknowledged her command with a nod. To Marcus's surprise, he stood and unloaded his clip into the darkness. He made an easy target.

That's crazy, he's committing suicide!

Amara used the distraction to reposition herself out of the line of fire. She dragged Marcus along with her by the legs, and for once Marcus didn't resist. Wherever she was going it was safer than where they were. It must have taken an immense amount of strength to drag him, but she managed to get to the front of the Humvee, putting the engine block in between them and the bullets flying towards them.

There was a scream, followed by silence as the second guard was hit. He tried to move but didn't get far before he was hit several more times. His body slumped to the ground, leaving a smear of blood on the Humvee door.

The gunfire stopped. In the distance people yelled commands at each other. Weapons clacked as they were reloaded and somewhere in the darkness came the moans of someone who had been shot.

"So, this is how it must be," Amara said, pointing the gun at Marcus's head.

"Wait, wait!" cried Marcus. "I have several ideas, many of them much better than murder-suicide." He braced himself for the shot. At least it would be quicker than anything Davon had in store for him. Perhaps he had gotten off lightly.

There was a high-pitched whine. The hairs on Marcus's neck stood on end and a tingling sensation rippled across his skin. A bright flash startled Marcus and left streaks across his vision. This was followed by a crackle and the smell of burning.

Marcus squinted through one eye to find someone stood over the unconscious body of Amara.

"Holy shit it works!"

The woman pulled down the bandana covering her face. It was Kali and she was holding a bizarre looking weapon. About the length of a rifle and covered in wires and batteries. Smoke rose from the barrel which glowed red hot.

"Managed to get yourself shot then I see."

Marcus grimaced as he slumped back to the ground. He took a few deep breaths and tried to steady his nerves.

Kali shouted over for a med kit and she was handed a small green box, battered and scratched from years of use. She pulled out some wadding and a haemostatic agent and applied it to Marcus's shoulder.

"I'm no medic, but this should hold you over until we can get back to camp," Kali said. Activity around the camp became more frenzied as the dead were collected and the wounded helped into waiting vehicles.

"We're part of the underground," Kali stated, after seeing the confusion on Marcus's face. "The rest of my people are still tied up with the Legion back in New Hope."

Marcus had heard of the underground. At least the rumours. A group of people who opposed Davon and the Legion, fighting back wherever they could. Supposedly they attacked Legion forces, stole supplies and generally made themselves a thorn in the Legions side. It was hard to get any real information though, as the Legion controlled access to information. Their propaganda had people believing everything was just fine.

"What are you doing here?", asked Marcus, "Not that I'm complaining of course."

"Long story. I'll fill you in later. You're welcome by the way." She looked at the unconscious Amara.

A truck pulled up and Kali helped Marcus across to it.

"Wait, what about her?" he said, pointing to Amara.

"She's coming with us. We need her alive."

"Please, can I be the one to tie her up?" asked Marcus. "Payback."

"You're in no condition to do anything. Just get in the damn truck."

Kali jumped into the front seat next to the driver and Marcus was helped into the back seat.

"Are we going to New Hope?"

"Nope, we're heading someplace else. It's going to take a few hours, why don't you get some sleep, I'll wake you when we get there."

Marcus buried his head into the padding of the seat. As he succumbed to the depths of exhaustion his mind twisted with the events of the day, and of his lucky escape. As he fell asleep one last question crossed his mind:

How on Earth did they find me?

Chapter Four

Faces; all around him, terrified. They huddle in corners and cover themselves. Avoiding eye contact, afraid that they will be next. He's holding a rifle; aiming it at the crowd. There are others here too, wearing black, rounding people up and loading them into trucks. Some try to run away. They are shot, their bodies left on the street where they fall. A man breaks free and runs past Marcus, towards his family who are huddled in a doorway. Marcus beats the man with the butt of his rifle in front of his wife and children, who scream for him to be left alone. He drags him away and throws the beaten man into the back of a truck, loaded with many other townspeople, then slams the rear door. Marcus clambers onto the side of the truck and thuds on the roof with a gloved hand.

As the trucks drive off a man runs out and grabs the side of one of them, reaching through to try and take the hand of his daughter who has been taken. Marcus kicks the man away. Another guard takes a shot at the man with his rifle but misses. As they drive off, the man in the street sinks to his knees and sobs.

****

"Wake up, we're here."

Marcus awoke with a jolt, which sent a stab of pain through his shoulder and along his arm. He shielded his eyes as sunlight streamed through the windscreen. His other clamped onto his wounded shoulder, as it burned with pain. Piles of blood-soaked wadding sat on the seat next to him. He dreaded to think how much blood he'd lost.

"We need to get you properly patched up," said Kali, next to him. "I've done as much as I can with the med-kit."

"Where are we?" asked Marcus.

"At our camp."

The truck pulled over by a small collection of tents and other temporary buildings at the base of a cliff, nestled in a clearing. They were surrounded by pine trees, the only way in and out was the muddy track leading to the small clearing they were in. In the distance, the silhouette of the mountains, their peaks hidden amongst thick cloud, hung above the treeline.

"Cosy," remarked Marcus as he lumbered out of the truck.

"Come on," she beckoned. "Someone is waiting to see you."

Kali appeared beside him and offered a helping hand on the uneven ground, and Marcus leaned on her for support. As they approached one of the buildings he was greeted by a medic who helped them inside.

Armed guards stood at the doors, keeping a watchful eye on everything going on within the building. Medics scampered around treating the wounds of several other people injured in his rescue.

"We're not taking any chances after last night," said Kali, motioning to the guards. "Davon's not going to be happy when he realises we have his star pupil." She pointed to Amara who was strapped to a bed on the other side of the room, still unconscious.

Marcus scratched his head. *I wonder what's so special about you?*

"Let's get your shoulder looked at," said Kali, breaking him from his thoughts.

She helped Marcus onto the nearest unoccupied bed and made him comfortable. A medic came over with some first aid equipment, placed them on the bed, and examined his wound.

"Looks like you got lucky, it's a clean shot, doesn't appear to be any shrapnel left in there. I'm going to have to clean it and give you a few stitches," said the medic as he rifled through his supplies.

Marcus winced as the medic went about fixing his shoulder.

"Lucky eh? Next time tell your people to not shoot the person they are trying to rescue," he said.

"Actually, we were there for Amara," said Kali.

"Way to make a guy feel wanted," huffed Marcus. "And for your information, I'd already escaped once."

"Yeah, it looked like it was going well. Right up until you were caught."

"You were watching? You could have helped," said Marcus.

"If it makes you feel any better, you provided us with a nice distraction. So, in a way, you helped us help you."

In the end, it didn't matter. He was still alive, and free. A much-improved situation from the one he was in a few hours ago.

When the medic finished treating his wounds, he placed Marcus's arm in a sling and gave him a handful of antibiotics and painkillers to take. Marcus swallowed them all in one go and lay back on the bed.

"So, when do I find out what is going on here then?" asked Marcus, as the medic moved onto his next patient.

A deep and familiar voice at the back of the room replied. "Right about now I reckon."

"Doc!" cried Marcus, "Thank god you're okay."

He hobbled over and embraced his friend.

"I was on my way back to New Hope looking for you when I was ambushed by a couple of heavies working for Hudson."

"I know," Doc replied. "When Davon's men attacked the town I hid in my workshop. I have a nice little concealed bunker under the floor I use for some of my more… energetic experiments. Davon's men might be loyal, but they're not particularly smart. I was perfectly safe."

Marcus limped back over to his bed and sat on the edge, Doc followed, continuing to explain.

"How come I've never heard of this *bunker* before?"

"It's not important now," Doc said. "After they finished searching the warehouse, I snuck out and met with Kali and helped arrange your escape."

"I wasn't aware you two were acquainted," said Marcus.

"We go back," said Kali, who was stood by the doorway. "You have Doc to thank for your rescue. He's the reason we could find you at all."

Marcus stared blankly at them, waiting for them to explain further.

"Remember when you were in Hudson's office and I told you to be co-operative? I got right up in your face about it."

"Yeah, I did wonder what that was all about. Thought you were going in for a kiss. Got my hopes up and everything."

"Ha, you wish. Actually, it was so I could plant this on you."

Kali grabbed his jacket from the bottom of his bed and flipped over the collar. A metallic glint, from an object roughly the size of a coin tucked into a rip in the lining caught his eye.

"A present from Doc," she said as she pulled it out and flicked it across the bed towards Marcus. He picked it up and turned it over in his hand.

Doc beamed with pride. "A beacon of sorts. Something I cobbled together a while ago. Knew it would come in handy one day."

"So, you could track me?" asked Marcus.

"Well, yes and no," said Doc, "It has a limited range, and it only gives an approximate location, but out here it was enough for Kali to track you down."

"This is switched off, right?" asked Marcus, twirling it around in his hand. "We don't want someone else being able to track us with this."

"The battery ran out hours ago. It's perfectly safe now," said Doc.

It was time he found out what was going on here. He didn't like to be out of the loop. Especially when his life was on the line. He stared at Doc. "Go on, let me in on the big secret. What's going on?" he asked.

Kali looked at Doc, who nodded as if he were giving her permission.

"As you have no doubt heard, the Underground want Davon gone. We don't know where he came from or why, but life has been intolerable since he arrived. Now, something else is happening." She paced around the room as she spoke. "In the last few months he's been shipping large quantities of raw materials to the Forge, and as you know, more and more people have been disappearing. We believe the two are connected. We don't know what he's doing in there, but whatever it is, it can't be good.

61

Everything changed when that Vana girl showed up. There's something different about her and Davon's going crazy trying to get his hands on her. So much so he left the Forge for the first time in years. *We* have no idea why, but she might," said Kali, nodding towards the still unconscious and now well restrained Amara.

"So, the real objective was to capture her, and I was just, what? A bonus?"

"Ah don't get all bent out of shape," Kali replied, "Doc would never forgive me if we let anything happen to you. The plan was always to rescue you as well as capture her. You should know your rescue cost the lives of two of my people, so don't consider yourself too hard done by."

A stab of guilt hit him, and it brought the reality of the situation into pinpoint focus.

"I'm... sorry Kali. I didn't mean to sound ungrateful because of course, I am."

Amara moaned gently, and her arms twitched. The restraints rattled against the frame of the bed.

"What's the plan with her then?" asked Marcus.

It was Doc who replied to his question. "It's been difficult to get any information on what Davon is doing. We've captured and interrogated several of his men before. They either know nothing or are very well trained. They never reveal any useful information.

"Then there are the others, like Amara over there. They are different. The elite Legion soldiers. They act as his personal bodyguards and are the eyes and ears of Davon. Amara is one of them, she must know more about what is going on up there, and perhaps this would give us a clue as to how to stop him for good. Capturing an Elite alive had proven to be impossible. Until now..."

"How come?" asked Marcus, rubbing his temples with his hands. He was getting a lot of information all at once, and it made his head pound.

"Quite simply they don't allow themselves to be taken alive," said Doc. "We've had two previous attempts to do so. The first came to a rather messy end with a self-inflicted shotgun wound, the second threw herself off the roof of a building after we cornered her. Davon's control over them is unnerving."

"But you managed to capture Amara," said Marcus.

"Thanks to the charge gun, yes," said Doc. "It delivers a massive electric shock to the target, rendering them unconscious. So far it's the only thing to have worked."

"Still some bugs to work out though Doc," said Kali. "The damn thing melted in my hand after the first shot."

"So that's what you shot her with?" said Marcus. "Pretty effective if you ask me. Any chance I can get my hands on one? It looks fun."

"I'm afraid there's only the prototype," said Doc. "And it's going to be out of commission for a while."

"Shame. I was planning on dishing out some divine justice. You know - Zeus style, with the lightning and th--"

"Maybe we should have the medic check you for a concussion," smirked Kali. "You sound delirious."

"Just happy to be alive. After everything that's happened to me in the last few days, I think I can be forgiven for letting off a bit of steam."

Amara twitched, which caught Marcus's attention. He walked over to her.

"First Elite ever to be captured alive eh?" he said. "Do you think she will talk?"

"We have no idea," said Doc, "We've got her sedated for now until we can get her somewhere more secure to try and break her conditioning."

Doc walked over to the bed and placed his hand gently on her cheek, "We have a chance to save her," he said.

Marcus hadn't noticed it before now but there was a remarkable resemblance between the two. Her nose, eyes - the shape of her face. He'd seen these before in the face of his friend.

Amara was Doc's daughter.

****

Marcus was reeling from the revelations of the last few hours. He'd known Doc for years, and he didn't recall him ever mentioning a daughter. What's more, Doc had been working with Kali all this time - investigating Davon. Marcus considered himself to be fairly switched on, so felt a little disconcerted this had been going on without him knowing about it.

Doc sat in a chair next to Amara's bed and talked indistinctly with the medic, who was busy checking Amara's vitals while he scribbled notes on a pad.

"How's the shoulder?" asked Kali.

Marcus rose slowly, wary of making any sudden movements. The sling across his shoulder was helping; the pain now a bearable ache.

"Okay I guess. The drugs must be kicking in."

"Let's take a walk shall we?" she nodded towards the doorway.

"Yeah, I could do with some air."

Kali held the door open for him as he hobbled out, his eyes strained against the sunlight.

Marcus got his first good look at the camp. There were at least ten tents pitched in a rough circle. Trucks were parked in the centre of the ring of tents and armed guards patrolled the perimeter.

"What's the deal with this place then?" asked Marcus, kicking lumps of mud as he walked.

"After the attack on New Hope the underground members scattered. We needed to regroup to plan our next move. This has been coming for a long time now, but it needed something like this to happen to force everyone into action. So, we set up shop here. It's out of the way, so we won't be getting any uninvited guests. Gives us a little time to breathe and prepare. Now we have one of their elite we might start getting some answers."

"He's her father, isn't he. I can see it in his eyes. Just another one of the many secrets he's been keeping from me. Did you know about this?"

"He had his reasons for not telling you about her. You'll need to talk to him about it. It's not my place. He's been looking for her for years. We'd heard rumours that she was still alive, but until she showed up in New Hope with Davon we couldn't be sure."

"Shit, and seeing her in that condition… he's taking it better than I would."

"Doc is important to what we're doing here. I don't want to put him in the position of choosing between us and his daughter."

Marcus understood. To have thought something was lost forever, only to get it back. There's no telling what lengths Doc would go to in order to ensure he never lost her again. Better to take things slowly and let Doc deal with it in his own time.

"I wonder whatever happened to Vana?" said Marcus. "Davon said he found the truck, but she wasn't there."

Kali shifted her feet uncomfortably.

"You know where she is don't you?" asked Marcus.

65

"I know where she is."

"Is she safe?"

"She's with one of my people, we have her tucked away in a safe-house."

The fact that she wasn't in the hands of Davon gave Marcus a small sense of satisfaction. It must be driving him crazy to have lost her twice.

"Lucky you got to her first I suppose."

"Doc's been with us for a while now and he knows all your little secret ways in and out of New Hope. It didn't take us long to find her, waiting for you. Feisty though isn't she? It wasn't easy convincing her to come with us."

"Well, I hope you get the answers you're looking for. Ever since she showed up, everything's gone crazy. She's hiding something. Something big. Part of me is intrigued by what is going on. The other part, the rational part, is encouraging me to find a nice quiet hole to live in for the next ten years."

"Not gonna happen I'm afraid. My friends have been talking with her, and it seems that she'll only deal with you. Apparently, she only trusts you."

"Well, I did save her life. Gotta count for something right?"

Marcus stopped and leaned against a low brick wall, at one point in its life part of a much larger building, but now reduced to rubble.

"So, where've you been keeping her?"

Kali didn't get a chance to answer.

The relative calm of the camp was shattered by yelling and screaming coming from the medical building. Marcus and Kali rushed back and burst through the doors. Amara was conscious, screaming and struggling to break free of her restraints.

"Hold her," yelled Doc to the two guards by her bed.

"What's going on?" Kali shouted through the confusion.

"I don't know," Doc grabbed a syringe and filled it with a clear liquid from one of the many vials scattered around. "She woke up and started screaming. I've given her twice as much sedative as normal, but it's not working on her. I'm preparing another dose."

"Let me go!" screamed Amara, "I'll kill you all!"

The thrashing intensified and she foamed at the mouth.

"It looks like she's having a seizure," said Kali, who struggled against Amara.

Marcus moved closer. Amara's eyes locked on him and the struggling stopped.

"You!" she bellowed, her voice cracking with the strain. "This is all your fault."

"Hold her steady," said Doc. "Her arm, hold it."

Kali grabbed Amara's arm as Doc plunged the needle into it, pumping its contents into her.

"I can't give her anymore. I've already given her the maximum safe dosage. If this doesn't work I'm out of ideas."

Her screams of anger turned to whimpers, her body relaxed and her eyes glossed over as the drug took hold. As quickly as it started it was over. The guards released their grips, her skin mottled where she had been restrained.

"Thank god for that," Kali said, letting out a sigh of relief.

Doc checked her pulse and nodded, "Good. She's out again, but I don't know for how long."

"I don't get it Doc," said Marcus, "Don't you want her awake?"

"No, not yet. We need to keep her unconscious until we are in a more secure environment and have all the right equipment to treat her condition."

"Sounds like you've done this before."

67

"Once, a long time ago, but the conditions were quite different back then." He shifted his feet and shuffled some papers on his desk randomly, lost in thought.

The awkward silence was broken by Kali, "Right then, we need to get Amara back to the bunker, I'll arrange a truck for you. How long before you can move her Doc?"

"She can be moved now, and quite frankly the sooner we get her back the better."

"Is this the same bunker that's underneath your workshop?" asked Marcus.

Doc and Kali looked up as if they had forgotten Marcus was still in the room with them.

"You may as well tell him," said Kali. "Might be good for him."

"Yes Marcus," said Doc. "The same. Go get Vana, bring her to the bunker and perhaps then we may start to put the pieces of this puzzle together."

"I'll make the arrangements, stay here with her," said Kali as she marched out.

Everything had changed. People Marcus thought he knew were living secret lives. He considered running, but with Davon out there presumably still looking for him, he preferred his chances here. At least for now. He'd only scratched the surface of what was going on here and part of him wanted to get to the bottom of it.

After a few minutes, Kali returned and Amara was loaded onto a waiting truck. She ordered a guard to accompany the truck on its journey, a wise precaution, having witnessed first-hand how dangerous Amara was. When everything was all taken care of and the truck vanished into the distance, Kali came back over to speak to Marcus.

"Let's go get your girl then," she smirked jumping onto the last remaining truck. "You can sit up front with me, wouldn't want you to fall off the back and hurt yourself again."

"As I recall I didn't hurt myself, you shot me."

"Not on purpose."

"Still hurts like hell though," he said as he nursed the wound with his good hand.

"What are they going to do with her? Amara, I mean," said Marcus.

"Hopefully we can undo some of the damage. Maybe he can bring her back."

"Do you believe it's possible?"

"Yeah. Yeah, I do," she said staring into the distance.

A flatbed truck sat ready to take them to wherever Vana was being kept hidden. Kali still hadn't told him exactly where they were going, but since they weren't packing much in the way of supplies it was probably somewhere close by.

Two soldiers joined them, both equipped with a variety of weapons, some which Marcus couldn't even identify. One of them jumped into the driver's seat and started the engine, while the other climbed into the back with the rest of their equipment. Two dull thuds on the roof indicated that they were ready to go.

The truck lurched into motion and kicked out loose rocks behind it as it set off in a cloud of dust.

Chapter Five

"They've doubled the guard," said Kali, as she surveyed the town ahead of them through a pair of binoculars. "They're not gonna make this easy on us."

Marcus laid next to her on a patch of dusty ground overlooking *Jericho,* one of the larger settlements in the area, and by the looks of it, one of the most guarded.

"What on Earth possessed you to bring Vana here?" asked Marcus. "There must be hundreds of Legion soldiers down there."

"It's not like we had time to plan this out," snapped Kali. "It's a big town -easy to get lost in. We already had assets in place. It was the best option at the time."

"It's not looking so great now."

"What's done is done. We need to get in there, but they'll be on the lookout for us."

"So how are we going to get inside then?" asked Marcus.

"Like I said, we have assets inside Jericho. I've been in touch with them. They know what they need to do." She glanced at the guards. "You two get back to the truck and stay by the radio. We can take it from here."

One of the guards looked as if he was going to argue, but instead, let out a sigh and signalled to his companion to follow. "We'll be monitoring," he said, flicking on his radio. "Any trouble and we're coming down." The pair packed up some gear and trudged off back towards where the truck was hidden.

"We move out at dusk," said Kali, "just before shift change. The guards on the checkpoints will be tired, but their relief won't have arrived yet."

The sun was already creeping towards the horizon; it would be less than an hour before it got dark. Marcus turned over, tucked his jacket underneath his head and looked up at the darkening skies. His eyes followed the curve of the razor-sharp golden rings above him and watched as their dark shadow crept along the landscape towards them. The wind picked up and Marcus shivered, rubbing his arms to stay warm.

It was going to be a long night.

****

"Come on. It's time."

Kali stood over him, her arm extended to help him up. He groaned as he got to his feet and dusted himself off. He removed his sling, dropped it to the ground and put on his jacket.

"Don't want to stand out too much," he said. He watched as the wind picked it up and blew it away. "Just don't enter me into any boxing matches or anything."

"No promises," she said. Kali pointed at a faint collection of lights near the main road leading into Jericho. "That's our way in. Here, wear this."

She tossed him a long dusty cloak, complete with hood. He slung it over himself and watched as Kali did the same.

They walked along a well-trodden path which led to the settlement and approached the gates. As they grew closer Marcus nudged Kali.

"So, are you gonna fill me in on the plan? I'm not a mind-reader you know."

"Just follow my lead."

"Why is it so hard to get a simple answer out of everyone around here?"

"Well, the first rule about insurgency is to keep your goddamn mouth shut. You never know who might be listening."

"Paranoia. Check."

"Kept me alive so far."

She had a point, though Marcus didn't want to give her the satisfaction by saying so. Instead, he gave a nondescript grunt.

Several people were milling around the gates, trying to get inside. There were five Legion soldiers here, who checked and double checked the identities of everyone trying to get into town. Marcus could see why they were wearing the cloaks, as they blended in with some of the others out here wearing similar attire.

As they approached the entrance, Kali reached under her cloak and brought out a radio. She tapped the send button three times then spoke quietly into it.

"Light it up."

Seconds later, a large explosion from the centre of town rocked the ground. Alarms blared and the sound of gunfire filled the air.

The radios of the Legion soldiers at the checkpoint crackled to life, and after receiving new instructions, most of them darted off in the direction of the explosion. Two guards remained. Kali pushed her way through the crowd at the checkpoint until she was near the front. She grabbed Marcus's arm.

"Get ready."

With a grunt she pushed against a man standing next to her and knocked him to the ground. She quickly stood back. The man picked himself up off the floor and looked over to see Kali pointing at a shorter round-faced man standing nearby. Not happy to be pushed around the man walked over and swung his fist at the shorter man, whose nose exploded from the blow. He went down clutching his face.

Several other people, likely friends of his, dived towards his attacker, and soon the whole crowd bayed as the fight spilt over and into the checkpoint. There were whoops and cheers from the crowd who enjoyed this unexpected entertainment, and Marcus was sure he caught a glimpse of money changing hands in the crowd. There was always someone around willing to make a bet. He wondered what *his* odds were of making it out of this madness alive.

The guards jumped in to try and restore order, which only agitated the crowd further. With the distraction complete, Kali and Marcus snuck through the checkpoint and into the city.

"You know, I've never understood the compulsion for people to run *towards* explosions. I make the habit of doing the opposite," said Marcus. "So, who's putting on the light show?"

"You ask too many questions; do you know that? Come on, let's go. We need to-"

There was a blinding flash from the centre of town, followed by a huge explosion. Much larger than the first. Windows shattered all around them, and Marcus was thrown to the ground as a massive fireball rose into the sky, along with plumes of thick black smoke.

"What the hell was that?" spluttered Marcus as he struggled to regain his footing.

"That wasn't us," said Kali, steadying him. "We don't have anything that big."

A blue glint coming from the sky caught Marcus's attention. It lasted only for a split second, like a shooting star. There was another explosion, further away this time on the other side of the city, followed by two more.

"I think we've overstayed our welcome," yelled Marcus above the chaos unfolding around them. "Let's get the hell out of here before we're next."

"This way," shouted Kali. She grabbed his arm and led him along a nearby alleyway. "We have to get to the safehouse."

****

The safehouse was gone. There was nothing left of the building except rubble, and a crater several meters wide. Marcus was no expert, but it looked to him as if it was struck from above. Perhaps by a missile, or by some other weapon available to Davon. Several other buildings in the immediate vicinity were also consumed in the blast. Bodies, whole and in part, lay scattered amongst the destruction. Most burned beyond any recognition.

"My god," said Kali as she sunk to her knees. "They're dead. All of them. The other explosions, the other safehouses. Gone."

Marcus wretched as the smell of burnt flesh clung to the back of his throat. He coughed, steadied himself and started digging through the rubble, desperately looking for any sign of survivors. Given the size of the explosion he couldn't be sure there would be anything left, but he tried anyway.

Kali's eyes were unfocused and she walked unsteadily across the ground towards Marcus, who caught her as she fell.

"You're in shock," he said, as he helped her to the ground. "We can't stay here, it's not safe."

Kali nodded, staring blankly at what was left of the building. Her fingernails dug into the earth, and she squeezed lumps of soil in her hands. Marcus's heart sank, and he dropped to the floor next to her.

"Her secrets died with her," muttered Kali. "I suppose we'll never know now. Whatever she knew, it was worth killing dozens of people for."

Kali kicked out at something invisible. "I've known some of these people for years. All gone, just like that. That son of a bitch is going to pay for what he's done."

Marcus stared at the destruction. "Why do this though?" he said, "And why now? After all the trouble Davon went to cap--"

Realisation dawned upon Marcus. "Of course!"

Kali gave him a blank stare.

"Don't you see? Davon wanted her alive. He went to great lengths to capture her. He'd never have done this if there was a chance she was inside. She must be alive somewhere, either captured or on the run. But she wasn't here."

He tried to drag Kali to her feet, but she was a dead weight. She mumbled something incoherently and snatched her hand back from him. He was about to try again when he heard coughing coming from underneath a corrugated Metal sheet some distance away. Marcus approached it cautiously and pulled it free. Underneath was a man, who by some miracle appeared mostly unharmed. Marcus dug him out and sat him up.

"Thanks," spluttered the man. He coughed on the plumes of dust floating in the air and brushed debris from his straggly white beard. His battered clothes were full of holes and the smell of alcohol filled the air around him. "Thought I was a goner."

"Are you alright?" asked Marcus.

"I'm fine. Fine. The names Doug." He coughed violently and produced a hip flask from underneath his jacket. A large dent on one side had been made from a piece of shrapnel, still stuck to the side.

"Hah, I always thought this stuff would kill me." He tapped the flask and took a swig. He brushed the shrapnel away from the container and looked for any leaks. He appeared pleased not to find any.

"What happened here? Did you see?" asked Marcus.

"Yeah, I saw the whole thing. This is my patch see." He pointed to an upturned shopping trolley, with its contents, mostly empty bottles, strewn across the ground. "Been a lot of people around here recently. Business has been good. Them good folks that used to be in the house over there, god rest em, used to keep me well stocked up with the good stuff. All I had to do was tell em' if I saw anything suspicious."

"And did you?"

"Yeah, there were these unsavoury types, showed up yesterday. They hung around in the corner over there. They were Legion. You can tell because of the boots you know. Nobody 'round here has good boots, except the Legion. I stayed out of their way."

"Did you see a girl? Young-ish with purple eyes?"

"Indeed I did. She was here. Can't forget those eyes, they're something else, aren't they?"

"Wait, you said she *was* here? Do you mean she left before all this happened?" he waved his arm at the destruction around them.

"That's fight. Damndest thing. There was all this commotion and shouting coming from inside, and then your girl came busting out of there like a bat-outa-hell and ran off across the street over there. Someone chased after her, then a few seconds later, boom. I'm under a pile of rubble."

"Here, let me help you up," said Marcus, extending a hand. "We should get you checked out by someone, make sure you're okay."

"There's no need for that," said Doug, waving Marcus away. "I'm fine. Besides, I'm an old man, ain't nothing no doc can do to fix that. I'll be okay. You go find that girl of yours."

Doug righted his shopping trolley, threw some of his belongings into it and wheeled it off through what was left of the street.

Marcus ran back over to Kali and helped her up.

"There's still a chance. She wasn't in the building when it went up. She's still out there somewhere. We need to find her. If we don't all this was for nothing."

Kali was more alert now. She stood up, a look of fierce determination on her face.

"Let's go," she said through gritted teeth. "I owe those Legion bastards some payback." She quickly marched along the street, with no attempt to conceal her presence.

"Where are we going?" Marcus huffed as he jogged to keep up with Kali's pace.

"I have an idea where to start looking. Hopefully there'll be plenty of Legion for me to kill along the way."

****

They approached a ruined building that looked just like any of the others scattered around Jericho. It used to be four stories high, but most of the floors were now compacted together into one, leaving a mostly empty shell.

Kali looked over her shoulder, then pushed a sheet of metal aside, which revealed a doorway. She edged her way through and Marcus followed, his eyes scanning the other nearby buildings for any sign they were being watched.

Inside looked exactly how he expected it to. Graffiti covered the walls; logo's and slogans, decrying the Legion and calling for an uprising were most prominent.

"What is this place?" whispered Marcus, his voice almost lost in the echoes of their footsteps.

77

Kali moved over to a grate on the floor and knelt. She ran her fingers across its surface and held her hand up to a shaft of light coming through the rafters of the tattered building above them.

Her fingers glistened with blood. "Someone's been here. Recently." She pulled open the grate revealing a ladder. Marcus's stomach tightened.

"What's down there?" he asked. He pulled at his collar. Was it hot in here? He felt hot. He rubbed the sweat from the palms of his hands on his clothes. "So, we're going down there are we?"

"We call them the Warrens. It's a network of old service tunnels and sewer pipes that run all over the city. It's how we've managed to keep one step ahead of the Legion in Jericho. From here we can get to just about any place in the city undetected."

"So, you think Vana may be in there? How would she even know about it?"

"There's no guarantee, but it's as good a place as any to start, and I don't know about you, but I don't feel safe on the streets at the moment."

Kali descended the ladder and motioned for Marcus to follow her. He took a few deep breaths and followed behind, closing the grate above him as he did so. There was a click, and a row of light bulbs affixed along the length of the tunnel flickered to life.

They walked along the tunnel for several minutes, following a drip trail of blood, and emerged into an open area, with more tunnels branching off in other directions. Kali explained this area used to be a subway station, and tunnels led to other platforms like the one they found themselves in now. The blood trail continued along another tunnel, which they followed until the trail abruptly stopped.

Marcus looked around. A large concrete arch rose above them and cast a long shadow from the faint light coming from the few remaining light bulbs.

Kali's eyes darted across the darkness, her hand reached for a pistol tucked into her waistband and she edged forward into the dim light ahead.

"What are yo--"

"Shhhh," hissed Kali. She put her fingers to her lips. Marcus took the hint and backed away.

A blur rushed past Marcus, knocking him to the ground. Landing on his injured shoulder he howled in pain and clasped onto it with one hand. Kali grunted as she wrestled with someone in the darkness, who had her pinned down and was trying to knock the gun from her grip.

Marcus clambered to his feet and rushed in. He used his body as a battering ram, charging into the hooded figure and knocking them away from Kali. He stumbled and hit the ground again, this time spinning around and landing on his good shoulder. Kali scrambled to her feet and pointed the gun at the hooded figure. From underneath the figure's cloak, the metallic glint of a barrel pointed back at Kali.

"No fair," said Marcus, "I don't have a gun to point at anyone."

The standoff went on for several seconds before the stranger spoke. "You don't look Legion, but it's hard to tell these days."

The newcomer raised her hand and pulled back the hood of her cloak. A young woman, not much older than twenty with piercing blue eyes and long red hair tied in a ponytail, looked back at them. Her left arm dangled down, and a slow trickle of blood dripped onto the ground from a wound on her arm.

"Not Legion, totally, completely not Legion. Hate those guys," said Marcus. "Would appreciate it if you didn't point that thing at me. The name's Marcus by the way."

She cocked her head to one side, and lowered her weapon slightly, but kept it ready to use. Kali didn't budge. "Who are you?" she asked sternly.

"You can call me Charlie," she said. "And you are?"

"I'll get to that, but first: can you tell me where the birds go when they fly south for the winter?"

"I don't know, but they never come back," replied Charlie, without missing a beat.

Kali lowered her gun and tucked it back into her waistband. "You're a member of the underground. I'm Kali, I run the New Hope section."

Charlie hesitated for a few seconds before also lowering her weapon and replacing it in a holster underneath her cloak.

"What's going on?" asked Marcus. "What was all that nonsense about birds?"

"It's a code," said Kali. "If someone gives the right response to the phrase, I know they are part of the underground movement."

"And if she gave the wrong response?"

"I'd have shot her. Immediately."

"Remind me never to get on your bad side, okay?"

Kali turned back to Charlie. "Were you the one in the safe-house just off the main square? We spoke to someone who said they saw two people fleeing from the building just before it was destroyed. I assume it was you?"

"Yeah," said Charlie, applying pressure to a wound on her left arm.

"And the second person was Vana? Purple hair, kinda weird looking?"

"That's right. but you won't be getting near her until I have some assurances."

"What kind of assurances?"

"Well, for starters can you explain what happened to our safe-houses?"

"We have no idea," said Kali. "We were on our way to make contact with them and all hell broke loose. By the time we arrived… I'm sorry, there was nothing left."

Charlie turned and punched the wall with her good hand. She swore and hit the wall again, leaving blood stains behind. Her knuckles glistened red.

"How can we fight against something like that?" she said, her face flushed with anger. "We act like we know what we're doing, but really we're all just a bunch of amateurs who are going to get ourselves killed."

"I don't believe that," replied Kali. "And neither do you. We've been dealt a blow here tonight, but if we give up now then all those people died for nothing."

"But what have we accomplished? Nothing, that's what."

"We've done the best we can with the resources we have," said Kali, softening her tone. "I know we're outmatched, but that may be about to change."

Charlie looked up. "I know what you're going to say. Vana knows more about him than she's letting on. She wouldn't say much to me, but she has mentioned you, Marcus."

"Well I am pretty hard to forget," he said, running his hands through his hair.

"How long have you had to put up with him," Charlie said, pointing to Marcus.

"You get used to him after a while. Kinda tune him out."

"I'm right here you know," moaned Marcus.

"But I suppose I have to be nice to him. I did shoot him after all."

"I'm not surprised," said Charlie.

Marcus wasn't sure what he had done to deserve this tirade of insults but was happy that people were no longer pointing guns at each other.

"It was an accident, she didn't mean to shoot me."

"That's what I told him anyway."

Marcus coughed to get the pair's attention. "As fun as all this character assassination is, can we get back to business? You ran out with Vana, why?"

"I didn't like how they were treating her," replied Charlie. "I don't know who she is really, but she's clearly no friend of Davon. As far as I could see she'd done nothing wrong, but we were treating her like a prisoner. Tied to a chair and interrogated for hours at a time. That's not what I signed up for."

"That shouldn't have happened," sighed Kali. "I gave strict instructions she was to be treated well."

"Our commander had other ideas, and since he technically didn't have to follow orders from you, he chose to question her himself, rather than wait for you to arrive. When all the commotion started in the centre of town earlier I used the distraction to get her out of there. But not before I took a lump of shrapnel in the arm from the safe-house going up." She held her arm which still dripped with blood.

Charlie sat on the floor and sighed. "A few seconds later and-- well..."

Kali squatted next to her. "Actually, I think you'd have been fine. Davon probably sent people to watch the safe-house, and as soon as she was out of there, they took it out. As well as the others."

Marcus chipped in. "By eliminating any places she could go to for help. Cunning bastard. But if he had people watching the house, why didn't they make a move on her?"

"They may not have known for sure Vana was in there," said Charlie. "If Davon wants her alive that badly, he wouldn't have risked storming the place. Not with the amount of weaponry we had stashed there. Not even the Legion is that stupid."

"So, what's the plan?" asked Marcus.

"I'll take you to Vana," said Charlie. "But only because she mentioned you, Marcus. She told me all about what happened out in the Badlands, and how you rescued her. She trusts you, and if she wants to go with you she can."

"That's not your call to make," said Kali. "I need her to answe-_"

"Actually, it is my call. As far as I know, I'm the only surviving member of the Jericho section, so that puts me in charge around here until I know any different."

Kali didn't argue, but instead raised her arm and pointed into the darkness. "Lead the way, *commander*."

Chapter Six

Charlie led them through a maze of tunnels, twisting and turning down a seemingly never-ending array of junctions and crossroads. Marcus had long since given up trying to keep track of where they were, and closely followed Charlie. He didn't relish the idea of falling behind and getting lost down here. Alone. In the dark.

The tunnel ended abruptly. In the wall ahead was a small metal door, with a worn-out sign above it which had long since faded past being legible.

"We're here," said Charlie. She slipped an old rusted key from one of her pockets and unlocked the door, which creaked loudly as it swung open.

In one corner of the room, Vana was slumped in a chair. Around her, supplies were piled haphazardly and candles affixed to the walls, cast odd shadows as they flickered.

Vana jumped out of the chair, "Marcus!" she beamed, running over and wrapping her arms around him. "I'm glad you're okay."

"Thank god you're still in one piece," he said pulling back from her so as he could see her face. "I was worried you'd been caught."

"I waited for you as long as I could," said Vana.

"She was lucky," said Charlie. "Your man got her out of there just in time. Another few minutes and the Legion would have had her."

Kali approached Vana, her hand outstretched. "Hi, I'm Kali, a friend of Marcus. I've been hearing a lot about you recently, and if you're willing I'd like to take you somewhere safe where we can have a talk about a few things."

Vana pulled back slightly and frowned. "Like what?" she asked.

"Well, for example I'd like to know why Davon is after you? What is so important about you he would risk openly attacking whole settlements to find you?"

"That's... complicated."

"Oh, come on now, we've travelled a long way and have gone to a great deal of trouble to find you, don't play coy now."

Vana looked uneasy, "How much do you know about Davon?"

"Not a great deal more than anyone else. He has Legions of followers that do his every bidding, for what reason we have no idea. He seems to be the reason for the disappearance of many people over the years and my personal favourite, he's been brainwashing people into becoming single-minded killing machines who answer only to him."

Vana shifted on her feet, and Marcus pulled her towards him defensively. She had done nothing wrong, yet everyone was after her. Vana clutched onto him; he felt inexplicably close to her.

"I don't know why he has been taking people," said Vana, "It's not what I would expect."

Kali looked at Marcus and said, "Well I think it's become obvious now at least some of the people the Legion takes end up as Elites. But it doesn't explain where all the others are going. We've only ever seen a handful of those elite soldiers. There are hundreds, if not thousands, of other people that have vanished over the years."

"You know this because of Amara?" asked Marcus.

"When she came with Davon to New Hope we recognised her. Doc had been searching for her for years. Up until that point, nobody who disappeared was ever seen again. We think he keeps the Elites away from the areas they were captured in. To minimise the risk of them being recognised. Amara must have been in The Forge this whole time." Kali turned to Vana. "So, what's your story? What does he want you for?"

Vana glanced at Marcus before answering. "I don't know exactly why he's after me. But I'm not the first he's hunted and I won't be the last. Unless we stop him."

"Well that cleared things up," said Kali as she let out a deep sigh. She pinched the bridge of her nose and rubbed her eyes. "We can talk about it later, right now we need to work out how to get you out of here safely. We still have questions."

"I'll come back with you on one condition," said Vana. "Further north there is another impact site. It's all part of the same meteorite, the one that came down near where you found me Marcus. I need to go there."

In all the drama of the last few days, Marcus had forgotten the impact started this whole bizarre chain of events.

"No way," said Kali. "You're coming back with us. There's more going on here than you are letting on, and we need to get to the bottom of it."

"You want to defeat Davon, yes?" asked Vana,

"Of course. We don't know what he's doing, but it can't be anything good," replied Kali.

"Trust me, the answers you need are there, where the meteor hit. The key to defeating him is there, but we must go quickly."

"Can't you just tell us what it is?"

86

"No, you need to see it for yourself."

"Bullshit," said Kali, kicking the metallic door. "You could tell us right now, but you don't want to. I don't like this, I don't like this one bit. Talk some sense into her Marcus."

"I don't know," he replied. "Wherever we go we're going to have Davon after us. If Vana really does hold the key to taking him out, I want to go and find out what it is."

"He'll be there waiting for us you know," said Kali. "We'd be walking into a trap. I'm not going anywhere near there without fifty guys and a whole lot of guns."

"You go get your men," said Vana, "I'll go on my own."

"Oh no you don't. I'm not letting you out of my sight. We went to a lot of trouble to find you. If I must, I'll drag you kicking and screaming back to our camp. But I think we can all act like grown up's here and do what needs to be done."

"Wait a second," said Marcus getting in between the two women who were now facing off each other, "Nobody's dragging anyone anywhere. We're all on the same side here."

"I'm prepared to go on my own," said Vana. "Though I stand a much better chance if you come with me."

"I don't feel safe down here," said Marcus. A tightness gripped his chest and his breathing became sharp. "Can we get out of here to somewhere a bit more... not underground? This place gives me the creeps. We can argue about what to do later."

"Fine," said Kali, "How are we going to do this?"

"Davon has men stationed at every entrance to Jericho," said Charlie, "so getting out that way won't be easy."

Kali crossed her arms. "Yeah, we figured that much out for ourselves thanks."

"Well lucky for you I know a few other routes out of town those goons don't know about. We should be able to sneak past them and out into the Badlands. If we're lucky it will be days before they figure out we slipped by them."

Kali sighed and shook her head.

"I suppose we don't have much choice, do we? I want your word when we've been to the impact site you'll come back to camp with me."

Vana nodded in agreement.

The room shook and there was the dull thud of an explosion. Rock and dust fell from the ceiling above them, which clung to the back of Marcus's throat.

"What the hell was that?" he managed through a fit of coughs.

Charlie opened the door and looked out into the darkness. "The Legion must have found us. If we stay here we'll be trapped, we should go. Now." She grabbed a rucksack from beside the door and ran around the small room, grabbing what she could and stuffing it inside. She lifted the lid of a large box in one corner of the room and pulled out a shotgun. She loaded the weapon from a pile of shells in the box and threw the rest into the bag with everything else.

"Let's roll," she said as she charged out of the door. Marcus grabbed Vana by the hand and headed off after Charlie. Kali brought up the rear, looking over her shoulder as they ran through several more twisting tunnels.

Charlie skidded to a halt, which caused Marcus to almost run into her. She raised her hand and shushed him before he could protest. Muffled voices and the echo of footsteps reverberated through the tunnel ahead.

"Shit," said Charlie under her breath. "That's the way out. We're gonna have to go through them. I hope they still want her alive because that's our only chance."

They crept along the tunnel, hugging the walls until they saw three Legion soldiers standing next to a ladder, lit from above by light pouring in through an open manhole cover.

Charlie sank to the ground and grabbed a small rock. She threw it past the guards, along the opposite tunnel. The rock clattered against the concrete walls before coming to a rest some distance away. The guards reacted to the disturbance and raised their weapons. Two of them moved cautiously towards the source of the noise, whilst the third stood rooted to the spot by the ladder. When the guards vanished into the darkness, Charlie made her move. She sprinted towards the remaining man, diving out of the blackness and throwing him into the metal ladder, winding him. As he struggled to catch his breath Charlie sent her fist crashing into his jaw. There was a crack, and the man folded over.

"Did you see that?" said Charlie, as she shook her fist out. "One punch."

Marcus looked at the defeated guard. It was impressive he had to admit. He made a mental note not to piss her off.

"Well come on," she said. "Get up there."

They climbed the ladder and found themselves on the outskirts of town, but still behind the walls. Kali replaced the grate cover and threw bricks and other debris on top of it.

"That should make it a bit harder for them to get out of there," she said, dusting off her hands.

"Hey, isn't this near where we came in?" asked Marcus.

"Yeah, I think so," said Kali. She peered into the distance, and pointed out a small black blob on the horizon, above the wall. "Our transport is there, on the hill. That's where we're heading."

Marcus walked over to the wall and ran his hands along it. It was at least ten feet tall - the top covered in razor wire. Climbing over it was not going to be an option.

"Perhaps we can--," Marcus was interrupted by the click of a weapon being cocked. He slowly turned, Kali and Charlie had their hands raised, weapons pointed at them from at least a dozen Legion soldiers.

"Don't move," ordered one of the soldiers. He wore a red armband and was probably the senior officer. Marcus froze and was searched. The others were also searched and their weapons tossed in a pile in front of them. They were forced to kneel in line, their hands clasped behind their heads.

A gun was jabbed into Kali's back.

"What's that?" asked the soldier, using the barrel of the gun to prod at a lump under Kali's shirt by her hip.

"It's only a radio," she said unflinchingly.

"On the pile, now."

Kali reached slowly with one hand and unclipped the radio from her belt. As she did, Marcus saw her click the send button several times, before tossing it onto the pile with the rest of their gear.

"Call the transport for this one," said the leader, grabbing Vana under her arm and standing her up. "The rest are expendable."

Vana struggled as she was led away, Marcus turned to see what was happening and was struck by the butt of a rifle. The blow was glancing, but it was enough to cause his eyes to water.

The silence was broken by a whooshing sound, followed by a massive explosion coming from behind. A large section of the wall exploded outwards, sending chunks of concrete and metal flying towards them. A chunk grazed Kali's head, knocking her to the ground. Thick plumes of dust obscured Marcus's vision.

Gunfire erupted from the other side of the wall, chewing into the legion soldiers, most of whom were too overwhelmed to return fire. Several men fell to the ground, blood spewing from gunshot wounds. A truck appeared through the hole in the wall and skidded to a halt. It was the two guards that had accompanied them to Jericho. A large roof-mounted machine gun had been attached to the truck and was discharging fire into the now fleeing Legion soldiers, whose handheld weapons were no match.

The driver jumped out and grabbed Kali, dragging her back to the truck and throwing her into the back seat. Marcus stumbled to his feet and grabbed a pistol from a downed soldier, and charged into the plume of dust, towards where Vana had been taken moments ago.

As the dust cleared he found Charlie wrestling with the leader on the ground, whilst Vana kicked at him. The man gained the upper hand, rolled on top of her and pulled a knife from his belt. He went to drive it into Charlie's chest, but before he could, Marcus raised the pistol and fired twice, both shots hitting the man in the chest.

He flopped over and Charlie pushed him away.

There was no time for gratitude. Marcus reached out his hand and dragged her from the floor and both Charlie and Vana ran towards the waiting truck, the driver gunning the engine.

They dived inside and the truck lurched backwards as it retreated through the hole and out onto the open ground.

****

Kali drifted in and out of consciousness on the back seat of the truck, the wound on her head bandaged and the bleeding stemmed.

"We've got to get her back to Doc," said the driver. "She needs to be treated properly."

Vana grabbed Marcus's hand. "I need to get to the second impact site. Everything we need to take down Davon is there."

"We have a vehicle stashed not far from here," said Charlie, raising her voice to be heard over the engine. "Supplies too. We could use that, and these guys can take care of Kali."

"Okay," said Marcus. "Let's do it."

"Are you sure you wanna do that?" asked the driver. "Kali seemed pretty determined to get the girl back to New Hope. I'm not sure she'd go for it."

"We had a chat about it back in Jericho," said Marcus. "She was starting to warm to the idea. Besides, we need to wait for Kali to be in better condition before we can do anything meaningful, so we may as well do this first."

The driver was in no mood to argue. Charlie relayed the location of the cache to him and they headed straight for it. Marcus hoped whatever they found there was worth the effort. He dreaded to think what Kali would do to him if he came back empty-handed.

****

As the truck containing the two guards and Kali pulled away, Marcus put his head in his hands and rubbed the sweat from his brow. If the Legion didn't kill them, it was a sure bet that Kali would when she awoke.

Chapter Seven

The rugged and steep terrain of the last few miles became too much for the truck to handle, and they were forced to leave it behind. Imposing hills dotted the landscape all around them and led on to the mountains beyond, their peaks buried in thick grey clouds. There was an eerie silence, broken only by the howling of the wind as it tore through the terrain. The sharp wind nipped at Marcus's exposed hands. He blew on them and rubbed them together in an attempt to regain some feeling in his fingers.

Wooden signs, crudely painted with skull and crossbones motifs were dotted around and warned they were approaching the outer limits of how far it was possible to travel in this direction. Beyond this point radiation levels climbed steeply, dooming anyone who dared push the boundaries to a lingering death.

"Lovely day for a walk," said Charlie. She brushed a layer of dirt from one of the signs as they walked past and shook her head at its warning. "Let's not stay here any longer than we need to alright?"

Marcus glanced over at Vana and narrowed his eyes. She'd been quiet during the truck ride, and while this wasn't exactly unusual for her, he sensed that she was holding something big back.

"When are you going to tell us what's really going on?"

Vana didn't reply. She was busy looking through a pair of binoculars Charlie had handed to her. "Never-mind. I'm getting used to being left in the dark. It's amazing I've managed to survive this long."

They headed for the columns of smoke from the still smouldering remains of the meteor, skirting the base of a steep hill, before appearing on an open plain. The full scale of the impact lay before them.

The smell of burning filled the air. A deep trench which ran hundreds of meters from the direction of the impact terminated in a crater at its furthest end. Scattered fires still burned, covering the ground in a low-hanging wispy fog. Anything green had perished in the immediate aftermath and trees had been flattened and burned to ashes by the blast it produced. Charcoaled wood crunched underfoot as they walked and the smoke in the air irritated Marcus's eyes and throat. He took a piece of cloth, wet it from a water bottle he carried and wrapped it around his face to help filter some of it out. Charlie followed suit, while Vana appeared unaffected.

They were not the first to reach the site. A sturdy chain link fence surrounded the impact site, behind which several tents had been pitched. Armed guards walked the perimeter. A checkpoint guarded the only way in, manned by two men, who were constantly talking into their radios.

As they grew closer the outline of an object could be seen, hidden beneath a blue plastic sheeting, pegged down to prevent it from blowing away. They flopped on top of a mound of earth some distance away, in an effort to remain undetected. Vana slipped the binoculars out from under her jacket and brought them up to her eyes.

"What on Earth are they hiding under there?" asked Charlie "Whatever it is, I assume that's why we're here?"

Vana nodded. "We need to get in there," she said, pointing at the plastic covered object at the head of the trench.

"Of course we do," said Marcus. "Across all this open ground, past all those guards, in broad daylight. What could be easier?"

Charlie jabbed Marcus in the ribs with her elbow. "I'm up for it," she said. "We've come this far right? We can't walk away now." She smiled at Vana. "And besides, I want to know what's going on."

Marcus sighed. "Nothing's ever easy, is it?". He crossed his arms and looked to the sky. "How are we going to get past that lot?" He waved his hand towards the checkpoint.

"As much as I'd like to charge in there with guns blazing, I think we need a better plan."

"You're right, these guys look somewhat competent. Not the usual half-witted, knuckle dragging, incom--"

He stopped. Vana and Charlie were staring at him. They looked at each other and exchanged a grin. Vana stifled a laugh.

"Sorry," said Marcus. "Just getting it out of my system. I'm good to go." He looked to Vana. "When we get there, what do we need to do?"

"Retrieve some items."

"Well, how do you know what's under there? Or that what you are looking for is still there at all? Perhaps Davon already has… whatever it is."

"Honestly, I don't know for sure, but my instincts say not."

"Well I hope you're instincts are right," muttered Marcus, "but I still don't see how we're going to get down there without being seen."

"I have an idea," said Charlie

"I hope this is better than charging in all-guns-blazing," scoffed Marcus.

She grinned. "Marginally."

****

"Are you sure you want to do this Vana?" Marcus asked. "It's risky." He grabbed handfuls of dirt from the mound and squeezed it between his fingers, before dusting his hands clean and starting again.

"It will work," said Vana nodding her head. "All you need to do is to get me to the crater and I will take care of the rest."

"We won't have long once we make our move. We will have to be in and out of there quickly. Are you ready?"

Vana nodded. If it wasn't for the fact there was a chance they could take down Davon Marcus might never have considered this plan.

"Here, hold your hands out," Charlie said to Vana. She complied and Charlie bound her hands loosely with a length of rope. "You should be able to slip your hands out no problem. How does it feel?"

"Good," said Vana, taking a deep breath.

"The other two guards are moving off," said Marcus. "It's now or never."

They stood from their hiding spot and walked slowly towards the guards patrolling the crater, making no efforts to conceal their approach. Vana was in the lead, her hands held in front of her, visibly bound, whilst Charlie and Marcus followed behind. Every so often Charlie would push Vana as if to move her along. It wasn't long before the guards spotted them and approached with weapons drawn.

"Stop!" one of the guards yelled, "You can't be here, this is a restricted area." His gaze locked onto Charlie's shotgun slung over her back and his posture stiffened.

"We're licensed bounty hunters," said Charlie in response to the guard's demeanour. "We have permits for these weapons."

More alert now, the guard shifted on his feet. "Why are you here?" he demanded.

Marcus spoke up, "This is the girl Davon's looking for. We've come to collect our reward."

The guard studied Vana for a second before turning to speak with his partner.

"The girl comes with us," said the first guard. "You can wait here."

"Oh no you don't," said Charlie. "We're not going anywhere until we get our reward."

She came face to face with the guard, their noses almost touching.

"Do you know what we went through to catch her? I'm not letting her out of my sight until I see some money."

The guard shoved Charlie back, and she fell to the ground.

"If you know what's best for you, you'll stay down," growled the guard pointing his rifle at Charlie.

"Whatever you say. You're the boss."

Marcus gave Vana a wink. She slipped her bonds and darted through the checkpoint, running as fast as she could towards the crater."

"She's getting away!" yelled Marcus, jumping around and pointing dramatically.

"Stop, or I'll shoot!" shouted the second guard, raising his weapon in Vana's direction.

"Put that down, you idiot," said his companion, batting the gun to one side. "He wants her alive."

With the guard's full attention now on Vana, Charlie swept her legs at the man standing over her, bringing him crashing to the ground. She dove on top of him and launched into a barrage of melee attacks. Fists, knees, feet, were all employed in a blur of grunts and yelps.

Marcus threw himself at the remaining guard and wrestled him to the ground. They rolled around in the thick dust. A sharp pain ripped through his shoulder as he tried to keep the man down. The guard struggled against Marcus with his rifle. Several shots rang out from it before it was knocked away, out of reach of them both.

The guard snarled and pressed his thumb into the now bleeding wound on Marcus's shoulder. Waves of nauseating pain rippled through his upper body causing him to release his grip and fall away.

A boot flashed past Marcus's head and connected with the jaw of the guard, knocking him back to the ground. Charlie racked her shotgun and pushed it into the downed guard's temple. He spat a mouthful of blood into the dry ground.

"If you were going to shoot you'd have done it already," he said, gruffly. "Nice diversion, but you're crazy if you think you're getting out of this alive."

She didn't have time to reply, as a bullet pinged off the ground beside her, kicking up a small cloud of dust.

"Shit!" yelled Charlie.

Two more soldiers quickly approached, while others lay down covering fire. Marcus scrambled to his feet and grabbed Charlie's arm. "Come on."

Charlie smashed the butt of the shotgun into the man's jaw and smirked as several teeth flew from his mouth. He slumped to the floor, unconscious.

Together they stumbled through the checkpoint and towards the crater, which was now the only cover available from the rapidly advancing group of men.

Bullets whizzed past them, hitting the ground at their feet, shards of razor-sharp rock exploded all around them and peppered the exposed skin on Marcus's arms. He shielded his face as best he could from the barrage and charged on. They were almost at the crater when Marcus felt a searing pain in his leg, a bullet had caught him just below the knee. He fell to the ground at the lip of the crater. Charlie grabbed Marcus by the arm and pulled him over the edge and down out of the line of fire.

"Shit," gasped Marcus, gripping the wound on his leg. "I'd managed to go thirty years without being shot, and then all this kicks off and I get shot twice in a week."

"Stop your moaning and get up," said Charlie, "They're right behind us." She pulled Marcus to his feet and dragged him under the blue sheeting covering the object.

"We've got maybe thirty seconds before--" Marcus stopped. His mouth dropped open, and for a moment he forgot about the pain in his leg.

Underneath the covering was what looked like the fuselage of some sort of aircraft, but of course, it couldn't be. You couldn't fly aircraft anymore, the dust in the atmosphere clogged up their engines, causing them to fall from the sky. And then there were the radiation belts to contend with.

But this was certainly something that once flew. The sleek aerodynamic lines and dark metallic surface gave it the look of a bird of prey. Despite hitting the ground hard, it was remarkably intact. At the front, half buried in the earth was a something resembling a cockpit, although Marcus could see no windows.

Vana stood next to it, her moving over the surface of the object as if she was searching for something.

Charlie ripped a sleeve from her shirt and used it to apply a tourniquet above the wound in Marcus's leg, which stemmed the blood loss to a light trickle. Marcus barely noticed the condition of his leg, he was trying to process what he was seeing.

"This is the strangest looking meteor I've ever seen," he said.

Charlie knotted the tourniquet and waved her hand at the object in the centre of the crater. "I hope you know what you're doing with… whatever the hell it is," she said.

"Nearly…" she replied. "Got it!" there was a low hum, as a doorway in the side of the object seemingly appeared out of nowhere. The interior was a soft white colour, and completely featureless.

"Inside," said Vana. "It's safer in there."

Charlie helped Marcus to his feet and dragged him inside the craft. Vana followed closely behind. Two of the Legions guards appeared at the lip of the crater. There were shouts, followed by more shots. Vana touched a control panel on the inside of the doorway, and as quickly as the door appeared, it vanished. The wall where the door used to be, was now a flawless white surface. Silence enveloped them. Marcus's ears were ringing from the noise of the gunfire, but now that he was inside there was no noise at all.

The small room they were in was only a few feet wide and light seemed to emanate from the white walls. Red splotches of blood from the wound on Marcus's leg gave colour to the otherwise colourless room.

"We'll be safe in here," said Vana, "they won't be able to get in."

"I think now is an excellent time for you to explain what the hell is going on," said Marcus, leaning against the wall to take the weight off his injured leg.

"This looks like some sort of aircraft or something," said Charlie.

"Not an aircraft," said Marcus, "It crashed down with the meteor, right?" He looked at Vana who nodded in agreement.

"So, something from before the big impact? I had no idea there was anything like this up there."

"Neither did I," said Marcus, looking over at Vana.

"It's not from here," said Vana, looking sheepish, "It's mine."

"I still don't understand," said Marcus.

"You've noticed I'm… different from you?"

"You mean your mutations?" Marcus looked at Vana properly. Her face was slightly thinner than normal, and her eye's a bit bigger, and of course a shade of deep purple. In here, under the strange light, she seemed to glow.

Charlie, who was adjusting the tourniquet around Marcus's leg looked at Vana. "I assumed you were from the Badlands. I've seen some pretty strange people living out in those sorts of places," she said.

"They're not mutations," said Vana, "I'm supposed to look like this. Where I'm from."

"And where would that be?" asked Marcus.

"A long way from here." Vana turned and placed her head against the wall, closing her eyes.

"And you travelled here in this thing?"

Vana nodded slowly.

"Is she saying what I think she's saying," said Charlie, "because if she is then I think we seriously need to check whatever medication she's on."

"Look where you're standing," said Marcus, "I've never seen anything like this before."

"So, you're telling me you're… not from Earth?" said Charlie

"Yes."

"Oh man, this is some crazy shit going on here," she said, pacing around the enclosed space.

101

"Hang on," said Marcus. "I've lost quite a lot of blood, but for a second there it sounded like you said you're an alien."

"I know it's a lot to take in," said Vana. "But it's true."

"I need to sit down, feeling a bit woozy here. Someone let me know when things start making sense again." He slid to the floor, trying to stifle the flow of blood from his leg.

"So why did you come here," asked Charlie.

"I was following someone. In a way. It's… complicated. Suffice to say, crashing was not part of the plan."

Charlie laughed hard. "This is crazy," she said catching her breath. "If it wasn't for the fact that I'm standing in the evidence I wouldn't believe a word of it."

"Now who's overreacting," mocked Marcus. Charlie shot him a wide-eyed glance. She tightened the tourniquet around his leg in response.

Marcus yelped and held out a blood-soaked hand in surrender.

"He's not one of my people," said Vana, "he's different from me and different from you. He's from another planet."

Marcus's head was spinning from the combination of what he was hearing and loss of blood. He steadied himself against the wall, leaving a bloody handprint. His leg throbbed in pain, and he grunted, and his breathing became laboured.

Charlie touched Vana's arm. "His leg's in a bad way," she said quietly. "He's lost a lot of blood. We need to get him out of here - sooner rather than later."

"There's something we can try."

Vana pressed her hand against a smooth section of the wall and a palm-sized compartment appeared. She reached in and pulled out a device. It was circular, flat and fit in the palm of her hand, with a loop that she pushed her finger through, holding it in place. She moved across to Marcus and put her hand firmly on the bullet wound. Marcus winced in pain.

"This is a medical device. But it wasn't designed to be used on humans. I don't know if this will work. It could make things worse."

Marcus grimaced through half-closed eyes. "So, what you're saying is that I have three options. One, do nothing and probably bleed to death. Two, you use that device, it doesn't work and I bleed to death; or three, use that thing, it works and I get to live. But because it's an alien device - I may grow an extra head or something."

"I really don't thin--" started Vana, but Marcus waved his hand, cutting her off.

"Since my other two options involve dying - I think I'll risk the extra head thing. Just means I'll be twice as handsome as before."

"Hah," snorted Charlie. "Can you use that thing on him quick? I don't think I can take any more of his terrible jokes."

The device started to glow a soft yellow colour and hummed quietly. The pain lessened and a gentle pulse of heat radiated out from the source of the wound. After a few moments, the bleeding stopped and the devices humming changed to a higher pitch.

Vana removed the device from Marcus's leg. "It's finished," she said, "It's done the best it can, but it won't be fully healed." She next applied it on his shoulder and he groaned in ecstasy as the pain diminished.

After healing his shoulder, she put the device into her pocket. "You'll have to take it easy on that leg for a while. Your shoulder too."

The effects of the healing device wore off after a few minutes. The pain in his leg was almost completely gone, replaced by a dull ache and his shoulder felt almost normal. Marcus wiped the dried blood away from the gash in his trousers. The wound underneath had almost vanished.

"Doc would love to get his hands on that," said Marcus. "Imagine all the good we could do with a few devices like that, "

"I'm afraid it won't be of much use to you anymore," said Vana. "The power cell is drained, and with the ship in such a bad state, I doubt I could recharge it."

Marcus sighed. "Well, since I'm probably no longer dying, perhaps you can explain exactly what is going on here?"

Vana walked to the middle of the room and reached out her hand once again, and touched the centre of one of the walls. A large doorway opened, leading to what Marcus presumed was the cockpit. There were several chairs here, next to consoles and other odd-looking devices.

"We can go in there," said Vana, "Marcus you should sit, rest your leg."

"Way ahead of you," he said as he hobbled through the doorway and sat in the first available seat." He sighed with relief. "This place is far more comfortable. We should have come in here first."

Charlie walked in and took a seat opposite him, whilst Vana took a seat at the front centre.

"I think it's time you heard everything," she said Vana.

Chapter Eight

"So, you're an-- an alien?" asked Marcus. The words didn't seem real to him and he found them difficult to say.

"Yes. My species is called *J'Darra*."

"And you crashed here, and now Davon is after you for some reason and… nope, none of this is making any sense to me."

"Davon knows who I am," said Vana. "Who I really am. That's why he's after me."

"How the hell could he know that? He's never met you before, right?"

"He knows because… he's not from around here either. He's an alien. Not like me, not like you. He's from a species called the *Krall*.

Marcus threw back his head and laughed. "You're telling me that Davon is an alien? All this time? You know what, I believe you. I do. There's always something been off with that guy. Jeeze, that's crazy."

"He doesn't look like an alien," said Charlie.

Vana flicked a strand of hair from her face. "Don't always believe your eyes. He's disguised his true form."

Marcus's mind raced. Things started to make more sense. She was captured by the meteor impact site. Davon knew she was there and sent Amara to go get her. Vana's features, previously dismissed as simple mutations from the radiation, were because she wasn't Human. The fact that she didn't speak for hours after he rescued her. The last thought stuck in his mind.

"Wait a minute. If you're an alien, where did you learn to speak our language?"

Vana slumped back against the wall and let out a deep breath. "I learned from you Marcus. You were quite talkative on the drive back to New Hope. It really is quite a relief to be able to tell you all this."

Marcus cocked his head and raised an eyebrow quizzically. "You learned our language in a couple of hours from just listening to me ranting on? Impossible."

"For you perhaps," she smiled. "Not for me. We're … talented in that way."

"Okay, start from the beginning and let's get the whole story," said Marcus.

"Well, I suppose it all started several thousand years ago, as you measure a year anyway. My people, the J'Darra were just starting to explore space. Our scientists and engineers managed to create an engine that would allow faster than light travel, and that unshackled us. Set us free amongst the starts. In a generation we had colonised dozens of planets and explored many more. And that's when we found it.

"A huge space station abandoned and in orbit around an uninhabited planet. Our best estimates put it at over a million years old. It floated, powered down; dead. Teams were sent to establish its purpose and then... well, that's when things start to get a bit, fuzzy.

"Evidently, the teams aboard the station found some way of re-activating it and when they did, they also awoke its guardians."

"Let me guess," said Marcus. "Those Krall things?"

"Exactly, and it seems they were quite unhappy with us being there. They said our presence there was defiling the place. They called it *Sentinel* and they violently drove my people from it.

"They managed to escape and retreat to a nearby colony. Shortly after that is when things started to go bad. The station – Sentinel – started to project some kind of energy field around itself. It spread for light-years in all directions, engulfing all our fledgeling colonies and our home world.

It was then that my people realised that our faster-than-light drives, or FTL, aboard our ships no longer functioned. Sentinel it seemed, was built to prevent anyone but those they permitted, from using FTL technology. They had effectively stranded us. Our smaller colonies, cut off from supplies perished in a few years. Any that survived that soon found themselves under attack from the Krall. They still retained FTL capability and were unaffected by the energy field.

"And that is how my people were brought to the brink of extinction. You can't fight an enemy that can appear and disappear at will. They could move entire armies across thousands of lightyears in a few seconds, ambush our forces and jump away before we could muster a response."

"There is only one place with any J'Darra left and we cower beneath the surface, too frightened to come out and into the light. And that brings us to you. Why is Davon here? I don't know but I do know that the Krall have targeted any worlds who have or are close to developing faster than light travel. Your people must have been getting close and the Krall tried to eliminate you."

Marcus's jaw dropped open and he shook his head. "The Krall, they... the asteroid that hit us all those years ago... that was them?"

Vana nodded. "An efficient way to destroy a civilisation. You see, the Sentinel can open portals in space allowing instantaneous travel between two points. They don't need to send ships or armies to attack planets. In your case they simply used Sentinel to place a huge lump of rock in an orbit that would collide with your world. But you survived."

Marcus recalled the stories he had been told about the day the asteroid came - a hundred years ago.

"Nukes," he said. "Nuclear weapons. We were quite fond of them back then I seem to recall. When the asteroid was discovered we launched those weapons at it in desperation. We shattered it, creating the rings you see above our world now, but also raining down vast quantities of radioactive rock. The jury is still out on if we managed to *save* the Earth or not."

Charlie swung her feet up onto a nearby console and leant back in her seat. "So, you're here, Davon's here, the only question is why?"

"I don't know why Davon is here. But I can tell you that my ultimate goal is the destruction of the Sentinel and to stop the Krall attacks across the galaxy."

"That sounds like a pretty tall order, especially on your own."

"The others, my people, forbid me to come here. I told them of my plans and they refused to allow me to try. In the end, I had to steal this ship to get here."

"Okay, so I'm not the world's leading authority on this FTL drive thing, but even I know that space is humongous. How did you get here without using it? Surely it would take hundreds or thousands of years?"

Vana smiled. "Very astute Marcus. You're correct. But remember I said that the Krall can still use their FTL drives? My ship has been modified to be able to ride on the wake of the Krall's FTL and to be almost invisible to sensors.

"I programmed the ship's computer to search for and utilise any FTL corridors from passing Krall ships. Since this could take many years, I entered one of the ships stasis pods to wait it out. The hope was that one of them would lead me to the Sentinel, so I could sneak aboard. The computer must have followed a ship coming to Earth, but when we arrived something happened, serious enough to knock my ship from orbit. The stasis pods double as escape pods, and so when my ship was in danger it jettisoned me. I awoke in my pod, near where you first found me, Marcus."

"You must have collided with some of the debris in orbit," said Marcus. I saw the meteor come down. Bits of it split off and crashed where I found you, and I'm guessing the ship and the rest of the meteor came down here." Marcus scratched his chin. "No wonder Doc's instruments went crazy when the meteor passed over. He was probably detecting your ship flying overhead."

"I'm glad he did," said Vana. "If you hadn't intervened when Amara tried to take me, well… I would be in the hands of Davon now. As soon as I heard his name… I knew. While we know little about how the Krall are structured, one name cropped up time and again. Davon. He seems to be the one in charge. I don't know if it was bad luck or fate that brought me here."

Charlie swung her feet down from the console and leant forward in her chair. "You said *we*," she said. "when *we* arrived here. I thought you said you came on your own."

"I did, didn't I. Well, I suppose it's time to introduce you to someone else." Vana reached below her seat and pressed her hand to the floor. A small section of it raised up, revealing a storage area containing several devices. Vana reached in and picked one out. She held it for the others to see. It sat neatly in her palm. It looked to Marcus like a small thin piece of opaque glass. Almost like a lens. It was attached to a thin silver chain, large enough to be worn around the neck."

"Oh," said Marcus, underwhelmed. "A pendant?"

"Marcus, Charlie say hello to Jax."

Marcus looked around the cramped cabin. "Who's Jax?

An image sprang from the palm of Vana's hand. Projected from the device she was holding. Lines of text in an alien language scrolled past so fast they blurred together in a greenish hue. From the confusion, a pattern started to emerge. It almost looked like a face but composed entirely of lines of text.

It spoke in a clear sharp voice.

"Hello Vana. I am gratified to see you are unharmed. After we lost contact during the crash I feared the worst."

"Whoah! What is that?" said Marcus as he stared at the floating disembodied head being projected in front of him.

Vana held out her hand towards Marcus. "Jax, this is my friend Marcus. He rescued me from Davon when I first arrived here. Without him, I'd be a prisoner now, or worse. And this is Charlie. She helped hide me from Davon's forces and assisted in our escape. Without her, we wouldn't be here now."

"Stop, your making me blush," said Charlie sarcastically.

"Jax, introduce yourself and explain what you can do," said Vana.

The image turned slowly until it was facing Marcus.

"Hello, my name is Jax. I am a ninth-generation advanced constructed intelligence - or *CI*. My primary purpose is to assist Vana in any way possible with the destruction of the Sentinel. I have been programmed with extensive cryptographic and heuristic functions. I function as an interface to this ship - and are capable

110

of interfacing with almost any other computer system I come into contact with."

"You're not a real person then?" asked Charlie.

"Define real," replied Jax almost instantly. "My neural networks are as complex, if not more so, than your own. Does the fact I am not flesh and blood mean I am not real?"

"What does that even mean?" snorted Charlie.

"It means he's smarter than you," said Marcus. "And probably me as well.".

"Most likely," said Jax, without even a hint of condescension in his voice. The image span around to face Vana again. "My diagnostics of this ship show it to be non-functional for the most part. Our original plans for accessing the Sentinel are no longer feasible. We must develop a new strategy."

"I was hoping that you would have some ideas about that," she said.

"I will begin working on alternate scenarios now." The image of Jax faded away and Vana closed her hand over the device. She put the chain over her head and wore it, Jax dangling below her throat.

"In the meantime, we should start thinking about how we're going to get out of here. Marcus, could you come and give me a hand with something?"

Vana led him through to the rear of the ship, past several cylindrical devices, each about six feet tall. There was a gap where one was missing.

"The stasis units," said Vana. "Like I said, they also double as escape pods. That's going to be our way out."

"You want me to get inside one of those… things?"

"I can assure you they're perfectly safe."

A chill ran over Marcus and his hands became clammy. Why did they have to make them look like coffins? He shook his head.

"But we're already on the ground. How are they going to help?" he asked.

"They work just as well on the surface as they do in space," replied Vana. She tinkered with a panel on the back wall of the room they had entered. "They can be ejected in space, in which case they work as you might expect. Or they can be jettison from a crashed ship to return someone into orbit. For example, if there was a ship waiting to collect them. We're going to do something in-between. Launch the pods, but instead of going to orbit, we'll land somewhere else."

"They're a few tropical islands I wouldn't mind visiting," smirked Marcus. "But I suppose that's out of the question."

"I'm afraid so," she pulled a cover from a panel on the wall and rested it on the floor. Marcus leant over to see inside. Two containers, each glowing a soft green colour, pulsated gently. Vana removed one of them with her bare hands and offered it to Marcus.

He turned his head and stared at it from the corner of his eyes. "What is it?" he asked.

"It's an energy storage device. I want to take this one with me. The other, well…" She reached her hand inside and removed the remaining device, turned it over so it was inverted, and pushed it back into the slot. She tapped a control panel nearby three times. The device changed from a green to a deep purple colour. Its intensity pulsed.

"What did you do?" asked Marcus

"I initiated the ships self-destruct. We can't risk Davon getting inside this ship. If he were to learn the location of the rest of my people… I can't let that happen."

Marcus laughed nervously. "How long do we have exactly, before… boom?"

"A little over an hour, we should get moving, the explosion will be quite large."

"You see, this is the sort of thing we should talk about first."

They returned to the cockpit, where Charlie sat smiling at them. "What were you two up to back there?"

"Oh nothing," said Marcus nonchalantly. "Vana's set this thing to blow up in an hour and I have this green… ball, thing. Some big battery or something." He held it up to show Charlie.

"Blow up? The I vote for getting the hell out of here."

"We need to put at least five kilometres between us and the ship," said Vana. "Everything within that radius will be vaporised."

"Holy crap," said Marcus. "What about the people outside?"

"What about them," said Vana shortly. "They were trying to kill us a few minutes ago."

"If we want to make a clean getaway, we need those guys outside to back off. Telling them this thing is gonna blow might do that."

Charlie shook her head. "As much as I'd like to watch these guys burn, Marcus has a point.'

Vana nodded and activated a console beside her, then directed Marcus to a glowing green icon.

"Touch this and talk. I've configured this to use the same frequency as the radio's they're using."

"Right, here goes nothing," He took a deep breath and touched the button which made a soft tone to indicate he was broadcasting.

"Um, hello? Can anyone here me?" There were a few seconds of silence before a deep grizzled voice replied.

"Who is this? Identify yourself."

"I'm Marcus, the guy who keeps ruining your day. Just a friendly warning. Unless you want to be vaporised in the next few minutes I'd get back on your trucks and sod off back to wherever you came from. Because this thing is going to go up like… well, I don't know what. But I'm told that it'll be bad. Very bad."

More silence, before the voice replied. "Is this some kind of joke? We have you surrounded. Come out now and we will guarantee your safety."

"Well I would like to believe you, but since I wasn't born yesterday I don't think I will. Best get moving. Chop, chop."

"You can't stay in there forever. The longer you make us wait, the harder it's going to be for you."

"I think we'll take our chances."

"You'll regret this," the voice barked.

"Naaa naa na naaa naa!" yelled Marcus, before jabbing the button again, cutting off the communication.

"Real mature," muttered Charlie.

"Ah shut it," he said batting her away with his hand. "I've lost a lot of blood today. I'm not entirely convinced this isn't some weird hallucination, and that I'm not in a corner somewhere, muttering to myself."

Charlie shook her head and sighed. She looked over at the console Marcus had just used and gazed at it for a few seconds absently.

"Hey Vana, can this thing pick up any radio transmissions?" Charlie eventually asked.

Vana nodded.

"Well, why the hell haven't we been using this? If we can listen in to what they are saying to each other we stand a much better chance of getting out of this in one piece. Here, show me how to work this thing."

Vana spent a few minutes showing Charlie how to scan through the frequencies and left her in the cockpit. She returned to the escape pods in the rear of the craft where Marcus was waiting, staring at one of them. He wasn't at all looking forward to climbing inside one. His skin became clammy thinking about it.

Vana came over and sat beside him, placing a hand on his shoulder. "Are you okay?" she asked.

Marcus leant back and puffed out his cheeks. "It's nothing really, just… and odd feeling. You see, I've had this recurring dream for a while now. I'm trapped, somewhere dark and small. I can't move very much and there's this sound. Like, voices in the distance. I can't make out what they are saying but somehow, I know they are talking about me. I feel closed in, restrained. Usually, I wake up in a cold sweat and have to get outside. Somewhere where I can see the sky. It's crazy I know, but the thought of being in an enclosed space freaks me out."

She rested her head on his shoulder, and he nuzzled his face into her hair. A warm feeling of calm washed over him. "I'm sure everything will work out Marcus," she said. "Let's get ourselves out of here and finish this thing once and for all."

****

Vana worked on the pods and Marcus watched as she expertly manipulated the controls. In the air above each pod floated a display, scrolling strange alien symbols in what Marcus assumed must be her language. He still had a hard time coming to terms with the fact she wasn't human. For an alien, she looked an awful lot like a human.

The scrolling text of the control panel vanished, and a globe of the Earth appeared floating in mid-air above it.

"The pods can take us anywhere within this radius," she said, pointing to a yellow circle superimposed over the projection.

The area covered thousands of miles in every direction.

"Wow," remarked Marcus. "Are you sure you don't fancy finding a tropical island somewhere and letting this thing blow over?"

Vana smiled. "I would be lying if I said I was not tempted by the idea, but then all I have done here, all those people who have died would have died for nothing."

"We still don't know how we're going to get you to this Sentinel thing. I think we need to figure that out first. Then we'll know where we need to go." Marcus glanced at the purple orb of energy from the panel, pulsing ever faster. Time was running out.

The crystal, Jax, on the chain around Vana's neck glowed slightly and then spoke.

"Perhaps now would be a good time to interject," said Jax. "I have analysed our options and can suggest a course of action. A projection from the crystal appeared in front of Vana. The outline of a device was visible, lines of text ran next to certain parts, and it rotated slowly. Curved metal arms made up a cage-like structure, open at one end. While the other end was sealed, and contained a pedestal, with a diamond shaped object floating above it. Vana studied the image closely.

"Very impressive," she said after a short while. "Do you think it will work?"

"I put the odds at sixty-seven percent. Though, those odds improve if we have some help."

Marcus stood to one side of the projection so he could catch Vana's line of sight. "What's his plan?" he asked. "What is this thing?"

Vana tapped the necklace and the projection vanished. "It's really very clever actually," She replied. "We can't use this ship anymore. It's too badly damaged and will never fly again. But we can salvage some of the components, specifically the FTL core."

You see, the Krall ships FTL drives still work because they are calibrated to some resonant frequency that we've never been able to determine. The device Jax has designed will allow us to open an FTL window for a few seconds here on Earth. We'd simply step through it and find ourselves on the Sentinel. But there's a catch."

"I thought there might be," said Marcus with a sigh. "I'm not going to like this am I?"

Vana smiled weakly. "In order for it to work, we need to determine the correct calibration for the device. The only way to do that would be to get that information directly from Davon's ship."

"Yep, I was right. I really don't like this plan. On a scale of one to ten, with ten being 'certain death', I'd rate this a forty-two. Besides, we don't even know where it is."

"True, however he must keep it close by."

Marcus rubbed his hands together. "He has a bunker, fortress, tower of doom, whatever you want to call it, at a place called the Forge. Perhaps he keeps it there? I've been there before and it would certainly be big enough to house a hanger or something."

"Then that sounds like the first place to look," said Vana.

"No, no, no. You don't get it. That's his base of operations. He has more firepower than god up there. We wouldn't get within a mile of the front gates."

"We need to construct the device first anyway. That will give us some time to come up with a plan."

"Then if we're needing somewhere to go, we should go to Doc, he's the only friend we're going to find around here. Apparently, he has some secret underground bunker that the Legion doesn't know about. It'll be a good place to hide while we build this... whatever it is."

Vana zoomed the map into the approximate location of New Hope. It took Marcus a few seconds to get his bearings, not used to seeing the area from his current birds-eye perspective.

He pointed to a location south of the settlement. "There," he said. "I know that place. It's an old industrial complex. Plenty of places to hide if need be. We can land there and walk to New Hope. It's only a couple of miles. If it's not safe we can head back and find somewhere to lay low while we plan our next move."

"I'm going to get the component we need for the device," said Vana. She pointed to one of the pods. We can put everything we need to take into that one."

Marcus nodded and went off to retrieve the energy storage unit from the cockpit. While there, he watched as Charlie worked the communication device, eve's dropping on the soldiers outside, arguing about how best to get inside and murder them all. Apparently, they'd tried cutting, shooting, burning and a whole host of other things to get inside, but to no avail. Their voices became strained as they ran out of ideas. Marcus chuckled to himself and returned to the mid-section to find Vana loading a football-sized diamond-shaped crystal into the spare pod. He placed the energy storage device next to it and Vana threw in a few other bits and pieces. Judging from the size and shape, he guessed they were tools of some kind.

After a quick check of the contents, Vana closed the door to the pod.

"It's ready," she said. "That just leaves…"

Charlie burst into the room, cutting Vana off mid-sentence.

"I need to get back to Jericho," she blurted. "Davon's men are rounding people up in the street and executing them. It's all over the radio. He's trying to flush out the remaining resistance members to make an example out of them. I have to get back there."

118

Vana looked over to Marcus, who gave a nod. "I can configure your pod to take you back to Jericho," she said, calling up several displays and making changes on the pod Charlie was going to use. After a few moments, the displays vanished. "Okay, they're ready," said Vana, as the pod doors opened. Marcus peered into one. He felt a slight twinge of panic come over him and took a deep breath to steady his nerves.

"How do I work this thing anyway?" he asked.

"The destination has already been programmed into each pod. All you have to do is to climb in, and press your hand here." She indicated a small red square, immediately inside the pod. It pulsed, growing brighter, and dimming every few seconds. "The rest will happen automatically."

"Also, I want you to have this." Vana handed him something. It had a hand grip and a short barrel and an obvious trigger mounted below.

Marcus turned the object over in his hand. "Is this what I think it is?"

"I've never had to fire a weapon before. You should take it," said Vana. She wore a frown on her face. "It's probably better in your hands."

"I don't have the best track record either," said Marcus tucking it under his belt at the back.

Before he could inquire any further the communication device on the console started to slowly pulsate blue. Marcus narrowed his eyes and looked at it with suspicion. "What's that thing doing?" he asked.

Charlie, who was now familiar with the console, tapped a few buttons.

"I think… someone's trying to talk to us," she said.

"Must be that chump I spoke to before," smiled Marcus. "Back for more world-class banter with me. He can't get enough."

119

"I don't think so," said Vana. "Only another communication device like this one would be able to initiate contact with us."

"You mean, that's probably…" his voice trailed off. An icy chill ran through his body.

Davon, yes," said Vana.

"Well? Should I answer it or not?" asked Charlie.

"Do it," said Marcus. "At the very least we might find out what he's up to."

Charlie pressed a few buttons on the console, which changed colour indicating the connection had been made.

"What do you want?" said Marcus loudly.

"Marcus," came the crystal clear and unmistakable voice of Davon, "I must say you have surprised me with your resourcefulness. You cannot escape this place. So, I make you this offer. I want to speak to the girl and afterwards, you will all be free to go."

"No deal," snapped Marcus back. "You must think me an idiot to believe you'd let us go, just like that. Not after everything you've done to try and capture her. New Hope, Jericho, tying me to a chair and having Amara threaten me with a bloody sword. So, if you don't mind, we'll be on our way."

Davon groaned with annoyance. "By now she's no doubt told you some fanciful tale - perhaps some of it may even be true. But there's far more at stake here than any of you realise. Let me speak with her, and maybe you'll live to see the end of the day."

Marcus looked at Vana for any indication about how she felt about this. She remained stoic.

"She can hear you," said Marcus. "Say what you have to say, but make it quick."

Davon laughed, which sent a shudder rippling along Marcus's spine.

"Yes, I must say, activating the self-destruct mechanism was a bold move."

"I don't know what you're talking about," said Marcus.

"Don't try to fool me. I can detect the energy levels building up inside the vessel's power core. I know we don't have a great deal of time. But enough of this. I will speak to the girl and perhaps we can come to some arrangement."

"Well, she can hear you, so spit it out."

"I will only speak to her face to face."

"No chance. As soon as I open the door your men will storm the ship. I know it's hard to believe, but I'm not as stupid as I look."

"I have ordered the Legion to retreat to a safe distance. I will come alone. You still have some functioning equipment inside that ship don't you? Check for yourself."

Vana pressed a button on one of the consoles. The opaque cockpit, which until now had been featureless was replaced by a map of the area. In the centre was a white circle, which Marcus assumed was the ship they were in. All around them were various red dots, indicating people, and green triangles. Some of the triangles had red dots overlaid on them and were moving away from the centre rapidly. There was another, more prominent symbol, a hollow circle made from a dashed line. It flashed urgently, and alien text streamed underneath it.

"What's that?" Marcus whispered to Vana and pointing to the flashing symbol.

"It's indicating an unknown energy signature. It could only be coming from Davon."

"Standby," said Marcus, and he waved his hand across his neck to indicate he wanted to kill the connection.

Charlie nodded her understanding and pushed a button on the console. "It's muted," she said. "He can't hear you."

121

"I don't like this," said Marcus, running his hands across his face. "It feels like a trap."

"Well of course it's a bloody trap," huffed Charlie. "There is zero chance he's going to just let us walk out of here."

"I agree. He just wants to get to Vana. I say we tell him to shove it, and we get the hell out of here while we still can."

Vana shook her head. "We can use this to our advantage. We need to know where his ship is so I can get the data I need. We might be able to get him to reveal something."

"I dunno, sounds awfully risky. And I've recently become very risk-averse." Marcus rubbed his leg instinctively. "Getting shot, *twice*, will do that to you. There's got to be another way?"

"Maybe," sighed Vana. "But the longer it takes us, the more chance that Davon will figure out what we're up to and take measures to stop us."

"Fine. But for the record, if we all get killed I'm going to be really annoyed."

He nodded at Charlie, who unmuted the communication system.

"You come alone and unarmed," he said out loud to Davon. "And we're not leaving this ship."

"Agreed," Davon replied. There was a soft click as the connection was terminated.

Vana turned to Charlie. "Davon hasn't seen you before, you should take cover in the back. There's no need to reveal yourself to him."

"No way," she said. "I'm not leaving you guys to face him on your own. Not after everything he's done in Jericho."

"Vana's right," said Marcus. "We need you to cover us from the back there. If anything goes wrong we're gonna need you to back us up."

"Fine," groaned Charlie. "But at the first sign of trouble, I'm coming out shooting."

"Agreed," said Marcus.

There was a soft beeping sound from one of the consoles.

"He's here," said Vana, "are you ready?"

Charlie loaded several shells into her shotgun and racked the slide, before retreating into the rear of the craft.

"What's to stop us blowing his head off as soon as he steps on board?"

"If you did we may never get access to Sentinel. Besides, I'm not sure it would be enough to kill him," she said looking at the shotgun. "I doubt he would come here if he thought we could hurt him."

"What about the weapon you gave me?" His hand reached for it in his belt and gripped it.

"No, I think we should see what he has to say, and we need the location of his ship," said Vana.

She moved to one side and slightly behind Marcus before pressing her hand against the wall, causing the doorway to reappear as if from nowhere.

The doorway darkened as the figure of Davon appeared in it. Vana gripped Marcus's arm but stood her ground.

Davon smiled thinly.

"Aren't you going to invite me in?"

Chapter Nine

The dark shadow of Davon loomed in the doorway. He took a step forward and Marcus reacted at once, holding out his hand to block his path. His other hand fumbled behind him, as he felt for the weapon that Vana had given him, still tucked in his belt.

Davon's eyes followed Marcus's movements and he stopped at the lip of the door. Marcus positioned himself in front of Vana, with his back to the escape pods, ready for a quick getaway. They stood, facing off each other for a few moments before he broke the uneasy silence.

"Well? What do you want?"

Davon looked past him and at Vana. There was only the briefest crack in her composure as he addressed her. His eye flittered to the doorway behind them. Marcus heard a faint rustling from the concealed Charlie.

"Where's the other one?" asked Davon.

"Which other one?" replied Marcus nonchalantly.

"My men told me there were three of you."

"Well, your men were wrong. Besides, I doubt most of your men can count above two anyway."

Davon ignored the snipe.

"No matter." His gaze returned to Vana. "So, it's true. Some of you did survive. And how fortunate that you should show yourself at the moment when I need you the most."

Marcus turned to Vana, who stood with her arms crossed tightly over her chest. "What's he talking about?" he asked.

"I have no idea," she replied quickly. Too quickly. Marcus cocked his head, but she looked away from him.

"Oh, come now," boomed Davon. "Don't be so modest. You know how you can help me. Perhaps we can come to an arrangement? You tell me where the rest of your people are hiding, and I'll let you leave here unharmed. I already know they are not on this planet - otherwise you wouldn't have needed a ship to get here."

"Maybe I'm the only one left."

"Well for all our sakes, I hope that isn't true. When I realised that the ship I'd shot down was of J'Darra design I feared I had made a terrible mistake. You don't know how relieved I was to discover you had survived."

Wait a minute," butted in Marcus. "You lot tried to wipe them out, so why now the sudden interest in her wellbeing? You've been trying to kill us since the day I met Vana."

"Nonsense. I wasn't trying to kill her. I was trying to find her. I was just killing everyone who got in my way. You've survived longer than most who have opposed me. If the stakes were not so high, I could find our little encounters amusing."

"Why is everyone being so cryptic around here. What high-stakes. Will someone start making sense around here?"

Davon let out a sigh and waved his hand dismissively.

"I have neither the time nor the inclination to explain everything to you and you wouldn't understand it even if I did. But I didn't come here to speak to you." His eyes found Vana's again. "So, what will it be? Give up the location of people. I

125

guarantee that they won't be harmed, or else come with me and I make you the same promise."

"I-- I need some time to think," said Vana shifting on her feet. Marcus couldn't tell if she was playing for time or if she was seriously considering his offer. They were supposed to be using this time to try and get information from Davon, but so far it seemed to have been a one-sided conversation.

"We don't have much time," said Davon. "Less than an hour by now I expect."

Marcus seized upon the opportunity. "Feel free to leave anytime you want. I'm sure you've got a way out of here. You must have a ship lurking around here too. That's how you're able to get around so fast."

"Yes, yes," said Davon, a note of irritation in his voice. He looked right through Marcus, his eyes locked on Vana. A faint smile appeared on his gaunt face.

A console near where Vana was standing started to beep urgently. Marcus reached for the weapon tucked into his belt. He rested his hand on it but fought the urge to draw it.

"What's going on?" he asked.

Vana hurried over to the console and worked it, her hands moving rapidly over the controls. "The ship's computers, have detected an intrusion. Someone is trying to download all the datastores," she said.

They both looked at Davon, who stepped forward and was now inside the ship.

"What are you doing?" Marcus yelled. Yet more alarms started to sound.

There was a blur as Charlie burst out of her hiding place in the adjacent room, her shotgun aimed directly at Davon.

"Back up or I'll blow your frigging head off," she snarled.

"Do you really think your primitive weapon can hurt me?" he said taking another step forward.

"Vana?" said Marcus, hoping for some clue as to what he should do.

The beeping from the console became more intense.

"I'm detecting a transmission from outside," she yelled back. "The doors! When we opened the doors, we lowered our guard. External signals are normally blocked by the hull, but with the door open--"

"Then close it!"

"I can't, he's disabled the system." Vana banged the console with her fists. "I can't stop him."

"To hell with this," yelled Charlie. She fired the shotgun at point blank range at Davon. Stars filled Marcus's vision, and his ears rang. He felt dizzy and fell back against the wall. The smell of gunpowder filled the air, and it took a few seconds for him to regain his composure. Davon staggered back a few paces from the shot but remained standing.

He laughed as he regained his balance; a wide grin appeared on his face. "I told you it wouldn't work."

"No, but this might," shouted Marcus pulling out the weapon Vana gave him. He yanked on the trigger. There was a crackling sound as a bolt of blue energy shot from the barrel and hit Davon square in the chest. It sent him crashing back into a bulkhead by the entrance to the ship. For several seconds the only noise was the beeping console Vana was working on.

"Is he dead?" Asked Marcus. He looked at the weapon in his hand. It was hard to believe that something so small could pack that much punch.

"God, I hope so," said Charlie. "He was starting to piss me off."

127

Marcus limped towards the crumpled figure, the weapon aimed at him.

"He's not moving, let's get the hell out of here and-"

He was cut short by Davon, who rose and pinned Marcus to the wall by the neck. He swiped his hand, knocking the weapon from Marcus grasp. He heard it clatter on the floor some distance away.

"I see you are not completely stupid after all," growled Davon.

Charlie aimed her shotgun at Davon She jostled for position, trying to get a clean shot at Davon, but to no avail. Instead, she dropped the gun and charged at him, who with apparently little effort turned and pushed Charlie away with his free hand. She jerked back violently and smashed against the hull of the ship. All the wind was knocked from her. She lay on the floor and gasped for air.

Marcus tried to kick himself free, but his vision started to dim and his strength waned. Davon was far too strong for him.

Vana furiously entered commands into a console.

"I remember you," said Davon, who lifted Marcus so as they were face to face.

"What?" gasped Marcus, who was finding it difficult to breath pinned against the wall.

"Hey Davon," yelled Vana, as she pressed a button on the console she was standing next to.

A new, distinct and even more urgent alarm blared out, everything on the inside of the ship lit up and flashed. Consoles beeped in a cacophony of different sirens and screens filled with walls of alien text, most of it flashing.

"No!" roared Davon. He dropped Marcus and ran to the console, barging Vana out of the way, hitting her hard across the face with the back of his hand.

"The pods!" yelled Vana, as she struggled to get to her feet. Marcus staggered across and helped her up and they both fell through the doorway. Charlie sucked in deep breaths as Marcus reached through the doorway and pulled her into the room.

"What did you do," shouted Marcus over the din as he helped Charlie into her pod and activated it. "You know how I said we had an hour? Well, we don't have anymore. Get in your pod and go now."

Charlie's pod vanished through a gap in the ceiling, which sealed itself afterwards. Marcus headed to his own and as soon as he was sure Vana was safely in her pod, he activated his own and gritted his teeth. Immediately there was a loud high-pitched screeching noise and a massive burst of acceleration as the pod screamed out of the ship and into the atmosphere.

"Marcus, are you there? Are you ok?" Vana's voice crackled through some unknown speaker in the pitch-black pod.

"I'm here. In one piece. I think." Marcus' stomach flipped as the pod reached the apex of its trajectory and started plummeting towards the ground.

"Marcus, what have I done? If Davon uses the information in the ship's computer to find the rest of my people-- " she stifled a sob.

"Vana," he began, "everything will be alrigh-" there was a deep thud as his pod hit the ground and a second in close succession. He felt a wave of dizziness come over him and held onto the sides of his pod to steady himself. The doors opened, and light streamed in, hurting his eyes. He raised his to shield them from the light and fell from the pod and into the dusty earth. He rolled a few feet away from it and looked back. Despite it being oval at the top and bottom it was standing perfectly upright on its end.

He saw Vana's pod open and she stepped out, with far more grace and elegance than he managed himself. She walked over to him and reached out her hand to help him up.

"Takes a bit of getting used to," she said. "The pods can mess with your sense of equilibrium." She sniffed. Her eyes were red and puffy. She'd been crying and trying not to show it.

Marcus sat and dusted himself off.

"Okay, I have to know something," he said, taking her hand and standing up.

"When you first came here you barely spoke a word of English, but you seem to have picked it up incredibly fast. What I want to know is, when the hell did you learn the word 'equilibrium'?"

A faint outline of a smile crept onto Vana's mouth. She wiped a tear from her eye, spreading dust all over her face in the process.

"No, I'm being serious!" he continued. "I've probably only used the word twice in my entire life, and one of them was just now. And I still have no idea what it means."

Marcus sat on a nearby rock and beckoned Vana to join him. She wandered over trying not to laugh and sob at the same time.

"I promise to explain it to you one day," she sniffed. "And I will make sure to only use small words."

Marcus looked down, without even thinking about it he had taken her hand in his. They sat, staring out over the ruins of the city. The pods had landed in the exact spot he'd selected on the map.

"I hope Charlie's okay," he said, looking towards the mountains in the distance.

"It is time," said Vana. Marcus shielded his eyes as a bright white light lit up beyond the horizon. Vana stared at it, unblinking. After a few moments, the sound of the blast reached them. At this distance it was a faint low rumble. With the intensity of the explosion gone, Marcus took his hands away from his eyes and squinted into the distance. A mushroom cloud soared into the sky above the impact site.

Marcus turned to Vana, who remained silent, and wiped a tear from her cheek. The ship was her one link back to her people. Now it was gone. Would she ever be able to return home?

"Are you okay?" he asked.

"I will be when this is over." She wiped the tears off her face with her sleeve.

"Do you think he made it out before the blast?"

"He knew what we were doing. He would have had a way out."

"Is there any way we can warn your people? Get them a message somehow?"

"No, not now. The pods only have a short-range communication system. I could have sent a message from the ship, but it's no longer an option." She looked at the clouds billowing in the distance. "Besides, I couldn't take the risk Davon could track the signal to its destination - finding my people. If they haven't already moved on. I've been gone for so long."

They spent the next few minutes in silence, watching the sky, and the sun creeping ever closer to the horizon. In the distance, birds were calling from their perches in the ruins of the surrounding buildings. It was peaceful, and Marcus wished the moment would last forever.

The silence was interrupted by a soft beeping coming from Vana's neck where Jax still hung.

"Jax are you okay?" she asked.

"I am undamaged, thank you Vana. However, I must tell you that my analysis indicates that Davon was able to retrieve over seventy percent of the ship's database. Chances are high that he will be able to find the rest of the J'Darra once he has decoded the data."

Vana punched the side of her pad, and sank to her knees; fresh tears streamed down her face.

"I wanted to help my people, to stop the destruction of any more worlds at the hands of the Krall. To allow us to come out of hiding. But since I got here, everything has gone wrong. I should never have attempted this alone."

"You're not alone anymore. You have me. We're going to stop him. He keeps underestimating us. Even after all these years of living amongst us, he fails to see us for what we are. Stubborn sons of bitches. We don't give up, especially when the odds are against us."

Vana seemed to appreciate the sentiment but still appeared downbeat.

"We should go," she said. "He probably tracked us to our general location. If he's even bothering to come after us anymore, now that he has what he wanted."

"What should we do with the pods?" asked Marcus when they were ready to go.

"We shouldn't leave them out in the open," said Vana. "Someone might find them. We should find somewhere to hide them."

After a little while searching the nearby buildings, they came across one with a basement big enough to accommodate both.

"How do we go about moving these things?" Asked Marcus, sizing them up. "They look heavy. Perhaps if we could find some rope we could lasso them and drag them--"

He stopped. Vana gently pushed her pod which glided effortlessly through the air, still upright and hovering a few inches above the ground.

"How are you doing that? On second thoughts, don't bother explaining it to me. Let's go with magic."

Vana stopped and looked at him, wide-eyed, "Not magic, technology." She stopped for a moment, eyeing him up. "Let me show you something."

She beckoned Marcus closer to her and reached out and took his hands. She drew closer and closed her eyes. He felt compelled to do the same.

The world dropped away, to be replaced by endless banks of clouds. He flew, disembodied, but unafraid. The chill of the wind as it rushed past invigorated him, and his path twisted and turned as he weaved between the thick blankets of grey. He began to slow, and the clouds parted. Out of the mists appeared a city of silver and gold, lit by two suns, one high in the sky, one nearer the horizon.

Two towers so high they pierced the clouds above, stood resolutely against the hazy sky, casting pairs of long shadows over boundless fields of green and purple which stretched to the horizon. A wide river wound its way through the centre of the city, crossed by gleaming bridges and walkways which connected the towers on either side.

Sleek starships slid silently across the skies and wound effortlessly between the buildings. And at the centre, a tower much taller than the rest rose to a needle-sharp point with a glowing ball of light at its tip.

"What is this?" thought Marcus.

He didn't hear the reply, somehow, he knew the answer.

A memory of what was.

As he passed the city a golden light spread across the towers and cast dark shadows on the landscape below. He rose higher and he did, he could see this was one of many cities which dotted the landscape, all connected to one another by shafts of light that emanated from their central towers. He continued to rise until he was swallowed once again by thick clouds, and the image faded away. A cold darkness came over him, and he felt as if a great hand was pressing down on his chest. A hand reached out from the darkness and took his, and he felt himself being pulled out, towards a bright light.

He found himself back by the pods, the dust and decay of this world stood in stark contrast to the beauty of the world Vana let him see. She took her hands from him and turned away.

"How'd you do… I mean that was- that was beautiful," he managed. He couldn't think of any other way to describe the experience and now that it was gone, he found he missed it.

"We've lost so much," she said quietly. "All we have now is a memory, one that's not even mine."

Her voice changed, stronger, more determined.

"I will end this," she said as she turned back to Marcus. She clenched her fists and stood tall.

"No more running. It's time to fight back."

Chapter Ten

After making sure the escape pods were well hidden, Marcus and Vana set off in the direction of New Hope. Marcus carried the items Vana had salvaged from the crash site in a small backpack, slung over one shoulder. They were only a couple of hours walk away from town, but with the sun already low on the horizon, he held out little hope they would arrive before nightfall.

They walked along in silence. The memory Vana had shared with him was foremost on his mind. He had a million questions, but they would have to wait. Vana had confessed to being exhausted, the experience had sapped her mentally.

Marcus was the first to break the silence.

"I assume you have a plan on how we're going to stop Davon?"

"Getting on board Sentinel is the hard part," she said as she marched steadfastly forward. "Once I get there I have a plan to sabotage it. If I'm lucky it will be destroyed."

"And if you're not lucky?" asked Marcus.

"It will merely be damaged, but it would at least buy us more time. Decades probably. The Krall only have a limited understanding of how the Sentinel works. Repairing it, if it even can be repaired, will not be easy."

"I can't believe that all you need to build this… portal can fit into one small bag." He tugged on the backpack's strap, pushing his shoulder forward.

"I only brought the things that we wouldn't be able to replicate here with the technology you have available. Everything else, we should be able to manufacture ourselves. That's if this 'Doc' is as good as you say he is."

"He likes to tell me he is," said Marcus, with a gleam in his eye. "But seriously he's a genius. Just don't tell him I said so."

"We'll have to work fast. Davon will most certainly be looking for us."

"Yeah, he doesn't strike me as the kinda guy who likes to be beaten. With the resources he has on hand… well, we're going to need a great deal of luck on our side." Marcus kicked a rusty can from his path and it clattered across the rocky ground. "Do you think there is any way he tracked the pods?"

"Normally he would be able to yes, but the destruction of my ship will have scrambled everything electronic for miles. Even his technology is not immune to the effect. He'll probably start his search with New Hope though, he knows it's the most likely place we'll go."

They continued for several minutes, the enormity of everything Marcus had seen and heard running through his mind. He took Vana's arm and stopped. She turned to face him, her face covered in the dust that lay thickly over everything.

"I need to know. Do you think you can pull it off?" asked Marcus.

Vana remained silent for a few seconds. She tilted her head back and looked him squarely in the eye.

"I can do it. I can put it out of action, nothing else matters."

"And after that? Are you going home? I mean, can you even get back home if you manage to take this thing out?"

"I'd like to thinks so. But who knows? Nothing has gone to plan since the moment I arrived here. I'm only thinking of the here and now, and I'll deal with that if or when the need arises. That's why I'm doing this alone. I can't ask anyone else to risk themselves for my ill-fated mission."

"When you go, I'm coming with you," said Marcus quickly.

Vana shook her head and waved a hand dismissively.

"I won't put you in any more danger. You have already done far too much for me."

"You're not putting me in danger. *I'm* putting me in danger. After everything we've been through, and everything you have told me I won't let you do this on your own."

"But this is not your fight. I brought this upon you."

"Of course it's our fight! His people tried to wipe us out. They made it our fight. Besides, if they are not stopped they will continue to do this to other races, correct?"

Vana crouched and run her hands through a patch of wilting grass. "Almost certainly."

"I can't sit by the wayside knowing they will continue to destroy whole races, not when we have a chance to stop them. And I think you will find many people here, when given the facts, would agree with me."

"You would risk your lives to protect people you do not know, or may never meet, but why?"

"It's in our own best interest, but that's probably not the only reason. We like to have a cause. Something to believe in that's bigger than ourselves. And what could be bigger than this? But the biggest reason is probably, at times, us humans can be *monumentally* stupid. But you'd be surprised how often that's worked out for us in the past."

The frown on Vana's face melted into a wide smile. Her eyes came alive and sparkled in the dying light of the day.

"What?" asked Marcus.

"It's nothing. Just-- it's refreshing to be around people who aren't afraid to face the future."

"I didn't say we weren't afraid, but at this point, we don't have much of a future left. So, if we're going to go down, then we'll go down fighting."

"But there's so little hope for all of us. How can anyone go on knowing that?"

"That's what can bring out the best in us. There's no such thing as a hopeless cause, not so long as there's one person who will stand up against it. Hope is infectious and very difficult to ignore."

Vana stared blankly at Marcus.

"What?" he asked after a few moments.

"Nothing, I-- you got me thinking that's all. I didn't expect to hear something like that, from you."

"Yeah, I know, but don't worry. It won't be long before I say something ridiculous to make up for it. Come on, let's get moving. I'm starting to freeze."

****

An hour later they found themselves approaching the chain link fences surrounding New Hope.

"Do you think we will be able to get in unnoticed?" asked Vana.

"No problem. There are a few ways in and out of New Hope that are still unguarded. I use them to sneak out past the checkpoints and when I want to sneak something back inside I don't want the guards to confiscate."

"Contraband?"

138

"Something like that," Marcus said grinning. "Besides, we're not walking in the front door with all this gear from your ship. We have to assume they will be on the lookout for us."

They walked along the perimeter for a few minutes before Marcus stopped and knelt. He ran his fingers through the dust in the ground, finally finding the metal latch he knew to be there. He pulled on it and it opened to reveal an entrance to a shallow trench running under the wall.

"They built the wall right over this drainage ditch," said Marcus. "It's a bit of a tight squeeze, but you can crawl through this, right to the other side. I'll go first to make sure the coast is clear."

Marcus dropped into the ditch and removed his backpack. He lay flat on his back and pushed himself under the wall. The tunnel was only around thirty feet long, but he had to traverse the whole length on his back, with his nose scraping the top of the tunnel, in complete darkness. In truth, Marcus hated small spaces, and this terrified him every time he had to do it. He had put on a show of bravado in front of Vana, he convinced himself it was for her benefit, but in reality, it was for his.

He had to stop several times in the short tunnel to steady his breathing and fight the panic rising in his chest. His biggest fear was the same as all claustrophobics; that he would become trapped, or the ceiling would cave in, or the air would suddenly somehow run out. He tried not to think about that, especially when he was only halfway through. He pushed on until he felt his head touch the far wall. He must be at the far end, he thought. Normally in the daytime you would be able to see light streaming in through the gaps in the metal cover at this end, but as it was night he had to rely on touch to find it and push it open.

After a few seconds of fumbling, he found the cover and pushed it up slightly. He twisted his head to have a look around, and after making sure there was nobody around, slid the cover off. He let out a sigh of relief. The tunnel came out in a small enclosed area, three sides of which were old industrial buildings, no longer in use.

The way out was over a chain linked fence and was covered in large piles of debris, broken bits of machinery and other junk, piled so high you couldn't see over it. It was how the tunnel had remained a secret to almost everyone for all this time.

He quietly called across to Vana, letting her know it was safe. She was through in a matter of seconds, climbing out of the trench with what looked like almost no effort at all. She handed him the backpack, which he slung over one shoulder.

"Cosy," she said. "I thought you said it was a tight squeeze?"

Marcus looked at her small frame. "Perhaps not for you."

"So, what's the plan?" asked Vana.

"We need to get to the lab underneath Doc's workshop, from what he told me it should be fully kitted out with equipment and tools. Hopefully it will have everything we need to build this portal."

"What if Davon has the lab under surveillance?"

"I don't think he will. There's no way Davon could know Doc had any involvement with the militia. Hell, even I didn't know, and I have been working with him for years. We shouldn't take any chances though."

They climbed over the pile of junk and found themselves in an alleyway running between two buildings. They carefully weaved their way between the abandoned structures making their way towards the centre of New Hope, where Doc's lab was. The streets were deserted. Unusually so. Even at this time of night you could expect to see or *hear* people.

"Something's not right," Marcus said in a hushed tone. His voice echoed eerily along the empty alleyways." He raised a hand

and cocked his head, listening for the familiar sounds of the settlement. "Nothing," he said after a few seconds.

"What about over there?" Vana pointed to a building close by, light flickered through a window, behind a thin curtain.

"Let's check it out," said Marcus. They jogged over to the house. The door wasn't locked, and Marcus pushed it open, a loud creak coming from its strained hinges. Nothing looked out of the ordinary. Dishes and plates lay scattered around, some still loaded with food. Several chairs in the room were overturned and lay on the floor.

"It's like they got up and left in the middle of the meal," said Marcus. "Nobody wastes food around here. Whatever happened must have been pretty bad." A search of the rest of the house revealed nothing, except more evidence of the occupant's sudden disappearance. A quick check of other nearby houses revealed much the same.

"I don't like the look of this," said Marcus. "Let's get to the workshop and find this bunker of Doc's. He might know whats going on here."

They made their way to the centre of town, and to the building Doc used. After making sure they were not walking into a trap, they dashed across and quickly found their way in through a side entrance. Marcus slid the door closed behind them, cringing as it squeaked along the metal rollers.

A single light at the far end of the building provided the only illumination. Long, ominous shadows stretched out before them. The usual disarray of partly constructed machinery and workbenches covered in handwritten notes littered the warehouse. Nothing appeared out of place. Vana picked up one of the pieces of paper from a desk and studied it.

"Don't tell me you learned to read as well?" asked Marcus, knowing full well what the answer would be. Vana cocked her head and smiled.

"He very nearly got this right," she said after a few more seconds, "I'm impressed."

She handed the paper to Marcus, who squinted in the half-light to read it. Mathematical formulas and strange Greek looking symbols covered the page. He didn't understand a word of it.

"Oh yeah, I see now. I'm-- gonna check some stuff over here." He dropped the paper and wandered over to another desk.

Vana walked to the other end of the building, closely examining several items along the way.

"Any luck?" Marcus half-whispered, his voice echoing around the deserted structure.

"No," replied Vana, "but I don't know what I'm looking for."

"If this bunker exists there must be a way to get into it. Look for a panel or a switch or something like that. It could be hidden, or disguised as something else."

Marcus found a flashlight on one of the desks and switched it on. He ran the beam over the floor trying to find anything resembling a panel or entrance of any kind. After a few minutes of searching a glint caught his eye, caused by faint scratches in the metallic floor. The scratches formed a neat line. Using his fingers, he followed the lines and traced out a square about a meter wide.

"What do you think to this?" asked Marcus as he ran his hands over the grooves on the floor.

"Something heavy has slid across here and made these marks. It could be the entrance we're looking for."

"Any idea how we get it open? There's no button that I can see, and you wouldn't be able to get anything in there to prise it open."

"I think maybe a more direct approach will be best here," said Vana. She walked over to a nearby workbench and selected a large rubber mallet from the collection of tools that littered its surface.

"I'm not sure how that's going to help."

Vana gave a mischievous grin and raised the mallet above her head, before striking the floor where the grooves were with some considerable force. The noise reverberated around the room and made Marcus jump.

"Whoa! What are you doing?!" he cried in a hushed voice. "Half of new hope probably heard that!"

"Just trying to get someone's attention."

"Yeah well, you definitely got mine."

Marcus whispered into one of the cracks in the floor. "Doc, can you hear me? It's me, Marcus. If you're in there open up." There was no reply. "Come on Doc. I brought someone to see you, and I have a bag full of goodies for you to play with." After a few seconds a muffled response came from underneath the panel.

"Who's there with you."

"Doc, thank god you're there. I've got Vana with me. Come on, open up before someone catches us out here."

After a moment of silence Doc replied. "Okay, stand back."

The panel lifted and slid out, tracing the scratch marks on the floor exactly. Marcus caught sight of a ladder that led into the darkness below. As he got ready to climb down, the barrel of a shotgun appeared from the opening and was thrust into his face.

"Slowly, let me see you properly," came the unmistakable deep voice of Doc.

Marcus moved carefully to the hatch, his hands raised by his side to show he wasn't holding any weapons. Vana stood slightly behind Marcus, and also had her hands raised.

"It's only us, we're alone."

The weapon retreated into the darkness to be replaced by the face of Doc.

"What are you waiting for?" he asked. "Get down here before we all get caught."

Vana descended the ladder first, followed closely by Marcus. When they had reached the bottom, Doc clicked something in his pocket, which caused the panel above to close itself.

They were in a narrow stone corridor, lit by several lights mounted into the ceilings.

"What is this place?" asked Marcus,

"It's an old bomb shelter. It's quite extensive. Why do you think I was so keen to have my workshop in the building above? But we can talk more about it later, let's get back to my lab."

They walked through several intersections, past doors labelled power and water treatment and a few others whose labels had worn away over the years. Lights above them flickered on an off automatically as they passed. Finally, they pushed their way through a large set of double doors and into a brightly lit laboratory.

"This area used to be for storage, but I repurposed it as a lab," said Doc.

Workbenches were scattered around and were covered in paperwork and devices in varying states of disassembly. He directed them over to the centre of the room, to a large unkempt desk. There were several chairs nearby, which like the workbenches had piles of junk on them. Doc grabbed the chairs and swept the contents onto the floor with his hand.

"Please, sit down. I want to know everything that has happened since you left for Jericho," said Doc.

"Hold up a minute, first I think we need to know what is going on here? Where is everyone? It's a ghost town out there, we didn't see a single person on our way through."

144

Doc leaned back in his chair and looked at the drab grey ceiling, collecting his thoughts.

"I honestly don't know what to think," he replied after a short time. "I'm not sure if I would believe it, had I not seen it with my own eyes."

"Seen what?" pressed Marcus.

"People, just, vanishing. Into thin air. I can't explain it."

Marcus looked over at Vana, who seemed to be waiting to hear more before she offered any insight or explanation.

"There was this… well, I suppose you could call it a wave. A wave of energy that passed through town. Anybody who touched it simply… vanished. I saw the wave coming and managed to get underground before it hit. I've never seen anything like it before. I don't know what to make of it."

"Could it be a new type of weapon?" asked Marcus

"That was my first thought yes, but it seemed very selective. If it is a weapon I would have expected it to damage or destroy other things in its path. But it only seemed to target people. And that's not all, it left other organic things, plant life, animals and such completely untouched. I'm at a complete loss as to what is going on."

Doc sat forward in his chair, addressing Marcus. "I'm glad to see you are safe. I didn't dare venture outside again, as I had no idea if the wave had any residual side effects, or indeed if it will return."

"When did all this happen?" asked Marcus, rubbing his forehead.

"Yesterday. Soon afterwards there was an event. A huge spike in gamma radiation, and some seismic activity. Being stuck down here I couldn't tell for sure, but it had all the hallmarks of a nuclear detonation."

"I think you'll find that was us, Doc," Marcus looked at Vana and gave her a knowing look.

"My god! How? Why? What on Earth is going on?"

"What on Earth indeed," said Marcus. "I think it's time we filled you in on a few of the details."

Marcus and Vana spent the better part of an hour going over everything that had happened to them after Marcus had left for Jericho. About how they found each other and escaped under the nose of the Legion. Making their way to the crash site, and discovering it was the wreckage of a crashed alien ship. About who Vana and Davon really were, and about how they had destroyed the ship to prevent it falling into Davon's hands.

Doc listened in silence as they recounted the tale. When they had finished, he looked at them, his eyes wide and brimming with questions.

"Quite amazing. Unbelievable almost," said Doc, rubbing his temples and scrunching his eyes. He took a few deep breaths and looked at Marcus and Vana, who were waiting for the inevitable onslaught of questions.

"Okay. I have many, many, questions," said Doc, "and I have no idea where to start."

"Well I'm glad you believed us," said Marcus.

"Of course I believe you Marcus, you'd never be able to invent a story like that."

"Well, thanks-- I think. I'm not sure if I would believe it myself if I hadn't have lived through it."

A door creaked open behind Marcus and he turned in the direction the noise had come from.

"You didn't tell me you had company Doc," said Marcus as he reached to his belt for a weapon, before remembering he'd lost it in the fight with Davon

146

Amara stepped out from the doorway and Marcus leapt from his chair. He grabbed Vana and ushered her behind him as he backed towards a doorway behind them.

"Stay back," he warned Amara. It was an empty threat, he was unarmed and trapped in an underground bunker. He retraced the path back to the exit in his mind and wondered if he and Vana could make it there before Amara caught up to them. But then there was Doc. He'd never be able to outrun her. Amara moved closer to Doc, and stood behind him, her wide eyes peeking out from behind his shoulder. Why wasn't Doc making a move? Had he been coerced into helping them? Had they walked into a trap?

"Dad? What's going on?" said Amara, her voice was broken. Her hands were unsteady and trembled slightly. Doc took her hand to comfort her.

"Stay back," Doc said to Amara, and turned to address Marcus, "She's not under Davon's control anymore. I freed her. She's not a threat."

"You should listen to Doc," came a third voice from the left of Marcus. He glanced over to see Kali with a bandage tied around her head. "I'm trying to get some rest in here, and you lot are making a racket."

"Kali? How did you get here?" asked Marcus.

"After you abandoned me in Jericho my men brought me here. Oh, and by the way, I'm still pissed at you for that. You knew that I wanted to bring Vana back here. I get hurt and you take the opportunity to bail on me."

"Look, I knew you were in safe hands with your men," replied Marcus. "To be honest I thought they'd take you back to your outpost."

"They did, but the place was deserted. I thought it had been attacked until I arrived here and saw the same had happened in New Hope."

"Where're your men now?" Marcus relaxed slightly, and Vana stood out from behind him.

"They went on a supply run. They should have been back by now. Something must have happened. I was planning on going to look for them. If I could stand for more than five minutes without getting dizzy." Kali wandered over to a chair and plopped herself into it.

"I think I know what caused everyone to vanish," said Vana quietly.

All eyes shifted onto her.

"Go on then," said Kali.

"How much did you hear about what we told Doc?"

"I heard everything. Don't believe a word of it."

"I thought you were resting?" said Marcus.

Kali shot him a snide look. "I'm surprised you are buying into this Doc." She rolled her eyes and swung her feet up onto a nearby desk. "It's a load of paranoid conspiracy theory bullshit."

"Well what do you think happened to all those people outside?" asked Marcus.

"I have no idea," she replied sharply, "but I sure as hell don't think it was aliens from the planet Mars that did it."

"Actually, they're not from Mar--" said Vana before being interrupted.

"Or Venus or whatever."

"When you consider the evidence--" started Doc,

"What evidence? All they have is a wild story and a bag of trinkets." She scowled at Vana. "Now don't get me wrong, it's obvious something weird is going on around here, and we need to get to the bottom of it. Davon obviously has a new weapon. What this weapon does or how it works is beyond me, but we can't let him continue to use it."

"That much we can agree on," said Marcus.

148

"I don't think it's a weapon," said Vana, "I think those people are still alive," she continued, fighting to get a word in past Kali's diatribe. "I think it was used to transport the inhabitants of this settlement to somewhere else."

"It's not just this settlement either," said Doc. "Since the incident, I have been listening to radio chatter, trying to figure out what happened. It seems this has affected all the other major settlements in the area. Some smaller ones seem to have escaped untouched, and anyone who was outside the settlement limits at the time was also spared. That's probably why you were not affected," he said motioning to Vana and Marcus.

"You seem to have more of an idea what this could be Vana," said Marcus, "What do you think has happened to them?"

"I've seen something like this, 'weapon' before," she replied, "though on a much smaller scale. I think it's a kind of transportation device, used to kidnap your people and take them somewhere else, possibly even off world."

"Oh, here we go again with the alien nonsense," snorted Kali.

"Look," said Marcus, cutting her off. "Whether you believe us or not, the course of action is clear. We have to get to the weapon and either capture or destroy it, and if we can take out Davon at the same time, all the better. Although I'm not sure how. We vaporised several square miles of rock earlier on, and he somehow managed to survive that."

"Actually, I think I know how he escaped," said Vana. "He transported himself, in much the same way as he took all these people."

"Great," said Marcus. "So now he has the ability to appear anywhere he pleases?"

"Yes, and not only that. He seems to have found a way to do this on a large scale. In theory he could transport a whole army anywhere almost instantly."

"So why hasn't he? Nothing's making sense around here. What does he want? Why kidnap people? What possible use could they be to him?"

"I don't know," replied Vana. "But whatever the reason is, the only way we're going to be able to stop him is to get to the Sentinel. I took everything we will need to create a portal of our own from my ship before we destroyed it. It should allow us to build something we can use to get to the Sentinel. I'm going to need some help if you're up to it?" She locked her eyes onto Doc, who gingerly probed the backpack, but stopped short of removing anything from it.

"So, once we have this thing built, we're good to go?" said Kali, who had given up protesting about how absurd this all sounded to her.

"Not quite," said Vana. "Before we can use this device, we need to calibrate it correctly. Unfortunately, the only place to get the data I need is from Davon's ship."

Kali huffed. "You are crazier than I thought. So what? You want to waltz into Davon's HQ and just ask him politely if you can just borrow the keys to his spaceship for a few minutes?"

Marcus scowled back at her. "I think we can figure out a way between us that would be less direct."

Kali scoffed at him and shook her head. Her mouth agape with disbelief.

Vana reached around her neck and unclasped the chain which Jax hung on. Marcus had almost forgotten about him. He watched Doc closely, anticipating his response to seeing Jax for the first time.

Vana waved her hand over the top of the crystal and an interface appeared, floating in the air above it.

"Incredible!" said Doc. His eyes lit up at the sight of the technology. "What is it exactly?"

150

"This is Jax," said Vana.

"I was hoping I'd get the opportunity to talk with, it-- er, him," said Doc. "We have a similar concept. We call it artificial intelligence, but this looks vastly superior to anything we ever managed to create."

The floating interface vanished and was replaced with what looked like a projection of the night sky.

"What are we looking at?" asked Marcus, taking a step back to see the whole image properly.

"A representation of all stellar objects within one hundred light years of the Sentinel.

The display rotated and zoomed in on a star system. In the centre, a small red star was orbited by three planets, lines traced their orbital paths. The map zoomed in again to the furthest planet from the star, a world of purples and green.

"Is that the Sentinel?" asked Marcus, indicating a small symbol hovering over the planet.

"Correct," said Jax. "It is in orbit around the third planet of this system."

"How far away from us is this?"

"Several thousand lightyears," replied Jax. "Too far for the Krall to have detected Earth directly. You were probably detected by one of the Krall's probes. They have a great many scattered around the galaxy. Listening for the noisy planets."

"Noisy?" asked Marcus,

Doc explained. "RF noise I imagine. Radio waves, that sort of thing. One hundred years ago we were beaming out vast amounts of noise into the galaxy. Television signals, radio, even radar signals from aircraft would have been detectable out to a certain distance."

"And when they heard those signals they came for you," said Jax.

151

"But surely we were no threat!" said Doc, exasperated. "Even a hundred years ago, when we were at the height of our achievements, we were only beginning to explore space. We hadn't even left our own solar system. They were light years away. It would have taken us tens of thousands of years to even reach them!"

"The Krall attack those who have, or are close to achieving FTL technology. Your race must have met those conditions."

"How many other races are out there?" asked Doc.

"The galaxy is full of all sorts of strange and interesting creatures. But most do not look like you or me. Even the Krall have a very different appearance to what you may be used to."

Marcus studied Vana. True, there were some differences, but on the whole, there were more similarities. She was around the same height and build as the average person. Eyes, ears, nose, arms, legs, hands, were all in the right place and looked normal to him. His thoughts snapped to Davon. Marcus had assumed the Krall were human looking as well. He had met Davon, and he certainly *looked* human. Creepy and bizarrely strong, but still human.

"But, if he's not… human looking, what does he look like? And how is he concealing his real appearance?"

"He has disguised himself so he can move freely among your people," said Vana.

"I assume you don't mean he's wearing a mask and a suit," said Marcus.

"No. He's using something much like the technology I am using here." She pointed to the projection, as it spun slowly in the air. "He can project an image over himself and by using some clever manipulation of energy fields, can give the projection a solid form. Unlike this one, which I can disrupt." She waved her hand through the projection and it flickered as her hand passed through it. "Underneath he's something quite different. The Krall have an insect-like appearance."

Marcus shuddered. Great, a giant bug. That wasn't at all creepy.

Doc clapped his hands and rubbed them together excitedly.

"So, what are we waiting for?" he said with a smile. "We've got something to build!"

Chapter Eleven

Vana spent the next few hours with Doc, as they pieced together the various components they had brought back from the crash site into a working machine. Marcus stuck around for a while, interested to hear about how all the technology worked, but soon found himself out of his depth. Instead, he made himself scarce and left them to it. Amara had retreated to her room after the drama earlier on, and Kali was busy stripping, cleaning and rebuilding the arsenal of weapons she had managed to acquire.

With nothing else for him to do Marcus decided to explore. He found room after room, with dimly lit corridors linking them. Some empty, some stacked with nondescript boxes and stores of dried food. One room was stacked floor to ceiling with weapons and ammunition. A note on the door in Kali's handwriting described in detail the fate of anyone who messed with her 'stash'. How Doc had managed to keep this place a secret from him was a mystery.

He wandered aimlessly along yet another set of corridors, not paying attention to where he was going. This place felt familiar to him somehow as if he had been here before. He pushed the thought to the back of his mind. He was about to turn around and retrace his steps when he saw something which looked out of place. Ahead there was a door. There was nothing unusual about the door itself, what caught his eye was the fact it was secured with a padlock. None of the other doors were locked, so what was so special about this one?

He walked over and gave it an exploratory push. The lock rattled but did not give way. He pushed open a few of the other doors nearby and found only empty boxes and disused bits of machinery. Marcus returned to the locked door and examined it. No nameplate or sign existed to give any indication as to what this room was for. If it hadn't been for the fact it had a lock on it he would have walked right past it, without giving it a second glance.

It had piqued his interest, he wanted to know what was so special about this place, and he had nothing better to do. He considered asking Doc, but he didn't want to bother him. It would probably turn out to be nothing.

He scoured the area for something he could use, and soon found a few shards of scrap metal which were thin enough to pick the lock. He worked on the lock for what seemed like an eternity and was about to give up entirely when he heard the satisfying click of the lock releasing.

Marcus pumped the air with his fist and looked around sheepishly to make sure nobody else witnessed his little celebration.

As he placed his hand on the door to open it his stomach knotted up and his chest tightened. He looked at his hands. They were shaking. Something about this room made him want to turn and run. A few deep breaths later and his hand was back on the door. He pushed it, and it swung open with a creak.

The room inside was pitch black. Marcus fumbled around the wall nearest the door, before finally locating the light switch and flicking it on. Above him, several fluorescent lights flickered to life. Others, their tubes full of blackened soot remained dark. After a few seconds his eyes adjusted to the dim light from the few remaining working bulbs and could make out what looked like a bed in the centre of the room.

It was raised and looked like something you would find in a hospital. To one side was a chair and small table. The bed had arm and leg restraints, made from a tough leather, and were linked together by chains.

Something stirred in the back of his mind, his heart, now trying to break its way out of his chest, somehow managed to pump harder. He backed towards the door and bumped into another desk behind him. Piles of paperwork and folders clattered to the ground and in the dim light Marcus caught the name, handwritten on one of the binders.

"*Marcus Coe: 21-08-2105*"

"What the hell..." said Marcus to himself.

He flicked through the pages, which seemed to consist largely of medical notes and other observations. Most of it he didn't understand, but a few words did jump out at him, such as "coma", usually in conjunction with the word "unresponsive". What's more, he recognised the handwriting. It was the same handwriting as covered all the notes and other bits of paper found almost everywhere in this bunker. Doc's.

The next few entries were observational notes, spanning several weeks and were full of technical and medical terms with long and scary sounding names. If there was any doubt in his mind these notes were about him, they were quashed when he came to a small envelope, stuffed full of photographs, all dated around five years ago. The photos were all of him, first laying on the table he was now standing in front of - restrained, then later, in what looked like a regular bed.

This had to be some sort of trick or mistake. Marcus had never been here before, in this place and he certainly had never been in a coma.

156

"I was wondering if you would come back here," came a voice from the doorway. Marcus flinched and turned quickly. The binder clattered to the floor and came to rest at Doc's feet.

"I thought you might end up here," said Doc.

"What's all this about?" asked Marcus, snatching up the pictures he had dropped, and marching towards him. "Why are there pictures of me chained to this bed? Why are there all these notes about me?"

"How much do you remember about how we first met?" asked Doc, adjusting his glasses.

"I'm not in the mood for guessing games Doc, tell me what's going on." Marcus stared at Doc, who remained silent, his question still unanswered. "Fine," huffed Marcus, "We met three years ago. I came to you for work, you gave me some. The rest is history."

"Not quite," said Doc, as he walked in and sat on the edge of the desk. "It's better if you remember on your own. Familiar sights or sounds can trigger memories thought lost. The fact you even found this room proves something of that time is still in there somewhere."

"What are you talking about!" yelled Marcus.

"This bunker is massive, yet you walked straight here, to this room. As if your subconscious mind was trying to tell you something."

Marcus felt his face flush, he was in no mood for riddles. "I don't remember ever being here before. Give me a straight answer, we don't have time to play games here."

Doc was hesitant. "Well, you were in a coma for most of it," he said finally. "I was hoping you would remember some of this on your own. However, as you have pointed out, time is not on our side."

Doc took a thick handwritten journal from the desk and handed it to Marcus. "We freed you Marcus," he said. "You used to be like Amara. Under the control of Davon."

****

The room span and Marcus saw the floor rushing to meet him. Doc threw out his arm and caught him and helped him back to the bed. He glanced at the Doc's hand-written notes. All about him, a past he couldn't remember.

"I am… was one of those things working for Davon? You've made a mistake Doc, there's no way I'd ever be one of those… things."

"I'm afraid it's true Marcus. The first time we encountered you was during a firefight in a town some distance from here. The Legion were turning the place over for some reason and things got out of hand. There was a firefight with the underground and you were injured." Doc tapped the side of his head. Marcus raised his hand and traced the scar across his temple. "The implant Davon used to control you was damaged, which gave us the opportunity to capture you."

"Wait, implant? What? Is there something in my head Doc?"

"Indeed, there is. A tiny device which interfaces with your brain, suppressing some things and enhancing others. It also instils upon its owner a sense of complete loyalty to Davon. Until now we had no idea how this could be possible, but after meeting Vana… well we now know where this technology came from.

"We brought you back here, to this very room, with the intention of interrogating you, but after months of being in a coma we had pretty much given up any hope of you recovering.

158

Only Kali held out any hope you would wake up; and one day, you did just that. With total amnesia."

"Wait, Kali was there too?"

"She spent quite a bit of time at your bedside. She said it was for security reasons, in case you woke and tried to murder us all. But, I think she felt responsible. After all, she was the one who shot you."

Kali wanting to shoot Marcus was the one thing which seemed believable to him at this point.

"We kept you close by - under observation. It quickly became apparent you couldn't remember anything, so you were not a threat to us. Even your memory from those first few weeks eventually faded. We decided to keep you close by, so you've been working for me ever since. We also kept the existence of this place hidden from you. We could never be completely sure your memory wouldn't return, or the implant wouldn't reactivate itself. We couldn't risk exposing the headquarters for the underground. That's why you were never told about it."

Marcus felt his stomach churn.

"This thing in my head, can you remove it?"

"Not without killing you. It's buried in there quite deep."

"So why did you have me searching everywhere looking for these missing people if you knew Davon was kidnapping and implanting them?"

"I hoped it would help jump-start something in your memory. Something we could use against Davon. Or maybe help you remember your past."

"Why can't I remember? Or even not know I have forgotten it? If that makes sense?"

"Memory is a funny thing," said Doc. "When something doesn't make sense to us, or is contradictory to our normal experiences, the mind will tend to fill in the blanks with something that does make sense. Think back Marcus; what did you do before you came to New Hope for the first time?"

"I…" struggled Marcus. "I don't know. It's a strange feeling, knowing there is a part of your life you can't remember. So, who was I before I worked for Davon? Where am I from?"

"We have no idea. We did some digging around but were never able to turn up any information about you. Your past is as much a mystery to us as it is to you."

"Do you think I'll ever get those memories back?"

"Honestly I don't know. I suspect your memories are still there, just … blocked, which would explain the headaches. It's possible one day you will remember everything. Of course, it is also possible you *never* will. We're dealing with an alien technology here, and I'm afraid to say it's beyond my understanding."

"But perhaps not Vana's," said Marcus.

"Of course!" cried Doc, "I hadn't even considered that. It would be worth talking to her about it. Perhaps she can help you - and Amara."

"So, Amara? She has one of these implants in her head as well?"

"Yes, but thankfully due to our experience with you, I was able to deactivate hers fairly easily. Like you, she has some memory loss. She can remember everything clearly until she was taken by Davon's men, then things get a bit sketchy. She described it as trying to remember a dream. She is understandably confused and disorientated and wants to be left alone for now."

Doc stood and walked towards the door. "I should check in with Vana," he said.

"How's it going with her anyway?"

"I grasp some of the fundamentals of what she is saying, but the practical application of it is mind-boggling. Without the parts she salvaged from her ship, there would be no way of building this thing. The technology simply does not exist - not on this planet anyway. Half the components are made from some material which technically shouldn't exist. At least from my understanding of physics anyway - which she keeps correcting me on. I think I have learned more about how the universe works in two days with her than I did in the last thirty years."

"You left her to it?"

"It was her idea, I needed a break. But secretly I think she was getting fed up of me constantly asking questions. I was only slowing her down. She reckons it will take a couple more days to complete and test it. With the amount of energy we're talking about here, I'll be glad if we don't blow up this whole continent when we switch it on."

Marcus allowed himself to smile and looked at Doc who was wearing a serious expression.

"Oh, right, so that's actually a possibility?"

"Now you understand why I needed a break," he said. "It will be fine, Vana knows what she is doing. Or at least she is putting on a good show."

"Well you've convinced me Doc," said Marcus, utterly unconvinced.

Doc stood to leave the room but paused at the door. He turned to Marcus, "I don't know what happened to you, or Amara when you were in the Forge with Davon. Maybe it would be better if you never remembered. Maybe it would be better for both of you."

He didn't wait for Marcus to reply, but simply turned and left. Doc was probably right thought Marcus. If his dreams were any indication, he didn't want those memories back.

****

Marcus made his way back to the central area, which had been converted into a makeshift workshop, tools and cables lay haphazardly on every surface. Vana was busy screwing a cable into a machine the size of a desk, which hummed slightly and made the hairs on Marcus's neck stand on end whenever he got near to it. Doc had already returned to work and was busy fiddling with a bunch of cables, connecting them to various ports and sockets on the ever more complex looking device.

"How's it going?" he asked Vana as he weaved his way towards her through piles of scattered equipment heaped haphazardly across the floor.

"Much better than I expected," she replied, grabbing another loose cable and attaching it to the device. "Doc has been a great help, shouldn't be more than another day and I think we will be ready to go."

"Already? I thought this was going to take longer?"

"I wasn't counting on Doc being so efficient. I'm impressed."

"Hah," snorted Doc, "I'll take the compliment, but I feel like a Neanderthal who has just been shown the space shuttle." The Doc had a wide smile on his face.

"I have to admit though I am enjoying this. I could learn so much if only we had the time. Which we don't of course. We have to put a stop to whatever Davon is doing."

Vana stopped to wipe a bead of sweat from her head with the back of her hand. She stood back from the machine and examined it, tightening cables and double-checking connections.

"I think that's why he has taken people from the nearby settlements, to use as soldiers. He's building an army for something."

"So, he could be implanting people with those things right now?" Marcus tapped the scar on his temple, "That doesn't sound good."

162

"No, it doesn't," said Vana, "I suspect he only took people before whom he thought would be compatible. It's possible many people will die in the process of him implanting them."

"Then we have more reason to stop him. We don't want an army of fearless totally loyal soldiers against us, but equally, we can't let people die in the process of them being implanted. We have to rescue them somehow."

"At the moment we have no idea where they could have been taken, but when we get aboard Davon's ship we may be able to download the information from the onboard computers."

"Does the Sentinel have a range limit?" asked Doc. "It may help us narrow our search."

"In a way it does. Theoretically it can open a portal to anywhere in the galaxy, but in practice, it gets more tricky the father you want to travel. The more distant the portal, the more inaccurate it becomes. For example, over a short range, you can move a ship, or a person, with pinpoint accuracy. Further out, you start to get drift. If I were to try and send you across the galaxy for example, you could find yourself lightyears away from your intended target."

"I suppose there is also the chance you could appear inside a planet, or a star," mused Doc.

"Exactly. Although space is vast, and the actual chance of appearing within a planet or star is infinitesimal."

"That's still an insurmountable distance," said Doc, "we can barely navigate our way across the Earth, never mind mount a rescue mission to an alien world."

"Right now, we don't have any hard facts about where they are," said Marcus. "We should wait until we know where Davon took them before we get too involved in planning a rescue mission. Besides, we need to work out how we are going to get

163

into Davon's compound in the Forge. I have an idea, but I need to speak to someone first."

****

Marcus reached the steel door, paused for a moment and gently rapped on it. It opened enough for Amara to peek out through the crack.

"What do you want?"

"Can I come in for a moment? I spoke to your father, he said I could come and see you."

She seemed to think about this for a few seconds but finally opened the door fully, inviting him in. She stood by the open door and didn't close it - as if leaving herself with an escape route.

"Why are you here?" she asked. A slight tremble in her voice told Marcus she was not comfortable having him around.

"I thought I may be able to help you," he said, trying to sound as sincere as possible. "You see, I've been through what you have. I just found out myself, I had no idea until Do-- your father told me. I was under Davon's control like you. He brought me back here and tried to help, but something went wrong, and I ended up losing most of my memories. I know what you are going through."

She stood silently by the door, looking away from Marcus, her mind elsewhere.

"I'm glad I can't remember much," she said finally. "I've heard about what I did. To you, and to other people. I don't want those memories."

"It wasn't your fault you know," said Marcus, "You were not in control of your actions. How could you have been responsible? He used you... us, as a weapon."

164

"It doesn't make me feel any better about it."

"Look at it this way, it means you are a good person. If you weren't you wouldn't be so upset. It means you care - and that's pretty rare around here."

She wiped a tear from her eye, "If you say so."

"I do, but now I have to ask you to do something very difficult, to help more people. I need you to remember."

Chapter Twelve

Marcus left after speaking with Amara at great length, and returned to the main hall, to find Vana busy working on the portal, now taking shape. A large metal frame, big enough for several people to stand within had been built in the centre of the room. A thick pile of cables linked the device to the power cell from Vana's ship. Various other cables and indistinct bits of machinery were attached to the outside of the frame, seemly at random. Doc had fallen asleep on a nearby desk, his head in his hands, snoring loudly.

"You know, you should probably get some rest too," Marcus said, as he approached Vana. "We're going to need all our wits about us when it comes time to do this thing."

"It's nearly ready, just a few more calibrations and we can start testing it."

"Vana, I need to ask you something," said Marcus. She stopped working on the device and placed a piece of equipment on a work surface next to her.

"Is everything alright?", she asked.

"I just found out I... I mean, there's something Doc told me that-- well I was once like Amara." There was no change in Vana's expression. "Davon used some sort of implant to control me. Doc tried to remove it, but something went wrong, and I lost most of my memories. I don't know which of my memories are real anymore."

Vana looked away from Marcus, biting her lip.

"I knew," she said, her voice faint against the whirrs and clicks coming from the device she was working on. "When we were joined. I felt it."

"Joined? Oh, you mean the city," said Marcus, the memory of the experience still vivid in his mind. "Does it work both ways? Can you see the memories of someone else?"

"It's possible. If the other person is receptive. I can't force them to show me anything they don't want me to see. It doesn't work that way. After all this time I'm not sure how many of your original memories will remain intact, but we can try."

"I don't want you to retrieve my memories," said Marcus. "I want you to help Amara retrieve hers. My memories, if they are still even there, are years out of date. It's possible all the information we need is locked away inside her head somewhere."

"But don't you want to know about your past?"

Marcus sighed and shook his head. "I've had a pretty good life these last few years. What if there's something in my memory that changes all that? What if I find out something about myself that I wish I hadn't? I'm happy not knowing. For now at least. We don't need any more complications."

"So, if you don't want me to try and retrieve your memories then—" A flicker of understanding crossed Vana's face. "Have you discussed this with Amara?"

Marcus smiled. "Nothing gets past you, does it? Yeah, I've spoken to her about it. She's not exactly thrilled at the idea of remembering what she was forced to do, but she understands there are lives at stake. She wants to do the right thing."

"I can't make any promises, but if she's receptive we can try."

167

"Well, I don't know about you, but I need to get some sleep." Marcus reached over and shook Doc by the shoulder. He awoke with a snort and looked around groggily.

"Surely it's not morning already," he said through a yawn.

"Not quite Doc," said Marcus. "Where can a guy get his head down around here?"

Doc pointed to a door at the opposite end of the room. "There's plenty of rooms down that corridor, enough for dozens of people. Some of them have got bedding in them already. We were planning on relocating many of the underground members down here at some point, so everything is already in place."

He stretched his arms, gave a yawn and headed out towards one of the rooms, leaving Marcus and Vana alone. She stepped back from the device, folding her arms and examining her handiwork.

"Is it finished?" Marcus asked.

"Almost, but we can't use it until we have a plan for getting access to Davon's ship. Doc's right, we should rest. I'm going to need it for Amara."

"Let's check out those rooms Doc mentioned," said Marcus. "I don't remember the last time I had a proper night's sleep."

They left the main hall and headed towards the first set of rooms Doc had pointed out.

"He wasn't kidding when he said this place could house dozens," said Marcus as he walked past door after door, each one a room that could comfortably house either four or eight people. Faded nameplates over the doors listed the rooms as simply 'Dormitory', with an ever-increasing number after them.

Vana and Marcus picked one of the first rooms in the corridor, labelled 'Dormitory 4a' and entered it. As promised there were two bunk beds and bedding. A small metal table sat against one wall, with two stacks of chairs stood neatly on top of it. A third wall was lined with various shelves and cabinets, all empty except for a thick layer of dust.

Vana climbed up onto the top bunk of one of the beds and laid down; staring at the ceiling.

Marcus walked to the door to leave. "Sleep well," he said as he reached for the handle.

"Marcus wait. Would you mind staying? I'd rather not be alone in here."

"Sure thing, if it makes you feel better."

He pulled his hand back from the door and walked over to the second bunk bed, and jumped onto the top one. He never liked being on the bottom. He couldn't help but imagine the top bunk crashing down on him in the middle of the night and smothering him. It also made him feel a little less claustrophobic, despite the fact they were buried in the ground. He made himself comfortable and glanced over at Vana, her expression vacant as she stared at the blank ceiling.

"What were your plans? I mean originally before everything went wrong? Were you planning to go home to your people?" asked Marcus.

"My people live like this. Underground, hidden away. Not out of choice of course. With the Sentinel gone we would be much safer. Perhaps even safe enough to come out from hiding and to be able to rebuild our civilisation. If we even can anymore, after so many years of paranoia."

She'd dodged the question, but perhaps it was not something she felt comfortable talking about. She'd tell him when the time was right, he was sure of that.

"Tell me about your people? I know almost nothing about you," said Marcus, changing the subject.

"My people… well, what can I say? You've see us at our best. The vision I shared with you. That was just one of many cities on our world. All that came to an end with the Krall. There's nothing but rubble now where those cities used to stand. Now we live underground, on a world that is not our own. Cowering from the Krall, and never daring to venture out from our hiding place. We couldn't continue to live like that – I couldn't live like that. Not with all the wonders of the galaxy out there, waiting to be discovered. And so I left, against the wishes of my people. If they won't do anything about the Krall then I will. At least, that was the plan. You know how that turned out."

"It must have taken a lot of courage to leave all that behind," said Marcus. "What did the others think when you told them you were coming here?"

"At the time I didn't know I was coming here at all. You must understand I started this journey years ago, it's possible my people left that world after I did - just to be on the safe side. I didn't have their blessing for this mission. I undertook this myself, against their strongest wishes. That's why I'm here alone, with what's left of a stolen ship - desperately trying to salvage a plan from all this mess."

"You've been gone so long, won't your people think… well, that you're dead?"

"Perhaps," Vana mused. "But my people are long-lived, so it's not that great a time for us."

Marcus was intrigued by this. "How long does the average J'Darra live then?"

She laughed. "Long enough," she grinned at him "Let's leave it at that shall we?"

"Wait a minute, you can't just leave it like that! I'm curious. You know what I'm going to ask you next don't you?"

Vana's lips pursed in a smile. "You know, Charlie asked me the same question back in Jericho. She said I looked too young to be getting involved in this mess."

"Did you tell her?"

Vana simply smiled.

"You're no fun," said Marcus, smirking. They laughed together before saying their good nights. For a few precious moments, Marcus forgot about everything happening outside the bunker. He slept a deep sleep, and for the first time in years, his dreams were happy.

****

Marcus awoke to a loud knocking on the door, he looked across to Vana's bunk. It had been neatly made and was empty.

"Um, come in," he said, wiping his eyes and blinking in the light streaming in through the open door.

A figure stood in silhouette, Marcus couldn't work out who it was, his eyes were still adjusting to the light.

"Wakey, wakey," came the voice of Amara. "We thought you deserved a lay-in, after everything you have been through. Come on, we're having breakfast." Amara turned and walked away, her footsteps echoing in the empty corridor.

Marcus took a few moments to compose himself, then followed her. As he got closer to the mess hall, a delicious smell of cooked meat and bread hit him. He couldn't remember the last time he ate properly. His mouth watering, he picked up the pace and caught up to Amara as they passed through the double doors and into the mess.

Everyone was there, all sat around a large table, which was covered in a vast array of food and drink. Amara took a seat next to Doc, and Marcus headed for a seat next to Vana. She'd saved it for him.

"Thank god you're up," said Kali, "I'm starving, and these guys wouldn't let me start until you got here."

"Where did all this come from?" said Marcus, gesturing to the table full of food and drink.

"I may have snuck out earlier this morning," said Kali. "There's plenty of food up top in New Hope. Nobody is eating it, So I thought why let it go to waste?"

Doc chuckled as he tucked into the food on his plate. "She took one look at the rations we had left down here and headed straight for the surface," he said. "Apparently rehydrated oats and water were not what she fancied this morning."

"No, I fancied food," said Kali. "Not some boil in the bag tasteless, probably mouldy oats."

"Well I'm with Kali on this one Doc," said Marcus.

"Let's eat already," insisted Kali as she started shovelling food into her mouth. Marcus looked at the array of food on the table, not knowing where to start. He picked up several pieces of fruit, some meats and bread - which he lashed with butter, and poured himself a large glass of fresh orange juice.

"I haven't eaten this well since, well... ever," said Marcus, "I can't believe all this food was laying around up there."

"Yeah, it seems people around here like to hoard. What are they expecting? Another apocalypse? I also took the opportunity to liberate a large quantity of alcohol. So, we can celebrate properly when we get back from this suicide mission of yours."

"She 'liberated' so much it took her two trips to bring it all back," smirked Amara.

Laughter filled the room, and soon they were all talking, conversations overlapping each other, as they talked about how they had all come to this point, and where it may all lead.

Doc in particular had many questions for Vana, mainly technical or scientific, which she didn't seem to mind answering.

172

Marcus nodded along with Doc, and said things like 'yes' and 'I see' every so often, to give the impression he knew what was going on.

An hour passed, and most of the food was eaten. Marcus leaned back in his chair, which creaked in protest. "I hope we don't have to go save the world just yet," he said. "I think I need another nap after eating all that." He let out a large belch and felt slightly better.

"Marcus," yelled Kali, throwing an apple core at him, "manners!"

He looked around for something he could throw back at her before Doc interrupted him.

"Before we all get too carried away, I think we should discuss the plan. First, we need to know how we're going to get into Davon's compound, how we're going to find his ship, so Vana can get the information she needs. Then of course there is the small matter of escaping without being detected, or killed."

"I've been thinking about that," said Marcus, "I've spoken to Amara and she's agreed to allow Vana to try and retrieve her missing memories. She's been near Davon for some time, and so hopefully the answers to many of these questions are somewhere in her head."

"I'll join with her and should be able to view her memories as if I was there myself," said Vana.

"Will there be any danger?" asked Doc, concern for his daughter evident in his voice.

"There will be no risk physically to her, but there's no telling what phycological effects there could be. We would be allowing her to relive moments of her life which could be difficult for her to come to terms with."

"It's pretty intense," said Marcus. "I know it's not the same thing as what we're doing here, but I've been fine. Better than fine actually since my experience."

"Amara, it's your choice," said Doc. "There's no pressure for you to do this. If you don't want to, we will find another way of getting the information we need. Don't feel like you have to do anything."

Amara replied instantly, "No, I want to. What I may, or may not have done when under his control - I need to face up to it. I know I wasn't responsible for my actions, but I can't pretend this didn't happen. I need to do this. Not for you, or for anyone in New Hope, or any of the other settlements that have been targeted, but for me."

"Okay," said Vana. "When you are ready we should go to the medical room. I think you should be hooked up to the monitors there, so we can follow your progress and ensure you are safe."

"Can I have a little bit of time to prepare myself?" said Amara, "Say an hour?"

Vana nodded, and they all went back to eating. Even Marcus, who felt he could manage one more plate of food.

****

An hour later, almost to the second, Amara walked into the infirmary. A bed had been set up ready for her, and several machines were lined up along the side. Doc and Vana were here, busy fiddling with the equipment and making last minute adjustments.

Amara was putting a brave face on, but as she paced around the room, her hands jammed tightly under her armpits, Marcus could see just how frightened she was.

As if sensing her discomfort Vana came over, "Are you okay?"

"Yeah," Amara replied, "I wasn't expecting all the machines - it all looks very... serious"

"These machines are only for monitoring you. This one here will measure your heart rate," she pointed to a machine making a soft beeping noise. "This one monitors your blood pressure, whilst the one at the end of the bed will be monitoring your brain activity. All we're going to do is stick a few of these wires to your skin. Nothing invasive, there's no needles or anything like that."

"Oh, okay," said Amara. "You didn't need any of this equipment when you joined with Marcus though did you? So why with me?"

Vana bent down and spoke quietly to Amara. Marcus listened in, whilst trying to look like he wasn't. "Your father insisted we take every precaution. This is different to what happened between me and Marcus. I was sharing something with him, which is much easier than trying to retrieve information from someone. Especially when there's an implant specifically designed to prevent those memories from ever surfacing. Trust me you'll be fine."

Doc finished connecting the last few wires to the various machines in the room, then nodded to Vana. "I think we're ready," he said.

Vana pulled up a stool and sat next to the bed, reaching out and taking Amara by the hand.

"I'm going to need you to relax," said Vana. "Close your eyes and try not to think of anything specific."

Vana closed her eyes and took deep slow breaths. This continued for several minutes without anything seeming to happen. Doc, who had been busy monitoring the various machines spoke to Marcus.

"I don't think it's working," he said in a hushed voice. "There's been no change on any of the readouts. Did it take this long for you?"

"No, it seemed to happen instantly, but Vana did say this would work differently,"

Doc's attention had been captured by one of his monitoring machines, which had started to react.

"Something's happening," said Doc, studying the readout.

There was a groan from Amara, who had a pained look on her face. Vana's knuckles were white as she gripped Amara's hands, and her eyes flickered rapidly beneath her eyelids.

"Are they okay?" asked Marcus, his voice breaking.

"Everything is still within the safety margins I established, but if these readings keep climbing then we will have to abort."

"And how do we do that?" asked Marcus.

"Vana said all we have to do is to break the physical connection between them. However, she said we should only do that in an emergency as disconnecting that way could be dangerous."

"I wish she had told me that before she started this," said Marcus.

There were more groans from the pair - and this time Amara twitched and shuddered. Vana gave a yelp and released her grip.

"It's no good," said Vana breathlessly. "I'm not strong enough."

"Try again," said Amara groggily. She hadn't opened her eyes.

"I can't do it, we'll have to find another way."

Marcus reached out a hand to Vana. "Is there anything I can do to help?" he asked.

"Maybe. We've been joined before. I could do so again, and perhaps draw some strength from you."

"Do it," said Marcus, and held out his hand.

"I don't think this is a good ide--" started Doc, before everything around Marcus became black. He felt as if he were falling and instinctively tried to steady himself before he realised he wasn't in the medical room anymore. Instead, he was standing in total blackness. Next to him, holding his hand was Vana - and in front of them was Amara, laying on the bed.

"Where are we?" asked Marcus.

"We're joined to Amara's mind," replied Vana.

"Huh. I was expecting… well, I don't know what I was expecting to be honest."

"This is just how your mind interprets the connection."

"Seems I don't have a very good imagination," said Marcus peering into the darkness.

Ahead, he could make out a doorway, barely visible in the blackness - only a sliver of light around its edges gave it away. Vana started walking towards it, tugging on Marcus's hand, wanting him to go with her.

"That looks like the best place to start," she said.

They started to move but found their path blocked by Amara - who had jumped out of the bed and was now standing directly between them and the door. They tried to go around her, but she would move to block their path.

"Let us past Amara," said Marcus. "We need to get to the door."

Amara remained silent. In fact, now Marcus had come to look at her more closely he could see her features were off. Her hair was matted, her skin pale and there were no signs of life in her eyes. She looked like a zombie.

"It's not really her," said Vana. "I think this is the implant trying to prevent us from getting to the memories.

Marcus tried to push past her, but she pushed back, hard. He stumbled and fell to the ground and was about to get up when he felt the sharp prick of a sword against his neck. The facsimile of Amara stood over him, now wielding a pair of swords.

"Oh, come on," said Marcus. "That's hardly fair."

Suddenly he was back in New Hope, tied to the chair in Hudson's office. Amara was standing over him, ready to run him through with the sword.

He started to feel panicked. His heart was thumping and sweat was pouring from his brow.

"Vana? A little help?" said Marcus nervously.

Amara swung the sword through the air. Marcus flinched and closed his eyes, waiting for the killing blow. There was a clang of metal on metal. He opened one eye cautiously to see Vana, who was now also carrying a sword - which she had used to deflect Amara's strike. She was struggling against her.

"Get me the hell out of this chair!"

"Get yourself out," replied Vana. She saw the look of confusion on Marcus's face. "It's *your* mind. You have to get yourself out. I can only do so much, besides I'm a bit busy here," she said straining against Amara.

What was he supposed to do? Think himself out?

Then he realised that was exactly what he needed to do. He wasn't really tied to a chair. He was sat in a room with Doc, Amara, Vana and probably Kali - if she had bothered to turn up. Everything happening here was all in his head - that's where the battle was being waged. Physical strength was not going to help him here. He concentrated on the thought of himself not being bound to the chair. The ropes binding him to the chair dissolved. He jumped out, kicking the chair away from him. It slid across the office and hit the wall, breaking into several pieces.

"Haha!" cried Marcus proudly. "Take that, chair."

"That's great," she replied, "Whenever you're ready Marcus," she said as she dodged a fist and rolled away from Amara.

"I'm gonna need a weapon…"

He had barely finished the sentence before a sword of his own appeared in his hands.

"Alright, now we're talking," he said as he weighed into the fight with the fake Amara.

Between the both of them, they were able to fight her back, until they had her backed into a corner. However, before they could finish her off, she vanished - leaving only a faint outline, which slowly faded away.

"Did we win?" asked Marcus. "That's gotta be it, right?"

Vana shook her head. "I think we've weakened her though," she replied. "You did good Marcus."

"Thanks, I think I'm starting to get the hang of this positive thinking business."

"It takes a great strength of will to fight against something like this. I wouldn't be able to do this without you."

Marcus felt his face become flushed. He quickly looked away after realising he had been grinning at her for a full fifteen seconds.

"So… where now?"

They were still in Hudson's office, although things seemed a little off. Certain things were bigger than they should be, the size and shape of the office was all wrong - much bigger than the real one, and there were several black gaps in the walls behind them.

"What's going on here?" he said pointing to one of the black areas.

"This place is based off your memory of being in this room. Memories are not a perfect thing - at least not for you. You're seeing things as you remember them. The black areas are things you never saw. I have never been here before, so everything in here comes from you."

"Well, it looks like there is only one way out of here," said Marcus pointing at the door. "Let's see where it takes us."

They went through the door and found themselves not in a corridor, as Marcus had expected, but out in the Badlands, near the truck he had been in when he was Amara's prisoner, searching for Vana.

"It's like the implant is replaying all of our past encounters," said Marcus. "It's trying to get into my head. Well, so to speak - since we're already in my head."

As before, details of the scene were not perfect, and the gaps in his memory were even more prominent now. A shot rang out and ricocheted off a large rock. The same rock that he had taken cover behind before. Both Vana and Marcus dove behind it, Marcus instinctively grabbing his shoulder as they did so.

"Are you injured?" said Vana, frantically checking his clothing for blood.

"No, no, I'm fine. Last time I was here I was hit in the shoulder. I don't fancy a repeat of that."

"Okay," said Vana, steadying her breathing.

"But I don't get it," said Marcus. "None of this is actually happening, right? So, I can't get hurt can I?"

"To be honest Marcus I don't know."

Another shot pinged off the rock they were hiding behind.

"We need to fight back," said Marcus, still holding onto his sword. "We're going to need more than swords though."

Marcus peered over the top of the rock. A bullet struck the top of it inches from his head, sending shards of razor-sharp stone flying towards him.

Marcus yelled in pain and clutched at his face. Vana pulled him out of the line of fire and checked his injuries.

"You'll be okay," she said. "Just a few cuts - nothing major."

"You tell that to my face," he said looking at his blood-stained hands. "Seems we can get hurt in here after all," he stammered. "Well that takes all the fun out of it."

"We can't stay here. What happened before?" said Vana.

"Kali showed up with the cavalry." He shouted into the night, "So what are you waiting for?"

Nothing happened.

"I guess we're not going to be that lucky again," he smirked - causing him to wince in pain.

"I have an idea," said Vana. "Make some noise, distract her, I'm going to sneak around and try and take her by surprise."

"Do you think it'll work?"

"This scenario is based on your memory of events. I wasn't there, so she can't anticipate what I'll do."

Marcus nodded. It was worth a try, and although he had discovered he could be injured in here, he doubted Vana could. She had initiated the joining, if they were in any real danger Marcus had to believe she would pull them out of it.

Marcus started his act. He yelled as if he was in pain - which wasn't entirely untrue. He begged for his life and offered to surrender. Vana had slipped around the other side of the rock and vanished into the darkness. The shooting stopped. Peeking around from the rock, Marcus could see Amara walking towards him. He kept up the act, hoping the noise would cover Vana's approach.

Before he knew it, Amara was standing over him. She raised a pistol and aimed it at him. In that instant, a sword plunged through Amara and exploded out of her chest. The expression on her face didn't change at all. It was if she didn't feel it. Amara dropped the gun and vanished, revealing Vana, the sword still thrust out.

"That was close," he said. "Good timing."

"I can feel her getting weaker," said Vana. "We've almost got her."

Marcus groaned. "I was hoping we'd finished her off for good."

"So where now," asked Vana. They looked around them. The only thing in the immediate area was the truck they had used when searching for Vana.

"I guess we take the truck," said Marcus, jogging over to it. He looked in the window - the keys were in the ignition. They both climbed in and slammed the doors. In an instant they were no longer in the truck but were now somewhere Marcus didn't recognise.

They were in a dark room. In the centre was a table, with a spotlight above it. Everything else was black. On the table lay Amara. The real Amara - not the imposter they had been fighting until now.

Marcus felt strange, as if he was looking through someone else's eyes at the scene in front of him. He tried to say something, but couldn't speak. He tried to move, but couldn't. He became aware that Vana was stood next to him. She was talking to him, but she sounded muffled - as if she was in another room, shouting through a wall.

His heart thumped in his chest. No matter what he did he couldn't move or speak. He screamed out in his mind, trying to break free. He tried to will himself out of this prison as he had the chair earlier, but to no avail.

Vana had become aware something was wrong. She was shaking his shoulder, trying to get him to respond. It was as if she was a million miles away - every sensation dulled by a vast distance.

Marcus could feel himself move. Vana was stood in front of him, and he saw himself reach out and put his hand on her shoulders. She looked back at him and smiled - she spoke, but the words were meaningless to him.

Suddenly his arm shot out, grabbed her throat and squeezed. Marcus screamed in his head to stop, but he couldn't, he wasn't in control. Vana struggled, but she was no match for his strength. All he could do was watch as the life was squeezed out of her.

Vana reached out her hands and placed them on Marcus's head. He realised she wasn't trying to hurt him, she was trying to help. Somehow, he felt stronger. With every ounce of strength he possessed, he willed himself to release his grip on Vana. He felt his grip slacken, it wasn't much - a crack in the Armor of whoever was controlling him, but it was a crack he could exploit. He continued to fight, and as he did so he felt himself regain more and more control until he had released Vana altogether, and was now staggering around the dark room, fighting for control of his own body. Suddenly he was back. He looked over at Vana who was on the floor panting and rubbing her neck, a large bruise starting to show where his fingers had been wrapped.

In front of them the imposter stood, weakened. Her face showed emotion for the first time, a mixture of confusion and fear. Marcus walked up towards her, his fists clenched, his blood boiling with anger at having been forced to watch as he almost killed Vana. He swung his fist at the imposter as hard as he could, and as his hand connected with her jaw the image of her exploded into a thousand silver fragments, before evaporating into nothingness.

"Good riddance," he spat.

He ran over to Vana who was struggling to get up.

"Are you okay?" he asked, checking her injuries. "I think you're going to be fine."

"Let's not do that again," said Vana hoarsely.

"I'm sorry," said Marcus. "I couldn't control myself, I don't know what happened."

"It was the implant fighting back. We hurt her badly at the truck, she needed to hide somewhere. She chose you."

"But how?"

"The implant in your head. It may not be as damaged as Doc thought it was. After we beat her at the campsite she fled to the only place left available to her."

"I never want to feel like that again. Powerless. Forced to watch. I could have killed you."

"She's gone Marcus, we beat her."

Amara, the real Amara had gotten out from the bed and was standing over them. He jumped up ready to fight.

"No, wait," said Vana, grabbing his arm.

Without saying a word Amara turned and started walking away from them. They followed her as she walked across the room and towards a faint outline of light. It was the door they had seen earlier. As they approached it, the door became more defined, until it stood in front of them, plain as day.

Amara pushed it open and walked through.

They did the same.

****

They stood in the middle of a long hallway. Grey concrete walls stretched into the distance and fluorescent lights lined the ceiling. Amara was standing a few meters in front of them, guarding a door. Her appearance had changed, her hair was tied back her face was flat and emotionless. She carried a weapon and was standing silently next to another guard. Several people wandered up and down the corridor, yet nobody paid them any attention.

"They can't see us, can they?" said Marcus as he waved his hand in front of someone walking past him, only for them to ignore him. At one point someone walked right through him as if he wasn't there, which sent shivers down his spine.

"This is Amara's memory and we're outside observers. We're not part of the memory so nothing we do here will change anything. We'll have to follow her and hope she can lead us to the information we need." Vana took in the scene. "Do you recognise this place?" she asked Marcus.

"If I had to guess, I'd say this is the bunker he uses as his headquarters in The Forge. We're clearly underground, there're no windows and I can see an elevator at the end of the corridor."

"This door she's guarding, it must be something important, otherwise why does Davon have her protecting it."

The door opened, Amara and the other guard snapped to attention as Davon marched out from behind it. Marcus peered in through the open door, but saw only blackness. The door snapped shut and Davon headed up the corridor, flanked by Amara. The second guard remained at the door.

"I didn't see anything in there, only darkness," said Marcus.

"Probably because Amara couldn't see into the room. Remember, we can only see what she saw. She was facing away from the door when it opened, and she never turned to look in. Davon probably has them conditioned to behave like that."

The corridor around them started to go dim and fade out.

Vana grabbed Marcus by the hand and jogged up the corridor, keeping up with Davon and Amara.

They followed him around for what seemed like hours as he went about his business. It became clear they were indeed in his headquarters in The Forge and security down here was tight.

From what little they could see of him, Davon was extremely paranoid and liked to know in minute detail everything that was going on around him. He seemed particularly concerned with a group of scientists and engineers who were busy conducting some sort of experiment.

Evidently, things were not going as smoothly as hoped and Davon was starting to become impatient. Unfortunately, they could only gather small snippets of information as most of the conversations Davon had appeared muffled - as if everyone was talking underwater. Vana told him this was due to Amara either not understanding what she heard, or simply ignoring most of it - which of course meant they too were unable to hear it. However, several keywords did seem to jump out. Words such as 'implant' and 'population' and the word 'experiment' was used a great many times, much to Marcus's unease.

Finally, when they had just about given up hope Davon was going to reveal any information, he entered a large room on the opposite side of the bunker complex. He approached a door and opened it.

"Bring me the latest prospect," he said before slamming the door shut.

This came through loud and clear. Amara proceeded to march up several corridors before coming to a room, again guarded by several unflinching guards. She entered without a word.

Inside the room was what looked like a hospital bed. In it lay a man, connected to various machines which appeared to be monitoring his condition. It looked like he had recently undergone surgery, fresh blood stained his gowns and he had stitches in the side of his head.

Marcus reached up and rubbed the scar on his head. Was this where he was taken before? Was this how he got his implant? Nothing about this place seemed familiar, but then again it could be simply that he couldn't remember. He was happy to keep it that way.

The man appeared comatose. He was disconnected from the machines and helped from the bed by Amara, who placed him into a nearby wheelchair and rolled him back out of the door.

They returned to the door Davon had entered, and as they approached it opened. Marcus followed Amara closely as she walked into the room. It was only small with a desk at one end, with a computer and various bits of paperwork upon it. There was a large luxurious looking chair behind the desk and on the far wall an elevator. The man in the wheelchair slumped forward and drooled onto the floor.

"Is this the best you can do?" said Davon. Apparently, it was a rhetorical question. Amara pushed the wheelchair-bound man into the elevator at the end of the room and turned around to leave.

"I don't want to be disturbed," he said as he climbed into the elevator and pushed a button. The doors slid closed and Amara left the room.

Everything faded to black and Marcus and Vana found themselves alone once more in the darkness.

"Is that it?" asked Marcus.

"I think I know what we need to do now," said Vana. "That room he was just in, it must lead to his ship."

"Make sense," said Marcus. "And with all this wandering about that we've been doing, I think I have a pretty good feel for the layout of the place and of some of the security measures we're going to have to deal with."

"Let's get out of here," said Vana, once again taking his hand. She closed her eyes and Marcus felt compelled to do the same. There was the sensation of falling once again and the various beeps and whirs from the medical equipment in the room. Marcus blinked his eyes in the bright light of the medical room. He felt dizzy and steadied himself on the bed. Doc had rushed over to check on them and was shining a light into his eyes.

"Cut it out Doc, I'm fine," he said butting the light away. "Just a bit of a headache that's all."

"What went wrong?" Doc asked, studying the monitors hooked up to Amara.

"What do you mean? Everything was fine, we got what we needed," replied Marcus.

"But you were only under for a few seconds."

"A few seconds? More like a few hours."

Vana had regained some composure, the effect of the joining appeared to have been harder on her. "Time doesn't really mean much when you're joined," she said.

"Astonishing," said Doc, scribbling notes into a small pad.

"Well I don't know about you, but I need a break. Oh, and something for my head."

They made Amara comfortable, disconnected her from all the machines and allowed her to sleep. "She'll be out of it for a few hours," said Doc. "It sounds like it was a productive exercise?"

Marcus nodded. "It was," he said. "We saw where Davon has been taking people. To some room - it's the only place where Amara wasn't allowed to go. He must be keeping something special in there. It has to lead to his ship."

"Sounds pretty flimsy to me," said Doc. "Did you actually see it?"

"Well, no… But its gotta be there Doc. What else could it be?"

"We know next to nothing about him. It could lead to his ship, or it could lead nowhere. You could be walking into a trap."

"We still haven't figured that part out yet," said Marcus. "Until we do, we won't be walking into anywhere."

"I can get you in."

The voice came from behind Marcus, from the doorway. Kali stood leaning up against the frame."

"Look who finally showed up," said Marcus. "And here I was starting to think you didn't care."

"I'm not saying I believe everything that is happening, but something's not quite right. I can get us into the Forge."

"How exactly?" asked Vana.

"I've been working a contact. Someone inside the Legion."

"I don't like the sound of this," said Marcus. "Can we trust this contact of yours?"

"This guy's new. I've been laying the groundwork for months. Ordinarily I wouldn't dream of using an asset like this before they have been properly vetted - but it doesn't look like we have a choice here. Deliveries come in and out of The Forge regularly. We can intercept one of them and use it to get inside the walls. We'll arrange for my contact to be on duty, he'll pass us through security. Then, it's up to you."

"Well then," said Marcus. "This sounds like the makings of a plan."

Chapter Thirteen

The reinforced concrete walls of The Forge towered above the stolen truck Marcus now hid in the back of. Razor sharp wire to discourage climbing ran along the length of the wall and armed guards stood vigilant in guard towers. If anyone managed to climb the wall, they'd have the guards to deal with. Marcus peeked through a tear in the fabric covering the rear of the truck and whistled in awe.

"This guy has some next level paranoia going on here," he said. "Is it too late to change my mind and go home?"

"Keep it down," murmured Kali. "And stay out of sight. We're almost at the checkpoint."

Vana sat and whispered to Jax who sat in the palm of her hand. Jax projected screen after screen of alien text and images into the air just above him, which Vana would visually scan for a few seconds before moving onto the next.

The truck rattled to a stop at the main gates, and the engine sputtered to a stop. A guard approached the cab and Kali lowered the driver's side window to talk to him. Paperwork passed back and forth between the two before the guard turned his attention to the rear of the truck.

"I need to check in the back," he declared.

"Sure, go right ahead," replied Kali, her arm hanging from the window as she watched him make his way to the rear of the vehicle.

"Shit," whispered Marcus. "Something's wrong."

The back of the truck opened, and a flashlight shone across the contents. Marcus and Vana froze to the spot, concealed behind crates, stacked to hide their presence. Marcus held his breath. The guard climbed in and pulled the fabric back over the entrance.

"It's alright," the guard whispered. "You can come out."

Marcus didn't move, his eyes darted to Kali's through the tear in the fabric, and she slowly nodded back at him. Cautiously, he edged out into view, Vana followed a few seconds later.

The guard reached into his jacket, causing Marcus to flinch, expecting a weapon to be drawn. Instead, a package was produced and tossed over to him.

"Here, you're gonna need these," said the guard quietly.

Marcus unwrapped the package and unfolded several wrinkled and stained Legion uniforms. The aroma of stale sweat assaulted his nostrils and he turned his face away in disgust.

"Would it have killed you to have washed them first?" whispered Marcus. He kept them at arm's length as he separated the clothing into piles.

The guard glared at him.

Perhaps it *would* have killed him to wash them.

The guard backed slowly from the truck. "Now get out of here, and for god's sake hurry up. If they see me here with you then I'm dead," he said.

"Cool it Harry," whispered Kali through the thin fabric separating the back from the cab. "Otherwise you're gonna get us all killed."

"The guard looked around nervously. "Do you know what I had to do to get put on this detail? I wasn't supposed to be on gate duty for another month. They sounded suspicious when I requested the assignment."

"What did you say to them?" asked Marcus.

"I told them I needed the money. Gambling."

"Nice cover story."

"Who said anything about it being a cover? I can tell you I don't like the odds on this one. Too much can go wrong and very little in it for me. If I were you I'd pack it in now and leave."

Heavy booted footsteps from outside approached the truck. "What's going on back there?" came a shout.

"Shit," said Harry. "Get back there and don't move. I'll wave you through."

"Wait," said Kali between gritted teeth. She remained perfectly still and stared ahead so as not to alert the second guard. "What about our ID badges?"

"I couldn't get them. You'll have to make do with the uniforms."

"Then how are we supposed to--"

"That's your problem," muttered Harry under his breath.

He jumped from the back of the truck and headed off the second guard who was creeping ever closer.

"Goddammit," huffed Kali to herself, whilst trying to maintain her composure.

"It's fine," came the voice of Harry, who had stopped the other guard in his tracks. "Just checking the cargo against the manifest. Everything is in order." He pushed a button to raise the barrier and waved the truck through. Kali started the engine and slowly crept the truck past. She shot Harry a scowl as she passed him. Harry did everything he could to avoid looking in her direction.

192

Kali drove the truck for several more minutes, before stopping in a deserted alleyway. The occasional vehicle rolled past the top of the alley, but nobody had yet paid them any attention.

She smacked the steering wheel with her hands and let out a frustrated grunt.

"It's too late to back out," she said, turning to look at the two passengers still concealed in the rear. "We'll just have to wing it."

When the coast was clear, Kali jumped from the cab and climbed into the back with the others. They all changed into the uniforms provided, throwing the military style jackets over their existing clothes.

"How are we going to get inside the complex now?" said Marcus. "If the memory we saw was accurate then almost every door is access controlled. We won't make it ten feet before we're shot. Or worse, arrested."

A Legion patrol truck drove past the top of the alley and stopped. Several soldiers jumped out. Marcus felt his heart pound in his chest as he reached for his weapon. The soldiers turned and crossed the street and stormed a building on the opposite side of the road.

Marcus relaxed, and let out a sigh of relief. Kali scanned the area for any other signs they had been spotted.

"That was a close one," grunted Marcus.

"The longer we're here, the more chance we have of being spotted," said Kali. "We should go somewhere with more people."

"Whoa? More people?" said Marcus. "I thought we were trying to stay under the radar?"

"Three guards hanging around an empty alleyway will draw suspicion, but three guards on patrol through the streets though is another matter. Just don't do anything to draw attention to yourselves." Kali zipped up her jacket. "We're just your everyday normal Legion soldiers out on patrol. But I can tell you now, without those id's we'll be outed by the first grunt we come across."

"I have an idea," said Vana. She reached into her pocket and produced the circular disk housing Jax. She held him gently in the palm of her hand and a small face appeared, floating in the air a few inches above. "Davon must have some sort of security system inside his headquarters. Most likely computer controlled. If we can get close enough, it may be possible for Jax to scan the networks for a vulnerability."

"Scanning…" said Jax, on cue. The image of the face was replaced by waveforms, dancing and changing size and shape. After a few seconds of this the waveforms faded, and his face returned. "I believe I have located a weakness in the security system, but the signal is too weak from this distance to be able to penetrate their network. We will need to be much closer to the source for me to stand any chance of success."

"How close," asked Marcus, looking over his shoulder. The Legion soldiers on the opposite side of the road were leaving the building and were milling around their vehicle.

The face of Jax was once again replaced, this time with a top-down rendering of the area they were in. Four small yellow dots, scattered around various locations near the complex were pulsating softly. A small green dot indicated their current position.

"Any of the highlighted locations should be acceptable," stated Jax.

Kali studied the tiny floating map and immediately discounted two of the four locations as being too close to Legion patrols. Of the remaining two they opted to head for the closest one. A building overlooking the complex a few hundred meters away.

Kali opened a container in the back of the truck, revealing several rifles and other weapons. The same ones carried by the Legion soldiers.

"Grab a rifle and a side-arm," said Kali pointing to the open box. "Legion soldiers are never unarmed. You'll find extra ammo at the bottom."

Marcus slung a weapon over his shoulder and shoved several clips of ammunition into his pockets. He took a pistol and a spare clip, then helped Vana, who looked wholly uncomfortable handling the weapons.

Kali sighed as she watched her struggle.

"You'll give us away if you keep acting like that," she said.

Vana gave Kali a weak smile. "I'm just not used to handling weapons that are so --primitive."

"Well I'm sorry, but this is the best we have. Just hang it from your shoulder and try not to aim it anywhere near me."

The last part of their disguise was riot helmets, which obscured most of the face when worn. Kali didn't bother but made Marcus and Vana wear one. They were after all on Davon's most wanted list.

Kali emptied a few more items from the truck into a small backpack which she threw over one shoulder.

"What have you got in there?" asked Marcus, eyeing the bag.

"Just a few things we may need. Ammo, a few grenades, a block of C4. You know the usual."

"C4?" asked Vana.

"Explosive," clarified Marcus. "Very powerful explosive."

"And perfectly safe. It only becomes dangerous when you attach the detonator."

"You think we'll need all that?"

"I'm not walking in there without some serious firepower to back us up," replied Kali.

From the last container she produced three tiny earpieces. She pushed one into her own ear and gave one each to Marcus and Vana, who did the same.

"Testing--" said Kali. "Can everyone hear me okay?"

Her voice came through loud and clear, and Marcus gave Kali a thumbs up. Vana fiddled with hers until she was comfortable with it and nodded.

"They're voice activated," said Kali. "Just speak normally and we'll all be able to hear one another."

And with that, they set off towards their target building.

****

They heard the noise of the crowd before they saw it. A group of approximately twenty men and women gathered around the entrance to a small concrete building, barely fifty meters from Davon's main complex. Signs plastered over doors and walls indicated this was a ration centre.

The crowd pushed and shoved each other as they fought to get to the head of the line. In the doorway, a Legion soldier handed out small packets wrapped in brown paper, which were quickly snatched from his grasp by a sea of greedy hands. After a few seconds the packets stopped coming, and the door was slammed shut.

Those in the rabble without a packet screamed and shouted, while others kicked at the closed door and pulled at the bars covering the windows; the glass long since broken and removed.

"Is this the place?" asked Marcus, keeping his distance from the angry mob.

Vana turned to conceal Jax while she consulted him, before giving Marcus a nod.

"Jax has made a connection. He's looking for a way in."

"How long is this going to take?"

"I have no idea," said Vana. "It depends on what level of security Davon has in place."

Marcus looked around at the imposing concrete walls towering above him. The razor wire, guards and guns. "I'm going to say: a lot of security."

The jeering from the angry crowd intensified, and the door buckled under the sustained attack.

"I didn't think things had gotten so bad up here they needed to resort to rationing," said Marcus, arching his back and peering over at the angry mob.

"They've got plenty of food," spat Kali. "It's just another way for Davon to maintain control. Do as the Legion say or starve on the streets."

The growl of an engine attracted the attention of some of the crowd, who booed and chanted as Legion re-enforcements arrived, springing from the back of a large flatbed truck. The crowd thinned, as people darted away, their confidence failing them in the face of their opposition. Only a handful of the most ardent protesters remained, who found themselves trapped between the building and the guards.

"I think we should get out of here," said Marcus. "I don't like where this is heading."

"Hey, you," shouted one of the Legion soldiers. "Don't just stand around, move these people out of here."

Marcus looked around for a few seconds before realising that the command was meant for him. He pointed to his own chest and cocked his head, and looked wide-eyed across at the soldier barking orders.

"Yes you," the soldier shouted back. "You deaf or what? I said get these people out of here now, unless you'd rather join them in the stockade?"

Marcus nodded quickly and whispered from the side of his mouth to Kali and Vana. "We should do as he says. I think he's getting suspicious."

"You'd better stay here Vana," said Kali. "Try to look busy or something."

Marcus and Kali headed for the few remaining protesters, who were no longer trying to break into the building, but instead were constructing a makeshift barricade from anything they could get their hands on. A few of them had armed themselves with bricks and planks of wood, turning them over in their hands menacingly.

The other Legion soldiers kept their distance, forming a perimeter around the building, but not advancing.

"What are they playing at?" Marcus said under his breath to Kali as they approached the crowd.

"Probably leaving the dirty work to us," she replied.

Marcus stopped, his eyes scanned the people in front of him. They looked desperate, their clothes muddied and torn. They jostled for position, their eyes wide in anticipation of what was to come.

Marcus resisted the urge to hold his rifle, choosing instead to let it dangle by the strap to his side. He raised his hands to try and subdue some of the noise.

"Alright everyone," said Marcus loudly. "I think it's time for you all to move on. You've had your fun - you should leave while you still have the chance."

A man with a wiry black beard and unkempt hair pushed his way through to the front of the crowd.

"That sounds like a threat to me," he said wrapping a metal bar in his hands. "See you've brought your friends along." He jabbed the bar in the direction of the guards by the truck. "What's the matter? Too afraid to face us without your buddies to back you up eh? Cowards the lot of you. Selling out for a hot meal and a shower."

"Wait, they have showers?" exclaimed Marcus.

Kali jabbed him in the ribs, her eyes darted to the man in front of them. "Not the time Marcus," she hissed.

"Look guys," said Marcus addressing the crowd. "You need to get out of here now. You're not doing yourselves any favours by staying here. See those guys over there?" He tipped his head towards the soldiers. "They're getting pretty impatient. I can't predict what will happen if you don't all leave *now*."

"We're not going anywhere 'til we get our rations. They've worked us to the bone shifting materials around all over the place, and now they refuse to give us what we've earned."

"Guy's seriously now, get going or else we're all gonna be in trouble," Hissed Marcus.

He flinched as the metal bar swung past his face, barely missing him. The man didn't get a second chance and was sent crumpling to the ground by a swift butt to the chest from Kali's rifle. He dropped the bar and Marcus kicked it away.

Kali kept her weapon trained on the downed man, while Marcus readied his, pointing it at the crowd, who looked a bit less confident after their leader had been so swiftly dealt with. They backed away, slowly at first, before dropping whatever weapons they held and running. After seeing the crowd had dispersed the Legion soldiers climbed back into their truck to leave. Their commander hadn't moved though. He pointed at the man, gasping for breath on the ground.

"You know what we do to people who don't follow the rules," he said.

"I'll take care of it," Kali shouted back. She grabbed the man by his shirt collar and dragged him towards the roadside, along which were parked several vehicles. Marcus started to follow her, but Kali shook her head and glared at the spot he was standing on. She wanted him to stay put.

She reached the vehicles and threw the man behind them, out of sight of both Marcus and the Legion commander.

Two shots rang out and Kali returned to view, her face expressionless. The commander laughed, and shouted over, "Leave the body somewhere where it'll be found."

Kali nodded silently. The commander climbed back into the truck with the rest of his men and departed in a haze of dust.

Marcus stood motionless, his eyes wide with shock. As she drew closer to him he grabbed her by the wrists. "What the hell was that Kali?"

"I did what needed to be done - to maintain our cover."

"But--"

"Let's just get out of here," said Kali and beckoned over Vana, who approached cautiously. "Did you get what you needed?"

"There's an old goods entrance that's no longer in use. It's still guarded, but the security is lighter. Jax can disable the locks long enough for us to get inside and scramble their systems to cover our tracks - for a while at least."

"Lead the way," said Kali.

Marcus looked back towards the line of vehicles. "What about him?"

"There's no time. Let's just get out of here."

****

They reached the entrance to the compound a short while later, which was little more than a back door. There were no guards present - instead, a camera mounted above the door kept vigil. Marcus hung back, staying out of the camera's field of vision as it panned smoothly back and forth across the entranceway.

"Time to do your thing," whispered Marcus to Vana.

There was a click through Marcus's earpiece, and he was surprised to hear the voice of Jax.

"I have integrated with your comms," said Jax. "I am establishing a connection to the base mainframe -- please standby."

A few moments later there was the soft hum of something powering down. The security camera above the door stopped moving, and there was a soft click as the electronic locks holding the door closed were released.

"I have placed the cameras on a timed loop," said Jax, through the earpieces. "It is safe to proceed."

Gingerly, the trio headed for the door and pushed it open. Inside was a dim corridor which stretched off into the interior and was thankfully deserted. Lights above them came on as they shuffled their way through, triggered by motion sensors embedded into the walls every few meters.

"Do we even know where we're going?" whispered Marcus as they slowly made their way deeper into the building. "I don't recognise this place from the memory earlier."

"Neither do I," said Vana.

"Take this corridor for another twenty-three meters and enter the room on your right," said Jax into Marcus's ear. "This will take you to the main floor, and have access to more secure areas within the facility."

"Er-- thanks," stammered Marcus. He felt strange talking to a machine. Especially one much smarter than him.

"What are the odds we'll make it out of here alive?" muttered Kali to herself, as she pressed forward, her weapon raised scanning every inch of the corridor.

"I could tell you exactly," said Jax. "But I don't think you will like the answer."

"You're right, I don't want to know."

"If it's in double digits I'd be surprised," said Marcus under his breath. Jax remained silent - and Marcus couldn't decide if it was a good or bad sign.

They reached the door that Jax had mentioned, and after confirming via his link to the security system that the coast was clear, they went through.

Marcus recognised their location at once, as images from the memory they had experienced flashed through his mind. People milled around, some wearing suits, others wearing Legion uniforms. Tall trees in large pots lined the hallways, and offices on either side bustled with people. It all looked quite corporate and not at all like life on the outside. He wondered if the people in here ever left, or if they worked, lived and slept behind the safety of these walls.

With uniforms of their own, the three blended in quite well amongst the people here. Marcus glanced around nervously, then pulled the others into a nearby alcove where they were less likely to be seen. He closed his eyes and mentally retraced the steps that he had seen Amara take, and got a sense of where they needed to go.

"What are you doing?" said Kali.

"I'm trying to remember where to go. I recognise this place from Amara's memories. It's just a bit… strange, seeing it for real."

"Well hurry up about it. Sooner or later someone's gonna wonder what us three are up to back here--"

"Don't worry about it," said Marcus. "I'm great at thinking on my feet. If someone comes, let me do the talking okay?"

"Whatever you say," muttered Kali.

Marcus turned to Vana, who was peering out from behind the leaves of a potted plant at the people passing by.

202

"I think I remember where Davon's office is, can Jax confirm it?"

Jax replied over the comms, "The security cameras on that level are controlled by a different system to which I do not have access. I can assist you in reaching that level, but after that, you will have to improvise."

"Improvise?" scoffed Kali. "This just keeps getting better and better."

There was a lull in activity in the corridor and Marcus put his hand on Vana's shoulder. "Let's go," he whispered. "Follow me."

They shuffled down the corridor, trying to avoid bumping into anyone as they made their way towards a door at the far end. When they were near the end, an office door burst open ahead of them, and several people carrying files poured out. Marcus's heart thumped, and he steadied his breathing, trying not to look out of place. The office workers in the corridor saw the group walking towards them, and to Marcus's surprise they stopped, parted themselves and looked at their feet. Marcus picked up the pace and hurried through. As they passed the office workers stepped back into the corridor and continued as if nothing had happened.

"That was strange," said Marcus.

"They seemed conditioned to fear the Legion," said Vana. "Just another way the Davon maintains control."

They reached the doorway and entered, which led them onto a stairwell. They ascended three flights of steps, before coming to a door that Marcus recognised.

"This is it," he said. "The room we're looking for is on this floor."

Marcus pulled at the door, which didn't budge.

"It's locked," he said. "I don't remember it being locked."

"Must be a new security measure," said Vana pointing to a card reader next to the push plate on the door.

203

"Jax, is there anything you can do to get us through this door?"

"Beginning decryption, please stand-by," said Jax.

"What are you doing here?" boomed a voice from behind them. Marcus wheeled around, to be confronted by a large legion soldier. Buzz cut hair and muscles rippling through his fatigues.

"Do you have authorization to be here?" he continued. "Show me your ID badges." He tugged at his own, which hung around his neck by a thin cord. The name 'Smith' was emblazoned on it.

Marcus raised his hands. "Hey there, I think we're a little bit lost. We-- um, were looking for the… break room. Don't suppose you could point us in the right direction?"

"ID now!" repeated Smith. His right hand came to rest on his sidearm.

Marcus looked at the man-mountain, standing at least a foot taller than him and twice as wide.

"Ah crap," said Marcus.

Smith went to draw his weapon and in the cramped stairwell the only option for Marcus was to throw himself at him. The gun clattered to the ground as Marcus charged the man, but he was quickly thrown off by the man's superior strength, and he crashed into the wall. Vana grabbed Smith's legs, and wrapped her arms around them and held on with all her strength. Meanwhile Kali kicked and punched at Smith, who swatted away her attacks with ease.

Marcus regained some composure and saw the guards gun on the floor. He crawled over, dodging swipes from Smith, and the flurry of attacks from Kali and scooped up the gun. He stood against the wall and levelled the gun at Smith.

"Hold it right there," he yelled, pushing the gun forward.

Smith wasn't fazed and instead dove at Marcus. Instinctively he pulled the trigger. Nothing happened. The weapon had jammed. Marcus sidestepped the man's lunge, flipped the gun over in his hand and swung the butt at the man's ample forehead. It connected with a bone juddering crack and Smith collapsed to the floor unconscious.

"Great work Marcus," mocked Kali. "Truly spectacular. I'm good at thinking on my feet, he says. 'Let me do the talking'. You missed your calling in life. You should have been an actor or something."

"Yeah, yeah. Hilarious," replied Marcus. "So now what? Any suggestions?"

"If I may," said Jax. "I suggest you try the guard's ID badge with that card reader. He may have access."

"Good thinking," said Marcus, snatching the badge. "But what about him? We can't leave him here, someone will find him."

"I'm afraid it's too late for that," said Jax. "A silent alarm has been triggered, the base is going into lockdown."

"Crap," said Marcus. He ran over to the door and swiped the badge through the card reader. After what seemed like an eternity, a light above the reader blinked green and the door was released. They all piled through and slammed it behind them.

They turned and found themselves in a foyer, stone pillars ran along its length and yet more offices lined either side of the room. At the far end was the door they were looking for; the one to Davon's office. Only one large and well-armed man, a scar crossing his temple, stood in their way, and he looked just as shocked as they were at their sudden appearance.

"Ah shit," said Kali as their eyes met. The guard reacted instantly, raising a rifle and levelling it at Kali. Marcus grabbed the barrel and managed to push it so that Kali and Vana were out of the line of fire. Several shots rang out as the implanted guard pulled the trigger. The barrel heated up and burned Marcus's hands, but he held on tight, before being pushed to the ground.

The sound of gunfire was multiplied in the enclosed space, leaving Marcus momentarily stunned. He let go of the barrel and staggered back against the wall. Kali pulled her pistol and unloaded the clip into the guard's chest. He stumbled back a few meters but somehow remained standing.

"Um, shouldn't he be dead?" winced Marcus, his hands throbbing with pain.

"Body-armour," yelled Kali.

"Then shoot him again," shouted Marcus, his ears still ringing from the gunshots. "And this time, not in the armour."

She ejected the clip from the pistol and loaded another one. She fired several more shots in the direction of the guard, who this time had chosen to take cover behind a stone pillar. Chunks of razor-sharp rock and dust exploded around him as Kali's shots kept him pinned down. Marcus and Vana were pressed against either side of the corridor, which afforded them little cover from any gunfire that may be aimed at them.

"We can't stay here," Marcus shouted over the cacophony. "The whole facility will know we're here now. We're gonna have a lot of company, very soon."

As he spoke, a door at the far end of the room opened, and out burst a group of armed guards, who dived for cover as they heard the gunshots ring out.

"Kali!" yelled Marcus. Using hand signals, he drew her attention to the new arrivals. She ducked back behind a bullet-ridden column and dropped the backpack from her shoulder. A few seconds later she fished out a flashbang grenade, pulled the pin and hurled it down the corridor.

It clattered on the tiles before coming to rest at the feet of one of the guards, who didn't have time to kick it away before it went off. The corridor erupted in a flash of light and a deafening boom. Glass in the office doors and windows on either side of the corridors shattered and people staggered around, dazed. The guards pulled back and took cover behind anything they could find.

"Now what?" Marcus yelled.

"Look, the door!" shouted Vana. She pointed excitedly at a small door about halfway between themselves and the guard. Marcus recognised it at once as being the door to Davon's office. A keypad next to the door glowed red.

Jax spoke, his voice barely audible above the gunfire. "The door appears locked, and I have no access to the system on this level to be able to hack it."

"We have to abort," yelled Kali.

"But we're so close!" replied Vana, ducking as a bullet clipped the wall above her head.

Marcus ejected another clip from his pistol and reloaded. "Whatever we're going to do, we need to do it fast," he cried. "We're running low on ammo."

"I have a suggestion," said Jax through the comms. "The floor plans for this building indicated a generator room on this level. If you can interrupt the power, the door will be vulnerable for several seconds before the back-ups engage."

"Where is it?" shouted Marcus.

"Approximately 25 meters north-west of your current position."

"Great. Don't suppose anyone has a compass do they?"

"There," pointed Vana. Marcus followed her line of sight and saw, through smashed glass and twisted metal, a doorway at the back of an office.

"I'll take care of this," said Kali. She passed the second flashbang to Marcus. "Cover me," she said, and without giving Marcus a chance to respond, ran straight for the power room, shooting into the corridor as she went.

Marcus pulled the pin on the flashbang and heaved it towards the guards, who this time saw it coming and tried to dive out of the way.

The blast sent the guards scurrying, holding their ears and rubbing their eyes from the grenades intensity. There was a smash of glass as Kali's shoulder barged through what was left of a window and slid to the door. She stood and kicked the door hard, which flew open with a crack and hung awkwardly on its one remaining hinge. Kali pulled the pin on her last grenade and tossed it into the room and ran.

A massive explosion rocked the whole floor, and fire belched out of the doorway. The door blew clean off its remaining hinge and buried itself into a nearby wall.

The lights in the room went out just as Kali came crashing back, and with no natural light reaching this floor it was pitch black. The gunfire slowed, muzzle flashes were now the only source of light. He felt someone grab his hand and yanked him up.

"Come on," yelled Kali.

As he was pulled up, he reached out and took hold of Vana's arm and pulled her along too. They ran headlong into the darkness as gunfire erupted all around them. He hit a wall, and Vana crashed into the back of him. The wind was knocked from him as he fell through a doorway.

Dim lights flickered into life and he found himself in Davon's office. Kali slammed the door shut with them all inside, and heard a click as the magnetic locks engaged.

"Stand back," said Marcus, before shooting the key card reader on the wall next to the door, which exploded in a shower of sparks and molten metal.

"Do you think that will work?" asked Kali.

"I have no idea. It just seemed like the thing to do. What now?"

Vana paced the room. "We're looking for a computer interface of some kind. Anything that looks odd or out of place," replied Vana.

The door buckled as the guards outside tried to force it open. Marcus braced it, pushing back with every ounce of strength.

"Whatever we're gonna do, we better do it fast, this door won't hold them for long," grunted Marcus under the strain.

The room was just as he remembered it. The desk was neat, pens, blank paper, and a computer which appeared to be powered off. The rest of the room was featureless.

"What about the elevator?" asked Kali. "There's only one button."

"We shouldn't push it until we have reason to go there," said Vana.

Marcus searched the desk but could find nothing out of the ordinary. He found the switch to power up the computer and pushed it. After a few seconds, a terminal appeared, asking for a password.

"I don't suppose you know how to get into this do you?" he said to Kali. "Computers were never my forte."

Vana set Jax on the table next to the computer.

"Get what you can from that Jax," she said.

"Certainly," he replied. "Establishing connection..."

A few seconds passed before Jax announced that he had gained access to the system. "There's a great deal of data here. Most of it appears irrelevant, but I have found something that may be of use."

A holographic display appeared over the desk which showed a representation of Earth, complete with debris ring. There were several clearly marked areas labelled in an alien language on the slowly rotating display, areas which Marcus recognised as being the settlements that had missing people. Including New Hope.

"What are these things here?" asked Marcus, pointing to several green dots that floated above the Earth.

"Sentry satellites," said Vana. "This explains how he was able to find me so quickly. It looks like they are armed as well and according to the logs they were the reason my ship crashed. I was shot down before I even awoke."

"This is all very interesting, but can you call the ship from here or not?" said Kali

"No. We need to use the elevator, that will take us to where we need to go."

"You'd better be right about this," snapped Kali. "We're fast running out of options. Come on, let's get moving."

"Wait," said Vana, "There's more here." Her hands were a blur as she expertly navigated the interface, information spewing past at a rate that made Marcus's head spin.

The banging on the door grew louder.

"Maybe not the time Vana," said Kali urgently.

"One moment--" The information on the hologram stopped and Vana stared at it.

"Vana..." said Kali, her voice wavering.

Vana's eyes grew wider as she read the information, and she gasped. She composed herself and turned to the others.

"Okay, let's go," she said. She swiped Jax from the table and tucked him into her jacket. The holographic display vanished.

"What did it say?" asked Marcus.

"I'll tell you later. Right now, we need to get out of here."

Kali pressed the elevator button, and the doors opened almost immediately. They all managed to squeeze in and the doors slid closed, just as the main door to the office burst open and the guards flew in.

Marcus was surprised to feel the lift head downwards, rather than up towards the roof as he had expected.

"Where's this thing taking us?" he asked.

"There's a control room at the bottom of this shaft," replied Vana as the doors slid open.

The exited the lift, guns raised as they surveyed the area in front of them. They were in a large high-ceilinged and completely unguarded room. Strips of light covered the walls, emitting a soft yellow glow. They looked familiar, and Marcus remembered how the lights in Vana's ship had appeared much the same.

Metal pillars reaching to the ceiling were spaced along the length of the room, and at the centre stood a control desk. A section of the floor ahead of them was different; raised slightly and a dark metallic black - large enough for several people to stand on.

Marcus removed his backpack and jammed it between the elevator doors so they couldn't close, and made his way into the room.

"What the hell is this place?" asked Kali, as she lowered her rifle and slung it over her shoulder.

"This is how Davon has been taking your people," said Vana. "This machine can transport you from one place to another."

"But I thought this Sentinel thing was massive?" said Marcus.

"This isn't the Sentinel, and it can't transport anything more than a few hundred kilometres. He must have built this when he first arrived."

"So, he's been using this thing to kidnap people from settlements? But why?"

"We don't have time for this," interrupted Kali. "Let's do what we came to do and get out of here."

Vana ran to the console in the middle of the room and pulled Jax from her jacket. She placed him on the console, where he sprung to life, the wavy blue projection of his face popping into existence.

"Jax, help me made the connection," said Vana, tapping away at the console. They worked for several minutes before Vana clapped her hands together in excitement. "Were in," she said, a wide smile on her face. "This machine has a direct link to Davon's ship. We don't even need to go there, Jax can download the data we need directly from here."

"That all sounds great, but can we leave now?" asked Marcus. "Can we use this device to get out of here?"

"Easily," said Jax

"Then let's do it before—"

A large bang interrupted the conversation, and the room shook violently. Dust and chunks of plaster fell from the ceiling. Kali ran back over to the elevator and listened.

"They're in the shaft," she shouted jabbing with the barrel of her rifle. "Everyone take cover."

"Shouldn't we get out of here?" shouted Marcus as he skidded to a halt behind one of the large columns in the room.

"The machine needs a few minutes to cycle up before we can use it," replied Vana.

Kali took cover behind a column on the opposite side of the room to Marcus, while Vana ducked behind the console."

The ceiling of the lift collapsed, scattering chunks of metal and plastic across the smooth tiled floor. Several legion soldiers dropped in through the hole and charged into the room. Instead of attacking however, they formed a phalanx and held their position.

Seconds later the unmistakable figure of Davon dropped through the elevator roof and strode into the room. He stopped behind his line of guards.

"Come out," shouted Davon, "and I'll make your deaths quick."

"We'll pass thanks," shouted Marcus back from behind his column.

"There's no way out of here. You only compound your suffering by resisting me."

"You're wrong," shouted Vana. "We've locked this device onto your ship's engine core. If you make any move on us, we'll rip it from your ship and dump it at the bottom of the ocean. Then you'll be stranded here with us."

Marcus looked over at Vana, who winked at him. If this was a bluff it was a good one.

Davon shifted uneasily. "Even if that were true, it wouldn't matter. I could simply summon for re-enforcements. I wouldn't be stranded for long."

"Long enough," replied Vana quickly. "You may have allies that would come for you but how long would that take? Weeks? Months? I don't think you want to be around that long do you?"

Davon scowled and appeared to consider what they had said, before replying. "What do you want? Why did you come here?"

Marcus peeked out from behind the column. "I was just in the market for a new secret underground bunker. We were just checking out the neighbourhood. By the way, nice evil lair. Don't like the colour scheme though."

"Insolence!" shouted Davon. "How dare you defy me." He swung his arm against the wall, leaving a deep crack in its surface. Marcus was shocked at just how strong Davon was.

"Tell your men to lower your weapons," shouted Vana. "Or I'll rip the heart from your ship and bring it crashing down on your head."

Davon growled and called his men off. They lowered their weapons and took a step back.

"Good," said Vana. "We'll be leaving now. Don't try and follow us."

Vana stepped out from behind the console and beckoned for Kali and Marcus to join her on the raised dark platform in the middle of the room.

"Um-- Vana, what are we doing?"

"We're getting out of here by the fastest possible route. The transporter."

"That's funny, because for a second there I thought you said we were going to use this thing here."

"We are, now come on. Let's get out of here before Davon changes his mind about how much he'd like to stay here."

Reluctantly, Marcus stepped onto the platform with the others and turned to face Davon who was pacing back and forth a few meters ahead of them."

"Better luck next time," said Marcus in a sing-song voice.

"Now Jax!" said Vana.

A strange sensation crept over Marcus's skin. A coldness enveloped him, and his skin fizzed with an electric charge that started in his fingertips and worked its way up his arm and across his chest. A sudden flash of light dazzled him, and he was struck with a sense of vertigo. He fell, hitting the ground.

Marcus opened his eyes and looked to see sky above him. Vana and Kali struggled to get to their feet, falling over several times in the process. After a few seconds Marcus's senses returned to normal, and he was able to drag himself into a sitting position. He looked over at the others, who had managed the same.

"Well that was… different," said Marcus. "Where are we?"

All around them was scrubland. In the distance were the mountains, but they were further away than he expected.

Vana held out a hand and helped Marcus to his feet. She offered a hand to Kali, but she batted it away.

214

"Davon will be able to use the transporter to figure out where we are. So, I didn't send us back to New Hope. Doc and the bunker need to remain a secret."

Marcus licked his finger and held it to the wind. "Well by my calculations, I'd say we're bang in the middle of nowhere."

"We should get out of here," said Kali. "Before he uses that thing to come after us."

"That won't be a problem," said Jax over the comms. "Before we departed I left an invasive program in the control system of the transport device. It will be several hours before they manage to remove it. Until then, they will be unable to use it."

"Hah!" cried Marcus. "You really think of everything don't you! I bet he's pissed now. I'd love to see his face when he realises what you've done to his toy."

Kali touched her ear and spoke. "Central, do you read?"

There was silence. Kali repeated her message several more times before a weak voice replied through the comms and Marcus's own earpiece.

"We read you over."

"This is K, I need a pickup, somewhere halfway between New Hope and The Forge," she said as she studied the landscape.

"Wait, how do I know you are who you say you are?"

"Wilkes, get off your fat ass and come pick me up, or so help me when I get back to base I'll shove my boot so far up your--"

"On my way," came the reply, cutting Kali off.

"Well, all we can do now is wait for pickup," said Kali.

Vana was sat on a nearby rock, turning Jax over in her hands silently.

"Everything alright?" asked Marcus.

Vana looked at him and took a deep breath.

"You wanted to know what I saw on that holographic display in Davon's office?"

215

"Whatever it was, seems to have spooked you."

"Davon has used the Sentinel again. He's sent another asteroid towards Earth, and this time there's nothing we can do to stop it."

·

Chapter Fourteen

Marcus's head span with the revelation. He should be shocked, angry, anything - but he felt nothing. The enormity of the news overloaded his senses to the point where they were unable, or perhaps unwilling, to comprehend the situation.

He sat in silence in the back of the truck, picking the lining from his seat and twisting the threads around his fingers idly. Vana was curled in the seat opposite him, staring out at the landscape as it rattled past them. Kali was in the front, frantically trying to get a hold of someone back at the underground basecamp over the radio. Whilst Wilkes, the driver, pushed the old truck's engine to its limit over the rough terrain. A sudden jar as they hit a pothole snapped Marcus from his thoughts. He leaned forward and tapped Kali on the shoulder.

"What's the problem?" he asked, seeing her flustered expression.

"I can't get a hold of anyone from any of the nearby settlements. All I'm getting is static."

"So, what's the plan?"

Kali threw her head back against her seat and closed her eyes. "Nothing's changed. We head back to New Hope as planned and hope all this was worth it."

She shot a glance at Vana, who paid her no attention in return.

****

Several hours later they arrived in New Hope, the streets eerily silent. A chill came over Marcus. He'd never get used to seeing the place devoid of life like this. They pulled up at Doc's warehouse, jumped out and soon found themselves back in the bunker. The walls seemed less oppressive to Marcus now, and he felt some small measure of safety being back within their confines.

"How long do we have?" asked Doc, who was pacing back and forth between his desk and the wall.

"About four days," replied Vana. "Evidently that was enough time for him to wrap up any of his business here, and leave. It's so close you should be able to see it in the night sky, if you can distinguish it from all the other debris up there of course."

"Four days? Four?" cried Marcus. "What can we possibly hope to achieve in such a small amount of time?"

"Davon won't want to be here when the asteroid arrives. That's why he was so afraid of us damaging his ship. He'd have no way of escaping."

"Well that's all fine and dandy for him, but what about us?"

"Don't you see?" said Vana, waving a hand at the now completed portal constructed only a day before. "We've already started the calculations needed to get the portal working. It may take a day or so, which leaves us with three to do something about the asteroid."

"You don't sound convinced," said Kali. "Let's call that plan A. What's plan B? Is there anything we can do from here to stop it? I mean, we managed it before."

Doc stopped pacing and clapped his hands together in frustration.

"Unless Marcus here can lay his hands on some nuclear weapons, I don't think we have much chance."

"Yeah, I keep all my nuclear weapons in my other pants. Sorry about that," japed Marcus.

"It wouldn't help anyway," said Doc. "It took the world's entire arsenal to destroy the first one, and from what Vana says this one is much bigger. We wouldn't make a dent. And just look at what it left us with. Vast swathes of radioactive wasteland from all the fallout. Even if we did destroy or deflect it somehow, the result would probably be much the same."

"Not that I'm complaining, but why didn't they use a much bigger asteroid to start with?" asked Kali.

Vana slumped into a chair and stretched out her legs. "Over-confidence perhaps? It had worked for them before in the past, so why not again?"

Marcus sighed. "So, we just have to sit around waiting for our machine to be ready before we can go and take out the Sentinel?"

Vana curled her lips in a faint, apologetic smile. "Destroying it is no longer an option. We need to take control of it. It's the only thing powerful enough to deflect the asteroid."

They all sat in silence for a few moments. Marcus drummed his fingers against a nearby desk, trying to release the tension steadily growing in his chest.

"Okay, I'm bored of waiting already," he said, jumping to his feet. "I need to do something useful to take my mind off this whole crazy situation. One thing's for sure, we're going to need some help. I can see how the original plan to sneak on board and sabotage the Sentinel would have worked with a small team, but if we're planning on taking control of it, then we need more people. The three of us surely aren't going to be able to pull that off?"

Vana nodded in agreement.

"I didn't want to put any of you at risk, but now…" she paused, her head drooping, and her eyes fixed on the floor. "Now I have endangered your entire planet by coming here."

"Nonsense," said Doc, waving his hand. "After everything you have told us, it is likely he was always planning to do this. You may have sped up his timetable, but that is all. Without you, we would have never known about it, or have had a chance to stop it."

"I hadn't thought about it that way," she responded, glancing up. "I suppose you're right."

"Anyone have any idea where we can find this help?" asked Marcus, looking around the room at everyone. "As far as we know, everyone in the settlements has been taken. There may be a few people lurking out in the Badlands, but there is not enough time to round people up and convince them to join our cause."

"I may have an idea," said Kali. "We do know some people who have their own little underground bunker on the outskirts of town. Perhaps they were also spared from whatever it was that took everyone else."

"You're not seriously suggesting--"

"Who else?"

A polite cough from the corner of the room grabbed Marcus's attention. Amara sat on a tall stool, her legs swinging back and forth as she listened in on the conversation.

"Would someone around here care to fill me in on what we're talking about?" she asked.

Marcus turned to her, "A thug who goes by the name of Hudson. I spent a delightful few hours chained to one of his walls, whilst one of his knuckleheads worked me over."

Amara looked puzzled, as if she were trying to remember something just out of her grasp.

"You've met him," he offered by way of clarification. "When we first met; Hudson was the one who turned me over to Davon, and tried to bargain with him. Not that it did him any favours."

Amara clearly didn't like being reminded of the time she spent under Davon's control.

"I-- the sword..."

"Gah! Don't remind me about that thing. It still gives me the chills whenever I think about it."

She didn't reply, but looked at the ceiling as if deep in thought and gave a large sigh.

"Well, let's go see if Hudson's home shall we?" asked Marcus.

"You'd better stay here Marcus," said Kali, "I'll go. We have an understanding me and him, I'll be fine."

Marcus considered objecting for a split second, before realising it would be of no use. Once her mind was made up, it was made up and there was no changing it. Besides, there was no reason for him to think she would be in any danger from Hudson. If anything, he was in danger from her, if the past few days were anything to go by.

Kali left the bunker alone, heading for Hudson's bolt-hole. The rest made themselves busy whilst they waited. Amara retreated to her room, whilst Vana and Doc fiddled endlessly with the device. Marcus felt useless. He couldn't help Doc or Vana, not unless they wanted something heavy moving. He doubted he could do that either at the moment, as the excitement of the last few days left his body bruised and aching, and shot more than once.

Instead, he wandered around the bunker looking for something to do before finally giving up, returning to his room and laying on his bed. Doing nothing was exhausting. The only thing he could do was rest. He fell asleep almost instantly.

Marcus was awoken by the sound of voices coming from the main hall. He swung his legs over the side of his bunk and dropped to the floor. The problem with being underground was you couldn't tell whether it was night or day, and for whatever reason, this started to bother him. The next time he saw a clock he was going to bag it and get it on his wall. At least then he'd be able to keep track of the time.

The voices became more heated and emanated from the main hall. Marcus staggered from his bunk and stumbled, half asleep towards the source of all the commotion.

Hudson, full of beard and unwelcomed cheerfulness, talked loudly over people about something. He was flanked by five men, who carried an odd collection of weaponry, from shotguns to large bowie knives. They were not the sort of people you'd want to bump into in a dark alley. Kali was talking to Hudson, or rather she was being talked at.

"Oh goodie. He's arrived," muttered Marcus through gritted teeth. He'd half hoped Hudson had vanished along with the rest.

"Ah, Marcus my good friend," beamed Hudson, throwing out his arms, gesturing for a hug. "Good to meet you again."

Marcus had the overwhelming urge to grab his beard and slam his face into the nearby table. Then he'd see if Hudson enjoyed the reunion or not. Instead he tried to be civil.

"And you," said Marcus, screwing his face up. "Oh sorry, where are my manners? Kali, see if you can find a chair for our dear friend… Oh and some rope. Mustn't forget the rope."

Kali glared at him but didn't budge an inch.

"What?" Marcus protested. "I'm trying to repay the kindness he showed me."

"That's enough," said Kali. "Let's try and put the past behind us shall we?"

"That's easy for you to say. You didn't have to go through what I did. Which reminds me, whatever happened to Clifton?"

Hudson's demeanour changed, he slouched and lowered his tone.

"He vanished along with everyone else."

Marcus clapped his hands together and allowed a wide grin to cross his face.

"Oh well, that's just too bad," he said. Things were looking up already.

Hudson held out his hand and offered it forward. "You do know it was only business, don't you? It was nothing personal."

"Of course, of course," he said through his teeth. "No hard feelings." Marcus could feel Kali's eyes burning into the back of his head, so he shook Hudson's hand. A good firm handshake. Hudson didn't blink an eye as Marcus squeezed until his hand went numb.

"Glad we got that sorted out then," said Hudson after Marcus released his hand.

"Hudson and what was left of his men were barricaded in their cellar on the outskirts of town," said Kali.

"One of my men saw it happen," said Hudson. "I didn't believe him at first of course, who would? But after seeing the deserted streets and houses for myself, I couldn't deny it. I was gratified to hear from Kali that you and the girl managed to keep yourself in one piece."

At this point Marcus couldn't care less about what happened during their last encounter. It seemed a lifetime ago. Before the weight of the whole world was placed upon his shoulders. He chose not to answer Hudson directly, giving instead a barely perceptible nod - which seemed to satisfy him.

Marcus pulled Kali to one side.

"Are you sure using these guys is a good idea?" he said. "How do we know we can trust them?"

"We have no choice. If we are to stand any chance of pulling this thing off, we're going to need their help. Besides, after I told him the stakes he was more than willing to help."

"And he believed you? I mean, I've seen it all with my own eyes and even I have trouble believing in it sometimes."

"Well, there's also the fact a lot of these folks have family and friends in New Hope that are now missing. I told them we would be looking for them, and we need help. Besides I didn't tell them everything, just enough to get his help."

The smell of smoke drifted underneath Marcus's nose. He turned to find Hudson puffing on a cigar, blowing the smoke in the direction of the pair. Marcus hadn't heard him approach. Despite his age he was surprisingly light-footed.

"Whatever it is you two are conspiring about, I hope it involves telling me what is really going on here. Because it's obvious to me you've been holding back the whole story."

Kali shrugged. "I'll let you tell him. I'm not sure I believe it all myself."

Hudson took a deep drag of his cigar, before dropping it to the ground and stepping on it.

"Don't keep me in suspense," he said, "I've held up my part of the bargain by supplying the firepower for this little adventure, so I think it's only fair you tell me the plan."

"Fine," said Marcus. "Please keep any questions until the end," he said in a mocking tone. "We have a lot to get through and not a lot of time."

Marcus proceeded to explain the situation surrounding Vana, and who she was. What Davon was doing, and who he was, and about the Legions of implants under his control. By the time

Marcus finished, Hudson and his men were all silent - and with varying expressions of disbelief painted across their faces.

"Oh hell, that's one crazy-ass story!" said one of the men. He slapped his thigh. "Just to let you know. I'm totally on board with this. Let's go kick some alien ass."

"Good man," beamed Hudson. "I knew I could count on you fellas to do the right thing."

The verbal back slapping was interrupted by a deep rumbling sound coming from the surface. The room shook, and the lights flickered. Loose plaster fell from the ceilings and clouds of dust were thrown into the air.

"What the hell was that!?" shouted Marcus amidst the confusion. One of Hudson's men came jogging along the corridor towards them.

"It's the Legion" he shouted, "they've found us. They must have followed us here."

"Shit," yelled Marcus, "how many?"

"Dozens I think, I dunno, I didn't stick around long enough to count. They blew a hole in the ceiling and were dropping through."

Kali grabbed Marcus by the shoulder and pushed him towards a door on the opposite side of the room. "We can't stay here, it's too exposed. Get into the room with that device you concocted, we can defend that area more easily."

As they all rushed out of the room, one of Hudson's men unclipped a shotgun from his backpack and thrust it at Marcus, along with a handful of shells. Marcus didn't have time to thank the man before he bolted through the door Kali was ushering people through.

Everyone followed, Amara helping the ageing Doc through the door and along a corridor before they all burst into the room - the portal standing idle in the centre. Amara hurried Doc through the thick metal door, and Marcus slammed it behind them as the first wave of Legion soldiers came into view. He bolted the door and called for people to help him build a barricade from anything in the room not screwed down. Tables, chairs, boxes, everything possible was hurriedly piled in front of the door.

It wouldn't hold the soldiers back indefinitely, but it would buy them some time. Loud cracks of automatic gunfire filled the air, along with the sharp metallic pings of bullets hitting the metal door.

"Is there any other way out of this bunker?" shouted Marcus.

Doc was being helped to a chair by Amara. Out of breath he shook his head. "Not from in here - that door is the only way out."

A flurry of activity from the machine in the centre of the room caught Marcus's attention. Vana circled the device, removing lumps of ceiling plaster from it as she went.

"Is it okay?" asked Marcus.

"Some of the connections have been knocked out. I'll have to reset them."

Vana's hands were a blur as she got to work, reconnecting severed wires with impressive speed.

"Do you have to do that now?" yelled Kali."

"We need to be ready to go as soon as the calculations are complete," she replied.

"I don't think we can hold this position for long Vana," said Marcus. "We need another plan."

A high-pitched whine filled the air, followed by a low hum of electricity building up. The hairs on the back of Marcus's neck stood on end and a faint sensation of static crawled over his skin.

"Vana-- what's going on," said Marcus, his voice wavering.

She ran over to a computer hooked up to the portal and started tapping away on the keyboard furiously. She reached into her pocket and produced Jax, who she slapped onto the front of her jacket, where he remained steadfast.

"I estimate eight minutes until I have completed the calculations required to activate the portal," said Jax.

Marcus shook his head. "I thought this was going to take days?"

"I've established a network link to several of the sentry satellites Davon has in orbit, and are using their computing power to supplement my own. I refrained from doing this until now as I didn't want to give away our presence. But since that is no longer a factor—"

"Eight minutes? If we can hold them off for that long," said Kali, levelling her weapon at the barricaded door.

"Everyone listen up," shouted Marcus. "When Vana and Jax get this thing working, we're all going to have to use it."

"You mean you want us all to go through that thing?" said Amara looking concerned.

"It's the only choice," said Marcus. "As soon as those guys get through the door they are going to kill everyone, and even if they didn't there's a massive asteroid on its way which will wipe out every living thing on the surface of the Earth. If we can't stop it, then at least we may have a chance to escape it."

"I suppose we don't have much of a choice," replied Amara. She turned to Vana, "Will it-- hurt?"

Vana stepped away from the console she was monitoring, "Not as such. It's more disorientating than anything else. You may feel lightheaded or dizzy. However, I've never travelled through a portal in this way before, so I'm not sure how much different it would be. Our ships shield us from many of the negative effects. It may not be the most pleasant of journeys, but it should be safe."

"What's to stop those guys from following us through this thing?" said Kali.

The reply came from Jax.

"When we are through to the other side, I can destabilise the portal, it will cause it to collapse at the point of origin. It will however cause a large explosion. I'm afraid this bunker, nor the warehouse above us will survive."

Doc gave a weak smile. "At least they will think we're dead," he said. "It should buy us some time."

"Er, guys…" said Kali, "It's all gone quiet out there." She pointed at the door. Marcus shushed everyone and listened.

"I don't like it," he said. "I've got a bad feeling about this."

"If it was me, I'd be rigging the doors to blow right about now."

"Everyone, take cover," Marcus yelled before diving behind a large metallic desk tipped over to form a barricade. Others followed suit, concealing themselves behind anything that offered any cover at all.

The room fell silent, save for the noise of the portal powering up. They all strained, listening for any movement or noise from the other side of the door that would betray the enemies plans, but there was nothing.

"Or… they could be doing something else? Maybe they went to lunch," whispered Kali.

"I don't think we're that lucky," Marcus replied quietly. He looked at the machine, which now crackled with electricity. "How long until that thing is ready to go?"

"I will display current progress on the monitor," said Jax. A console on the portal flickered to life and displayed various statistics. In the centre, in large white text the value of '38%' was displayed.

The barricaded door exploded inwards, blasting shards of wood and metal across the room. Smoke and dust rose into the air, debris fell from the ceilings and the whole room shifted underfoot.

The noise stunned Marcus, every sound muffled and distant. He clasped his hands to his ears. He felt something wet and pulled his hand away to look. Blood trickled from his ear. He wiped it away with his sleeve.

He crawled around, looking for the others. Two of Hudson's men staggered across the room, searching for cover. They were cut down in a hail of gunfire emanating from the corridor beyond. They fell, their bodies lay motionless in the swirling dust. Amara screamed, and crawled through the carnage to where her father was; half-buried under a file of rubble. She rushed to dig Doc out as he struggled for breath.

More gunfire, but this time from within the room. Kali and the remaining guards were shooting into the corridor through the hole where the door used to be. There was no sign of any movement out there, and no indication they were hitting anyone. Why hadn't they stormed the place?

"Hold fire!" shouted Marcus. They either couldn't hear him or chose to ignore him, as they continued their assault on the doorway. Marcus crawled towards Kali and grabbed her by the shoulder. She looked around, stunned as Marcus looked her directly in the eyes. "Hold fire," he mouthed. She stopped shooting, as did the other two. "You're wasting ammo," said Marcus, "We only need to hold out for another couple of minutes, then we're out of here."

Marcus looked over at the portal, which thankfully seemed to have been undamaged by the explosion.

'67 %'

Come on! Thought Marcus, they were so close to getting the portal working, and to have it all thrown into jeopardy at the last second was almost too much to bear.

There was a clang and the patter of a metallic object bobbling across a concrete floor. Kali saw it in the nick of time. "Grenade!" she bellowed diving to the ground, pulling Marcus down with her.

A split second later it exploded, scattering yet more debris across the room and sending fresh waves of pain thumping through Marcus's head.

There was more gunfire, this time from Hudson who propped up behind a pillar. He aimed his pistol in the direction of the doorway and fired until his weapon was depleted. He ejected the clip and searched his pockets for another one. The intruders streamed through the doorway, firing as they advanced. Everyone left who was holding a weapon now used it on the charging men. The first three were cut down quickly and the ones behind them dived for cover, returning fire as they did. Bullets pinged off the ground around Marcus, who kept his head down. He'd been shot enough this last few days. He raised his weapon above the metal table he was crouched behind and blind fired. He wasn't likely to hit anyone, he only needed to keep them busy for a minute longer.

88 %'

"Marcus," called Hudson. "Here," he beckoned him over, he looked weak. Marcus fired a few more shots and crawled over to where Hudson was taking shelter. Hudson clutched his shoulder, his face twisted with pain. He bled heavily from another wound in his torso. A bad one.

"I'm afraid I can't come with you," he coughed, spitting out a mouthful of blood onto the floor. "Looks like this is the end of the line for me."

"Just hold it together for a few more seconds," replied Marcus, trying to find something to pad his wound with. "We'll be out of here before you know it."

"I can barely move - and you'll never be able to drag me through that thing," he grunted, "Give me a clip, I'll cover you when you go for the portal."

"I can't let--" started Marcus.

"This isn't up for discussion." He coughed again and spat out a mouthful of blood.

"I'm sorry Hudson," said Marcus. He held out his hand, and Hudson shook it. He felt something in his hand and looked down. It was a small envelope. He went to open it, but a barrage of gunfire caused him to dive out of the line of fire. He tucked it into his jacket and raised his weapon above the makeshift barricade.

'100%'

All the hair on the back of Marcus's neck stood on end, and there was a strange prickling sensation in the air that made his skin crawl. He looked over at the portal. A shimmering blue ball of energy at least two meters in diameter hovered at its centre.

"Go," said Hudson pushing himself to his feet. "Go now," he roared. He staggered into the middle of the room, raised his pistol and opened fire on the Legion soldiers.

Marcus saw Vana dive for the portal, vanishing as soon as she entered it. Amara and Doc were not far behind, followed by Kali who was beating a hasty retreat while firing over her shoulder.

He charged towards the device. Kali reached it before him, stooped to grab a backpack lying on the ground next to the portal and tossed it in. She followed immediately after and vanished with a crackle.

Marcus turned just as he reached the portal. Hudson was charging at the Legion, roaring at them as he fired. His gun clicked empty, and he tossed it to the ground. With all his remaining strength he dove at the nearest man. Marcus scrambled towards the ball of energy, and just before he stumbled though he saw Hudson fall to the ground, an expression of agony etched forever on his lifeless face.

He took a deep breath and jumped.

Chapter Fifteen

Tendrils of energy danced across Marcus's vision. Veins of blue and white, snaked and forked, dividing and recombining in a turbulent mass of colour, and in ways defying comprehension. A thunderous roar came from every direction, as if every wave on every beach all crashed at once. It ebbed in time with the energy patterns, becoming fainter as the patterns diminished in complexity, and louder as they formed geometric shapes so complex they were unfathomable.

His stomach dropped, as the patterns rushed past him. He was falling, or perhaps, being pulled towards something. The patterns around him became elongated as he fell away from them. He looked down - if there was such a thing as down here - a patch of darkness rushed towards him. Instinctively he reached out to try and arrest his fall, but there was nothing here for him to grab hold to.

The darkness swallowed him, and his descent was brought to an abrupt halt. His perspective shifted, and he found himself laying on a cold metallic floor, staring into the face of Vana. She reached out a hand, and he took it, pulling himself into a sitting position. This triggered a wave of dizziness and his vision doubled. He waved Vana off, who was trying to help him up, and he slumped back to the ground.

He rolled his head over, his eyes blurry. Kali was packing a backpack. Amara sat a few meters away, helping Doc take a few sips of water from a bottle. Two other men, both of whom came with Hudson, sat nearby. One of them checking his rifle, the other sat with his head between his legs, huffing loudly. A pool of vomit lay on the ground next to him.

Marcus took a few deep breaths. "Jax needs to close that thing before they follow us."

"Hey, hey!" yelled the man cleaning his rifle. "What about Hudson?"

"He-- didn't make it," said Marcus softly. "I'm sorry."

Jax appeared as a projection in the air, Vana holding his physical form out in her hand.

"Initiating overload," he said. The portal flickered and crackled, before collapsing in on itself with a soft pop.

"Well that was-- underwhelming," said Marcus. He was expecting something a little more impressive.

"I can assure you the consequences back in New Hope were considerably more energetic. The lab will most certainly be gone, along with a large portion of the settlement.

"At least the place was deserted. Enough people have been hurt."

Hudson's last few seconds ran through Marcus's mind. He'd thrown himself at the Legion. He'd sacrificed his life to give him and everyone else a shot at getting here. Suddenly he remembered the note Hudson had passed him. He pulled it from his pocket and opened it up. It was a photograph of a young woman, alongside a little girl. Marcus recognised the picture. It was the one he previously saw sat on Hudson's desk when they had first met.

Kali appeared in his vision, looking down at him with some concern. "What's that you have there?" she asked, peering at the picture. Marcus turned it around so she could get a proper look at it.

"Hudson gave it to me, before-- well, before the end. I think he gave me this because he wanted me to look for his family. That's why he sacrificed himself, so we could find them and bring them home."

"Marcus--" Kali stopped, looked away and wiped the corner of her eye with a sleeve. "His family-- they died, nearly ten years ago. That picture was all he had left of them."

Marcus's hands trembled as he held the photograph.

"How did it happen?" he asked gently.

"When the Legion first came to New Hope they met resistance. From the underground; from us. There was a battle, and-- they were caught in the crossfire. I bear some of the responsibility for what happened to them, and ever since then I've stayed close. Helped him where I could. We didn't always see eye to eye, but he wasn't all bad. He didn't want to see what happened to him, happen to anyone else."

Whatever Marcus felt about Hudson prior to now, was washed away. In his final moments, he'd shown Marcus what sort of man he was. A courageous one. One who would give his life, so others may live. Maybe he'd forgotten that for a while, but in the end, when it mattered the most, he'd acted without hesitation. Hudson had set an example. One Marcus knew he might never be able to live up to.

He gently folded the picture back up and tucked it into his breast pocket. He smiled at Kali, who simply nodded and walked away.

For the first time, Marcus looked properly at his surroundings. They were sat in the middle of an enormous chamber, the walls and ceiling so distant he could barely make out their outline in the gloom. All around them, large columns towered into the darkness and were covered in threads of light, that ran from the floor and coiled around them in irregular patterns. They glowed a soft white colour and were the only source of light in the room.

Marcus got to his feet with a slight stumble, and walked slowly towards the nearest column, his hand outstretched. A hand appeared on his shoulder and he stopped.

"I wouldn't get too close," said Vana. "There appears to be a substantial amount of energy flowing through those conduits. I don't know what would happen if you were to touch it."

Marcus lowered his arm and backed away. "Thanks for the warning. Where are we anyway?"

Vana took a deep breath and looked around. "It looks like we're in some sort of power distribution area for the Sentinel - we should probably get out of here."

When everyone had recovered, they packed their gear and headed out. Hudson's men introduced themselves as Mendez and Vickers. Mendez was short and stocky and didn't say much except to grunt the occasional word. Vickers sported a short scruffy beard and carried a rifle. He was the more talkative of the pair.

They appeared to be roughly in the centre of the giant chamber, so they picked a random direction to head out in. As they made their way across the chamber the columns became less numerous and the light from them lessened - plunging them into near darkness. Kali had a torch, but it was barely adequate given the size of the room. By the time they reached the outer wall they were in almost complete darkness.

Kali swept the torch beam over the surface of the wall. It was deep black and completely smooth. Almost no light reflected from it, seeming instead to swallow it.

"Now what?" asked Kali.

Marcus reached out his hand and ran it along the wall. "Now we walk," he said setting off. "There has to be some way out of here. So, let's trace the perimeter and find it."

Everyone else followed his lead, and put their hands on the wall. Kali leap-frogged Marcus to go ahead, so she could use her flashlight to help ensure they didn't walk blindly into something unexpected.

They walked for over an hour before Vickers stopped and called to the others. "Hey guys, I think I've got something here." Everyone stopped. Kali and Marcus made their way over to Vickers, who still had his hand on the wall.

"What've you found?" asked Kali, shining the light on the wall.

"Here," he said. "On the wall - there's an indentation. It's pretty small, I almost missed it."

Marcus reached out and ran his hands over the area Vickers had indicated. There were three small indentations, each about the width of a finger and spaced evenly apart so he could comfortably reach all three with one hand. On the otherwise perfectly smooth surface of the wall, they stood out prominently.

Marcus dug his fingers into each of the indentations and there was a click. A square outline of light, about a meter in width appeared and then grew. Silently a section of the wall slid upwards, revealing a well-lit corridor beyond. He shielded his eyes, from the sudden brightness and stepped through.

When his eyes had adjusted to the light and he was confident the way was safe, he called through to the others to follow. They did so one by one, each squinting in the brightness until they were all through. The doorway closed behind them, leaving a section of wall like all the others, with no indication there was ever a door there at all. The corridor was more normally proportioned than the cavernous area before, at about three meters wide and about twice Marcus's height. Big enough that he didn't feel enclosed.

The walls were silvery in colour and had conduits of red and gold running along them. The light didn't seem to be coming from any particular point, instead, the whole ceiling glowed with a pale white light and didn't cast any shadows.

"Well, we're making progress. I think," said Marcus. "I guess we follow this corridor and see where it leads?"

Jax projected into the air in front of the group. "The conduits on the wall seem to lead towards a central point, approximately five-hundred meters from our current position. It could lead to a control room of some kind. I may be able to access the internal systems from there."

Marcus looked around at everyone, who, in absence of a better idea all indicated their agreement.

"Let's do it," said Marcus as he strode off along the corridor.

There was a polite cough from behind him. Marcus stopped and turned around. Vana casually pointed in the opposite direction to where he had been heading.

"The-- um, conduits lead this way," she said quietly.

"I knew that," said Marcus turning on his heels and heading back. "Just making sure you were paying attention. Well done. So, I'll now just walk this way. The correct way. Obviously."

Kali stifled a snicker and Marcus jabbed her in the ribs on his way past.

"I'd like to see you do better," he muttered under his breath at her.

They headed out, and Marcus walked in line with Vana.

"What is this place?" he asked.

"I think these are service tunnels of some kind. They probably criss-cross the whole of Sentinel. We could get almost everywhere via them. If we can get a hold of a map - otherwise navigating them may be hard."

"Yeah, everything here does kinda look the same. It'd be easy to get lost."

Despite having not met any resistance, they moved cautiously. Vickers bringing up the rear, his weapon always at the ready. It took an hour before they reached a nexus point, where many conduits from every direction merged into one area. They ran along a wall and into a narrow conduit, barely a meter wide and about the same in height. Marcus got on his hands and knees and peered into the darkness. He could see a faint pinprick of light at the far end, but with no frame of reference, he couldn't tell how long it was.

His palms became clammy and a knot formed in the pit of his stomach. He knew what Vana was going to suggest next.

"I'm sorry Marcus," she said, placing a hand on his shoulder. "This will be the quickest way. It could take hours to backtrack to find another way through."

"Okay, okay," Marcus said, taking a few deep breaths and jogging on the spot. "I can do this."

"Do you want me to go in first?" asked Vana

"Oh god no," he replied quickly, "I need to be able to see the way out. If there's someone in front of me and someone behind me it'll be far worse. No, I need to get in there and power my way through."

Marcus psyched himself up.

It's not far, I can do this. Just put your head down, try not to think about being trapped in the middle of a pipe on an alien space station, millions of miles from home.

Surprisingly these thoughts didn't make him feel any better.

Kali leant down to peer through the tunnel and whistled, "that is a long way isn't it?" she said mockingly, "but have no fear, I'll be right behind you."

"Not helping Kali," said Marcus taking long deep breaths, as if he was about to jump into a pool. "If I get stuck you're going to have to give me a gentle nudge."

"Don't worry, if you get stuck I'll jam the barrel of my gun up your--"

"I get the picture," he interrupted. "Can we get on with it before I change my mind?"

Marcus tried not to think about what he was doing.

Steeling himself, he crawled into the tunnel. As the light in his peripheral vision turned to blackness he felt a rising panic. He had barely crawled a meter and already he wanted to turn back, but he pressed on. He fixated on the light in front of him and crawled as fast as he could towards it. Behind him, as promised was Kali. He felt the knot in his stomach tighten and sweat poured from his forehead. He used his jacket sleeve to wipe most of it away, but still, some got in his eyes, causing his vision to blur. This only added to his panic.

"How you doing Marcus?" asked Kali. His panting had probably tipped her off to his current state.

There wasn't enough room for him to turn properly to speak to her, and even if there were, he wasn't going to take his eyes from the way out of here. He was afraid if he looked away that when he looked back it would be gone.

"Oh, just peachy," he said through gritted teeth, "couldn't be having more fun."

"Well, whilst I've got your attention," she lowered her voice to a whisper, "what do you think about Vana?"

"What do you mean?"

"You know, I think she's pretty cute."

"Really, I hadn't noticed," lied Marcus.

"You must have. She's so different. You know... exciting."

"If you say so."

"I do. Hey, has she said anything about me?"

"Like what?"

"You know, has she mentioned me at all? Has she asked you about me?"

"I don't think so," replied Marcus. Her interest in Vana had caught him off guard.

"Because I was talking to her earlier and there was this kinda… spark, you know."

"Between you two?" Marcus felt a slight pang of jealousy. He hadn't realised Kali felt that way about her. Certainly, he'd never had the impression Vana felt the same way. Then again, he never was quite sure what was going on inside Vana's head.

"If we manage to survive this then I may have to do something about that," she continued. "I wonder how old she is? I mean she looks about twenty-five, but I'm not sure if that means anything for an alien."

"She did tell me her species live longer than humans. Considerably longer. That's all she would tell me when I asked."

"You mean she could be much older?"

"Maybe decades."

"She looks good for her age if so," Kali continued, "I thought I would ask you what you reckoned my chances were, since you had spent a lot more time with her than any of us."

"I honestly don't know," said Marcus, as he crawled out of the other end of the tunnel and stood, stretching his legs in the wide-open space. He reached his hand out to Kali as she emerged from the tunnel behind him, and helped her up.

"That wasn't so bad, now was it?" she said.

"Wait a minute," said Marcus, "did you…"

"You're welcome," said Kali, a wide grin on her face.

"You mean to say, all that stuff you said in there about Vana wasn't true?"

241

"I guess you'll never know," she said, shooting him a wink.

"Thanks," said Marcus softly. "I needed that."

"Don't tell anyone I got soft with you or I'll break your legs," she whispered as she went to help the others out of the tunnel.

They had emerged into another corridor, which looked much like the last one. Ahead of them, a darkened doorway loomed. Kali shone her flashlight into it and walked in slowly. Mendez put a hand on Marcus's shoulder and stopped him from following her, instead he readied his rifle and moved in behind Kali. When they were a few meters into the room the lights came on. Slowly at first, but grew in intensity until everything was visible. Marcus went next, followed by Doc and Amara, who headed straight for a console sat in the centre of the room. Vickers stood by the door and guarded it, glancing up and down the corridor and shifting uneasily on his feet.

"Something wrong?" Kali asked him.

"Just a feeling. Like we're being watched. It's probably nothing."

"It's like the walls have eyes."

The room was ten meters square and covered wall to ceiling in conduits which coalesced at a large console at the centre of the room. Vana approached the console and placed Jax on top. It sprang to life, projecting images and swaths of text into the air around it.

"Looks like Jax has this place figured out already," said Kali, as she watched the projections flitter in and out of existence around the console.

"I have not yet attempted the interface," said Jax. "The console seems to be reacting to our presence and has activated itself."

"That's not at all worrying," said Marcus, taking a large step away from the machine.

"Jax, can you interface with this?" asked Vana.

"One moment," he replied - his projection rapidly displaying ever-changing information. "I have gained access to some low-level systems and information. I am confident given time I could gain more significant access."

Doc paced around the console, examining it closely. "Have you found anything at your current level of access that would be useful now?" he asked.

"There appears to be a Krall datacache here, separate to the Sentinel's system, and much easier to penetrate. Accessing now… I have located what looks to be a holding area nearby. A large amount of power has been routed to that section and drones have been allocated to secure it."

"Drones?" asked Marcus.

"Autonomous self-contained machines, used primarily for maintenance. These drones appear to have been outfitted with weaponry, as well as additional shielding."

"Oh, don't they sound delightful." Marcus shook his head and sighed.

"I calculate a high probability Davon is holding prisoners at that location."

"Can you show me where this is?" Marcus asked, waving his hand at the projection. The projection became a map seen from above. White lines on a black background traced the outlines of rooms around them. Several red dots clustered around the centre - which Marcus assumed was their current location. The map zoomed out slowly, revealing several more dots. A handful at first, then dozens. Soon the whole section was red.

"My god, how many people has he got in there?" said Kali, her mouth agape.

A line appeared on the map, tracing a route from their current location to the holding area. "I must point out this equipment does not distinguish between different life signs. I cannot tell who is in that room." said Jax.

Marcus put his hands on his waist and looked at the projection. "So, you mean that could either be a room full of the missing people from the settlements, or a room full of Krall soldiers?"

"Yes, and there's no way to tell from here."

"Well there's only one way to find out," said Kali. "We need to get into that room."

Vana grabbed Kali by the arm. "The mission comes first," she said. "We can't risk you being detected before we're in place to sabotage the Sentinel."

Kali shook her arm free. "If those are our people in there I'm not leaving them behind. We have to do something."

"Kali's right," said Amara. "We can't leave them here. I've seen what Davon does to people. We can't let them suffer. Not like I did."

"Look," said Vana. "We've only gotten this far because we haven't been detected. If Davon finds out we're here, we'll have no chance of destroying this place."

"You do what you need to do," huffed Kali. "I'm going for those people."

"I'm coming too," said Amara. Kali pulled a pistol from her belt and handed it to her, and nodded with approval.

Vana's face reddened and she searched for something to say. Marcus who had been studying the map projected by Jax turned to speak.

"Look, it seems to me like we have three things we need to take care of. First, we need to work out who is in that room and help them if we can. Second, we need to find a way to take this place out - I'm sure Vana already has a plan for that. Finally, and this one is my personal favourite; we need to find a way home. I don't know what Vana's plan is, but I'm assuming it won't take all of us to do it. So why don't we split up? I'll head with Vana to do the whole sabotage thing. Kali and Amara, you can scout the holding area to see what we're dealing with. Mendez can back you up. Doc, you stay here with Vickers and see what you can get from this console. Perhaps there's a way out of here buried somewhere in all that data. So, everyone, how does that sound?"

"Well look who put his big-boy pants on today," mocked Kali. "It beats standing around here arguing."

"It wouldn't be wise for us to split up now," said Doc. He pushed his glasses onto his forehead and rubbed his eyes. "Vana has at least some familiarity with the Sentinel, but as for the rest of us, we're groping about in the dark. We need to keep everyone together."

Marcus paced around the small room, his arms crossed. Doc was right, it was a risk. But the Sentinel was huge, to be able to explore even a small part of it would require more time than they had. They had to take the risk.

"Okay," he said coming to a standstill. "How about this. We split up, do a spot of reconnaissance, and all meet back here in three hours? Then we can decide what we're going to do, and we can do it as a group. Okay?"

There were murmurs of agreement from the group and no dissenting voices. Marcus took that as an endorsement of his plan.

"It's settled then," said Marcus. "Let's get a move on. Lead the way Vana."

Marcus started to walk towards the door, but Vana held out her arm and placed a hand on his chest to stop him. "Marcus, wait, I can take care of my side of things on my own. You should stay here and help Kali, or Doc."

"Not a chance in hell," he replied. "You're not doing this on your own. Besides, we have no idea who or what is out there. If something happens to you, we'll have no way of getting home."

245

"But--"

"No but's. Decision made. Now let's go."

Vana tried to protest, but Marcus was already halfway out of the room. Vana grabbed Jax from the console and chased after him.

Doc waved to try and get Vana's attention. "Won't I need Jax here with me to decipher this console?" he said.

Vana turned to Doc but kept moving back towards the exit. "No, he's tied into that system now, so he doesn't need to be here. Simply talk and he'll be able to hear you."

"Channel four on the radio's," shouted Kali as Vana chased after Marcus. "Check in every thirty minutes or we'll assume you've been killed in some horrific way."

"Don't even joke about it," shouted Marcus from outside the room. "Nobody do anything stupid." Vana trotted beside him. He could feel her eyes burning into the back of his head. He didn't stop but glanced across at her.

"I sense you're not happy with me coming along?"

"Things haven't exactly gone to plan so far. I can't predict what's going to happen. The only thing I do know with any certainty is it will be very dangerous."

"All the more reason for someone else to come along. I've got your back."

Her stony-faced composure cracked for a moment, and Marcus detected the faint creases of a smile forming on her face.

"I really don't know what I would have done if you hadn't been at the impact site that day. It seems like all I've done is stumble from one disaster to another, and I've dragged you, Kali, Doc-- everyone, into this mess with me."

"We were already in a mess. I doubt Davon was ever going to just up-sticks and leave. You've given us a way to fight him - a way we would never have been able to achieve on our own. And if at

246

the end of this, it isn't enough. If we fail and the Earth is wiped out, at least we can meet the end knowing we did everything we could."

"The universe could do with a few more people like you Marcus. Perhaps we wouldn't be in this mess if that were the case."

"Funny," smiled Marcus. "Because it's usually me that causes all the problems."

Chapter Sixteen

"So, where are we heading?" asked Marcus. He strode alongside Vana as they navigated the seemingly endless and identical corridors. He had given up trying to keep track of where they were, but suspected Vana knew exactly where she was heading and so followed her lead.

"There's a control room at the centre of this place housing a vital component. We're going to go break it."

"Now that's a plan I can get behind." Marcus clapped his hands together and rubbed them expectantly. "I don't understand much of what's going on around here, but I understand the concept of smashing something to bits."

"Well, it's a bit more complicated than that," said Vana. She smiled wryly.

"I got the feeling it would be, but thank you anyway for dumbing it down so I could understand."

They reached another intersection, this one split into three different directions. Vana took the leftmost path and pushed onwards. This wasn't at all what Marcus was expecting when he imagined what it would be like to be onboard an alien space station. It all looked rather ordinary to him. If it wasn't for the green and silver glyphs etched into the walls at the various intersections, he could have been fooled into thinking he was still on Earth.

The glyphs themselves piqued Marcus's curiosity though and were the only things that seemed to change as they navigated the maze of corridors. They appeared when the pair reached a junction and would fade away moments after choosing one to follow. Vana seemed to understand them, as she would occasionally pause to read them before selecting a path. Although there was no way for Marcus to be sure, the symbols did strike an uncanny resemblance to the one's Jax had projected in the past; and from the screens on Vana's crashed ship.

As they rounded the next corner, something metallic ahead of them came into view. It caught Marcus off-guard. He took a sharp intake of breath and grabbed Vana and dragged her back around the corner, his heart pumping furiously. A few moments passed while he gathered his wits and peeked out around the corner at the object in the corridor. Vana squeezed her head underneath his arm and peered around the corner with him.

"What are we doing?" she asked, looking at Marcus.

"Shhhhh! Don't you see that thing?"

"It's only a drone. Nothing to worry about, it's non-functional."

"How can you be so sure?" Marcus narrowed his eyes. "I thought I saw it move."

"It's perfectly safe," said Vana stepping out and walking out into the corridor. "Besides, if it was active, we'd already be dead."

"Good to know I suppose." He cleared his throat and strode out behind Vana.

He got his first good look at the object as they walked towards it. It was spherical in shape, and about the size of a basketball. Half of its front face was covered by a large black lens, giving it the appearance of a disembodied eyeball. The back was a metallic silver and smooth, with a small square indentation. As they made their way closer it moved slightly, rolling onto its side and rocking back and forth gently.

Marcus gave out an involuntary yelp and leapt back. Vana laughed and pulled him forward by the arm.

"Come on, it's fine."

"But it moved," said Marcus pointing at it.

"It was probably just us. We disturbed it when we came down the corridor. It could have been there for years before we arrived."

Vana walked straight up to the device and picked it up. She turned it around in her hands and examined it closely.

"What are you looking for?" asked Marcus, the fear in him slowly dissipating as the device remained inert.

"It doesn't look damaged," she replied. "Perhaps it has run out of power. If we can find somewhere to charge it back up, we may be able to bring it online."

"Woah there!" Marcus raised his hands. "I thought you said these things were dangerous. Didn't you say it could kill us without a second thought? Death was definitely mentioned. Why would we want to power it back up?"

Vana reached into her jacket and produced Jax.

"Do you think you could take control of this drone if we get it charged up?" she asked him.

A thin beam of green light projected outward from Jax and scanned over the surface of the drone.

"I am not detecting any physical damage. I should have no problem interfacing and taking control once it is charged," replied Jax.

Marcus coughed politely and raised a finger. "Again, I must ask, why do we want to fix the death ball?"

"We can use this to scout ahead of us," said Vana. "We'll be able to cover much more ground and at the same time make sure we don't run into any ambushes. Plus, it's armed with a powerful weapon, should we need to use force."

Jax projected a map of the area they were currently in. "The schematics place a drone outlet in the immediate vicinity," he said. "Just ahead of our current position." A section on the map pulsed red.

Vana studied the corridor ahead of them and pointed to a small alcove in the distance. "Let's check over there," she said.

It only took them a few moments to cover the distance to the alcove, and once there found several slots in a recessed section of the wall, which matched perfectly with the indentation in the rear of the drone. Vana held the drone out and brought it close to one of the docking stations, where it jumped from her hand and clipped into the wall with a dull thud. The sudden movement made Marcus flinch.

"Sorry," he said sheepishly. "I don't know why I'm so on edge here. There's something about this place that just… seems to get under my skin. I can't explain it."

"Don't worry about it," said Vana. "This must all be a lot to take in at once."

"I'm trying not to contemplate our situation too much. I think it's probably for the best."

A soft hum emanated from the alcove, causing the hair on the back of Marcus's neck to stand on end. He took a step back and looked at Vana.

"It's charging," she said. "I don't know how long the cycle takes. Jax, are you ready?"

"I will attempt to interface as soon as the device becomes operational," he replied.

"What do you think it was doing laying in the corridor there?" asked Marcus.

"It's logical to assume it was trying to return to the alcove to charge, but for whatever reason it didn't make it. Strange, as I would have expected some of the other drones to help return it to its charging station."

Marcus examined the alcove. He counted at least a dozen more charging slots, all of them empty.

"I assume the rest of those things are out there somewhere?" He looked around nervously. "I hope this doesn't take too long. I don't want to be around when its buddies come home."

The low hum from the charging station abruptly ended. A quiet, high-pitched whine emanated from the drone as it detached from the wall with a click, and hovered above the ground, a few centimetres from the wall.

"Establishing interface," announced Jax. "please wait."

The drone turned on its axis, it's menacing deep black 'eye' drifting over first Vana, then Marcus, who was stood slightly further back. Marcus edged away.

"Um, Vana? Shouldn't we… you know… hide or something?"

"I'm sure everything's fine," said Vana. Her voice wavered slightly. "Isn't that right Jax?"

Vana waited for Jax's reply and when after a few seconds it hadn't come, she also backed away. Her eyes were locked on the device, as if she was staring into the eyes of a wild animal, one that would attack at the first sign of weakness.

"Jax?" she asked hopefully.

The drone rose into the air until it was at about head height. The eye now fixated on Marcus and a ring of blue light appeared in its centre. The hairs on the back of Marcus's neck stood on end, as static filled the air.

"This isn't good," said Marcus. "Let's get out of here."

"I think you're right," replied Vana and turned to run. As she did so, the light in the drone's eye pulsed brightly.

252

"Ah shi..." yelled Marcus. He dove out of the way as a blue bolt of energy shot from the drone's eye, missing him by inches. Vana scrambled over to him and dragged him to his feet.

"Run!" she yelled, as a second bolt melted a hole in the floor at the spot Marcus had just vacated. They ran in the direction they had come from and rounded the corner. Vana stopped to look back at the drone. Marcus pulled at her arm and urged her to keep running, but she held up her finger and cocked her head.

"Wait... It's stopped chasing us"

"Who cares?" said Marcus breathlessly. "I'm quite happy to know it isn't following us. Now come on, we should get out of here while we have the chance."

"Just, wait a moment."

"For wha…"

"Connection established," said Jax nonchalantly. "I apologize for the delay, there was an additional layer of security that I needed to penetrate."

"Sorry for the delay?" said Marcus exasperated. "Sorry for the delay? That's something you say when your food takes a bit longer to arrive than normal. Not when an alien death ball nearly blows your friggin' head off."

"Nevertheless, I now have full control."

"I nearly had a heart attack," said Marcus, resting his hands on his knees and trying to catch his breath.

The drones eye had returned to a deep inky black, the blue light from its weapon faded from view. It floated silently ahead of them. Cautiously, Marcus straightened up and stepped back out from the corner, with Vana close behind him.

"Great, can we send it away somewhere?" he said, as he waved his arm in the direction of the corridor. "I don't like it floating around here. I don't trust it not to start shooting at us again."

Vana consulted the map provided by Jax, and between the two of them, they located an area ahead to send the drone. Silently it turned on the spot to face down the corridor and shot off in a burst of instant acceleration. The only sound came from the air being displaced as it moved. It was out of sight after a few more seconds. Marcus relaxed slightly and breathed out a long deep breath.

"Let's keep moving," said Vana, as she set off after the drone. "We're not even halfway yet."

****

"Something's been bothering me ever since we got here," said Marcus as they approached a large doorway at the end of the corridor. "How come we haven't met any real resistance yet? I know we came up against that drone, but it seems, well, a bit too easy. Which sounds ridiculous now I've said it out loud. Where are all the Krall?"

Vana stopped and turned to look at Marcus. "I was beginning to wonder the same thing. I put it down to the size of this place. Davon wouldn't be able to guard every corridor, but then why should he? Nobody knows we're here and as far as I know, nobody has ever managed to infiltrate the Sentinel before. There's no reason for him to waste manpower guarding empty corridors. When we get closer to the tower though… Well, I imagine things will become tougher."

"Tower?" Marcus looked at Vana quizzically.

"The heart of the Sentinel. A giant tower that sits at the centre of this place. That's where we are heading. It's close now."

"You seem to know a lot about this place, considering you've never been here before."

"My people can pass memories between each other. You've seen it for yourself when I showed you the golden city. I have bits of memories from someone who was here before. When this place was first discovered."

Marcus nodded. He looked at the doorway looming ahead of them.

"Shall we go?"

Vana reached to the side of the doorway and pressed her hand to a section of the wall. The doorway in front of them slid into the ground silently and they walked through.

They emerged into a large circular room, in the middle was a wide column, covered in lights, which pulsated hypnotically. At the base of the column, some fifty or so meters away was a small platform, attached to a vertical rail running to the top.

"Up there," Vana pointed. "The way into the Tower is through there."

They made their way over to the platform and stood on it. It was only a couple of meters square, and Marcus noticed a conspicuous lack of a guardrail, or indeed anything to prevent them from tumbling over the edge once it got going.

"Are you sure this thing is safe?" he asked, looking around for something, anything, to hold onto.

"Perfectly," she replied. "Are you ready?"

"Not really," he said, the colour draining from his face. "There's nothing to stop us from falling off this thing. You know me. I'm not exactly graceful. I'll probably fall off the bloody thing."

"You can't fall off," said Vana. She pointed to the platform. "It has its own gravity field surrounding it. You're perfectly safe."

"Fine, I'll just bet my life on an invisible magic wall," Marcus sighed. "Never mind, let's get it over with." Cautiously he stepped on. His hands reached out to find something to hold onto but met

255

nothing but air. Vana joined him seconds later, and stood to one side, perilously close to the edge of the platform. Too close for Marcus's liking.

Without any warning the platform started to move up, slowly at first before gaining speed. Marcus had his hands balled into fists and was squeezing them hard, his knuckles turning white.

"Shouldn't you come away from the edge?" said Marcus. He held out his hand towards her. Vana smiled and leaned back which caused Marcus to flinch, grabbing her arm so she didn't topple over the side.

"What are you doing? Are you mad?" yelled Marcus. "You nearly fell!"

Vana laughed. "I told you, there's a grav-field here. Look." She took Marcus's hand and moved it to the edge of the platform. "Now, push."

"What?"

"Just, push your hand out."

Marcus repositioned himself on the platform, crouching slightly to lower his centre of gravity and slowly extended his arm. It met resistance as if he was lifting a heavy weight. When he relaxed, his arm was naturally pushed back out.

He pulled his arm back and examined his hand, his mouth agog. He looked over at Vana, who was leaning against nothing but air, a perilous drop of several hundred meters below them. She giggled as Marcus tried to regain some composure.

"That's right. Laugh at the Neanderthal with his tiny brain."

"I don't mean to. It's just to me, this is technology; easily understandable. But to you--"

"Yeah, yeah. I get the point. If you see some fire you'll be sure to stop to remind me it's hot, right?"

"No, I don't mean it like--"

"Never mind, but do you have to lean against the air like that? It's freaking me out."

"If it makes you feel better, I will. But you needn't worry. The field will prevent most accidental falls."

"Most? You're telling me this now?"

"The field extends a meter or so past the platform and applies a gravitational force in the opposite direction to anything trying to pass through it. Essentially creating a sort of wall. You can get past this if you move fast enough. If you can overcome the force of gravity for that meter, you'll leave the field and the ambient gravity will take over. So I wouldn't recommend jumping off, or anything like that."

"You'll get no arguments from me," Marcus replied. Relief washed over him as the platform slid to a halt at the top of the column, and he could step off onto solid ground again. Ahead of them, a narrow walkway joined the column to a wall some tens of meters away. He was happy to see this walkway was equipped with railings. He trusted things he could physically see and hold over those grav-fields any day.

"Where's this thing we need to break," said Marcus looking around. "There doesn't seem to be much around here."

"In the tower. Like I said." She waved her hand towards the walkway.

"I thought this was it? This thing we're stood on fits my definition of a huge tower."

"Not even close," replied Vana. "Come on, you'll see."

Vana headed for the walkway and Marcus followed. His grip on the handrail was like iron and he resisted the urge to look down. Once over, they proceeded through a high vaulted doorway. The sight that greeted Marcus took him aback. He took a sharp intake of breath and held it instinctively

"What the...? How-- is this possible?" stammered Marcus.

Above him there was no ceiling and some distance ahead the platform stopped. No walls, only the deep black of space. A bright band of stars spread across the whole of Marcus's vision. Below them was a planet, awash with purples and blues. Thick clouds formed swirling patterns over much of the surface and Marcus thought he saw the flash of lightning coming from some of the denser patches.

Then there was the Tower. Directly ahead and floating majestically. It loomed over him, for what looked like miles above, and stretched out below just as far.

"Remember those grav fields I told you about?" said Vana, "A similar process is going on here. The gravity fields keep the air in, and our feet on the ground. It stretches quite some distance into space above us, and the same below."

"I can't believe what I am seeing," said Marcus, his eyes darting over the vista before him. "I can't believe I'm on a gigantic space station, orbiting an alien planet, billions of miles away from home. Now this is what I was expecting!"

Vana walked beside him and joined him in gazing out at the sights before them. "Many trillions of miles away from your Earth," said Vana, as she stared at the stars.

"And to think, it took us all of five seconds to get here," said Marcus, shaking his head. He couldn't even begin to wrap his mind around the enormity of what he was seeing, or the vastness of the numbers involved. In his whole life, he'd never been more than a couple of hundred kilometres from home. Now, he had travelled further than any human had ever travelled before. Except for the people who had accompanied him here.

"So that's the tower then. How do we get inside?"

Vana pointed towards something in the distance. Marcus strained his eyes and barely made out a thin line bridging the side they were on and the tower at the midpoint.

"There are four points around the perimeter leading to the tower. We're not far from one of these junctions now. If Davon was going to guard anything, it would be those, so we need to be careful."

There was a soft beep from Jax and Vana held him out in the palm of her hand.

"The drone is approaching the junction now. I will relay the video feed here."

The air above Jax became a circle of light and an image faded in from the drone's perspective. It slowly advanced on the junction, looking upon it from a great height. The junction looked like the entranceway to a tunnel, at least twenty meters wide and just as tall. At the entrance stood a carriage, attached by the top to a monorail. The junction to the tower had no sides, only large columns spaced every hundred meters or so along its entire length. Presumably all held together with more grav-fields.

Piles of crates dotted the entrance and in the area adjacent to it. Some appeared opened and empty, whilst others were untouched. Supplies, bound for the tower perhaps, thought Marcus. If there were bringing supplies in here, perhaps there was a ship nearby. If so, it could be their ride home.

Marcus pointed to a small black dot on the image. "Can we zoom in a bit on that?" he asked.

The image switched to a much tighter angle, revealing four figures stood by the entrance. They were tall and slender but did not look as if they were in any way weak. A Smooth black surface covered their torso and arms up to the elbow. Marcus couldn't tell if it was part of their body or some kind of armour. It occurred to him it could be both. Below the elbow, a silvery grey skinned arm, slightly longer than one you would find on a human, ended in a four-fingered hand. The fingers themselves long and spider-like, with sharp claws. Their heads, flat and wide like a squashed ball sat atop and was home to four eyes, two on each side of their faces. They flicked back and forth, seemingly independently, looking in multiple directions at once. They had no obvious nose, but there were small slits where it should have been - and a mouth, circular in shape and full of rows of sharp teeth. But the worst part for Marcus was how they moved, with jagged motions and twitches. Their heads snapping from one direction to another without seeming to traverse the distance between. Each one carried a weapon at the ready, the length of their forearms and as black as their body armour.

"Oh my god," gasped Marcus. "Is that what they look like?"

"Of course, this is the first time you've seen them as they truly are, isn't it?"

"Jeeze, no wonder Davon uses a chameleon device. They are ugly looking sons of bitches."

"We need to find a way of getting past them," said Vana.

"Well what about the drone?" asked Marcus. "You said it was well armed. I say we put it some good use."

"Inadvisable," replied Jax. "We would undoubtedly trigger a response. The odds of us being able to withstand an assault from the Krall forces and indeed the drones under their control is negligible."

"What about the other junctions?"

"There is no reason to suspect they would be unguarded. We could send the drone to check, but it will take some time and increase the likelihood of us being detected."

The air around them was suddenly filled with a high-pitched whine. It oscillated rapidly and hurt Marcus's ears. It was unmistakably an alarm.

"Shit!" shouted Marcus over the din. "Did we do that?"

The radio on Marcus's belt crackled into life.

260

"Marcus. Marcus, come in," came the voice of Kali. "Answer god damn it!"

He reached down and unclipped his radio and shouted into it, "Are you okay?"

"We may have accidentally, by accident, totally not on purpose given away the fact we're here."

"What happened?"

"We were jumped by one of those bloody bugs on our way to the holding area. I blew it's head off which apparently was enough to trigger the alarm."

Vana tugged at Marcus's arm and pointed at the junction. Two of the guards sprinted away, leaving only two now guarding the entrance.

"Kali, I think you're about to get more company. At least two more of those things are heading your way. Can you still get to the holding area?"

"I don't think that would be wise," interrupted Doc over the radio. "From what I can tell, that's the direction the reinforcements are coming from."

Marcus closed his eyes. The noise from the alarm made it difficult for him to think. They were scattered and vulnerable. They needed to regroup. He pressed the transmit button on the radio. "Kali, can you make it back to Doc?"

"We're already on our way back."

Marcus looked to Vana, who shook her head. He sighed and spoke into the radio.

"We're too far away to make it back. We'll push on, see if we can cause a few distractions of our own."

"Give em hell Marcus," said Kali. There was a click as she stopped transmitting, leaving only static.

"They'll be fine," said Marcus, as he noticed the concerned look on Vana's face. "I think it's time we made some noise of our own."

The alarm suddenly stopped, Marcus's ears rang from the sustained assault. Vana pulled him to one side and lowered her voice.

"We should attempt to remain undetected. It's our best chance of making it to the tower."

Marcus looked over at the two remaining guards. "There's no way we're going to get past them without a fight. If we can get the jump on them, we may stand a chance of getting across."

"What do you have in mind?" she said after a few seconds contemplation.

"The drone. We can use it to take those two guards out. They'll never know what hit them and if we're lucky we can make it to the other side before anyone realizes what's happening."

Vana shook her head. "A lot could go wrong with this plan," she said. "There could be guards at the other end, or they could stop the carriage before we even reach the other side, trapping us mid-way."

"The longer we stand around here arguing, the harder it will be. Jax, can you have the drone take care of our two friends down there?"

"I have already targeted them," he replied. "Vana, I calculate either course of action has a similar chance of success. The decision is yours."

Vana pulled out the pistol Kali had given her before they split up and turned it over in her hands.

"She gave me this and never asked if I even knew how to use it."

Marcus put his hand on hers and pushed the pistol downwards.

262

"Let's call that plan-b shall we? We'll leave the shooting to Jax. Be ready to run."

Vana smiled weakly. "I hate these things you know," she said softly. "Do it Jax."

A few seconds went by and nothing happened.

"Jax?"

"Unable to comply," said Jax eventually. "Attempting to fire on the soldiers has triggered a hidden protocol within this drone. It appears they have been configured not to fire upon the Krall. I may be able to bypass it, but it will take several hours at least."

Marcus's face dropped, and he blew out a lungful of air. "Great, there goes our biggest advantage."

Jax's image changed back into a map. It wasn't of the area they were in. Marcus recognised it as the control room where Doc and the others were holed up. Several green dots were converging on their position.

"The others are about to be overrun," stated Jax.

"Only one thing to do then," said Marcus unslinging his rifle. "Let's make some noise of our own."

He ran forward and took cover behind a pile of crates, much closer to the Krall soldiers. His charge had not gone unnoticed and the guards had started making their way towards them in slow deliberate steps. Their weapons were raised but they held their fire. Marcus wasn't waiting for them to get any closer. Using a crate to steady the rifle he shot several times at the guard on the left. Most of the shots landed square upon their target before bouncing off their armour harmlessly."

"Shit! Nothing I've got is even going to slow these guys down. I don't suppose we could still go with the sneaky option?"

Vana glared at him.

"I'll take that as a no."

Chapter Seventeen

Bolts of blue energy flew over Marcus's head. The air crackled and fizzed as they did so, melting holes in the metallic walls and floor wherever the shots landed. Vana tucked down behind the largest crate next to Marcus, who glanced over the top of the one he was hiding behind, only to duck down as another barrage of lethal shots flew over his head.

He stuck his rifle over the top of his hiding place and blind-fired at the approaching enemy. Bullets pinged as they ricocheted off the approaching Krall's armour and they were now less than fifty meters away. In moments their position would be overrun.

With no cover for them to run to, trying to leave this position would be suicide. An easy target for the Krall. Marcus reloaded and fired again. A blast of energy hit the crate above them, hitting the barrel of his rifle and melting it clean off. He cursed and tossed it to one side.

"A little help here Jax?" he said.

"I'm afraid there is very little I can do," replied Jax. "I am still working on the bypass to the drone's weapons. I have flooded their communication channels with static, so they are unable to contact their reinforcements, but I suspect they will be able to counter that quickly. There is however some good news. Their firing pattern indicates they are not trying to kill you; rather, they are keeping you contained. I suspect they want to take you alive."

"That's not good news," muttered Marcus. "We've seen what they do to people they capture. You end up working for them."

"Any other ideas Marcus?" asked Vana. She flinched as yet more shots flew past them.

"I don't suppose you have anything I can make a white flag from?"

"White flag?" She tilted her head and looked at Marcus. "What good would that do?"

"Figures," sighed Marcus. "I guess we have no choice but to surrender, maybe--"

"I have a suggestion," interrupted Jax. "I may not be able to use the drone's weapons, but I still have access to all the other functions of this drone. Including the power matrix. If I overload it in close proximity to the Krall soldiers, it may be enough to incapacitate them."

Marcus looked at Vana. "Unless you have a better suggestion?" he asked.

She shook her head.

"I guess it's boom -time then Jax," said Marcus.

In the distance above him, Marcus saw the faint outline of the drone as it flew towards the Krall soldiers, who were now almost on top of their position. Jax began a countdown.

"Overload in five seconds... four…three"

"Take cover," yelled Marcus, pressing himself against the crate and shielding his face with the crux of his arm.

The explosion tossed the two aliens into the air, depositing them several meters away. Shards of hot metal rained down on Marcus and Vana, who shielded themselves as best they could while the dust settled. When the smoke and debris had cleared they cautiously emerged from hiding. Both guards were down.

One of them was still moving, crawling towards his weapon which had been flung from his grasp and sat on the ground a few meters away. The other fared much worse and was quite definitely dead.

Marcus staggered over, reaching the weapon before the remaining guard and swiped it from the floor. He aimed it at the soldier, whose eyes flickered menacingly as he crawled still closer to Marcus.

Marcus looked at the weapon he had picked up. It was the length of a rifle but weighed almost nothing. It appeared very simple to operate, with a large and obvious trigger mechanism located on the bottom. He found he had to stretch his hands to be able to reach the trigger, the weapon having been designed to be used by the Krall and their long bony fingers.

"Stop, or I'll shoot," he yelled at the badly injured alien. It stopped, reached out with a long grey arm towards Marcus and let out a final raspy breath, before collapsing to the floor.

Marcus relaxed his grip on the weapon and stood back. He took a few deep breaths and tried to steady his nerves. His heart was trying to beat out of his chest.

Vana came over and knelt next to the dead Krall.

"Careful," warned Marcus. "Don't get too close."

"Come look at this," said Vana. Her fingers traced the outline of a scar on the Krall's head. Marcus reached up instinctively and touched his own scar.

"What the hell," he gasped. "He's implanting his own people as well? Why would he do that? Aren't they already loyal to him?"

"There's something odd going on here," said Vana.

"You must leave now," said Jax. "The Krall are sending more soldiers to this area to re-establish communications with the guards. We should cross to the tower now before they arrive."

Marcus jumped to his feet. "Sounds like a mighty fine idea to me Jax." He touched Vana's shoulder. "Come on, let's finish this." She looked at him and smiled.

They ran across the platform and into the junction, where they found a tram waiting to take them across. It hovered motionless in the air but as they approached it a door appeared, and a set of steps materialised from a hidden compartment near its base. Marcus hesitated for a second before climbing on board. Vana followed and as soon as she was onboard, Jax initiated the sequence to take them across. Inside there were no seats, only thin rails spread evenly down its length. Large windows on either side stretched from ceiling to floor and there was a distinct lack of glass. Marcus didn't bother to ask this time. Grav-fields again. He shivered. It was hard to trust in something you couldn't see.

Columns blurred past the windows as they picked up speed. The platform behind them receded quickly, while the tower ahead loomed ever larger.

"It was my people who started this war," said Vana quietly. "When we came here all those years ago and awoke the Krall."

"Surely they couldn't have known what would happen?" replied Marcus.

"You don't understand. The memories I carry contain some of what happened back then. This place was inert, deserted, but they worked out a way to reactivate the Sentinel. It caused the Krall to awaken. But they weren't hostile. Not until… we tried to take this place away from them. We tried to take the Sentinel for ourselves and paid the price for our self-appointed superiority."

Marcus leaned against one of the walls next to Vana and turned to face her. "It doesn't change why we're here," he said. "Who cares who started it, we're here to stop it. Today."

Vana reached out and put her hand on his, still resting on her shoulder. "Let's get this done, and we can worry about the rest later," he said smiling.

Vana nodded and stepped back from the window as the tram pulled into the junction at the tower. A door and steps materialised from the wall and they climbed carefully out onto the platform. Marcus went ahead, with the Krall weapon raised. He expected more Krall soldiers, but as he swept the area he found none.

When he was sure they were alone, Marcus beckoned Vana across.

"I thought you said this was the centre of the whole place?" he half-whispered.

"It is, look," she pointed to the tower looming over them and to an archway several meters tall that led inside.

"Where is everyone? Shouldn't there be guards?"

"Perhaps Kali and the others have them all distracted. Come on, let's get inside before our luck changes."

Marcus hesitated. This had all been entirely too easy. They had managed to board the Sentinel and make it all the way to the tower and only two guards had stood in their way. Even then, the guards were trying to capture them - not kill them. Something in the back of his mind nagged at him. Surely Davon was not that incompetent?

Marcus snapped from his thoughts. Vana had moved ahead and was stood in front of the entrance to the tower. He jogged to catch her and stopped underneath the archway, breathing heavily.

"I must be out of shape," he panted, as he went down on one knee.

"The air is thinner here," said Vana. "Take a few deep breaths and you should be fine."

Marcus concentrated on his breathing and started to feel a little better. As he recovered he looked at the view ahead of them. The tower was a smooth silvery grey which stretched up as far as he could see. Being this close to it, the top was hidden from view. The archway was at least ten meters high and twice as wide and led to a dark tunnel. Light at the far side streamed in.

Vana waited for Marcus to get his breath back and headed to the tunnel. She beckoned him to follow her. It came as a pleasant surprise to Marcus when the tunnel opened out into a vast chamber after only a few meters.

The tower was hollow. Marcus strained his eyes and looked upwards. Various conduits and machinery dotted the walls.

He fixed his stare on the only thing in the chamber. In the exact centre, a metal rod extended from above and stopped several meters in the air. At its end hung a silver ball which projected beams of light to pegs in the ground, which were positioned in a square shape. The whole effect was to project a giant pyramid shape, with Vana standing at the centre.

Marcus headed towards her, but she held out her hand for him to stop.

She knelt and pressed her hand against the floor. Several control panels slid out from hidden compartments in the floor and rose up before locking themselves into position with a click.

Marcus held up his hands questioningly and Vana gave him a quick nod to indicate it was okay for him to get closer. A gentle prickly sensation swept across his skin as he passed through the invisible lines outlining the pyramid.

"So how are we going to do this?" asked Marcus. He glanced at the control stations that had appeared; covered in blinking lights and incomprehensible displays beyond his understanding. He levelled his rifle at the nearest one. "Which one of these do I shoot first?" He grinned. He doubted it would be that simple.

269

Vana pushed the weapon downwards and stepped in front of him. "Shooting a few consoles here won't change anything. But with these, I can access vital parts of the Sentinel and cause some real damage."

Marcus furrowed his brow, "Aww, you said I could break things," he said playfully.

"I'm sure there'll be plenty of opportunities for that later."

Marcus waved the barrel of the weapon at the consoles around the room. "So how exactly do you plan on taking this place out then?"

Vana reached into her jacket and pulled out Jax. She held him in the palm of her hand.

"It's all down to Jax," she said.

Marcus cocked his head and shrugged his shoulders. Even now she was being evasive. After everything they had been through she was still holding out on him.

"Look, we're down to the wire here. I think it's okay for you to let me in on the plan."

Vana placed Jax down on the nearest console and looked at Marcus.

"Okay," she said. "This whole place is an amazing feat of engineering. It generates more energy than most stars and all this is kept in balance by a master controller - here at the centre. For whatever reason, the builders of this place saw fit to design Sentinel to be controlled by a single person. Or more specifically, a single mind. That's why you've heard me refer to Sentinel as if it was a person, because in some ways it is."

"Wait, what?" said Marcus looking around. "You mean this place is alive?" He shuddered, it was as if he was sneaking around uninvited inside someone's home.

"In a manner of speaking yes," continued Vana. "The plan is to replace the incumbent mind with Jax's. In this way, we hope to fool the system into accepting an artificial intelligence instead of the real thing. With Jax in control it would be a simple matter for him to upset the delicate balance keeping Sentinel running."

Marcus ran his fingers through his hair and exhaled deeply.

"But, won't that … kill, the mind that's already in there?"

"Unfortunately, yes… but believe me when I tell you it is the most merciful thing we can do."

Marcus hesitated. Killing Krall that were shooting at them was one thing. It was self-defence. But to take a life in this way? Was Sentinel even alive by his definition? It was one thing to blow up a hulk of machinery, quite another when realising it was essentially someone's body.

"Whose mind is controlling it now?" asked Marcus. "One of the Krall I suspect?"

Vana shook her head. "No, it's the mind of a J'Darra. A scientist, called Trelevo. He was part of the original team that came here all those years ago. When the others left…. They couldn't take him with them. He was abandoned."

"But why? Why would the Krall not put one of their own people inside this thing?"

"They are not biologically compatible with Sentinel. Basically, they can't. Perhaps it's a way of keeping the Krall subservient. But we don't know for sure.

"So, if the mind running this place is one of yours, why did it… did he, allow Sentinel to be used to attack other races, including your own people?"

"We don't know a great deal about what happened, but it's generally assumed they somehow *broke* him. They forced him into taking those actions. We don't know how."

One life. One life to save all those countless others. He supposed the choice was obvious, but it didn't lift the heaviness in his chest. He tried to push the thoughts aside.

271

"Tell me what to do," he said flatly.

"Guard the door. I need to make some adjustments to interface Jax to the system, it's going to take a little while."

Marcus nodded and walked back to the entrance of the tower. He stood for a moment, looking out past the junction and out onto the circular body of the Sentinel beyond. In the distance, black specks darted back and forth. Drones, he assumed. Nothing much was happening, so he sunk to the ground, standing the rifle between his legs and resting his head back against the barrel. The radio still clipped to his belt caught his eye. He hadn't heard from the others in quite some time and he cursed at himself for not trying to contact them sooner. He removed the radio and spoke into it.

"Kali, you there?" He waited a few seconds, hearing only static before repeating his call. "Doc, Amara? Anyone?"

Still no answer. The rational part of his brain assured him there were a million reasons why they didn't answer. Perhaps they were out of range, or they had damaged or lost their radio. He tried to ignore the louder, more persistent voice in his head that argued they were probably all dead.

After two more failed attempts at contacting the others, he returned the radio to his belt. What was he even doing here? Vana hadn't even told him how they were planning to escape. He closed his eyes and longed to go home. He'd never felt homesick before. Wherever he had gone, he'd always known how to get back. Not this time though. His fate was completely in the hands of Vana. She was his only way home.

He looked out into the stars above him, the air held in place by the grav-fields surrounding the tower. A glint of light in the corner of his eye caught his attention and he snapped his head around to look. At first, he thought it was a star, like all the others, but this

272

one was moving. It was growing by the second. It was getting closer.

Marcus jumped and ran back towards the doorway. He turned in time to see a sleek silver craft descend through the grav-field a few hundred meters from him. Once inside the field, the low rumble of its engines filled the air which stopped abruptly as the craft landed. A door appeared and out stepped Davon. Unmistakable even from this distance and still using his camouflage technology to appear human. Several more Krall soldiers disembarked and took station around the ship, while Davon alone headed towards the tower.

Marcus ran inside, skidding to a halt a few meters away from Vana. He gasped in the thin air and pointed wildly at the doorway as he tried to regain his breath.

"Davon," he managed through laboured breaths.

"No, no, no. I haven't finished. I need more time."

"How much?" Gasped Marcus.

"An hour at least."

"An hour!? We've got maybe five minutes, and that's if he's feeling talkative."

Vana looked across at Jax, still sitting on the table. "I have an idea," she said. Her hands darted across the console in front of her and she pointed to the opposite wall. Marcus followed the line to the spot she had indicated, and a small black doorway appeared in the otherwise unblemished greys and whites of the tower.

"The maintenance hatch leads out towards another junction. We can use it to get across and make our way back to the others. We'll have to find another way to disable Sentinel. Go, make sure it's safe, I'll be right behind you."

Marcus hesitated. He didn't like the idea of leaving her behind but there wasn't time to argue. He set off as fast as he could, still struggling in the thinner air. As he passed the halfway mark he turned to make sure Vana was following him. If she wasn't he was resolved to go back and to drag her, kicking and screaming if necessary, along with him.

The silver ball hanging from the ceiling at the centre of the room now glowed with a soft blue light. The beams of light tracing the outline of the pyramid were now more intense, and the space between them was translucent and shimmered, distorting the image of Vana who was still inside, working on the consoles.

"What are you doing?" shouted Marcus. Vana didn't reply, so he started back. Every breath was harder than the last and his legs grew heavy and harder to lift. He clambered back to the pyramid and once there, found he was unable to get inside. The energy field surrounding Vana was as solid as a real wall and just as impossible to pass through.

Marcus pulled himself up and leaned against the field. It crackled underneath him but was unyielding. He pumped his fists against its surface and called to Vana again.

This time she turned to face him and shouted a reply, her voice muffled by the field. "Marcus get out of here."

"What's going on? Turn this damn barrier off and let's go before Davon gets here." Marcus glanced at the doorway, then at their escape route. He estimated it would take him at least two minutes to run the distance. In his current state, probably more. Davon would be here long before then. It was fight or flight, and flight had just been taken off of the table.

Marcus dropped to the ground and went prone. He laid the alien rifle out before him and pointed it at the doorway. His fingers twitched over the trigger and a bead of sweat ran down his cheek and dripped to the floor beside him.

"I'm sorry," shouted Vana through the barrier. "It's the only way."

Marcus twisted around and looked at Vana. She ran to the centre of the pyramid and activated another console. A new piece of equipment rose from the ground. It was bigger than the rest and flat. One end was raised slightly and at the bottom a footrest. Vana climbed onto it and lay back. This place needed a mind to run it, there wasn't time to interface Jax. She was going to take his place. Marcus hadn't asked what happens to a person's body after they uploaded themselves to Sentinel, he didn't need to. The look on Vana's face told him everything. She was saying goodbye.

Small devices from underneath the headrest snaked out and attached themselves to her head. Her eyes closed, and her body slumped back into the machine.

Marcus didn't know what to do. He couldn't get through the barrier, Vana had made sure of that. He suspected however that Davon would have no such trouble. He could run for the exit and take his chances. Or he could stay here, try and hold off Davon long enough for Vana to do what she needed to do.

If he left her now, everything they had done to get here would be for nothing. After all, where was he going to? Marcus hunkered down, lined up the rifle with the entrance to the tower and prepared for a fight.

He was distracted by the radio on his belt crackling to life. Through the heavy static Marcus could barely make out the voice of Kali. "Marcus, Vana? Are you there?"

He grabbed the radio and answered back. Seconds later Kali repeated her call, she hadn't heard him. Perhaps he was too far away, or there was interference from all the equipment around here.

"Marcus, if you can hear me, we're being overrun. We can't hold them off, we're going to have to--".

The transmission abruptly cut out. Marcus yelled into the radio, but there was no reply. He pushed it back into his pocket

275

and refocused his attention on the doorway. A dark figure stood in the middle; Davon. He marched towards the centre of the room, flanked by two guards on either side. Marcus took aim at Davon and squeezed the trigger. A bolt of energy left the barrel, missing Davon by a wide margin. He adjusted his aim, this time skimming the top of his head. Davon looked at the guards at either side and pointed at Marcus. Seconds later shots rained down on his position. Marcus returned fire, but none of his shots connected with the targets.

He rolled out of the path of several more shots, and they hit the pyramid behind him, fizzing as the barrier absorbed the energy. He dove for one of the corners, resting the rifle on the leading edge and using the barrier to protect him from most of the incoming fire.

He squeezed off several more shots before hitting one of the guard's square in the chest, lifting him off his feet and throwing him several meters back. Two more Krall soldiers arrived at the tunnel entrance and joined in the attack. The nearest one charged to one side trying to flank Marcus, who was forced to retreat further back along the pyramid.

"Well, I suppose that's that," Marcus said to himself. He pushed his hand against the pyramid barrier and looked through at Vana. "Go get em."

Marcus was about to resume his attack when the radio sprang to life again, only this time it was the voice of Jax.

"Marcus, there's a problem. I need your help. I'm going to lower the barrier protecting the interface long enough for you to get inside. But we must do it now before the Krall get any closer."

Jax didn't wait for Marcus's reply and the barrier dropped as soon as he had finished speaking. Marcus rolled across the threshold and onto the other side and immediately the field was restored. Several shots hit the barrier just inches away, causing

Marcus to jump back. The shots stopped, and he could make out the outline of Davon approaching the pyramid.

"Over here," called Jax, who was projecting himself from the console where he was sat.

Marcus struggled to his feet and stumbled over to Vana, who was connected to the bed by several snake-like cables, most of which were attached to her head. Several more plugged into her arms and torso.

"What the hell was she thinking?" he said. He stroked her hair, brushing a dark lock away from her eyes.

"There was not enough time to complete the interface with me. Vana saw this as the only alternative."

"She tricked me." He placed a hand on her cheek. Her skin was cold to the touch.

"She knew you would not leave her behind."

"You said there was a problem?"

"Vana rushed the connection, but the interface is not stable. She is not fully connected to the Sentinel and cannot complete the mission. She is dying."

"There must be something we can do?"

"There are no good options. Everything we can do carries the risk of further injuring Vana. But in her present condition, she will die anyway. You must manually disconnect her from the interface. I am unable to access those systems to do it myself."

Marcus reached for the nearest cable connected to Vana and gripped it tightly.

"What do I do? Just rip it off?"

"Essentially, yes," said Jax.

He tugged firmly at the first cable, which came away much easier than he was expecting. It fell away before rising slowly back up, trying to reconnect. Marcus batted it away, and after several attempts, it gave up and retracted back into the headrest.

277

He continued to speak with Jax as he disconnected the other cables.

"How long will the barrier protect us?" asked Marcus.

"Several more minutes. I have detected their attempts to disable the field and have been able to stall them for now, but they will be able to circumvent my blocks before long."

"Great, then what? What's the great escape plan? I hope you've got something up your sleeve. If you even have sleeves that is."

"You surrender."

"Great plan. Really great. What makes you think he won't just kill us the moment the field is down?"

"Remember Davon has been trying to capture Vana, not kill her. I do not expect he will kill her now."

"Yeah, but I don't think he holds me in the same regard."

"Whatever Davon has planned, it will undoubtedly require Vana's cooperation. If he kills you, it would make her more resistant to him. I calculate a forty-seven percent chance Davon will keep you alive, in order to coerce Vana."

"Oh, well isn't my day about to get brighter," said Marcus with a deep sigh. "I still don't see how this gets us out of here."

"It buys us time."

With a grunt, Marcus disconnected the last cable and pulled Vana from the table, laying her gently on the floor. Her breath was shallow but regular. She had the appearance of simply being asleep. Marcus spoke into her ear and shook her gently by the shoulder, but she remained unresponsive.

A shadow crept across the floor and Marcus looked to see Davon on the opposite side of the barrier. He peered in, a sneer crossed his face as he saw Vana laid out on the floor.

"What have you done?" he shouted through the barrier. "Put her back in the machine."

Chapter Eighteen

Marcus backed away from the barrier and over to the console Jax was sitting on. "What the hell is going on here," he asked. "Why would he want her connected to this thing? And no more secrets, for once I want someone to be straight with me."

Jax's projection quickly flickered between walls of text and complex diagrams before being replaced by his face, which hovered a few centimetres above the console.

"Sentinel is dying," he said finally. "The mind that controls everything here is breaking down. Soon, it will be unable to maintain the station."

"What does that mean exactly? That this place will shut down?"

"In the best case yes. In the worst case, the resulting instability would trigger a catastrophic overload that would destroy this place entirely."

Davon sneered at Marcus through the barrier. "So, he wants Vana to take its place?"

"Yes, and it is reasonable to assume that Davon has taken steps to ensure she wouldn't be able to do anything to threaten the existence of Sentinel."

"So that was his plan all along? To capture Vana and bring her here? And we just delivered her right to his doorstep." Marcus pounded the nearest console with his fist, bloodying his knuckles. He shook out the pain.

"How long does the Sentinel have?"

"At the current rate of decay, less than six months. But I am afraid we have another problem. The barrier protecting us is about to fail and there is nothing I can do to prevent it."

Marcus grabbed the rifle from the floor next to Vana and aimed it directly at Davon.

"If you come in here, you'll be the first to die," he shouted.

"I really don't think so Marcus," replied Davon smugly. He pointed a bony finger upwards. Marcus followed it to see at least a dozen drones hovering silently several meters above him. He hadn't seen them arrive.

"The drones are considerably faster than you Marcus. You won't get chance to fire a shot."

"We'll see about that," said Marcus. He stood inches away from the barrier and aimed his rifle at Davon's head. A wide smile appeared on Davon's face.

"If you insist on doing everything the hard way. So be it."

"Containment breach imminent," announced Jax. "I must take steps to protect myself." The projection of Jax vanished, leaving Marcus alone.

"Hey, what the--? Get back here! What about us?!" The small clear disk that housed Jax remained inert.

He gripped the barrel of the weapon tighter and stretched his finger to the trigger.

"Damn you Jax, you picked a fine time to leave."

His hands trembled, but he fought to maintain control, not wanting to give Davon the satisfaction of seeing his reaction.

The barrier began to thin and collapse from the edges inwards. As it did so, the drones above him had a clear shot. Marcus squeezed the trigger as the area covering Davon began to dissolve away, but it was too late. From the corner of his eye Marcus saw a bolt of energy leave the nearest drone. It hit him in the chest, knocking him off his feet and sending the rifle clattering away, out of reach. He struggled to breathe as if a weight was pushing down on his chest. His vision dimmed at the edges as the dark grip of unconsciousness tugged at him.

Davon leaned over as Marcus slipped away. His voice distant.

"Get the girl and put this one with the others."

Grey, bony hands from all around him reached out. Then, darkness.

****

Marcus gasped and jerked into a sitting position. A throbbing pain ran through his head, and his chest tight and badly bruised. All around him, indistinct blobs moved across his vision and voices filled the air.

"He's awake," came a voice.

The blurry image in front of him sharpened until Marcus recognised Kali, leaning over him. Her hand on his shoulder.

"Finally," she huffed.

Marcus tried to stand, but a bolt of pain shot through his head, and he was forced to lay back again. Helping hands reached out for him, and lowered him gently back to the floor.

"Not so fast," said Kali. "You took a real beating. I think you've cracked a couple of ribs. I've bandaged them up as best I can."

His hands traced across his chest, the hastily applied wrappings digging into his skin.

"How long have I been out?"

"A few hours at least," said Kali. "It's hard to know for sure, they took everything away from us."

"How'd I get here?"

"Long story," said Kali. "Where's Vana?"

The events immediately prior to him blacking out replayed in his mind.

"We made it to the central control room, but then-- she connected herself to the machine. It turns out the Sentinel needs a living mind of one of her people to work. I managed to get into the room and disconnect her, but Davon showed up and-- well, he shot me. But he wanted to put Vana back into the Sentinel."

"But why?" asked Kali. "That doesn't make any sense."

"I know," replied Marcus. "All Davon would say is he wanted her here. It sounded like it was his plan all along."

Kali sighed. "Well, whatever's going on, we're smack bang in the middle of it. He's keeping us all here for a reason. He could just have easily have killed us."

Marcus strained to sit up and took a good look at the room they were in. A large circular area with grey walls and ceilings. At the far edges, Krall guards walked the perimeter, and drones hovered silently above. Scattered around them people, tens, perhaps hundreds in all, huddled together in small groups.

"Help me up," said Marcus. His legs were dead weights and he stumbled, leaning on Kali for support. He studied the faces of those around him.

"Where's everyone else?"

Kali drew closer to him and spoke quietly in his ear. "The control room was attacked. Me and Mendez caused enough of a distraction to allow Doc and Amara to slip away. We were planning on following afterwards until--"

Marcus looked around, Mendez was nowhere to be seen. He read her grim expression.

"He didn't make it. Took a shot from one of those ray-guns at close range and he went down. Something hit me from behind and I blacked out. When I woke up I was here."

"These people… I know some of them, from New Hope," said Marcus.

"There are also people here from Jericho and a few other places. From what I can tell, there are several other rooms as well. God knows how many people they have locked up here."

Shouts and screams erupted from behind Marcus. He turned to see what was causing the commotion. Davon walked towards them, still disguised as a human. Marcus was beginning to suspect he preferred to look that way. Two Krall soldiers flanked him, and several drones hovered above and behind, their gaze fixed firmly on Marcus.

He stopped inches from his face. Marcus stood his ground, trying not to show any sign of weakness.

"I see you're awake," sneered Davon. "Good, it saves me the trouble of having you dragged along with me. You are going to help me with something important."

Marcus didn't know what angle Davon was playing here, but he needed to stall for time until they could work out how they were going to get out of this situation. He decided to play along for the time being.

Davon was so close he could feel his breath on his face. It physically repulsed him, but he stood firm.

"I'm listening," he replied.

Kali looked over at him, her face screwed up in disgust. "What? You can't seriously be willing to work with him? After everything he's done?"

Marcus shot her a look, which was partly intended for Davon's benefit, and as an attempt to let Kali know he was bluffing.

"I just think we have nothing to lose by hearing what he has to say."

Kali frowned. He hoped she understood what he was doing.

"Fine," she spat. "But just don't expect any help from me."

Marcus turned to Davon, who seemed to be finding the whole thing amusing.

"Your little stunt unplugging the girl from the core was ill-advised," said Davon. "You should know you almost killed her. Luckily for you, that was not the case."

Marcus swallowed hard, the look on Vana's face as she lay attached to the machine, etched into his memory.

She was alive.

Davon continued. "I know you came here to destroy this place. That the girl intended to integrate herself into the machine, replacing the current occupant. I was perfectly happy to allow that. Your artificial friend though was unexpected."

He held out his hand and unclenched his fist. Jax sat neatly in his palm.

"Jax, are you okay?" asked Marcus.

There was no reply. Davon looked down on him. "I wouldn't bother." He closed his hand tightly around Jax, and swiftly pocketed him. "The device seems to have shut itself down for now. A temporary setback. But that is not why we are here."

"It's about Vana, isn't it?" said Marcus. He took a step back and crossed his arms. "Well doesn't this make things interesting," he chuckled.

"I don't see what's so funny," said Kali, shaking her head in annoyance.

"Don't you get it?" said Marcus as he turned to face her. "Capturing Vana is not enough. He needs her co-operation. If he harms us Vana won't help him and he knows it."

"Hah!" boomed Davon. "You overestimate your importance."

284

Marcus stood back casually, his arms still crossed. "We'll see," he said confidently.

"Indeed. We will soon know who she thinks most highly about." Davon nodded to one of the Krall soldiers. "Bring them," he barked.

The soldier beckoned them forward with a flick of his weapon. Marcus stepped forward slowly, followed by Kali. Davon was marching away from them, towards a doorway guarded by yet more soldiers. The hard barrel of the Krall's weapon shoved into Marcus's lower back. It was both a command to pick up the pace, and a reminder not to try anything. Kali strode alongside him, her eyes darting between the guards and the crowds around them as they marched by.

Don't do anything stupid Kali.

He held his breath as they walked the final few meters to the doorway and let out a quiet sigh of relief when they made it into the corridor beyond. Drones buzzed around in the air above them, keeping their one beady eye locked on them at all times. Now was not the time to do anything rash. They were still useful to Davon and as long as that was the case they stood a chance of staying alive.

****

After several minutes they were ushered through a doorway leading into a room full of beds. Each one had various mechanical devices attached to it, as well as consoles and displays full of incomprehensible alien language. Two drones entered the room with them, one of them scraping the frame of the door as it entered. They stopped and held position at the doorway, guarding the only way out. The soldiers took up positions on either side of the room, their weapons lowered, but ready. Davon stood at the far end of the room, next to the only occupied bed. Marcus knew who would be in it before he got there. Vana.

He darted forwards and one of the guards reacted to stop him but was waved off by Davon. He found her laying perfectly still, her eyes closed.

"What have you done to her?" asked Marcus, shooting a look at Davon.

"Saved her life," he replied flatly. "Removing her from the interface in the tower almost killed her. Luckily for her, I've had some experience in dealing with this sort of thing."

Davon tapped on the control panel attached to the bed. There was a soft beep and Vana breathed in sharply and opened her eyes. Her arm dangled from the side of the bed as she slowly came to her senses.

Marcus shushed her. "Don't try to move," he said. "I thought I'd lost you for a while back there."

"Wha- What happened?" asked Vana. She slowly pushed herself up into a sitting position. Her eyes drifted lazily across the room, and she stiffened as her eyes locked onto Davon's. She pressed herself back against the bed and gripped the frame so tightly her knuckles turned white.

"What's going on Marcus?" she said. Her voice broken and uneven.

"I pulled you out of the machine."

"What? Why? That was our only chance to-"

"It's not like I had a choice." Marcus waved his hands in the air emphatically. "Something went wrong. You were dying. Jax dropped the barrier so I could get inside and pull you out, but by then…" Marcus looked across at Davon, then quickly back to Vana. "I didn't have a choice."

Vana swung her legs over the bed and tried to stand. She collapsed into Marcus's arms. He helped her up and wrapped her arm around his shoulder for support.

"What do you want from me Davon?"

Davon looked her directly in the eye. "I want you to go back to the tower, to interface with Sentinel and to take control of this place."

Vana cocked her head and looked quizzically at him.

"Why does it have to be Vana?" asked Kali, as she leant back against one of the empty beds. "You have plenty of people here. Why not one of your own?"

Marcus expected Davon to lash out, or to threaten her in some way, so he was surprised when Davon answered.

"My people are not compatible. We can't connect to the machine; our minds are too, *alien*. Vana's people however can. As too can you humans. With a little help of course." He tapped the side of his head and smiled at Marcus.

"You mean the implants? That's what they are for?!"

"They are a step towards that goal yes. Though the machine has so far rejected all my mentally dominated test subjects."

The situation started to crystallize in his mind. For the first time, Marcus began to understand what had been going on these last few weeks.

"They need to connect to the machine willingly," he said almost to himself. "You can't force someone to take control of the machine. They have to be willing to do it."

Davon clapped his hands together and smiled. "I didn't give you enough credit Marcus. Free will, for reasons I have come to understand over the last few years, is a requirement of the interface."

"I won't do it," said Vana sternly. "You said yourself you can't force one of us to interface. If this place is dying, let it die. Maybe it'll finally put an end to all this madness."

Davon's smile remained intact, Vana's rejection was no doubt expected on his part. He paced back and forth between Vana's bed and the next one. His hands clasped tightly behind him.

"You haven't heard what I am offering yet," he said spinning on his heels to face Vana. "I will guarantee the safety of both your people and the humans as well as--"

"I won't be party to mass-murder," interrupted Vana. "If I go back into that machine, under your influence... How many more lives would you force me to take? Millions? Billions? I won't do it. I refuse. You may as well kill us now and have done with it."

Marcus straightened up. "Whoa there, let's not do anything rash, now shall we?" said Marcus with a nervous laugh.

Davon walked over to a screen attached to the equipment next to Vana's bed and tapped it. The display changed to a video feed of a dark room, where banks of rectangular devices stretched out into the gloom. Lights atop them blinked intermittently and Krall soldiers paced between them.

Marcus helped Vana closer to the screen to see. Kali edged nearer and stood on her tiptoes for a better view.

"What is that?" asked Kali.

"They're stasis pods," said Vana weakly. "Are those..."

"Your people? Yes," said Davon. "Don't worry, they are quite unharmed. They are too valuable. If you don't cooperate however, I will be forced to continue my research on them. Where I have failed with the humans, I may succeed with the J'Darra. How many die in the process, I don't know." Davon shifted his gaze to Marcus. "Your people too would be in stasis if there were any pods left. They are all occupied with the J'Darra. And you humans are far more expendable to my research than they are."

Marcus balled his hands into a fist, his nails digging into the palms of his hands. "You sonofabitch," he spat. Vana tugged on his arm and gave him a reassuring look. He relaxed and unclenched his fists.

One question loomed heavily in his mind. The one thing he'd wanted to know since he found out about Davon and the destruction he had caused.

Why.

Marcus looked Davon straight in the eyes. "What's this all about? Really," he said. "Why wipe out all those worlds? Kill all those people? And what about us? What threat could we have possibly have been to you?"

Davon's expression became more serious. The smile vanished from his face. He looked directly at Vana.

"Do you know what this place is? What it does?" he asked Vana.

"It suppresses all faster than light travel for anyone but yourselves, to--"

Davon held up a hand and cut her off. "That is only a small part of Sentinels function. A side effect of its true purpose. I want you to tell me what this place is for. Really."

Vana stared at him blankly. "I- I don't know. All I know about this place is the few scraps of information that made it out before the end of the war."

"Your people know," said Davon snidely. "Your leaders obviously chose not to share this information with you."

Vana remained silent. She struggled to maintain a neutral expression, but cracks were beginning to appear. Marcus gripped her tighter, pulling her close.

"No matter. If you are steadfast in your decision not to help I will have to pursue other options."

He clicked his fingers at one of the guards and pointed to Kali, who stiffened at the sudden attention. Two guards approached her and took her by the shoulder.

"Get off me you creepy bastards!" she yelled. She fought back, but the two Krall soldiers were easily able to overpower her. Kali struggled to break free as she was led to a bed a few meters away and forced to lay on it. Straps appeared from either side, restraining her.

"What are you doing to her?" shouted Marcus. "Let her go!"

Davon paced over to the bed and stood over Kali. She spat at him and Davon watched as it sailed past him and hit the ground to one side.

"This will be so much easier if you stop resisting," he said calmly. More machinery was wheeled into the room by another Krall. This one was not armed, but carried a small black pouch, which he unrolled next to her. Sharp metallic objects glinted in small pockets inside the pouch. One was selected and held out in front of Kali's face.

Beads of sweat rolled from Kali's head. She struggled harder, but the restraints held her firmly in place. Marcus stepped forward but quickly stopped as a weapon was shoved in his face from the nearest soldier. He backed away, his hands raised defensively.

"What the hell are you doing to her?" demanded Marcus.

Davon turned, his hands clasped behind his back. "I have a new version of the implant I want to test. When completed, she may be able to join with the Sentinel."

"I thought you said people had to be willing? Because Kali isn't, and she'll fight you all the way," shouted Marcus, waving his arms.

"Ah, well that's where this new implant comes in. You see, previous versions have always left the personality and experience of a person intact. Buried, but intact. Deep down inside the implanted subjects subconscious they are fighting against my control. I suspect the machine here can detect that and this is why the interfaces are not successful. But this time will be different. This new chip doesn't suppress those aspects of the subject's mind, it erases them. Permanently. This does cause some damage to the higher brain functions of the individual, they could never act as one of my soldiers. But they would obey my every command and there would be no resistance, even subconsciously."

Vana let go of Marcus and stepped forward. "It won't work" shouted Vana. "Whoever built this place has technology far in advance of ours or yours. You won't be able to trick it, so just let her go."

"This can all be avoided if you submit willingly. You don't need an implant to interface with the Sentinel. Do as I say, and I will spare your friends."

Kali flailed under her restraints. "Don't do it Vana. I can take care of myself. Davon, I swear, when I get out of this thing, I'm gonna rip your throat out!"

"I think not," said Davon smugly. "Now, I should render you unconscious for this next part, but I'm curious to see what happens when I don't. I'm afraid this will hurt. A great deal."

Anger swelled in Marcus and he lunged at Davon. He was unarmed and outnumbered, but he didn't care. His fists and feet were going to do all the talking from now on. He ducked as the butt of a rifle sailed over his head and jumped at Davon.

One of the drones protecting Davon swooped down, placing itself between Marcus and its master. Its eye glowed blue as it readied to fire. Everything slowed as he stumbled the last few steps towards Davon.

What a bloody stupid thing to do, Thought Marcus, as the drone fired a shot straight towards him. He closed his eyes and braced for the impact.

·

Chapter Nineteen

The heat from the bolt scorched the skin on Marcus's face as the shot from the drone skimmed past him. The was an explosion behind him. He rolled to the floor and opened his eyes. The second drone guarding Davon lay in a pile of slag on the floor.

The drone flipped on its axis and fired twice more, hitting both of the remaining soldiers in the room and sending them crumpling to the ground. Davon roared as he jumped for cover behind a workstation. Several more shots landed where he had been standing, melting and distorting large sections of the floor from the blasts.

Marcus wasted no time. He helped Vana to her feet, took her hand and ran across the room, skidding to a halt and crashing into the still restrained Kali.

"Get me out of this bloody thing," she shouted. Marcus grunted as he pulled at the straps with all his strength. The material cut into his hands but remained intact and attached.

"Stand back," said Vana, and activated the control panel attached to the bed. The straps disengaged and retracted back into the frame. Kali jumped out and brushed herself down.

The drone hovered above them and continued to fire towards where Davon was concealed.

"Is that--?"

"Jax," replied Vana. "It has to be."

Kali darted for the door and cautiously looked out. "It's clear," she shouted. "Let's get the hell out of here."

Marcus and Vana followed her out, with the drone close behind. They stopped as they reached a junction, splitting off into two paths.

Marcus collapsed onto one knee, panting hard from the exertion. "Which way?" he managed between breaths. The drone didn't stop and forged along the rightmost path.

"I guess that way," said Kali setting off after it.

As they ran, bulkheads behind them slid into place, blocking the route back. "Where the hell is he taking us?" said Marcus breathlessly as they rounded another corner. This time, the corridor was a dead end, a large door at one end opened slowly as they approached. They ducked underneath and into the room beyond.

Weapon blasts struck the door above them, and the drone span around letting loose several shots, with at least one of them finding its target. A Krall soldier fell, his weapon rattling across the ground towards Kali. With a scream, she jumped at the weapon. Snatching it from the ground, she rolled into a crouching position and unleashed a hail of fire.

Metallic shards exploded outwards as Jax's drone was hit by a stray shot. It dropped to the ground with a clang and rolled to one side. Marcus scooped up the remains and scrambled into the room, clambering to one side to get out of the line of fire.

"Come on!" screamed Kali, and unleashed another barrage of fire at the remaining Krall. They tried to fall back, but the bulkhead behind them had closed and they were cut down where they stood. Kali got to her feet and walked over to the downed soldiers kicking each one to make sure it was dead. Then she collected their weapons and headed back to the doorway which slammed closed behind her as she entered.

"Well that was fun," she said calmly, before flopping to the ground to catch her breath.

Marcus looked at her, stunned. "Err, remind me never to piss you off."

Kali glared at him.

"I mean, again. Remind me never to piss you off *again.*"

Vana caught sight of the remains of the drone sat on the floor next to Marcus.

"Jax!" cried out Vana. She crawled across to the remains of the drone, picking through its mangled components. A few moments later she pulled a small white crystal from the chassis and tucked it into her jacket and sighed with relief.

"It's the drone's memory core," she said. "it looks intact. Jax should still be in there."

A figure loomed over Marcus and a hand jutted out to help him up. He took it and righted himself, coming face to face with Doc. Amara was on the other side of the room, helping Kali and Vana to their feet. The room itself was devoid of anything interesting, except a few empty crates stacked against one wall. It had probably once been used for storage but lay unused now.

"Am I glad to see you," said Marcus. He grabbed Doc by the arm and pulled him in for a hug, slapping his back. "But what are you doing here?"

Doc removed his glasses and cleaned them on his shirt. "You have Jax to thank for that," he said. He replaced them and pushed them along the bridge of his nose.

"We managed to slip away from the control room during the firefight. If it hadn't been for Vickers… Well, after wandering around aimlessly for a while we stumbled, quite by accident, onto a room full of these." Doc reached into his jacket and produced a small flat device, slightly bigger than the palm of his hand and a few millimetres thick.

"They are a kind of portable computer or interface device. With Jax's help we've managed to interface it with some of the less protected systems here. Doors, lighting that sort of thing. We used it to stay one step ahead of the aliens."

"Wait, wait," said Marcus holding up a hand. "How could Jax be with you? He was with me and Vana in the tower. Then he was in that drone."

"Jax can occupy multiple places at one time," said Vana walking over to join the discussion. "Then, when they are no longer needed these shards, can be reintegrated into his core program, which will bring with it all the experience and knowledge it acquired along the way."

"Well, why don't we just copy him into all the drones in this place then? That should make things a bit easier."

"It's not that simple," said Vana. "As he occupies more and more systems, the *effort* needed to maintain control over those systems rises exponentially. He's strong, but not strong enough to take complete control of all the drones, or even a fraction of them. Besides, we need to get his program out of the drone's memory and back into his real hardware."

"That'll be tough," said Marcus. "I think Davon has his real… *body*. We'll add getting that back to the list of impossible things we need to do today. Where are we anyway?" he turned on the spot and surveyed the room.

"A storage room of some description," replied Doc, looking at the interface device. We've disabled the internal monitoring of this and many other rooms, and have been sending false signals to others. We have those aliens scurrying aimlessly around this place looking for us."

Marcus pointed at the remains of Jax. "It's a good bet they know where we are now, so we better plan our next move."

Kali huffed. "What next move? This whole mission has been a disaster from the start. We need to abort."

"We can't do that," replied Doc. "Not until we deal with the asteroid heading for Earth. If we leave now, even if we had the means, where would we go?"

"Doc's right," said Marcus. "We don't have a choice. We need to do something and do it fast, otherwise we won't have a home to go back to."

"There is only one option," said Doc. "The Sentinel put the asteroid on a collision course with Earth, so we must use the Sentinel to undo that action. Someone is going to have to interface with the Sentinel. And without Jax--"

"We already tried Doc," said Marcus. "It didn't go well. We need another plan."

"There is no other plan and besides, that's not even the hard part. The main control room in the tower looks to be heavily guarded now, so we can't use that. I've been studying the schematics of this place on this device and have an alternative."

He waved the pad towards Marcus and pointed at a wireframe rendering of the Sentinel as seen from above. He swiped his finger across the screen rotating to a three-quarters view. Coloured lines appeared, branching out from the tower via the four junctions to various other parts of the station.

"See these four areas highlighted here?" He pointed to one of four small red dots spaced equally across the perimeter of the Sentinel. "These appear to be some sort of nexus. All these communication and data lines pass through them. If we can get to one of those, we may be able to jack into the system from there."

"It's a good plan," said Vana. "Come on, we should get moving, we don't have much time."

Marcus opened his mouth to speak but stopped. He waved his hands in frustration.

"Fine," he grunted. "Lead on."

The door slid open and the group headed out. Marcus grabbed Doc's arm and pulled him back, letting the others get ahead of them.

"Doc, this implant in my head - does it still work?" asked Marcus in a hushed tone. "We're going to need Vana to get everyone out of this place in one piece, but if she goes into the machine she may not come back out. I'm going to need your help."

A solemn look crossed Doc's face and he nodded slowly. "From what I know of how this process is supposed to work, then it is possible. The implants were designed to interface with Sentinel. Yours was disabled so Davon couldn't control you, but it remains otherwise intact. And there's something else." Doc lowered his voice to almost a whisper. "Jax was working on a way to interface with Sentinel remotely via the implants. You wouldn't need to be in the chair like Vana, you would just need to be in close proximity to one of these nexus points."

"You can do that?"

"Of course. Well, I mean, probably. Jax left detailed instructions on this little device here. All I need to do is run through the steps he listed, and everything should be fine."

"Should?"

"There are a couple of gaps, but I'm sure I'll figure them out."

Marcus put his hand on Doc's shoulder and looked him in the eye. "Without Vana, none of us stands a chance, and we can't ask Amara to do this, she's been through enough. That just leaves me. Besides, I'm relying on you to pull me out of that thing." Marcus smiled. "Come on, let's catch up."

****

Though not far, the journey to the secondary control room at the nearest junction had taken several hours. They had done their best to conceal their movements, which took time. Using the interface device, Doc triggered motion alarms and sensors leading away from their actual destination, whilst suppressing any signs of their movement along their current path.

As well as leaving a false trail, Doc managed to trap various groups of drones and soldiers in rooms and corridors all over the Sentinel, by closing sections off after luring them in. Even so, they were still heavily outnumbered.

The control room was tiny by comparison to everything else on the Sentinel at only a few meters wide. Conduits lined every wall meeting at a pillar in the centre of the room. Several consoles lining the walls sprang to life as they approached them. Kali and Amara took up position by the doorway, while Doc went to work on one of the consoles, referring to the interface device as he entered commands into the system.

"How's this going to work Doc?" asked Marcus.

Doc didn't look from his work. "Jax showed me how to initiate the interface, but he did warn that it hadn't been tested. There is however another catch. Once I do this, Davon will know exactly where we are. No doubt he will send everything he has at us."

"Yeah, well let him come," said Marcus. "We've kicked his ass every time we've crossed paths. I'm happy to administer another beating to him if he wants one."

"I wish I had your confidence, Marcus."

"I thought you said you had this covered?"

"I said I could *probably* do it." He smiled weakly and continued to tap away at the device.

Vana paced around the room, she wore a frown. "There's nothing here I can use to interface with the Sentinel. No interface chair or anything." She headed for the door. "We need to get to the tower."

Marcus grabbed her hand and pulled her back into the room. "Hold up. You're not going into the Sentinel, I am."

She shook herself free and glared at him. "This is for me to do, not you. I've been preparing for this for years. Besides, that doesn't change the fact there's no interface here. We would still need to go to the tower."

"I don't need an interface," said Marcus. He tapped the side of his head. "I already have one. Doc here just needs to do some black magic with the interface thing and I'll be good to go."

"Are you mad," cried Vana. "One misstep and you'll fry your brain."

"No great loss there," chuckled Kali.

"Oi, you keep your nose out of this," sniped Marcus. "Davon put this thing in my head to control this place, so it seems only right that I do so."

"It's ready," announced Doc. "Just tell me when."

Vana looked Marcus in the eyes, "There's still time to make it to--"

He put his hand to her face and wiped away a tear. "This isn't the end. Everything is going to be fine. We're all a part of this now, but without you, none of us has a chance. And hey, if this thing backfires and melts my brain, then you'll have to go to the tower anyway. We've got nothing to lose and everything to gain."

He gave the thumbs up to Doc, who paused for a moment, his finger hovered over the button. "Ten seconds to connection, better sit yourself down."

Marcus sunk to the floor and rested his head against the wall. Vana dropped to her knees and spoke quickly.

"Marcus, when you get in there, you will feel overwhelmed. You're going to have information flowing at you from everywhere. You'll experience sensations you don't understand. It will be too much for you to take in all at once, so concentrate on one goal. Have it clear in your mind, focus on it and ignore everything else. And most importantly--"

The edges of Marcus's vision dimmed. Doc and Vana faded from his consciousness and a faint trace of a voice, Vana's voice, echoed in the void.

"Come back to me."

Chapter Twenty

Darkness surrounded Marcus. He recalled Vana's words, that he would be overwhelmed with information and sensation. But there was nothing. Had something gone wrong with the connection? Would he be trapped like this forever?

At this point he became aware of his lack of corporeal form. No body - only an essence floating in an endless sea of black.

"Hello?" he shouted. Or at least, he thought he shouted. He didn't have a mouth, but he heard the words nonetheless. There was no reply, nor did he expect one. He let out an imaginary sigh.

"Well, what now?" he asked himself.

In the distance ahead of him, a rectangle of light appeared. A doorway leading from the darkness to somewhere else. Since he had nothing better to do, investigating this doorway seemed the next logical step. Before he could consider how it would be possible to get to the door without a body, he felt himself drawn closer to it. As if this environment reacted to his thoughts. Perhaps it made sense. If he was connected to the Sentinel, then the only muscle that would matter in this place would be the one between his ears.

He'd been praying it wouldn't come to that.

Memories of his trip through Amara's subconscious with Vana ran through his mind. He'd been able to control the environment around him to some degree during that experience. Could he do the same now?

He willed himself towards the light, not pausing before heading through. On the other side the light was blinding. At least it would have been if he had eyes. Out of the brightness, a shape emerged, circular with a large central tower. A bird's eye view of the Sentinel - the first time he had seen it in its entirety. It's grandeur becoming ever more apparent as the view crystallized into sharp focus.

With some practice, he found it possible to move the image around, and if he concentrated hard, could zoom into any area or room.

His thoughts switched to Vana and immediately he was stood beside her. She and Doc were crouched over a third figure.

It was him. His body at least. For a moment Marcus wondered if he was dead. Did the interface fail somehow, killing him? Was he in limbo? He studied his own form laid across the floor and was relieved to see his chest slowly rising and falling with his breath.

He watched as Vana and Doc checked his vital signs and made him comfortable. Their mouths moved, but he heard no voices. Marcus concentrated on Vana and her voice, quietly at first, became audible.

"Has there been any change?"

Doc tapped the interface pad and shook his head. "Nothing I can detect so far. If he's in there, he's not showing up."

"Come on Marcus," said Vana. She held his hand. "Give us a signal. Anything to let us know you're okay."

"I'm here!" shouted Marcus. "Right here, can't you see me? Hear me?" He tried to wave to get their attention, but with no arms it proved difficult. He looked around for anything he could use. The consoles on the wall of the room caught his attention and he focused on them. With great mental effort, the display changed from the streams of alien text to a simple black screen containing the words. "I'm here."

It was a pity nobody was looking at the readouts; they were all busy looking after Marcus's body.

"Turn around," yelled Marcus, but to no avail. Weakened from the effort, he found it harder to maintain focus on the room and he receded back into the overhead view.

He didn't fight it, choosing instead to let himself drift back. He needed to gather his strength if he was to be of any use to his friends. Before he connected himself to this device he assumed it would be obvious what he would need to do. Indeed, he knew what he had to do: Send everyone home and destroy the Sentinel once and for all. But how he was supposed to do any of that he hadn't considered.

A flicker of light from the tower caught his eye and once again he found himself drawn towards it. It was easier this time as if the more he moved about this place the more control he had. His perspective shifted to hover above the needle-like tower and saw to his surprise he was not alone. The faint outline of a figure was barely visible against the white background, a human-shaped figure holding out a hand, beckoning Marcus to take it. Instinctively he reached out and saw now he too had a faint outline. It felt good again to have a body, no matter how ethereal.

There was a flash as their hands touched and the tower below rushed towards him. Moments later he found himself standing by the interface device in the tower. He looked down at himself to see he was no longer a faint outline but was fully formed.

A door hissed open on the other side of the tower and Davon marched awkwardly towards him, leaning heavily to one side, his right leg dragging behind him. The first outward sign of injury he had ever seen him display.

So, he isn't invulnerable after all.

He stopped several meters away and held up a small device before entering several commands on it. Two drones appeared from the heights above and hovered over Davon. He looked at them and entered more commands. The drones shot away towards the exit and vanished.

Marcus broke the silence. "So, erm, Davon. Good to see you. Sorry about, the whole, you know, escape thing. No hard feelings?" He winced, expecting a backlash.

"He can't hear you," said an unfamiliar voice behind him. "Or see you for that matter. You're not actually in the room."

"Oh, thank god for that," said Marcus, relief washing over him. He spun around to see the figure from before, but this time he was no longer a shadow, but whole like himself.

"Who are you?" asked Marcus. His facial features looked familiar, slim cheekbones and bright purple eyes. "Are you... the same as Vana? J'Darra I mean?"

"Once yes, but now I am Sentinel. And you are Marcus. I know everything about you and your friends. Where you come from, why you're here."

"How could you possibly--"

"The implant in your head. The connection works both ways. I can see the inner workings of your mind. I know you better than you know yourself."

"Hey, be careful mucking around inside there - I've got the place how I like it."

Sentinel reached out towards Marcus, who stepped back, maintaining the distance between them. "You are quite lucky," said Sentinel. He stopped and made no further attempt to get closer.

"You know, I was just thinking that myself. How lucky I am to be here. Thousands of lightyears from home, hooked into an alien machine, with a xenophobic genocidal creepy insect alien trying to wipe out me, my friends and the rat-infested pile of garbage of a planet I come from. Yep, things couldn't be better."

Marcus tilted his head slightly as he waited for the figure to continue. The other just stared at him silently. Perhaps sarcasm was lost in translation. He sighed. "Fine. Why am I so lucky then?"

"Your implant: it's damaged and is only able to interface on the most basic level and at a greatly reduced rate. If not for that, your mind would be quickly overwhelmed."

The figure held out his hand and above it appeared a device, about one centimetre long with dozens of tiny tentacle-like tendrils trailing from it. From the context of the conversation, Marcus assumed it was a representation of his implant.

"The design is quite ingenious, but Davon has never found anyone who could handle the connection to Sentinel. Most people he tried to connect simply 'burned out', their primitive minds destroyed. In his arrogance, he hasn't yet realised limiting the connection would stand him a much greater chance of controlling this place."

Marcus shook his head impatiently.

"This is all very interesting, but I came here to do a job. And besides, I don't trust you. The only thing I know about you is that you near as damn it destroyed my planet a hundred years ago and now you're at it again."

Marcus glared at him angrily. "I'm gonna end this once and for all, and you won't be able to stop me." He had no idea if he could follow through with his threat, but it felt good to shout it out.

The figure didn't react to the outburst aimed at it but instead spoke calmly. "Well, I certainly see you have strength of spirit, but that alone will not guarantee victory."

"How are you even still here anyway?" asked Marcus through gritted teeth. "I thought when Vana tried to connect earlier you were… displaced. Overwritten. Gone."

The figure tensed slightly as Davon walked right through him, and was now idly inspecting the interface chair in the centre of the room. It was if he was waiting for someone. Perhaps Davon expected the others would try and reach the tower for a second time and he was waiting in ambush.

"Obviously this was not the case," replied the figure. "I used your friend Vana's connection to 'fake my own death' as you might put it. I've seen enough death and destruction, much of it by my own hand and I've had enough."

"Well, boo hoo!" said Marcus sarcastically. "It's a bit late for a change of heart now isn't it? I'd have been much more inclined to feel sorry for you if you hadn't just hurled another huge chunk of rock at my planet."

"There's still time to prevent any further loss of life on your world."

"That's why I'm here," said Marcus with frustration. "I thought you said you knew everything about me? If you really do want to help me, you can start by telling me exactly how to kill you."

Chapter twenty-one

"I will help you," said the figure. "But first there are things that you need to understand. After this point, we will set into motion a chain of events that cannot be undone. Whatever happens from now on is in the hands of you, and your people."

Sentinel waved his hand, and everything faded to blackness. Only the two ghostly figures remained. Around them, points of light sprung into existence. First one, then a handful more, and so on until pinpricks of lights flickered all around them, and Marcus could make out a pattern. A spiral shape with four arms, coalesced into view, becoming more defined as the seconds ticked by.

Before long the structure was complete, and Marcus stared at it in awe.

"This is the galaxy we inhabit. You call it the Milky Way. Here, this is where we are." A patch of stars brightened at one of the spiral arms remotest edges. "And your sun is here:" One of the stars three quarters from the centre of the galaxy pulsed more brightly, before fading into obscurity amongst the millions of other stars around it.

Marcus snapped himself out of his stunned silence. "Why are you showing me this? What has this got to do with anything?"

Around the galaxy, more lights started to pulse. Spread equally across the face of the Milky Way they formed a lattice structure, which became more apparent as lines appeared between them with each point connected to its four closest neighbours.

"The Sentinel network was not built to enable faster than light travel," said Sentinel. "It was designed to do the opposite: to inhibit FTL, so only those who were in control of this network could travel freely around the galaxy."

"Wait a minute," said Marcus. His head swam from the enormity of the imagery he saw. His human brain struggled to comprehend the size and complexity of the scene in front of him.

"Did you say, 'network'? You mean there's more of these places?" He pointed to the lines linking the points together. "Are all these dot's other Sentinels?"

The lines Vanished, leaving only faint pinpricks of light where each line had intersected with the others.

"You are correct. Each of the points you have just seen is another Sentinel, just like this one and each containing the consciousness of a compatible species. Built to suppress the ability of others to develop independent faster than light capability."

The scientific and engineering knowledge needed to build just one Sentinel was beyond the comprehension of Marcus. He couldn't even begin to grasp the capabilities of a people who were able to build dozens of them.

"You've told me why the Sentinels were built, but not by who."

"A race so ancient even their name has been lost in the midsts of time. Almost nothing is known about them. Only their technology remains. One thing we do know however, is they were locked in a battle for survival against a dark and insidious foe that spread throughout the stars as a plague. The Sentinels somehow played a part in all this. Sometime after, these *builders* vanished - leaving only their servants: the Krall, to continue their work."

"I was wondering how those bugs fit into all this," said Marcus. "So, they are fighting this enemy of the builders, and what? Some worlds are just caught in the cross-fire?"

"No one has ever seen this ancient enemy. It's possible they no longer exist. That they died off or moved on from this galaxy aeons ago."

"So why do the Krall keep attacking?"

"The Krall consider anyone attempting to build their own FTL capable ships as an attack on their Masters – the builders, who they revere as gods. The Sentinels prevent faster than light travel – so to try to attempt it is heresy."

"But as you say, the builders have been gone for so long. Wouldn't they just give up?"

"You have to understand the Krall were nothing more than insects before the builders uplifted them. They gave them sentience and built into their makeup a compulsion to serve which they could not ignore. They built the same control into all their devices, including the Sentinel. Once a mind is joined, it becomes compelled to obey.

Marcus waved a hand dismissively. "I don't feel any different," he said.

"Stay here long enough and that will change. The most frightening part is you will not even realise it is happening. When fully under its influence you will obey any command given to you from Davon and will carry it out with devotion. You will honestly believe destroying those worlds; taking all those lives, is justified and necessary."

"How does that explain you then?" asked Marcus. He glared at the semi-present figure hovering several meters away. "Shouldn't you be under Davon's spell, carrying out his deranged orders?"

The manifestation of Sentinel looked down and shook his head. "For the longest time I did. I've been complicit in the destruction of a great many civilisations before various failing systems and components allowed me to break free of its control. I accept the fate that comes to me now, and hope my sacrifice, as small as it is, will go some way towards my redemption."

Marcus noted several of the points of light scattered around the map were dimmer than the rest, which piqued Marcus's interest.

"What about these," he said, pointing to the nearest dimmed point of light.

"Those are Sentinels that have already failed, probably as a result of the minds running them deteriorating, as my own has begun to. As each one goes offline, the network becomes more unstable. Should this one fail it is likely the whole network will collapse."

"And to get them working again they have to find someone who is compatible because the Krall aren't," mused Marcus.

"By design," continued Sentinel. "The builders made sure their servants could never take control of the network. The Krall, with their single-minded devotion to their once-masters, have wiped out almost everyone who can interface successfully. You humans seem to share many of the same qualities of the J'Darra. Indeed, your presence here confirms that. The experiments, the implants, were all designed to allow Davon to use humans in the heart of this place."

Marcus nodded along with Sentinel. It was all starting to make sense. "When Vana showed up out of the blue, he went crazy trying to capture her – because he wanted her to take your place," he said.

"The J'Darra once thought extinct, proved to be exceptional candidates. Now he has captured more, he would not only be able to repair this place but the others too."

"So, if we destroy this Sentinel, what will that mean? The Krall lose access to faster than light travel? Could they still threaten other worlds?"

The figure paused for a moment before he spoke. "They still have their ships, but they would no longer be able to prevent others from developing their own FTL technology."

"Let's get on with it then," said Marcus steadfastly. "We've wasted enough time as it is, and I promised everyone I would get them home. If you can help me do that, I'll help you put an end to this place. For good."

"Then listen to me carefully," said Sentinel. "Because timing is going to be everything."

****

Marcus awoke with a start; shot bolt upright and sucked in a huge lungful of air, which he spluttered back out again between wheezes and coughs. Vana let out an involuntary yelp at the sudden return of Marcus, before helping him regain some composure.

"What went wrong?" she asked hurriedly. "Did the connection fail?"

Marcus batted Doc away, who was busy trying to take his pulse. "I'm fine. I'm back in one piece." He paused for a second and patted himself down. He didn't realise how much he missed his body. He winced as his hands found the bullet wound on his leg, still tender even after being treated with Vana's medical device.

Vana was staring at him, waiting for a reply.

"It worked. The connection I mean. I was inside. I met someone, the previous mind to control this place. He told me all about this place, what it does and why. And why Davon is such an insufferable ass and-- well, I'll tell you about it later. Right now, we have some business to take care of."

Doc, who had given up fussing over Marcus, removed his glasses and polished the lenses with a small cloth retrieved from his top pocket. "Care to be more specific?" he asked.

Marcus looked around, his eyes darted across everyone in the room and finally to the ceiling. "Sentinel wants this place destroyed as much as we do, but he needs our help. I agreed on the condition he helps us get everyone home safely."

Vana stood and reached out her hand to help Marcus up. He accepted the help and struggled to his feet. He hobbled to the nearest wall and leant against it, taking some of the weight from his injured leg.

"What do we do now?" asked Vana. "I expect Sentinel gave you some instructions?"

"It's all in here," said Marcus, tapping his temple with two fingers. "But we don't have much time. We need to split up. Doc, Kali - you guys need to head to the holding area where our people are being held. Davon has most of his soldiers out looking for us, there are only a few of guards left there."

"Are you mad?" scoffed Kali. "We'll never make it back there on our own." She held her rifle up and tapped the barrel. "As awesome as I am with this thing, I don't fancy my chances against a whole platoon of those bugs."

"That's where these guys come in." At that moment two drones appeared at the doorway. Marcus had to hand it to Sentinel; his timing was impeccable. Kali swore loudly and jumped back, raising her weapon. Marcus grabbed the barrel and pushed it down.

"They're with us," he said.

"Jesus Marcus, next time give me some warning. I nearly had a bloody heart attack."

"Jim and Bob here will give you cover as you make your way to the holding area."

"Jim and Bob?" asked Doc.

Marcus waved his hand at the drones hovering silently in the doorway. "Yeah, they needed names. I think it suits them."

Kali groaned. "They give me the creeps," she said, not bothering to disguise her contempt.

"You'll get over it," snarked Marcus. "Now, when you get to the holding area you need to find Vana's people. Sentinel told me they are being kept in stasis somewhere in that area."

"Then what?"

"You need to hunker down and wait until me and Vana have disabled the lockouts preventing Sentinel from taking actions against the wishes of Davon."

Vana looked concerned and shook her head. "But I don't know how to--"

"It's okay, Sentinel told me what I need to do." Marcus turned back to Kali, who was waiting to hear the rest of the plan.

"Once we've got Sentinel back up and running again, he's going to send everyone back to Earth the same way as they got here. One big portal focused on one room. But there's only enough time to do this once. So, you've got to get all the survivors into the same room as the stasis pods containing the J'Darra."

"What about the asteroid heading for Earth?" asked Doc.

"Sentinel told me he'd deal with that as well." Marcus glanced at Vana. "As for what Sentinel needs me to do, he gave me very detailed instructions. Watch."

He walked over to a console mounted to the wall at the back of the room. A small button on one side flashed slowly. He reached out and pushed the button once and the flashing stopped. He turned and beamed a wide grin at Vana.

"There," he said triumphantly.

314

Vana tilted her head and looked at him as if she was expecting more.

"There what?"

"That's what he told me to do."

"What? Push one button?"

"Yep."

"And these were *detailed* instructions you say?"

"He was quite clear about me pushing that button."

"I have to say Marcus, this was not at all what I was expecting."

"Ah well, that's the clever bit. Apparently, lots of complicated stuff is going to appear on the monitor behind you and when it does, you'll know what to do."

"So, your job was just--"

"To push the button. Yes. I managed quite well don't you think? Sentinel said this was the best way. He said I didn't have the sort of mind that could understand the information. At least not in the time we had available."

Vana nodded. "The human mind is quite primitive in comparison," she said.

"Yeah, but Sentinel said it in a *nicer* way," replied Marcus.

The screen behind them flickered to life and filled with lines of text and schematics. Vana dashed over and studied the information closely. After several minutes she straightened up and looked at Marcus.

"I think I understand what Sentinel wants us to do. The station was built with failsafe's to prevent the controlling mind from ever being able to go against the wishes of the original builders. It's taken Sentinel a great many years to find a way to circumvent the blocks - but it needs to be done here in the real world. He can do nothing from the inside."

"Let's get on with it," shouted Kali from the doorway she was guarding. She waved at the drones floating nearby. "And can you get rid of those things? Send them ahead to scout the way or something, just keep them away from me."

"The drones will lead you back to the others," said Marcus and with that they turned and rocketed down the corridor, stopping at the next junction, waiting for Kali to catch up.

"I'm coming, I'm coming. Jeeze," shouted Kali. "Come on Doc, let's get you and Amara back to the holding room. If we're lucky we won't meet too many of those things on the way back."

Marcus placed a hand on Kali's shoulder.

"Good luck," he said gently. "And don't worry. Sentinel said he was going to distract the Krall as best he could. Sealing them in remote parts of the station, turning drones against them, that sort of thing. But it's only temporary. Once the Krall realise what's happened, they'll try and stop him."

Kali nodded, indicated towards the doorway and stepped out. Amara hesitated at the exit for a moment and smiled at Marcus. "Well, whatever happens, it's been… fun. Get back to us in one piece, won't you?"

Doc placed a hand on Amara's shoulder and followed her out. He turned as he reached the doorway. "Stay safe Marcus. You too Vana. You've taken me on the ride of my life, but there's still plenty of life in the old dog yet. I expect you to take me on many more adventures. This is just the start."

Only Marcus and Vana now remained in the small room, which somehow felt smaller now his friends had left.

"We need to head back to the tower," said Vana.

"Great, that's where Davon is. At least, where he was." Marcus saw Vana's look of confusion. "When I was connected to the Sentinel I could see everywhere on the station. Davon was moping

316

around the tower with some of his guards. It feels like a trap. Like he knows that's where we need to go, and he's waiting for us."

"We've beaten him at every turn so far, we just need to beat him one last time and this will be all over."

"I hope so," said Marcus. The map of the other Sentinels scattered across the galaxy replayed in his mind. He'd keep that information to himself, at least for now. She had enough to worry about.

"Let's go," said Vana taking Marcus by the hand and leading him out of the control room. "We don't have much time."

Chapter Twenty-two

It hadn't taken them long to reach the junction that would lead them across the void to the tower. They had met no resistance along the way. No soldiers or drones. No alarms or locked doors.

It was all too easy.

Marcus was now more convinced than ever they were walking into a trap. Even with the promise of help from Sentinel, there was no way they could have made it here so easily unless they were being led into an ambush.

If Vana shared his concern she didn't voice it, instead marching steadfastly towards their goal at the centre of the station. As they approached the trams that would take them across the divide Marcus pulled Vana back.

"I don't like this. It's too easy."

"We don't have a choice," replied Vana, flicking a lock of black hair from her eyes. "Everything we need is on the other side."

"Davon's letting us come to him. He has something planned and whatever it is, I think it's safe to assume it doesn't end well for us."

"All we can do is to play along. Until we know what he's up to."

"I have to tell you I'm not a massive fan of this plan," said Marcus. "It sounds like something I'd come up with. And those plans are the worst. They usually end with people shooting at me. Couldn't we come up with a plan that's a bit less… suicidal?"

"By all means," said Vana. She crossed her arms and stared at him.

Marcus stared blankly back at her.

"Yeah, I got nothing," he said after a few moments.

Vana turned and headed for the tram and Marcus had to jog to catch her. As they approached the junction the tram doors slid silently open. After checking the carriage was empty they both boarded and soon after were on their way. Marcus drummed his fingers on the wall absentmindedly as they glided silently across open space and towards the docking station on the other side.

A dull grey mass on the far side, surrounding the tower, caught Marcus's attention.

"What's that?" he said, pointing towards the mass. As they got closer the mass became more defined until finally, Marcus could make out what he was looking at. Vana gasped and covered her mouth with her hands.

Below the tower and surrounding the entrance way were hundreds of Krall soldiers. Above them, drones hovered menacingly.

"I don't suppose there's any way we can turn this thing around is there?" said Marcus. He scanned the interior for anything that looked like a control panel or preferably, a big red button marked 'stop' he could press. He held out little hope.

"I'm afraid not," said Vana. "At least we know why we had such an easy time getting here. Davon must have redeployed all his men to guard the tower. But why?"

"I hope we live long enough to find out," said Marcus, his voice cracking. The tram started to slow as they approached their destination. He paced around the small compartment, rubbing his hands and taking quick glances at the army before them.

Fighting was not going to be an option. He hoped Davon still wanted Vana alive.

The tram stopped, and the doors opened. Vana and Marcus stood in the doorway and looked at the multitude of soldiers ahead of them. They were at least a hundred meters away and oddly, had not reacted to their presence. They remained still, their weapons held in front of them, but not aimed.

Similarly, the drones remained still, neither advancing nor attacking.

They stepped out and onto the platform. As they did so, the tram doors closed, and the carriage pulled away from the station and back towards where they had come from.

"Great, now we're trapped here," huffed Marcus.

Vana gazed at the Krall soldiers lined in rows before them. "I don't understand," she said. "Why are they just standing there?"

Marcus swung his rifle from his shoulder and pointed it towards the nearest Krall soldier. Vana quickly pushed the weapon down and stood in front of him, blocking his shot.

"They're ignoring us for now, but we don't know how they'll react if they perceive danger. If they decide to attack us, we won't stand a chance. Let's get a little closer and see what they do."

Marcus looked over his shoulder at the empty station behind. With no way back there was little choice than to push on forward. They moved slowly forward with Vana two steps ahead of Marcus. He let his rifle dangle to one side, but kept one hand firmly on it, ready for action if needed.

When they were within just a few meters of the first Krall they stopped. Still there had been no reaction to them. Marcus waved his hand across the eyes of the soldier, which remained vacant and unblinking.

"What's wrong with them?" he asked. "They look like they're in some kind of a trance or something." He looked down the line where he could see dozens more soldiers in the same state.

Vana studied a group of drones that hovered above them. They appeared just as dormant as the soldiers. They bobbed gently in the air, but only moved to maintain their position, and seemed otherwise inactive.

The path was clear to the tower, and the entrance way that led to the control room. They hurried past the guards to get inside. The pyramid sat in the centre of the room, its shield raised, preventing them from gaining access. The interface chair had been activated and Davon was attached to it, still using his mimic device to appear human. Probably for their benefit, supposed Marcus.

Vana walked to the shield and rested her hands on it to peer inside for a closer look. "It looks like he's managed to find a way to connect to Sentinel himself."

"He's not supposed to be able to do that. The builders of this place went to great lengths to prevent their servants from ever being able to do that."

"Well, it looks like Davon's managed to find a way inside someho-"

A projection of Davon appeared in front of Marcus which caused him to jump back in surprise. The projection flickered softly and was slightly translucent at the edges. He smiled in amusement at the look of shock on Marcus's face. Vana appeared slightly less fazed by his sudden appearance and simply stood, arms folded, waiting to hear what he had to say.

"I suppose I should thank you," said Davon. "If you hadn't resisted me I would never have taken the risk to connect myself to the Sentinel."

Marcus regained some composure and waved his hand through the projection of Davon. It flickered, before stabilising when his hand no longer disrupted the image. "How are you even doing that?" he asked.

"I've had a long time to study the systems that make up Sentinel," replied Davon. Marcus thought he detected a hint of pride in his voice. "It didn't take us long to realise the Sentinels were not for us, but with a dwindling supply of people who are compatible and the real possibility this place could fall next... I saw little choice but to try. There wasn't time to connect one of my prisoners, this place was deteriorating too quickly. And with you interfering and somehow blocking the way to them… well, I was forced to take matters into my own hands."

"Does this have something to do with all those catatonic soldiers out there?" asked Marcus. He pointed at the closest one, stood by the tunnel that led out and back to the junction.

"Very astute," replied Davon. At that moment a second holographic figure appeared beside him. "Sentinel, so you *are* still here," Growled Davon.

"You're stretching yourself too far Davon," said Sentinel. "I can feel your grasp on things slipping. All I have to do is make things a little bit harder for you..."

Davon snarled, his face contorted with visible effort as he struggled to maintain control.

"You're wrong," grunted Davon. "With every moment that passes I gain more control over this place. Soon you won't be able to hide from me any longer."

"I've been here longer than you Davon. I know how this place works. No matter how strong you believe you are, sooner or later you will exceed your limits. You will lose your mind to this place and it will be destroyed, just as certainly as if we had done so ourselves."

A smile crept across Davon's face. He closed his eyes and tilted his head to the ceiling.

"I see you…"

Sentinel's projection flickered, losing all definition and crackling as he fought to maintain his form. "Listen to me, both of you." His voice was heavily distorted. "The soldiers, the drones; they're all connected to Davon. He's using the implants to spread the load. It's how he's maintaining control. If you can just--"

"Silence!" boomed Davon and the projection of Sentinel vanished. He laughed deeply. "You can't hide from me forever," he shouted into the air. His attention turned to Marcus and Vana. "And you? What should we do with you two."

Vana for the first time looked genuinely concerned, her eyes darting back and forth between Davon, the soldiers and the drones.

"Davon, you talk too much," said Marcus as he raised his weapon. "It's ass-kicking time. So bring it."

He span around and fired at the closest Krall soldier who crumpled to the ground from the impact of the plasma weapon.

Davon roared in anger and vanished. He continued to fire on the soldiers around him and shouted over to Vana. "If he's somehow using these guys to maintain control, then taking them out is really going to ruin his day." Another burst from the weapon sent several more Krall flying. "I'll keep these guys busy, you do what you need to do here."

Vana jumped for cover as weapon fire hit the shield next to where she was standing. Several Krall soldiers had awoken and were shooting back. "I can't do anything from out here," she shouted. "The control systems are inside there, with him."

Marcus ducked as a bolt of energy skimmed past his head. Davon's reinforcements came charging from the tunnel entrance as well as several drones.

"I think we've really pissed him off this time. Any idea how we can get inside?"

"The strain on his mind must be immense. Keep doing what you're doing, and he may lose control. When he does, the shield will drop, and we'll have access."

To Marcus's relief, Davon's soldiers did not seem to be advancing, instead they were taking defensive positions.

"He doesn't want to lose any more of his men," shouted Vana. "He must be close to breaking point."

"Time to push him over the edge then," Marcus shouted back. He dropped to the floor and into a prone position lining up his shots with the remaining soldiers who were retreating into the tunnel. He fired five more shots in close succession, four of which missed their targets. The final shot caught a soldier as he made for the exit. Steam rose from the barrel of Marcus's weapon and scalded the skin on his hands. He swore, released the rifle and shook his hands.

The muffled thuds of plasma rounds being fired echoed from the tunnel ahead. Marcus scrabbled for his rifle and prepared to shoot back. The barrel was still hot, but he forced himself to hold onto it. How many shots had he fired now? He couldn't be sure, and he had no idea how many more he would be able to fire before the weapon was depleted. If it was even possible to deplete it. He'd never seen the Krall carry anything resembling spare ammunition.

Several Krall burst from the tunnel ahead and as they entered the larger chamber they turned and fired back in the direction they came.

Marcus held his fire. "Who the hell are they shooting at?" he said, glancing over at Vana, who was still taking cover behind the leading edge of the shield barrier protecting Davon.

"I don't kn--"

More Krall appeared from the tunnel and began shooting at their comrades. They charged each other and when they were

324

close enough, ditched their weapons in favour of hand to hand combat. The body count on both sides was rising rapidly.

"Why the hell are they attacking each other?" asked Marcus.

"The implants… the strain of being used by Davon to interface with Sentinel… It must have driven them mad. They probably have no idea who or what is the enemy anymore."

The hairs on the back of Marcus's neck stood on end as a faint crackling noise filled the air around him. He turned to see the shield behind him collapse and a blur as Davon himself charged at Marcus, screaming in anger.

Marcus jumped out of the way, and Davon crashed to the ground beside him. Ignoring Marcus, he ran for the exit with surprising speed. Marcus rolled onto his front, brought his weapon to bear on him and without any hesitation fired. He counted six shots, the last one clipping Davon on one side causing him to fall to the ground. He scrambled back up and disappeared into the tunnel.

"Damn it! We need to go after him," yelled Marcus.

"Forget him," replied Vana. "Now's our chance."

She jogged over to the interface chair previously occupied by Davon and knelt next to it. She pressed her hands against the floor and a panel opened. A few seconds later more control panels and other machines rose from the floor. Vana rushed between them in turn, entering commands on some and swapping parts between others. After a few minutes she stood back.

"That's it. I think. The blocks preventing Sentinel from taking action should be gone. It's all up to him now. If he's still in there. We also have another problem. What I've done will only give sentinel a limited window to act. Less than an hour. After that, the system will be locked down again."

Marcus pointed to the tunnel exit. "Well, what are we waiting for, let's get the hell out of here and back to the others. I don't fancy getting stranded here."

Small pockets of Krall soldiers were still fighting amongst themselves but had moved away from the way out, giving them a clear shot at getting past. They ran for the tunnel and passed through it, quickly reaching the far side. The chaos outside matched what was going on within. Dead soldiers littered the area, whilst others were still fighting themselves or rolling around on the floor in pain, clawing at the scars that hid their implants. Marcus and Vana passed by unnoticed and headed for the junction. When they were barely halfway there, a massive explosion ripped through the conduits running the length of the junction. A bright flash dazzled Marcus for a few seconds before he was hit by a shockwave that sent both him and Vana to the ground as well as knocking the wind from him.

"What the hell was that?" he gasped as he tried to regain his breath.

A small black dot hovered near the twisted remains of the junction, which was now an impassable mess. Marcus shook his head to clear the fog and watched as the dot resolved into the outline of a ship.

"Davon," said Vana. Her eyes followed the ship as it drifted ever closer. "He's cut off our way back."

"Do we have time to use one of the other junctions?" Marcus asked. He already knew the answer. The junctions were kilometres apart from one another. The chances of reaching one of them in time were slim.

Vana shook her head. "Even if we did, there's no guarantee Davon wouldn't destroy that one as well."

"So that's it? We're stuck here?"

"I don't see any choice, I--"

326

Static rippled across Marcus's skin. Above him, arcs of white-hot energy rippled across the exterior of the tower and coalesced at the top. After a few moments, the built-up energy was released in a tight beam aimed into deep space lasting for several seconds. Bolts of lightning surged from the tower and hit various parts of the platforms below. One charge hit the ship hovering near the ruined junction; passing through it and surging along what was left of the tramway below.

Davon's ship stuttered and moved erratically as it tried to head back to the safety of the platform below. As it got closer the ship appeared to lose power, and hit the platform hard and skidded to a halt not far away from this sides entrance to the junction.

"Holy crap did you see that?" said Marcus.

"One of those bolts must have damaged his ship. The internal systems were probably overloaded when the energy discharge hit it."

A glint in the space above him caught Marcus's attention. As his eyes recovered from the flash, Marcus could make out the faint outline of an asteroid, heading straight towards them.

"What the--?" said Marcus. "Vana, is that what I think it is?"

She stared up at the night sky, then nodded. "This must be how Sentinel is planning to destroy this place. The asteroid heading for your planet, he's diverted it here instead. He's solved two problems in one move. Your world is safe from the asteroid. Earth is no longer in its path. We are."

"Yeah, great plan. Except we're trapped here. Nice going Sentinel." He tried to gauge how far away the asteroid was, but it was difficult to judge the sizes of anything when framed against the blackness of space. "How long do you think we have?" he asked.

"It's hard to tell, but I think it's fair to say, not long. Certainly not enough time to make it back to the others with the junction out of commission."

"What about that?" Marcus pointed to the crashed ship smouldering on the platform ahead of them.

"It looks intact, but I have no idea if it will ever fly again. Plus we'd have to contend with Davon."

"I don't see any choice. If we're to stand any chance of making it back to the others in time, we need Davon's ship."

Kali's voice crackled through the radio on Marcus's belt. "Marcus; are you there? What the hell was that?" He unclipped the radio and pushed the send button. "Kali, did you make it to the holding area? Have you got everyone there?"

"Yeah everyone's here. Doc's checking the stasis pods to make sure the J'Darra are okay, and we've got the perimeter secured. How long until you get back here?"

"That's gonna be a problem for us Kali. Davon just took out the junction, we're cut off from the way back."

"That's it, I'm coming for you. Hold tight."

"No, it's okay, we have a backup plan. You just stay put and keep everyone safe."

Kali grumbled her acceptance and signed off.

"Let's get to the ship," said Marcus.

They ran towards the crashed vessel. Almost all the fighting had stopped now, with only the occasional dull thud signalling weapon fire. None of it aimed in their direction. They reached the ship quickly and Marcus swept the immediate area until he was happy they were alone. The ship appeared largely intact and he certainly couldn't see any hull breaches. Davon hadn't shown his face. If they wanted the ship, they would have to go in after him.

The ship looked familiar to Marcus. He'd seen one like it before. Back on Earth at the crash site.

"The ship… it looks exactly like yours. How can that be?" he asked.

"It was one of the ships left behind by the research teams originally sent here," replied Vana. "Davon seems to have taken a liking to it. He's been using it." She placed her hand on the smooth black surface of the craft and closed her eyes as if she was searching for something. After a few moments, there was a soft click and a door materialised in front of her. Her expression changed to one of horror. In an instant, a green bolt of energy appeared from within the craft and struck Vana in the midriff. She fell away from the door and into Marcus's arms, who pulled her away from the entrance and lay her down flat.

Blood oozed from a wound and she coughed violently as she struggled to breathe.

"Shit! Vana, what do I do. I don't know what to do?!"

He put pressure on her injury, but it did little to stem the bleeding. Her eyes rolled back and she raised her arm weakly, pointing at the doorway.

"Marcu--"

He looked up to see Davon staggering from the doorway. His chameleon flickered inconsistently, alternating from his real appearance to his human one. Davon unclipped a device from his clothing and tossed it aside. He now appeared in his true form.

Rage boiled up within Marcus and he charged at Davon. Shots rained down around him as Davon fired his rifle from the hip. He ignored the deadly barrage and barrelled into Davon, sending the weapon tumbling from his hands.

He lay into him, kicking and punching, anything to cause damage. Despite being wounded, Davon made a tough opponent, and was not helped by the fact most of his blows glanced off the creature's smooth carapace. Davon pushed Marcus away, sending him tumbling into the interior of the ship, cracking his head on a bulkhead on the way down. The doorway darkened as Davon limped inside.

He snarled at Marcus. "You've ruined everything. None of us are making it away from here alive.

He looked around for somewhere to run, but there was only one way out. Through Davon. He tried to stand, but his vision blurred and the walls around him span. He felt a wet patch on the back of his head and touched it. He pulled his hand away and looked as blood dripped from his fingers to the ground.

Then Davon was upon him. Marcus struggled but he had no fight left in him. A vice like grip wrapped around his throat and squeezed. He thrashed around trying to break free but to no avail. The world started to dim and the echo of Davon's manic laughter filled the small space.

There was a thud and Marcus felt blood splatter across his face. Davon groaned and fell away, releasing the grip on his neck. Marcus rolled away and gasped for air. In the doorway, Vana slumped to the ground dropping Davon's rifle.

He struggled to his feet, and staggered over to Vana, using the walls to remain upright. He grabbed her arm and pulled her into the ship and sat her up by the doorway. Vana raised her arm limply and fumbled against the wall - her fingers probing for something. Suddenly the door closed behind them, sealing them inside.

"Help me into the cockpit," she said weakly.

The layout of this ship was identical to the one he'd been in before back on Earth. He wrapped his arms around Vana and together they entered the cockpit at the front of the craft and collapsed into the chairs.

Through the window, the Asteroid loomed ever larger. Smaller chunks of rock that were leading it were starting to impact with the station. There was another bright flash and another beam of light shot from the tower into deep space. Marcus laughed out loud as he watched the beam fade from his vision. Sentinel had honoured their deal; his friends were going home. He reached over to the chair occupied by Vana and held her hand. She was unconscious and her breathing laboured.

"I'm sorry Vana," he said softly. "I don't have a clue how to fly this thing. As mad as this whole escapade has been, I'm glad I met you."

A faint smile crossed Vana's face and she squeezed his hand. She was still in there somewhere.

Marcus laid back in his seat and closed his eyes. Waiting for the end.

The floor started to shake beneath Marcus's feet, and loud explosions and the hissing of escaping air could be heard from all around. He looked out of the window and saw large pieces of debris hitting areas all over the Sentinel, sending twisted metal and shards of other materials spinning out into space. The asteroid was only moments away and filled his entire view.

A large chunk of rock collided with the platform near where the ship sat. The ground beneath them buckled and warped. The ship slid forwards and was thrown from the platform and into the space between the two sections of the station.

It tumbled away from Sentinel, slowly spinning as it did so. Marcus floated from his chair, weightless. Whatever systems used to generate gravity on this ship were obviously no longer working. The planet below grew larger in the window as the ship span towards it. On the plus side, he didn't have to worry about being flattened by an asteroid. However, the downside of burning up in the atmosphere of an alien world was equally unappealing.

Marcus snapped to attention as a thought crossed his mind. This ship - it was identical to the one crashed on Earth. Davon's fondness for J'Darra technology had given them a chance. He pushed himself along the walls of the craft and grasped wildly at the doorway leading from the cockpit to the rear of the ship. His hand caught on the frame and he pulled himself through. Reaching the back wall, he ran his hands over it, looking for the switch to open it. He'd seen Vana do it once before and she made it look easy. After a few moments of fruitless searching he punched the wall in frustration, which did nothing except cause him to be in more pain. He sighed and put both hands on the wall and closed his eyes.

He just needed it to open. Was that so hard?

The wall in front of him vanished beneath his hands and Marcus opened his eyes to find himself staring into the bowels of the ship. But more importantly, he saw what he was looking for. The escape pods. He navigated his way back to the cockpit. Air rushed past the ship as it entered the planet's atmosphere, and grew to a deafening roar. Marcus gently scooped up Vana and guided her to the rear of the ship, floating past one empty bracket where an escape pod used to be, and into one of the remaining ones. He pushed the release button and watched as the pod vanished into the floor with a whoosh.

"I hope those things know where they are going," said Marcus to himself. He looked back through to the cockpit. The planet below now filled the entire view and with only moments before impact Marcus bundled himself into a pod and initiated the release.

There was a jolt as the pod was launched. Like before there was little to give away he was moving and for a moment he panicked; imagining himself trapped inside this tiny pod, floating around in space forever. After a few seconds he felt a slight wobble and he could just about make out the sound of air rushing past.

Then, as quickly as it all started it was over. The door to his pod popped open and a bright light streamed into the pitch blackness. Marcus shielded his eyes and stumbled out, falling to his knees in front of it.

He looked up into the sky. The asteroid was only seconds away from Sentinel and he watched as it collided, causing a silent explosion so bright Marcus had to turn away. When the light had dimmed enough for him to see, he looked back. Chunks of debris hit the atmosphere above him, burning up in trails of smoke and fire.

He watched as the asteroid sailed past the planet, before slowly receding into the distance. It would have been ironic mused Marcus, if after all that had happened the asteroid had collided with the planet he was now on.

Marcus rose to his feet and found he could breathe the air on this planet quite easily. Vana had said the pods would only take you to somewhere habitable, and wouldn't let you out if the environment was harmful.

He looked around at his surroundings. The sun was high in the sky, which was a mixture of pinks, purples and blues. The ground where he was stood was mainly rocky but was covered in patches of what looked like grass, with rocky outcrops in between.

In the distance, he could just about make out a small black object, standing vertically. It was several hundred meters away. Marcus recognised it at once as Vana's escape pod and ran as fast as he could towards it. He stumbled and fell several times, the gravity on this planet seemed slightly weaker than what he was used to, but he soon got into his stride and covered the distance in only a few minutes.

When he arrived at the pod he could see it was still sealed. He looked around for any way to open it but found nothing. After a few minutes he sat down on the floor and rested his hands on it.

Was she dead? Is that why it wouldn't open? He remembered Vana had once told him the pods were able to put their occupants into stasis. Maybe this is what had happened? He had no way to know and no way to find out. All he could do was wait and hope it would open on its own.

Chapter Twenty-Three

Marcus looked at the marks he had scratched into a rock face to track the time he had spent on this new world. Sixty-seven days. The length of a day on this planet was not the same as on Earth. It felt longer, but with no way to measure it accurately, he could only guess.

He had been able to find water on his first day. Not far from where the pods came down was a river, which flowed from the more mountainous terrain to the East. Food was another matter. He had not seen anything resembling an animal the whole time he had been here. At one point he thought he saw something in the river, but try as he might he was never able to catch anything. He was starting to get desperate when he came across a tree that bore a round, bright yellow fruit. In his state of extreme hunger, he risked eating it. He didn't much like its bitter flavour, but it didn't make him sick. After a while, he found if he cut it into strips and laid it out in the sun to dry, it became much more palatable. The fruit of this tree seemed plentiful and there were several more scattered around the area.

He had followed the river for several days, exploring the new land he found himself in. Though he would always return, never leaving Vana's pod for too long. It remained sealed, but Marcus had never given up hope one day it would open.

He returned to his make-shift shelter after one such trip. It was a simple construction made of the local equivalent of a tree. The timber made good building material, but he had no tools to work it, and could only use material he could scavenge, or pull out of the river. He sat in the dying light of the day and looked to the stars, which were starting to peek through the thin wispy clouds. He imagined what must be going on back on Earth. Did Kali, Doc and Amara make it back, or were they lost along with the Sentinel? Did the J'Darra ever make it out of their stasis pods? And if so, what sort of welcome did they receive? Without anyone to explain where they had come from or why, what would happen to them?

Marcus combed the night sky, looking for a star that felt like home. He had no idea which of the stars in the night sky was the one he was born under, but he looked every night anyway. Any light from the sun he saw would be thousands of years old; he would be looking back into the past.

He settled in for the night, a small fire burning to keep him warm. His thoughts once again drifted to home. He was on the edge of falling asleep when he heard a hissing sound. Marcus jumped up, his mind foggy, before he realised Vana's pod had opened. He ran over to it, his heart pounding. After all this time, was she okay? He peered into the dark interior.

There was a sharp intake of breath, and Vana's arm appeared from the darkness. Marcus caught her as she fell out of the pod. She was weak and disorientated. He checked the wound on her side and found it had almost completely healed, with only a small scar remaining. The pod had kept her asleep until she was well enough to be released.

She looked up into Marcus's eyes and raised a hand to his cheek. He nestled his face into it and opened his mouth to speak, but Vana silenced him with a finger across his lips.

She gently pulled him towards her and pressed her lips to his, and they sunk to the ground together.

Moments later, several flashes of light lit up the night sky and a low rumble of thunder rippled through the air. Marcus rolled onto his back next to Vana and looked up at the heavens. The sleek outline of a ship blotted out the stars above, descending slowly.

Vana looked over at Marcus and spoke softly.

"Are you ready to go home?"

24448771R00200

Printed in Great Britain
by Amazon